The Journey of Lyght and Path of Color

A.O. Zephryes

DEDICATION

For my Aunt Donna and my wife Tamsyn, the two most caring and supportive women I've ever met. I love you both more than you'll ever know.

ACKNOWLEDGMENTS

I'd like to take this opportunity to thank my amazing friend Laura Ridings of Iron Clad Designs for designing my book cover. She is, in a word, awesome.

1

Her name was Pi, a Quasi, and she was ready to stop leaping. She wanted to go home to her own HomeSpace. Pi's breath left her four lungs, thickly crystallizing in swirls around her like reverse steam clouds. Her fur was now thoroughly frosted as the foggy air clung to her gray and tan coat, shedding icicles as her body moved through the thorny brush protecting the rocky outer rim of the Northlands.

As she leaped from jagged rock to jagged rock, the thick meaty pads of her sinewy, wide two rear paws, which served as both her keel and balance as well as her propulsion engines, had begun to rub slightly raw, and felt as if they would stick and capture her to quartz and granite at any moment halting any additional progress towards returning her to the comforts to be found in the deep caves nestled beneath ground ahead. She wished for nothing more than to nestle in her bedtime nook and fall asleep listening to the whirring of lyght lamps and feeling their warm heat waft through the interconnected caves known as the Eastern HomeSpace. Pi had spent the last few days delivering a coded message to the elders at the three other HomeSpaces: South, West, and North, but wanted nothing other than the comforts of her own home now. Pi was tired of all this quick travel, her aching body even more so.

The remaining time took roughly ten dats from the rim, seven with her speed, but she was quite tired and knew that tonight would take longer. The past few days had been the longest of her young life, but also the most exciting. Having to alert the other HomeSpaces of a Beckoning was a great honor. But not knowing why the meeting of the various clans' elders was taking place was frustrating to no end. There had been hushed whispers throughout the caves about a prophecy left by the elders since she was a small pup. She only hoped this upcoming meeting of the dens was one of salvation and not of ruin. Pi pushed on, soldiering through her weariness to leap in long, graceful bounces across the earth and through the misty sky in front of her.

Pi slid to a stop, landing on a smooth, slick patch of marble quartz, her talons clicking against the hard rock. Something caught her large topaz eyes in the snowlight. Up ahead, she saw the first traces of flickering yellow lanterns signaling the mouth of her HomeSpace and the Quasi leaper now knew home was now in sight. She reached into her pouch with her two elongated forearms to warm her talon nailed front paws for a moment and then removed the last ration of the carrot bread her brother, Rex, had sent her off with and ate it slowly, savoring it while thinking of what type of stew would be waiting for her at home, left in its cobble pot being kept warm on the hearth.

Finishing up the rest of the carrot bread, Pi took a long, deep breath before leaping forward in the sky towards her favorite place: home. When she arrived, Pi found herself dismayed she had been met by no one eager to hear of her latest adventure. Her younger brother, Rex, was the first to approach her at the Main Gate, guarded by Bugle sentries. Bugles had been in service to the Quasi since the first Quasi rescued them from a barren island on the Shining Sea nearly three millennia ago on the Great Journey across the Shining Sea.

That journey had brought the Quasi to this place, Arkelia's last continent, and here they remained with nowhere left to go. The Quasi and Bugles were all that remained of civilization on Arkelia. The horrid MaRuu did not count as they were just vengeful blood thirty creatures. There was nothing civilized about them in the least.

Rex was close to her in age and carried with him a long white streak through his brown fur that had given him the ability to stand apart from the rest of the clan, who held only tan and gray markings. Impish sometimes, but always in high spirits, he was Pi's friend as well as her brother. The two were inseparable and being away from him for this long was one of the main reasons she was so very happy to now be home to share with him her latest adventure.

"Loving you, sister!" Rex exclaimed, the greeting he always shared with her.

She smiled. "Loving you too, Rex! How are things?"

"Not shabby, for sure," he replied with confidence. "We've been waiting to hear if the other clans are coming to meet. That's the whispers going around, anyways. So? Are they?"

"They say they will come. All of them. After each Elder read the message from Ichabod, none hesitated to say 'Aye'."

Rex eyed Pi up. She was tough to read sometimes, even for him. She was often staring in the distance looking at one thing but thinking about something else entirely. Being three planet turns older than him, Rex was proud as proud can be of his big sister. Since their mum and dad passed, it was only in each other that they were able to grieve and move on from such a sad thing as death. She nurtured him and he gave her strength. Scout, Pi's life partner, and her friend Rhi, a Bugle, helped round out their motley quartet and offered just as much support as two entirely polar opposites possibly could!

"Thinking about the Council?" Rex asked.

Pi snapped out of her gaze. "Oh, wait. What's this now?"

Rex chuckled with a snort. "Welcome back to planet Arkelia. What's going on up there, sister?"

Pi scrunched her face. "Dinner. What are we having?"

"I made veg stew and carrot bread, your favorite."

Pi snorted a chuckle. "It's the only thing we ever have, Rex."

"Like I said," Rex replied, "Your favorite!"

Pi smiled. "I get my sarcasm from you, you know."

"I know it, sister. Did anyone tell you about Scout yet?"

She leaned towards him. "No? Why? What happened to him?"

"They sent him out on a scouting right after you left. He really should have picked a better nickname than his occupation, you know?"

"Where to?" Pi leaned in closer still. "I thought I was the only one allowed to leave HomeSpace."

Rex shrugged, as he often did instead of answering when he did not have an answer to provide.

"You're a lot of help... not," Pi mused.

"He said they sent him on a secret mission, that's all," Rex replied. "Come on, your supper's waiting for you. You must be famished."

They returned to their smallish burrow and nestled into their nooks to eat in silence. Pi devoured her first two helpings and was halfway through her third when her long ears began to twitch.

"Who is it?" she asked moments before a long shadow danced across them.

3

"Still one to have a leaper's good ears, I see," an older Quasi mentioned from beyond the outer door in his usually gruff voice.

It was Ichabod the High Elder, their leader. He had chosen Pi as a Leaper since her pup days, in addition to keeping her mostly out of trouble in and around HomeSpace. His fur bushy and gray, Ichabod wore a thick fabric coat and carried a long walking stick engraved with ancient carvings of the first six Journeyers who had saved the Quasis from extinction a millennia ago.

Rex was of a different sort, not one who was intended for adventure or trips far from home. He tended to be quite nefarious in leaving behind a trail of trouble when he was in high spirits. Laughably, Rex becoming their homemaker was a bit of a surprise as he settled down after his pup years. Quasis can always change, Ichabod would say, once they truly find their way. Rex had become quite the homebody and an excellent caretaker of their burro den once Pi and Scout begun being sent out on Leaps. His cooking was next to none in the HomeSpace.

"Ichabod, you overestimated how long that trek was going to take me," Pi said drolly. "According to you, I shouldn't have been back for another two days."

"And yet, you still completed the journey two days faster than it took your father, and that was the reigning record time… until now that is."

Pi smiled. She liked when Ichabod made mention of her parents, especially when it meant she had broken another of her father's Leaping legacy records.

"Come for my famous stew, Ichabod?" Rex fetched another clay bowl from the hutch.

"Sadly, not tonight, Rex," Ichabod replied, his stare never leaving Pi. "I've come to speak with Pi regarding her and Scout's missions. You've become quite the good secret keeper so if Pi wants you here, I will begin."

"You don't even have to ask, Ichabod," Pi said proudly, eyeing Rex. "You already know my answer."

Ichabod smiled. The bond between these two was impenetrable… for now. This news might change that.

He settled into the large sack chair on the side of Pi and Rex's nooks.

"First, I'll have you know that Scout has returned safely from his, er, scouting," Ichabod said, raising his paw to his mouth. "But no questions about that now."

Pi found herself growing squirmy with anxiousness. Rex was not far behind, looking as if he would soon fall over from leaning too far in towards Ichabod.

"The Quasi have been tasked with communicating with the great Quasi Spirit to keep the balance of nature in check and Arkelia going around her at a pace that allows us to harvest the vegetables and use the Lyght Veins to power our civilization. This is what the prophecy calls 'The Balance'.

"Each millennia brings its own challenges and obstacles, and as you and many others have noticed, the snowquakes and the lyghtning showers have been - "

"Increasing?" Rex added, looking to Ichabod for approval.

Rex was met with a noticeable sigh and nod from the Elder... and an unmistakable glance to hush. This was serious business.

Ichabod ran his paws along his walking stick, as if retracing the journeys that took place that led to this very moment in time. He felt winsome.

"Your father believed he would be the one to be asked what I am about to ask you, Pi, but those MaRuu marauders made this your burden, child. I have tried to find a way to choose another, believe me I have, but the Spirit has willed it and I can't seem to find a way around asking you to undertake something you are not suited for in the least."

"I am no child, nor pup, Ichabod," Pi stated plainly. "Tell me my destiny or let me ask you, am I the Chosen One of the prophecy? The fastest, smartest Quasi?"

Rex leaned in further still, using his hind paws to stop himself from toppling over, in rapt attention.

"Yes, Pi, the Spirit has summoned to be the Journeyer," Ichabod replied. "This burden is one of the gravest pieces of news a Quasi has ever been told, one of danger and calamity, struggle and sacrifice. If you refuse to go, which I would completely understand and encourage, I will gladly find another. There is Battler named Dee who I'm sure would--"

"Yes!" Pi exclaimed, startling Ichabod nearly out of his seat.

Ichabod seemed flabbergasted. "Pi, er, this is a grave and solemn-"

Pi leapt to her hind paws and outstretched her left front paw to Rex, who slapped it in turn. "Yah!"

"Pi, please sit back down, this is a task no one--"

She wasn't hearing any of it. She was exuberant and joyful unlike any time in her life. She had always felt different, not really special, but definitely different. Pi could tell from a young age, just how her parents and the elders treated her with a near deference, that she was being groomed for something the others were not.

Fast was never fast enough for her. Smart was never smart enough. Wisdom was never wise enough. She always wanted more, out of herself and also out of life. Now she knew she was right. She felt adrenaline pump through her body in nervous excitement.

"Pi!" Ichabod chastised. "Pay attention and heed me!"

Pi puffed her chest fur before returning to her seat.

"Thank you," Ichabod said. "Now stay there."

He glanced at Rex. "That goes for you too."

Ichabod reached in his front pouch and removed a silver and gold chest plate adorned with an odd shaped violet stone in its middle, etched with the language of the Elders throughout.

He held it out towards Pi.

"This is the Arkelian, Pi," Ichabod said. "Within the Violet Stone lies the soul of our very planet. Whoever wears the Arkelian will embark on the Journey of Lyght with the very essence of Arkelia with them to offer sacrifice to the Quasi Spirit to keep the planet in orbit for another millennia. You have been chosen for this quest by the Spirit itself and I will assume, you will think heavily before undertaking this to be your journey and yours alone? This is not something to enter into brashly, Pi. I would gladly hold on to the Arkelian and find another alternative to this. I truly wish that--"

They were suddenly interrupted by a loud thud outside their burrow. Ichabod quickly returned the Arkelian to his pouch right as a large, slightly fluffy and rotund Quasi appeared before them.

"Scout, the MaRuu must hear you coming from five clicks away," Ichabod muttered. "I take it you retrieved the parcel from the Western HomeSpace?"

"Aye," Scout replied, offering a salute of sorts with his right front paw. "Was told the job was done, so what better place to go than that which offers the best stew in the Caves?"

Ichabod rose to his hind paws. "We'll continue this later, Pi. I'm off for now knowing where you stand. Stay close to home these next few days, all right? None of your jaunts off across the Rocklands."

Rex snorted. "Not likely..."

Ichabod furrowed his brow. "At least stay within a click or two so you can see if you've been beckoned. Wish I could stay for some of Rex's stew but as you can imagine, I have a lot to get sorted. I'm off-"

"But I have questions!" Pi replied. "You can't go and drop that on my plate and then just set off, Ichabod. That's not fair."

Ichabod nodded. "Not fair at all. Such is life, Pi. As you will learn soon enough. And I have more to say before you leap into anything all willy nilly as you tend to do. Enjoy this time with your mates. But keep your head clear and your heart strong. Good night."

Ichabod did not wait for a response before departing, leaving Scout as bewildered as he was since returning from his own leap.

"What was that all about?" Scout asked, making his way to the stew kettle and grabbing a bowl and spoon from the nearby ledge.

"You know I tell you everything, love," Pi said in Scout's direction, "but for the first time in my life I think I'm going to keep this close to the pouch for a bit. How was your mission?"

"It was... odd," Scout replied after filling his bowl with stew and sitting next to her. "They sent me to retrieve... something, which I of course did. Neither here, there, nor back here again would anybody tell what it was I was bloody transporting though. All this mystery lately, and now the same from you? Am I that bad at keeping secrets?"

"Yes," Pi and Rex replied in immediate unison.

"Ah, well, truth be told right there I see," Scout replied, digging into his stew. "Fair's fair."

Pi smiled. Her life partner had hearts almost as big as his mouth. Until she better understood what the future would hold for her, she was not going to risk jeopardizing the fate of the planet and her people to Scout's inability to keep anything of any importance to himself. She watched him eat in near silence, making eye contact a few times with Rex, but mostly just watching the lyght lamps dance with the shadows on the burro walls. She was incredibly tired and felt her eyelids droop more and more as the time paced on.

Rex noticed this. "Hey, you," he said to Pi. "Why don't you and Scout tucker down for a nap after all that leaping? I'll tend to the supper dishes."

Pi looked at Scout, his mouth adorably half-covered in stew bits, and met his loving, gentle glance. "Sounds dreamy to me."

"Makes two of us then," Scout replied. "You're an ace, Rex. Thanks mate."

The tired couple retired to their shared bed shelf and quickly fell quiet in each other's paws, Scout thinking of what could possibly be important enough to make Pi start to keep secrets from him no matter how bad he was at keeping them and Pi wondering how long she should wait before sharing her news with Scout. Both of these thoughts slowly slipped away as their aching musculature reminded them both how physically drained they were. Sleep, and a deep and restful one at that, arrived shortly thereafter leaving the soft and calming whirring of the lyght fans the only thing left awake in the dark, warm burro.

2

The next morning, Pi awoke before first light. She slipped out of Scout's comforting embrace, grabbed a few pieces of carrot bread and a flask of sweetwater from the hob, and made her way out of the burro. Walking quietly through the interconnected maze of caves, tunnels, and burros that made up HomeSpace, she wondered if the other Quasi would find it comforting or upsetting that the millennial turn was happening right under their noses and that she, a young female courier had been chosen as the one to represent them in concert with the Sun. An orphan, no less.

She thought to the MaRuu attack that claimed her parents, and her friend's Rhi's also. The Quasi and Bugles, Rhi's race of humanoid beetles with shiny, gold skin and crystallized butterfly wings, had set out on an expedition to colonize the SouthLands in an attempts to stop the Southern HomeSpace from becoming too overcrowded as more and more sought shelter from the dangers of the Storm Plains and the ever-increasing static Lyghtning Fields as the planet grew more and more unstable as the Sun turned an ever-increasing, pulsating hue of purplish blue wreaking constant havoc on the surface.

From the only four that escaped, the Bugle leader Bha and his mate, Bor, and Scout's parents, they learned the MaRuus had attacked only once, at night from every angle and direction in one blistering, coordinated attack of cunning and force. It was a devastatingly effective slaughter that let the Quasis and Bugles know once and for certain that the Far Lands were never to be travelled to, far less made into homesteads.

9

"The dead do not tell ghost stories. Only the living."

Pi shuddered. The Midnight Massacre, Ichabod said often, was more of a message and one intended to keep what little peace was left between the three remaining species on Arkelia. It served its purpose and had been respectfully heeded, with those who were lost venerated as heroes who would never be forgotten in time or history. Every Autumn, on the anniversary of the Return of the Four, red and black awnings were draped throughout HomeSpace and a remembrance vigil held in their honor.

"We live to remember their debt. We will never ever forget. All of us here honor their death."

Scout's parents, Bud and Fay, lived the rest of their natural lives out on the far side of HomeSpace, away from the hustle and bustle of the greater community in near solitude. Scout's relationship with his father was a difficult one. Bud, an ornery Quasi for his whole life, was incredibly hard on his only son, believing him to be too soft and quiet as Scout grew from his pup days.

They shared a name, Budder, and Scout was called Buddy as a child and into his teens which he despised. As soon as he took on his role of a Scout, he took that as his given name and never looked back. Fay tried her best to shield Scout from his father's relentless criticism, but it had left deep emotional scars to this day, sixteen planet turns after Bud's death by self-intoxication.

Scout was ferociously close to Fay and became a near shell of himself when she passed two planet turns ago from the Cold, a flu-like illness that killed many elderly Quasi each year. It was only Pi asking Scout to be her life partner and asking him to live with her and Rex did Scout slowly return to a sense of normalcy in his life. He still had days where his spirits were dampened by the loss of his mother, but they had grown few and far between. Between Pi's love and support and Rex's brotherly friendship, Scout had finally become proud of who he was and what he could be... the best Quasi scout ever.

Scout's Auntie Addy, his mother's sister, lived in Elder Care, with the other older Quasi who could not tend to their own medical needs, not far from their home burro. He doted on her and took care to heed her advice on all things for her wisdom was held in high esteem throughout HomeSpace. She was slipping away from life faster now, and Scout made a point to see her as often as he could in between scouting missions. Pi too would call on her for counsel or simply to chat with a parent, as they both thought of her. She was, in a word, lovely.

It was here that Pi was on her way to. She felt that Auntie Addy deserved to be the first to know her secret and hoped she would offer advice and wisdom on her future endeavors. Pi had known she was different than her pup mates ever since she could remember, not to mention her ability to learn the Bugle language in a matter of days which made her friendship with Rhi that much more special because she had in turn learned the Quasi dialect at the same speed. She had always been the wisest of any who came in contact with her, and to be so down to planet about it made her who she was, a friend to all.

Her hearts were pure. She never gloated about her attributes nor thought better of herself, she just felt different and not conceited in any way. Auntie Addy often said that was what she enjoyed about Pi the most, her humility and grace. They shared that trait in common. Pi relished speaking with another female who knew more than she let on around the tribesmen. With a glint in the eye, they studied and learned from all they came in contact with, without others realizing they were doing so. Being as smart as they were was their shared secret, save Ichabod, who saw the promise in Pi from a young age too.

Between the two of them, Pi learned everything from the stories of the Ancients to Arkelian sociology and philosophy. As a young orphan, she was truly blessed to be taken under their shared tutelage. And now, as a young adult she knew why. She was the one who would represent her people to Sun to plead to restore the planet to its earlier more prosperous glory, fertile and fresh from the ending to come.

She was being asked to sacrifice herself to try to save their world. This should scare her, but it strangely brought Pi an odd sense of peace and a sense of reckoning with herself. It was this she wished to speak to Auntie Addy about the most. The anticipation of sharing her news with the closest thing to a mother Pi ever had made her hearts beat ever that much faster as she reached the Elder Care burros. She couldn't wait to share her news with Auntie.

As Pi passed through the last set of burros before reaching Elder Care, she thought to how her fellow Quasi lived, believing their world would one day just... end, without hope for their species, the Bugles, or their planet. They were taught from puphood that the story of the Journey of Lyght was now no more than hushed folklore, a dream not worth dreaming for.

Hope, that curious notion tied to every spirit's very existence, was a fickle thing to Pi. She knew that hope was double-edged, both a blessing and a curse for to want to hold on to one's life was in a way greedy and yet, a propellent of desire to strive to spring eternal. Eternity, they were taught, was were those who had lived went when they left their mortal vessel behind, as Auntie Addy had described often and was not subtle in longing for "her next voyage" as she called it.

That gave the Quasi the peace of mind they needed to go about their lives but for Pi it wasn't enough, as most things often weren't. She always wanted more... knowledge. Pi truly wanted to understand anything and everything she discovered or came across, which was one of the reasons Auntie Addy had taken to her so deeply since the first time Scout brought her with him to visit her so many planet turns ago. It was Auntie Addy that informed Pi that although she loved her nephew dearly, it was Pi's visits she came to cherish most.

She would regale Pi with stories of the Arkelia of her youth and teach her of Quasi antiquity while Pi would share remembrances of her frequent off burro leapings, the state of the upper world, the lightning fields, and the other tribes' goings on. Their visits always ended with Pi having to pry herself away for fear of missing out on lunch or supper, depending on when she was able to spend time with Auntie. Seeing the soft light of the Elder Care burros begin to reflect of her retinas, Pi grew more excited, wondering what Auntie Addy would have to say when she heard the news of the journey.

She checked her pouch to make sure she had remembered to bring the carrot bread treat. Feeling the wrapper with her long thumb and forepaw, Pi smiled. Auntie loved Rex's carrot bread almost more than she loved Rex.

***

Rex slipped out of his nook while it was still dark, which was unusual for him. He, like Scout, tended to sleep well until the lyght lamps were shining brightly through the caves on their regular schedule that kept the Quasis regulated on the same rhythm of the planet's storms which pulsed across the sky above from morning until nighttime. With the Sun now shrinking back on the light it shared with them, the static energy this caused helped keep Arkelia moving in turn, if Pi and his professors from school were to be believed.

He and Scout had other ideas but kept quiet when his sister, Miss Believe Everything You're Told in School was around. She mocked their theories of conspiracy and mysticism. To quote Pi, "If it hasn't been proven, then it's not true."

Rex and Scout, in their simple countering, would just add, "Yet."

Rex smiled thinking of this. How he loved them both. Rhi, well, she sure had spark. That was for sure. A little too much, in his opinion but he, Pi, and Scout, well, they had a good thing going now. They were the triumphant trio! Pi said that with Rhi's addition, they made for the terrific team and Rex let her have it so as to include her lifelong friend into the mix so as not to exclude her. He had learned that compromise was the best weapon in his limited arsenal to maintain a healthy relationship with his very knowledgeable, highly opinionated sister and her fiery, feisty little friend, Rhi. Oh, those two were a pair all right. The heavens couldn't stand in their way when they decided upon something.

Scout was smart. He had never bothered trying. He somehow found Pi and Rhi's bond admirable from the start and never tried to cut in or claim any sort of dominance away from them. Rex on the other hand spent countless and fruitless planet turns trying to usurp Rhi and have Pi all to himself. It wasn't until he took Scout's advice and began calling on Auntie Addy for advice that he came out of his childish ways and began to appreciate the unbreakable bonds of friendship found in life. "Friends are the family that we choose, Rex. Never forget that," Auntie would say to him frequently until it sunk in.

When Rhi visited the Bugle enclave to the North for sentry training five planet turns ago, Pi peppered Rex and Scout with endless things they either didn't care to understand or better yet, care to give any thought to in the first place. She was also noticeable glum, like she was somehow missing a piece of her soul. When Rex realized she was, he had a new appreciation for his sister's relationship with her best friend. It was the love of having a sister, something neither he nor Scout could provide.

After that, Rex gave them wide berth and stopped being jealous of their bond for it was entirely different of the bond he shared with Pi as a sister and with Rex as a surrogate brother. The four completed each other in different ways... and Rhi's way might be to bluster and fluster about but Rex learned to love her all the same. She might say differently on the surface but deep down, Rex knew Rhi loved him too... or at least his cooking.

Rex smiled at the thought as he entered the cooking room, noticing a half loaf of carrot bread missing from the serving table. Pi had gone to Auntie's. This didn't surprise him. Of course, she would tell Addy of the news that came from Ichabod last night. Addy, although in Elder Care, was held in the highest esteem throughout the burrow for her near mystical way of providing comfort, support, advice, and hope to any and all who would sit beside her bed and hold her paw. He just wished Pi had asked Rex to join her.

Peeking his head into Pi and Scout's sleeping nook, Rex saw his brother's large body curled up still fast asleep. Typical. Pi always had to do what she wanted, when she wanted, and usually alone. It was an odd way to live one's live when the Quasi way of life was one based on being a close-knit community and sharing all of life's offers with each other in the close proximity of their HomeBases. Everyone spent their time in the company of each other so frequently, it was almost frowned upon the way Pi tended to keep to herself, but her compassionate and curious ways bode her goodwill from others.

Rex had grown so used to living in his older sister's shadow that he would often forget the pangs of jealousy that peppered his thoughts from time to time on their given roles in life. Under Addy's tutelage, Rex tried to be nothing but proud for Pi and happy to be the Burro Keeper, safely out of danger and harms ways but still, there were times he secretly wished he was leaping side by side with them on one of her and Scout's jaunts out of HomeSpace and across the barren lyghtning fields of Arkelia's surface. Then he would remember how much he despised the cold, blistering winds and forever modulating temperatures when he had gone and quickly brushed the pangs of longing away once again.

To the outside, Rex knew he had come to be viewed as laid back and easy going and he secretly felt guilty that his thoughts on many things would make him out to be an imposter of sorts. He truly was grateful for his life, but the death of their parents left him with a dark streak, tainting his self-view. If such violence and sadness was in the world, what type of a world really was it? This question continued to go unanswered.

Discovering that Pi, his sister, was being chosen as the Journeyer, made both perfect sense and yet scary and sad news. The thought of her saving the planet for another millennia smashed right up against his petrifying fear of losing her forever, causing him to toss and turn all night with hardly any sleep at all. So much so that the sound of Scout letting out a loud yawn nearly sent him through the burro's ceiling.

"You going to eat that bread or just keep staring at it, mate?" Scout asked, wiping sleep from his eyes before returning his spectacles to his snout.

Rex grimaced for a brief clip. "Shut up, Fluffer."

"I don't like when you call me that, Rex," Scout said plainly, pouring himself a tankard of sweetwater.

"I know," Rex replied, grabbing the hunk of carrot bread he had cut for himself and moving past Scout into the living area to increase the lyght fan whirrers to heat the burro and take a seat to eat his breakfast next to the hearth.

"Why do you think I call you it?" he asked Scout mischievously.

Snout snorted. "If you weren't such a good cook, I'd flatten you like one of those light, fluffy, delicious graincakes you're going to make me for breakfast this morning, Rex."

Rex grinned. He loved his surrogate brother and their relationship, especially the part where they verbally rip each other to shreds on the regular. "Thanks. I'll take that compliment, thank you very much."

This interaction took his mind away from his thoughts and he settled down to eat. Taking a big bite, Rex savored it. He was a darn good cook.

***

Scout left the burro soon after finishing his breakfast. Waking up to find Pi gone was more than a little bit disheartening. Stupid, stupid secrets, he grumbled.

His stomach felt as full as his head did after the occurrences of the last few planet turn's events. Secret missions and secrets between them, the balance of their lives seemingly slowly slipping away with each new day. He sighed, trying to clear the burdens from his mind. These glum thoughts do you no good, he told himself, let them float away. But it was difficult to do so, all things considered.

He knew Pi well enough to know that if she, Rex, and Ichabod were keeping court, something big was on the horizon. Something... epic.

And if they wouldn't tell him for fear of him spilling the beans to anyone else, it made him heart sick. They could trust him! Of course, they could, he told himself. They just didn't.

Bounding up to the north quadrant, the Bugle enclave, Scout decided there was only one thing to do: see Rhi. She would know what he should do, for she knew how Pi thought better than anyone else in HomeSpace save Auntie Addy, who was where Scout assumed Pi had left their burro to go see if he had to place a wager on it. For a free spirit, Pi also tended to be quite predictable in her actions, motivations, and routines. She was as organized as a Quasi could be, which could both be an attribute but also a detriment in some instances.

Scout teased her from time to time about her lack of spontaneity, but Pi would have none of it: doing things the right way first meant not having to do them more than once, she would say to anyone who would listen. It was usually just Scout, as he was the only one close enough to her to nudge her in that way, lovingly. Their spars were mostly times to josh one another, as all partners do to keep things lively and interesting. Pi might have a long fuse, but Scout knew how to light it.

Reaching the nest of hives where Rhi lived, Scout once again marveled at the beauty of the crystalline, intricately spun designs in the webbed hives the Bugles made their homes. Tucked near pulsing lyght veins, the hives pulsed with all the colors of the rainbow in kaleidoscopic fashion that bedazzled Scout's eyes, the light flickering across them and nearly entrancing him. He knew this was how they caught their prey, cavegulls, to draw them in and kill them before they knew what hit them. Better them than me, Scout thought. "Rhi, Rhi, Rhi!" he called out loudly, the traditional three-time beckoning call of the Bugles.

A two-paw tall, silver and bronze skinned Bugle, with large rainbow hued wings popped out of one of the nearest hive entrances, flying out, her wings flapping gracefully, creating the illusion of being a moving prism. "Hiya, Scout! What's it all about?!"

Scout grinned. Rhi's energy was contagious. He was already feeling better.

"Came by for a stroll and a chat, if you're up for it," Scout said. "There's some goings on but, er, I don't know what going on. It's all very troublesome."

Rhi smiled, sighing. Oh, Scout, she thought. How couldn't you love the big lug? What a fluffy mess of a silly Quasi. "As sure as rain, it sounds. I'll be right down!"

Scout watched her reverse direction and return inside the hive. He listened to the banging and crashing inside the enclosure walls before Rhi returned yet again, this time making a nosedive for him and landing on his left shoulder.

"Think I'll let you get the exercise if you don't mind, Scout," Rhi said, plopping herself down into a sitting position. "I drank too much nectar last night and my wings feel like grain sacks if you know what I mean."

Scout chuckled. Of course, she did. Moderation and Rhi were two words that did not mix well together. There had been many a night he, Rhi, and Rex drank their more than fair share of nectar while Pi played them woodwind music but sometimes it seemed that Rhi, even though so much smaller in size than them, would out drink them tenfold, relatively speaking. To see her attempt to fly at the end of one of their nectar nights was a sight to be seen, mostly for her raw inability to admit any sort of defeat...ever.

Watching her flitter skyward only to violently corkscrew from side to side before falling back to the ground could be hard to watch, if it wasn't so darn side-splittingly funny of an exercise to behold. Many a nectar night ended with a banged up Rhi asleep in the corner of the burro sleep space between theirs and Rex's hovel, muttering obscenities before trailing off into a heavy buzzing noise that would linger on the ear for hours.

All said, she was in top form and used nectar nights to unwind after long hours acting as the HomeSpace daytime sentry, which kept her close to all the hustle and bustle of cave life without being afforded the opportunity to join the other bugles sent to accompany the Quasi on their foraging missions, always keeping a lookout for MaRuu attackers ready to pounce. She groused often and more increasingly about the council members telling their covens one thing and then claiming the opposite when it came to burro business.

They thought they were avoiding the prying ears of the other Quasi by having their important gossip at the entrance to the burros but Rhi, with her incredible Bugle sonic hearing, heard it all. While Ichabod told the Quasi at large things were improving and a new spring was in sight, Rhi knew they were all lies. Ichabod was scared as heck, for the weather kept worsening, the lyght arteries losing strength, and the lyghtning fields growing less and less stable by the turn. It wasn't looking good for their HomeSpace and Arkelia in general for that matter.

The words 'grim' and 'dire' were used more and more frequently. Drinking softened the sadness, albeit at the expense of being angrier. Ichabod seemed to anticipate every bubble of trouble somehow, always knowing exactly what to say to keep his people in line. Rhi wondered if he was a fortune teller rather than a mystic sometimes.

"So, what do I owe the pleasure of you visit today?" Rhi asked as Scout leapt them away from the hives and towards the Northern Passage, an infrequently used tunnel that connected the HomeSpace to the nearest lyghtning field. It was beautifully lit by a bevy of amber lyght veins that bounced off the thick quartz scattered throughout, making the long tunnel appear to be a portal to another world.

"Can I talk to you about something that came up last night?" Scout asked, finding a thick set of low-lying rocks to leap onto, setting them down gently upon them.

Rhi smirked. "You already are, Scout. Go on then. Spill it. What's going on?"

"Rhi, I'm not sure what to do," Scout said sadly. "Pi and Rex don't think I can keep a secret. Ichabod, sure, I get it. He's the High Elder, but my life partner and my brother don't trust me to keep my mouth shut? I mean, come on!"

Rhi looked up at Scout, staring until he noticed her doing so.

"What?" Scout asked, caught off guard.

"You amaze me, Scout. Unreal you are sometimes, you big ball of fluffing. You came here to ask my advice on why they don't trust you with secrets by literally telling me they have some big secret in the process!" Rhi laughed so hard she was afraid her wings were going to fall off.

Scout went to say something, then stopped himself to consider what she said. Dang it, he cursed himself silently under his breath. They were right not to tell him what they were discussing after all.

"Frick," Scout muttered. "Gone and done it again. Serves me right, don't it, Rhi?"

"That it does, friend." She felt her inquisitiveness begin to hum throughout her small body. Juicy information to her ears was sometimes, but not always, better than the delicious, stupefying taste of nectar to her lips.

"Now you want me to tell you what I know." Scout knew what

came next. "Right?"

"Right again, you goof." Rhi flew up to match Scout's line of sight. "Start from the beginning and don't skip a detail. Every itsy-bitsy teeny weenie morsel of news in as vivid recollection as you can muster. Begin." She heard him sigh. "Now!"

"Promise you won't share a word of it?" Scout asked mawkishly, fearing the repercussions to come.

"NOW, SCOUT!!!" Rhi exclaimed, punching him in the front paw.

A hungover Bugle with an ear for gossip was not to be reckoned or reasoned with.

So, he began.

***

The Elder Care burros were truly something to look forward to for a Quasi in their older turns. Basked in warm, healing lyght arteries and decorated with lush pillows, beddings, and personal effects brought from their homes, the place was one half care facility and the other a shrine to its inhabitants. When a Quasi reached the age of two hundred turns, their frail bodies usually required near constant lyght warmth to sustain it for the rest of their mortal time.

The old were revered in Quasi culture, both for carrying the lyght spirit the longest and for the oral histories they shared of times long past. With the exception of Ichabod, they were not able to vote in the callings so as to stop them from voting against progress in lieu of how things used to be, their stories provided information to the young on how to avoid past mistakes.

Aunt Addy fell perfectly into the category of a wise sage to her brethren, as she was forced to retire from the burro life when she needed to absolve herself of personal freedom and enter into Elder Care. Her she sat, propped up with numerous hay pillows, her soft, grey fur now dulled and somewhat matted. Addy had also lost a great deal of the mane from the top of her head, laying her pinkish, white skin bare. Her right rear paw had grown infected from a bacterial infection after a life full of leaping and required amputation.

One of her hearts had also become infected and she was immobilized and in constant need of lyght energy to remain mortal. In poor health but good spirits, she welcomed visits like the one today from Pi, which made her feel like she was still connected to the world outside her bed, helping others live as she would: to the fullest.

Even more so when advice or council was asked for, although just being told stories of the life going on outside Elder Care were good too. But oh, how she loved being asked for help, whether it be for guidance or compassion. When Pi told Addy she was being sent on a leaping to the other HomeBases with a coded message, her aunt knew something big was afoot. Just not this. Who would, really? Gracious!

"I should have told Scout, I know," Pi said ruefully. "I just wanted your advice first. You know how scared he gets about big things."

"You did the right thing, sweetie," Addy replied, stroking Pi's front paw, comforting her.

"His hearts are nearly as big as he is, but his mind takes him to fearful places with news such as this. He'll be alright, though. He has no choice in the matter, and I'll tell him so. This isn't an opportunity you can turn away from, Pi. No female Quasi has ever been called from the for something such as important as this. You represent a change… and one long overdue if we stand any chance of…" Addy trailed off.

Pi leaned in. "Aunt Addy? Any chance of what?"

Addy sighed. "I fear say, Pi. I don't want it to affect you. This troubles me very much but," she paused, "it must be done. No two ways about it, I'm afraid. Oh child, I'm sorry."

Pi felt a knot in her stomach and a lump in her throat. Addy had never been anything but chipper and loving to her, but now, out of nowhere, she heard fear, sadness, and longing in her voice. "Addy, tell me. Don't hold out on me now. Please?"

Addy leaned back in her bedding. She took a large gulp of sweetwater for the carrot bread had long since been shared and finished between them. Seeing the look in Pi's eyes, Addy could honestly say it was the first time she had seen fear in her niece's eyes. It was unfortunate but necessary, sadly.

"For you to understand what I am about to tell you, Pi, I need you to know that the past is just that, gone and past. We only have the present. The future hasn't happened yet. What I tell you now is only meant to make you aware of how this present, there here and right now, is happening the way it is. I can't tell you for a lick what will happen next, but I can tell you what happened before in hopes you can gleam a different future for yourself and all of us as a result."

Pi was confused. What was Addy talking about? She studied her for signs of dementia, but Addy's blue eyes were razor sharp. This was for real. Pi bit her bottom lip, met Addy's stare, and nodded for her aunt to continue, wherever the story may go. She was ready for anything, or so she thought. "What is it, Auntie? Tell me."

Addy sighed. There would be no going back from this. "You have been taught lies, Pi. You and the others, you whole lives."

"About what?" Pi asked, a growing sense of shock in her stomach knotting it up.

"About everything really," Addy replied. There was no way to sugarcoat the truth that the truth they were taught since young age were mostly lies. "You were taught false hope, Pi. I am so sorry. You are being asked to undertake a suicide mission, I'm afraid."

"But... what?! Why?!" Pi finally stammered. Her head was spinning. Addy wasn't delirious... she was serious. What was this? A way to stop her from risking her life, perhaps? To stop her from being the one to extend the truce with the Sun.

Addy drank more sweetwater, sensing how upset her niece was becoming. Pi had already forgotten that Addy told her that she should accept Ichabod's request.

"Pi, my sweet," Addy finally said, "I didn't say you shouldn't go. But I want you to know the truth of what you are being asked to do and what happened to the past journeyers. I want you to have what they did not: the ability to make an informed decision. That is all I am offering you. The chance to choose wisely. You should always think twice in life, Pi. Never rush to judgement. Take the time to think things through from both perspectives: the emotional and the rational. So, take a moment and decide if you want to hear what I have to say... or if you've already made your mind up. The choice is yours, child. It always will be."

Pi leaned back, needing to think, and flopped her back against the cluster of hay pillows behind her. She watched Addy closely, studying the old Quasi for any sign that she was being daft. They shared this silence until it became uncomfortable for Pi. Too uncomfortable.

"Tell me," Pi said simply.

"There have been many Journeyers since we began keeping record, Pi. Countless of them. Hundreds maybe. We have been living on Arkelia for millions of turns, not thousands, dear. Each one told they were the first to be asked. And the whole time, Arkelia has been slowly dying as we continue to creep closer and closer to the Sun. There have never been any abatements or truces with the Spirit. We continue to wither and are forced to draw deeper and deeper underground to escape the conditions you see on the surface on your leapings. These missions have done nothing more than provide a dying planet's inhabitants false hope of salvation and a happy ending that just won't happen, Pi. It's a historical ruse wrapped in a religious dressing to appease to the masses. What you are being asked to do is to give your generation just enough hope to keep us going until folks start to lose it all over again. You've been living at the end your whole life. We all have. And they wouldn't have told you before asking you to sacrifice your life to keep the ruse alive for another generation in hopes the planet doesn't give out while any of us are alive to witness it. I'm sorry, Pi, but your quest is a lie."

It was Addy's turn to sit back, drink another gulp of sweetwater, and take a moment to rest.

Pi was numb. Her world and everything she believed was a lie. Hope had been turned maleficent, evil somehow. If hope was false, what could she believe in now?

"Believe in yourself, Pi," Addy said, as if she could read Pi's thoughts. "Believe in love. Believe in the love you share with others, me, your brother, Scout, your friends. Believe in that. Hope has always been a blessing and a curse, dear. For when there's nothing to look forward to, why would one want to keep on living, others would ask. I reply that to love life and those you share it with is better than having false hope in better days never to come. Love the now for the later isn't here yet. Be happy, Pi, and deciding whether you want to sacrifice yourself for the good of the four HomeSpaces and all of their inhabitants will then be a decision made wisely. Do this out of love for yourself and others and you will have chosen wisely. Do this out of a sense of trickery, skullduggery, and false hope, well, I won't let Ichabod pull that on you. I don't care if he's managed to get himself inside your head. You deserve the truth."

Pi felt dizzy. None of this made sense. None of it. The stories, the parchments, the altars, the quests, none of it true? Her head throbbed; her hearts pumping way too fast. This was too much.

"Drink more sweetwater," Addy instructed, motioning to Pi's goblet.

Pi gulped down half of the sweetwater and then sat in silence for a time. "How long have you known, Addy?"

"All the High Elders find out the true history of the failed journeys,

Pi. It is a bitter pill to swallow, isn't it?"

Pi nodded. "But what of the Violet Stone and the Journey of Lyght?"

Pi," Addy added with conviction, "just because something hasn't happened before doesn't mean that it can't happen now. If you do decide to take the quest, you can be darn sure I believe you might be the one to do it. Do you know how much I love you?"

Addy smiled, knowing the response but wanting to hear it anyways. "How much, Addy?"

"More than you'll ever know."

They embraced tenderly, sharing each other's warmth.

"I'm going to save the planet, Addy," Pi whispered.

Addy sighed. "I know it in my hearts. Now go find Rhi. I'm sure my nephew has spilt what he knows to her by now and her little Bugle mind is probably ready to pop. Your family needs you, Pi. You have much to accomplish in a short amount of time. And if Ichabod asks where you got your information from, you send him right to me. I'll deal with him, the stuffy bureaucrat and politician disguised as a Quasi of faith that he is. He holds a dark power over us I've never been able to quite put a paw on. I don't trust him."

Pi smiled. "Family first."

"You're darn tooting," Addy replied, smiling. "You listen to your hearts, darling. And to the hearts of our family of scrappers and scoundrels. Find strength in their courage to tell you what they think of all this, but I caution you to keep the truth to yourselves. False hope might be cruel, Pi, but it has served the Quasi for thousands of planet turns. If all knew the truth, it would end the last vestiges of what civilization we have left as a people. Which is why--"

"We can't tell Scout," Pi finished for her. "He'd blabber all over the burros before the next sun rose."

Addy took a deep breath. "His parents did a real number on him, Pi. You know this. He seeks his truth in the acceptance of others, never trusting himself to come to a decision of his own making. Without you guiding him, he would be a great danger to himself. If he ever thought you were going on a journey, which you now know is one never to return from, he will lose his bearings on the importance this holds for our people. I wonder how in Arkelia's name Ichabod came to choose you, as he knows this to be true. It could have been any number of the Battlers called instead. In my mind, this calls for a warrior. Not a leaper, especially one whose family relies on them as much as Ichabod knows you to do. This is all quite intriguing to this old mind of mine."

Battlers were the male Quasi charged with the defense of the HomeSpaces against MaRuu invaders, even though none had actually ever seen any battle. The MaRuu stayed far away in their own territories, and seemingly always had. But they were out there, and no one could definitively say they wouldn't escalate tensions some turn in the future. The Quasi, knowing the MaRuus' lethal and cunning ways, must always be at the ready for attack, no matter how small the chance might be. The best defense was having a lethal offense at the ready.

The Quasi who became Battlers were the biggest and bravest of all, who spent their time preparing their agile bodies for warfare every day, defending the territories in packs of six, carrying blades of sharp silver and bronze in their pouches, and wearing protective body armor to fell even the sharpest blow from reaching either fur or the skin beneath their thick tan coats. The Battlers were the toughest of the tough, and the bravest of the brave. Their personalities were as stoic as their gloried place in Quasi society.

Pi knew some of them, not well, but well enough they tended to have rocks for brains. Two exceptions were Dee and Chukk, the Battalion leaders and life partners. They were decent guys who seemed to be able to think for themselves. The rest just did as they were told and that was about it, really. She saw the logic in sending one of them to their deaths to be a glorious sacrifice for the populous at large the more she thought about.

"I have to admit it didn't exactly sound as if Ichabod was entirely thrilled with me being chosen, Addy," Pi added, thinking back to their brief conversation. "He spent the time we had warning me to think on it before accepting."

Addy scratched the long tendril of fur under her jawbone. "Something is afoot, Pi. For a woman to be nominated is nearly heresy. You know as well as I do how females are thought of in life. To serve and obey and all that garbage the men have spewed since time began."

Pi frowned at that simple truth. "What do you think it means? How did Ichabod decide?"

"Only Ichabod would know. I have no knowledge of it, sadly. So, what I think it means is that Ichabod has some serious explaining to do. And quick!"

Pi nodded. "The more you know, aye?"

"Now go find your buzzy little friend before she hits the nectar. You know how she gets."

"Drunk?" Pi chuckled.

"No finer a word for it, is there?" Addy smiled. "I can't say why Pi, but this is giving me a sense of hope that is in no way false. Maybe you were called for the very reason you hope you've been. But what do I know? I'm just an old, battered, and bruised Quasi holding on to this mortal vessel for as long as I can. I'm greedy for this life and for the love we all share with each other. To know you've been called for this honor and to still be considering doing so even now, knowing what it will entail, warms my soul. As it should yours. You're one in a million, love."

They embraced again, not really having any more to say. Pi didn't want to leave, but she wanted to see what Rhi and Rex made of all this... and how they could keep Scout off the scent for as long as possible.

Pi left the Elder Care burros more confused and apprehensive than she was before arriving, but with the information she would need to decide what the future held not just for herself, but for her family, and the rest of the Quasi and Bugles at large. It made both her hearts and her soul almost unbearably heavy with a mixed sense of foreboding and gloom unlike any Pi had ever known. Knowledge, it seemed, did not always yield good tidings.

***

Two shadows, one quite large and the other quite small, were cast against of the lyght artery cave nestled in the far end of HomeSpace, just near the Bugle nests.

"You're drunk."

"Again."

"You're drunk."

Rhi chortled. "No, I meant 'I'm drunk again'. Scout, you're a true pisser, you are!"

Scout chuckled. "Rhi, at this sad point in my life I will take that as a genuine compliment."

"And as such you should, my fuzzy friend!" Rhi exclaimed, finishing the last of her cup, now dry of sweet nectar. "So, what do we know, eh? Your girl and my sister have been asked... something..."

"Something important," Scout finished, his head buzzing with nectar. "Something too important to tell me, it seems."

Rhi found the strength to fly up onto his shoulder. Taking a seat by holding on to his floppy left ear for balance, she patted his shoulder with her other hand. "It's all right then, Scout. You know she wanted to tell you. She just knew you'd do what you did, mate. Come straight to me. Which you did, aye?"

"I'm not trustworthy," Scout groused. "Not enough for important things it seems. I couldn't even keep that there was a secret, er, secret. Dang it, Rhi. I'm hopeless."

Rhi chuckled. "That's not true and you know it. You have the biggest hearts in the burro. You just have the loosest lips too. You have to learn to find your natural instincts... and then listen to them."

Scout drained the last of his nectar, wiping the fur around his lips. "That package they sent me for... has to be a part of it. Has to be."

"Has to be," Rhi repeated. "So, what now? She knows that you know... something. And I'm sure she knows you well enough to know you'd go find and tell me about it."

"I guess we wait," Scout said after a moment's pause. "Not much else to do, is there?"

Rhi shook her head. "No, Scout, no. We ask. Let her tell us there's nothing to tell us so we can get a better read on her. I'm getting to the bottom of this. You and I both know she's with Addy right now figuring out whatever there is to figure out about this. For all we know, she'll come back *wanting* to tell us about it. So, what was it they sent you for? I know you peeked!"

Scout looked her in the eyes. "A parchment map and a very, very old one at that."

Rhi cocked an eyebrow. "And the plot thickens."

"Aye," was all Scout could muster. "Aye."

***

Rex hadn't left the burro all day, taking the time to clean the hovel with vigor. It helped him to clear his mind when life left him frazzled. And he was most certainly feeling frazzled after last night's events. Rex so very much wished things had just gone back to the usual goings on but no, of course not, he groused silently, finishing sweeping out the brambles and stray roots from the burro floors. Everything had to change, again, just when he, Pi, Scout, and Rhi had settled into a familiar routine of domesticated life.

Oh, who was he kidding? Rex knew there was nothing normal or predictable about those three. Scout might follow Pi around like a young pup and Rhi might drink like the biggest of Battlers, but none of them ever took the time to just stay at home in the quiet of the hovel and rest. They were always on the go, to and from, this way or that way, neither here nor there was ever good enough for any of them while Rex enjoyed nothing more than a steaming mug of root tea and the quiet, gentle whirring of the heat providing lyght lamps, which both circulated the air through the burros but also drew lyght and heat from the lyght veins which ran through the deep rock of the HomeSpace.

The lyght energy was the capillaries of the planet's very core, sustaining them, and healing and sustaining them as in Addy's case. It was one of the reasons Quasi lived for so many planet turns, as Arkelia itself feed them warmth. The yellowish color pulses and throbbed through the rock face and sparkled through the crystalline quartz deposits scattered throughout the rock face. They brought Rex constant comfort and peace.

Rex could not understand for the life of him why Pi and her mates wanted nothing more than to break free of the comforts of home at every opportunity. Not him, no sir. He loved the confines of the burro and the warm blanket of safety it provided. Save the leapings, scoutings, sentry duties, and courier chores for the rest of them, thank you very much. Being adventurous had gotten his and Rhi's parents killed. And now, it looked like Pi might very well follow suit if she went about accepting the Journey of Lyght as Ichabod had begrudgingly begun to offer her.

Something foretold since time began being dropped in his gregarious sister's lap just like that? Had Ichabod gone mad? Although he wouldn't say it aloud, Rex was shocked a female Quasi had been chosen... and by whom? And how? The more Rex thought and pondered all this, the more it seemed like a sick and twisted turn of fate rather than an opportunity to grant the Quasi another millennia of balance with the Spirit. The risk was just too heavy a load to bear, and he wasn't even the one tasked with accepting it or not. Could Pi decline this the way it seemed Ichabod had urged her to, Rex wondered? But would Pi decline it, even if she could? Not likely, Rex admitted silently to himself.

Rex placed the thicket woven broom back in the closet dug into the corner and took a moment to rub his temples. This was all becoming very troublesome indeed. Scout would lose it when he eventually found out. Oh, that was not going to be a pretty picture at all. Scout relied on Pi to keep himself together on a near spiritual level and the mere thought of losing here would very well send him over the side of a mental cliff, one that Rex doubted even he and Rhi together would be able to reel him back from. What was Ichabod thinking?

Rex poured sweetwater from the large clay jug they kept in the kitchen into a bronze kettle, then placed it over the hearth where the steam stove began to work its magic. Root tea, Rex thought, would sooth his frazzled nerves for the time being. In the time it took for the kettle to come to a boil, four longish petal plant roots added to a steaming, piping hot clay mug of sweetwater, and taking his first sip plopped down in his favorite pillow pile, Rex thought of at least three more reasons for Pi to decline what Rex for the first time called 'the curse of the Journey'. It would not be the last.

***

Pi was not ready to face Scout, Rhi, and Rex yet. She needed to clear her mind, and she did so the way she always did by pumping her hearts and lungs and by pushing her body to her limits on a leaping. She left HomeSpace through the nearest auxiliary channel entrances to the Elder Care, where Pi knew she had zero chance of running into Rhi as the sentry on duty. The bugle that she passed in leaving, Bor, was one of the four who returned from the expedition, but they had never spoke, so there was little risk of him saying he had seen Pi depart. She didn't like this newfound feeling of hiding herself and her thoughts from those nearest and dearest to her and was why Pi needed some time alone to sort some things out.

As the Sun slowly sank beneath the far horizon, the thick indigo storm cloud cover and the burnt blood red yellow dusk sky looming overhead ominously, the rainy mist coated the exterior of Pi's fur with a slick finish giving her the appearance of a noticeable shine. Pi began at a moderate gallop, her two hind paws propelling her in unison. She began to tuck into a proper leaping position, each of her leaps sending her higher and further than the one before. Hopping from one jagged rock formation to the next, leaping over ravines that had once supposedly carried raging rivers of sweetwater across the planet surface, Pi knew exactly where she was heading. The lyghtning fields were calling to her yet again.

A place of nature's raw and unadulterated power, the lyghtning fields were also a place few Quasi ventured, let alone return to more than once. The fear of experiencing the constant thumping of thunder mixed with the sight of blistering, yellow and red lyghtning rising from fissures in Arkelia's core, bounding and twisting up in the air in dizzying spandrels before being pulled back down to the planet and slamming back into the ground, sending out waves of heated static energy might be the how the planet generated the lyght energy that fueled the HomeSpaces but it was also what keep Arkelia in a constant state of storming. It was both terrifying and, to Pi at least, magical and pure. She came and sat on the cliff overlooking the fields often when she needed to think, losing track of doubts and worries in the rhythmic, pulsating energy bursts that filled her hearts and long ears. She found peace in the chaos.

The events of the past day spun in Pi's head, from when Ichabod sent her with the message to the three other HomeSpaces essentially telling her she had a glorified one-way ticket to what she now knew, courtesy of Aunt Addy, certain death. Yes, she would die a hero, but she would wouldn't be around to savor it. And knowing her partner, Scout would probably find some way to follow shortly thereafter. Rex and Rhi would suffer, sure, but they would persevere in time. Pi would be revered and remembered around the hearth as the nectar would pour in abundance. She sighed. This was all just too much, too soon. But how else do things like this take place, Pi asked herself? Time was a fickle and folly thing, wasn't it? One day you have all the time in the world and the next you've all but run out of it. A huge, twisty column of lyghtning suddenly erupted, slamming into the sky with more force than Pi could ever remember seeing. It was as if the energy was somehow intertwined with her troubled soul. As it came crashing into the surface, the thick rock and gravel beneath her paws shook from the impact so strongly that Pi had to steady herself.

Addy was right. The weather, even in Pi's seventy-seven planet turns, had continued to grow more and more unstable. The storm cycles had grown fiercer and the lyghtning eruptions larger, the rainstorms more ferocious, and the sweetwater lakes drier and harder to locate. Arkelia was dying... and for the first time, Pi realized that meant its inhabitants right along with it. From the planet to its people, Arkelia was running out of time just as Pi was in making a decision as what to do with the information she now had. They were intertwined and she wasn't too pleased about it. How rash and foolhardy she had been to be so excited about the promise of being the Chosen of the Journey. It wasn't an honor... or was it? She was so confused!

Hope, Addy had said, was a false promise of better days ahead but something the Quasi and Bugles needed to survive. If they had nothing to look forward to, they would lose the will to live. 'Hope,' Addy said in a near whisper, 'gives our souls fuel to fight the darkness surrounding us.' But false hope, Pi asked herself? What of that? Her quest would be a lie designed only to buy her people more time to live a lie. She thought of the pups under forty turns, shuddering at the thought of babies being born into apocalypse. What did they have to look forward to but a frightful and fear-filled death? This newfound sense of imminent mortality shook Pi to the core, not unlike the tremendous and violent constant streams of static lyghtning on witness in front of her. Intertwined indeed. Pi's soul was truly shaken, along with her very quasiality.

"Oh, Addy," Pi whispered. "Why in Spirit's name did you tell me such a horrible thing?"

The tears, gone for so very long, now streamed down her face and along her long snout, the salt from them puckering her cracked, trembling lips. She felt a heavy burden unlike any Quasi should ever have to reckon with now, a mixture of doom and pain unlike any other she had ever felt, not even after the death of her parents so very long ago.

As the lyghtning danced across her deep blue eyes and the booming thunder rippled through her eardrums, Pi found herself trying to find solace, the inner silence she spent years with Ichabod's tutelage to find and master. It escaped her now, the thoughts and fears of Addy's revisionist history swamping out the excitement to be the Chosen for the Journey of Lyght, Ichabod's ruse to keep the hope of the Quasi alive.

Pi, you have been chosen. Your fate with mine is now woven.

She whipped around, thrashing her long tail to fell the intruders behind her, only to find herself... alone? Pi used her keen eyes to scan her surroundings, seeing nothing but mist and lyght flashes in the dark. Whose voices had she heard?

Her fur bristled, defensively, turning thick and sharp, a quilled coat of protective armor. In one swift, graceful move, Pi grabbed the slingshot and a handful of burst stones from her pouch, arming herself in a near instant. Slowly, when she was sure she was alone, Pi cried out, "What is happening to me?!"

She did not receive a response to her liking. She heard only thunder and wind. Pi screamed the question again, louder this time, with the same result. After longer than she realized, Pi relaxed her quill armor and returned the slingshot and ammunition to her pouch, seemingly defeated. She took one last, long look to the lyghtning fields before deciding it was time to return home before she lost her mind altogether.

Secret-spiller be damned, Pi needed her Scout's soft embrace now more than ever. For only the second time in her life, Pi of the Quasi was scared. And she hated every growing second of it. As she spun on her hind paws and took off to return to HomeSpace, Pi wanted nothing more than to make sense of all of this growing craziness. She wanted to go back to that simpler time only the day before when Pi believed her world could be saved.

Behind her, a massive red lyghtning cluster smashed through the cloudy mist, lighting up the night before sending a massive shockwave rippling underneath Pi's paws as she leapt. Thrown to the ground, she turned around long enough to watch a humongous slab of earth flip skywards before slamming back into the ground, sending a huge cloud of dust and debris cascading out in all directions. It was if Arkelia was under attack from itself. Never before had Pi seen such fury or elemental rage from the sky upon the planet, nor any lyghtning that bright crimson hue before.

"Home...go home now," she said, willing herself up and getting back on the move.

Pi shook her head, pushing herself faster now. She hoped her speed and the sound of her journey back would allow her to keep what semblance of her sanity left just long enough to reach Scout... and then Ichabod. For the High Elder of HomeSpace had a reckoning unlike any ever witnessed in the HomeSpace coming his way from one particularly peeved off leaper to deal with, and Ichabod would not be let go until it happened. Pi just hoped HomeSpace would be there when she arrived.

3

Scout and Rhi were finishing the last of their shared nectar, not far from the Lyght artery tunnel where they had their talk, seated beneath the edge of the Bugle nests on an intricately carved stone bench when the HomeSpace suddenly seemed to be lifted into the air as if being raised out of the ground by the Spirit itself, before being immediately dropped back into the ground not a second later. The crash was an immense shockwave of sheer planetary power that sent huge clumps of earth and stone to be shook free of the HomeSpace ceilings and sent smashing to the quartz and clay floors beneath them.

They were both thrown to the ground after the first bouncing, with Scout instinctually shoving a shocked and dazed Rhi under the cover of the bench before the crashing sound and huge chunks of falling debris came a moment later. His act saved her life for certain, as a huge chunk of quartz fell right on top of her former position, sending a bomb of debris into the air around them.

"We're under attack! MaRuus invasion!" Rhi screamed to no one in particular before letting out the shrieking, shrill Bugler's Call, the sound of general alarm notifying HomeSpace of an impending attack of the MaRuus.

She was met with companion calls from the rest of her fellow Bugles, the sound so overpowering that Scout guessed it was bloody all of them, mixing with scary, shuddering noises of the ground in and around the HomeSpace resettling after the shockwave had passed by. Clumps of dirt and rock continued to fall, smaller than the first, sending plumes of dust in their wake.

Finally, Scout, lying on his stomach next to the bench and Rhi, reached back and muzzled her, his sensitive eardrums about ready to be ripped apart by the siren she was admitting at a frequency he couldn't believe even possible, and muzzled her. "Sush! Rhi, sush! For the love of Arkelia, sush yourself!"

It took a long moment, but when Rhi did stop sending the call she looked up with a look of fright and terror that sent shivers down Scout's spine. She looked at him, searching for any semblance of why any of this was happening. "Why would they do this?! Why would anyone do this to us?!"

Scout met her longing gaze with one of a reassurance he felt shocked to be experiencing. "We're alive and it's enough for now! We need to find the others! Fast! I need you to fly, little Rhi. Fly faster than you ever have before. Leave me here! Go find and save the others! Go! Go!! Go!!!"

Rhi snapped out of her daze in a heartbeat, replaced with a sense of strength she had no idea she had in her little bronze and crystal frame. To fly! Without saying a word, Rhi rolled out from under the bench and took off into the air so fast it made a loud POP sound that echoed throughout the artery tunnel in her blurry, streaky wake.

POP!

In Rhi's haste, she did not notice that Scout laying there pinned down, unable to move with a jagged edged, massive piece of quartz covering the lower half of his large frame, splattered with copious amounts of his blood on it, on him, and gushing out in growing pools across the ground. He need not think about it. He knew he was dying before help could come. Scout felt no pain, oddly, just a sense of sinking down into the earth beneath him as if he was becoming one with the silica and soil.

Lying there, he thought of Pi and how he wished she had told him her secret. Scout had a strong suspicion that it had to do with the map he was sent for and the whispers of the Journey being passed through HomeSpace. He knew in his hearts of hearts that Pi was not just his chosen one, but everyone's... Scout just wanted to hear it from her first. He understood though. Scout and secrets did not go well with each other. He so loved sharing exciting things with his family though. It gave Scout such joy to see happiness in others as he tended to find so little in himself most times.

But he knew in his hearts Pi would save them all and also that he loved her unlike no other he had ever known, and the promise of her journey still yet to come, more than life itself. Scout closed his tired eyes and felt like sleeping, the darkness sinking into the depths of his mind and soul, hoping he would dream of Pi for the rest of the eternity. He let out one last soft breath, whispered Pi's name, and let the darkness overtake him.

***

After the shockwave, Rex found himself huddled in a corner of the burro afraid to move for fear of another blast ready to rip through HomeSpace at any second. The burro, one of the closest to the surface of HomeSpace, had been largely saved from the destruction Rex could hear coming from the bowels of the caverns. There was yelling out for help at an almost constant rate, leaving Rex to start to venture out from his hiding spot only to return, scared, as soon as another large piece of ceiling came crashing down through the center cave that help the spiraling burros down towards the warm of the planet's depths. Rex felt the role of coward but could not shake it, just wishing that all he heard in turmoil and pain would be okay and safe again soon.

Rhi nearly slammed into him as she flew inside, crashing instead into the clay burro wall next to him. Falling the ground, Rhi quickly sprung up from the ground, her wings fluttering faster than Rex had ever seen, keeping the Bugle in perfect stop motion in the air. She appeared stronger and more with it than Rex had ever seen. Even in that instant of doom, Rex was eternally proud of Rhi for her composure in crisis. He was amazed at the difference between their opposing composures.

"You all right?!" Rhi asked worriedly. "Rex? Rex?!"

Rex snapped out of his admiring daze. "Aye, I'm all right! What in Arkelia's name happened out there? Where are the others?!"

"Scout was with me near the brunt of it. Saved my life, he did, Rex! Pushed me under cover before the ceiling crashed around us! Fearful no more, I say today!"

That didn't sound all that great for Scout. "Was he all right?"

Rhi nodded in the affirmative. "Aye! He sent me to save all of you. Told me to fly my heart out and I did without thinking. Didn't know I could fly so fast, Rex. Truly didn't. Have you seen Pi? Check on Addy and Ichabod yet?"

Rex swallowed hard. "Uh, no, not yet. I thought it best to, er, stay here to set up a meeting spot because it's safe here. You know? A meeting place while we gather ourselves back up."

Rhi nodded. "Makes good sense, Rex. Keep the faith and the light on. I can get places no Quasi can. Here's hoping Pi was with Addy and kept her safe when the rocks fell! I'm sure Ichabod was near in the Council Cave at the surface. Here's hoping! I'm off! --"

POP!

Rhi was gone, only the echo of her wake stream remaining. Rex's jaw nearly dropped. She was the picture of composure, compassion, and strength, unlike him, the cowardly Quasi huddled in the corner waiting to be saved. Rex couldn't believe Rhi could fly so fricking fast, either. He had never seen any Bugle move like that in his life! He thought now of others like Rhi was doing and set out to gather blankets, prepare food, and get ready for the return of his loved ones. Rex of the Quasi didn't have to be a coward if he didn't want to, he decided with renewed vigor and verve.

***

Rhi found the Elder Care in dusty shambles. It seemed as if whatever happened had been carried through the lyght arteries that warmed and powered HomeSpace, as well as gave sustenance and life to the inhabitants. This was truest for the elderly, as Elder Care was built into a large lyght artery deposit to bask the inhabitants in as much healing lyght as possible.

Today, now, that meant that it had suffered what might be the worst of the attack. Rhi felt tears welling up as she flew up, finding some of the Battlers she did not know digging away at the entrance, trying to clear a passageway large enough to enter through.

"Still not big enough, lads!" one of the Battlers called out, furiously digging way. "We can't get through to the elders in there!"

Rhi furrowed her brow. "You can't but I can!" she called out, surprising even herself at the volume of her voice. She buzzed past the awed Battlers

into the nooks and through the crannies to find Addy and any others that could be saved.

Of the ten odd elders and caregivers she estimated to have seen on her past visits, Rhi was able to identify most of the faces of the dead and wounded. "Help us…" the living called out, weakly and repeatedly.

"Aye!" Rhi called out. "The Battlers are coming! Hold fast, Quasi, hold fast! I'll bring sweetwater when I'm able!"

Rhi wanted to help every single one of the four she saw living right now, but she owed it to her family of friends to locate Addy first. There really wasn't more for her to do then act as a finder, anyways. Fly and report, yes. Lift heavy rubble and debris, sadly not so much. She wished she had the strength of ten Battlers right now, not realized she did in her heart and mettle to help. Such was how Rhi was working through this rubbish with such gusto. She wasn't thinking about it. Rhi was just doing what needed to be done the best she could, wishing every second she could do even more.

Addy's burro had been one of the smaller ones of the lot and Rhi hoped that help shield the old Quasi from the onslaught of falling rubble that came after the blast. Finding the burro's location, Rhi was thankful to have been mostly correct in her assumption. While there was a fair share of debris near the smallish entrance, the inner burro looked from the outside to be structurally intact for the most part. With the dust still heavy in the thick air, Rhi found her fluttering wings to be causing dust swirls all around her forcing her to land briefly to wipe the soot from in and around her purple eyes. She suddenly let out a cough to get the ash out of her lungs and mouth.

"Who, who is there?" Rhi heard a weak Aunt Addy struggle to call out into the darkness. She snapped to attention and buzzed into the burro straight away.

"Addy! It's Rhi Bugle! Are you okay?!" She came to a full stop in the air above where she remembered Aunt Addy's bedding pillows being laid out, although she could not see the elder in the dark.

"Down here, child," Addy said quietly. "Beneath you."

Rhi floated to the rocky ground, feeling only rubble beneath her small clawed and taloned feet. Where was she, dang it? "Addy? Where?!"

"Beneath... you." The breathing was labored and shallow, causing Rhi to shudder.

Rhi looked down, seeing nothing but the outline of jagged rock. She dove into digging furiously, her little arms flying back and forth almost as fast her crystalline, silver wings carried through the sky. "I'm coming! I'm coming, Addy!"

It was a futile effort, save for clearing away a small area from Addy's face so Rhi could see her through the shadowy darkness which engulfed them. "Addy, love. We're going to get the Battlers in here and we're going to save you okay?!"

"Save the young. I've lived my life, Rhi," Addy said in a near whisper. "What of the others? Scout and Pi? Rex?"

"Pi's not here?" Rhi asked, both relieved and scared. "Rex, he's fine by the by, well, dang it, Addy, we both thought she would be here with you?!"

"She was earlier, left not a dat ago," Addy informed her. I have a strong feeling you'll find her outside the burro. She had thinking to do. But what of my Scout, my darling boy. Is he safe?"

Rhi nodded in the affirmative. "For sure as light and right as rain, Addy! He saved my life! Got me under cover before the rocks fell. He sent me to save the others without thinking about himself for a heartbeat. Amazing, he is."

Rhi heard Addy sigh contently.

"A hero when called is a hero forever. He does me proud. You tell him that when you get back to him," Addy whispered. "And you tell him I love him more than he'll ever know."

Rhi felt tears welling up again. Addy was slipping away.

"I will, Auntie Addy, I promise," Rhi replied with absolute conviction.

"Tell Rex I love him and the rest of you all the same. All we have is love, Rhi. And tell Pi that's what she needs to guide her life's journey..."

Rhi nodded in affirmation. "I will, Addy. I swear it on my life."

"Love life and love each other..." Addy whispered softly, just loud enough for Rhi to hear.

Crying hard now, Rhi sobbed, "We will, we will, but you hang in there, Addy! You hang in there for us! Scout will be here soon!"

"He already is, child. I feel him in my hearts," Addy said after a long, uncomfortable pause. Blissfully so, if Rhi had to pick a word to describe how the elderly dying Quasi sounded as she mouthed the sentiment.

It was at that moment when Addona of the Quasi would speak no more.

Rhi found herself sobbing, the sound of the Battlers clearing away the debris behind her losing volume. All she heard around her, was a gnawing, deadly silence filling both her ears and her heart. Life had lost meaning in less than a click and she, nor her world, would ever be the same again.

***

Pi made it as far as the collapsed remains of the HomeSpace side entry she had used to leave earlier to know calamity lay ahead. She leapt as fast as she could along the outer rim of rocky hills above HomeSpace to reach the main entrance a click and a half away. Pi trimmed the time to just under one click through a speed she was previously aware she was capable of achieving, leaving the sound of loud THUMPS and dust clouds behind her, even extending the winged flaps beneath her front paws on more than one occasion to glide quickly down embankments rather than slow down to navigate them judiciously. Home, she needed to go home. To her Scout, to her brother, to Rhi, to Addy and to Ichabod, Pi wanted to see them all safe and sound right here and now!

Breathing heavily, Pi willed herself to keep her composure, nearing the HomeSpace entrance which had clearly been heavily damaged in the whatever it was that Sun had just rained down on them from the heavens above. Seeing no Bugle entries, Pi saw only a battalion of weary, saddened Battlers, armed with silver blades and shields in front of them. Each warrior's fur, even with their quill armor extended to shield their bodies from attack's harm, was dirtied with soot and sand. They looked absolutely rubbish, both inside and out.

"How bad?" Pi called out, nearing them without slowing down. "How fricking bad?! NOW!"

"Hundred dead, at least, Pi!" the nearest Battler, a broad, thick Quasi named Dee whom Pi often caught eyeing her with passing glances when she spied him reading parchments in the HomeSpace Circle on his off time, called out in response. "Get your fur to the Elder Care! It fell hard! Rhi Bugle's there!"

"Watch for falling debris too! Still some hanging from roots coming down, Leaper!" Dee's mate, Chukk called out.

"Aye!" Pi barked, whizzing past them in a near blur. "It wasn't MaRuu! It was a lyghtning blast!!!"

After she raced by, Chukk turned to face Dee. His jaw was slack. "Did she say this was lyghtning?!"

Dee eyed the indigo and yellow sky above, thick clouds strobing with color in the distance and the rain coming down thicker now. He loosened his quills, relaxing his terse musculature a bit but still ready to fight if need be, and counting the dits of time between the thunderclaps and lyghtning streaks. They were coming in a quickening barrage he silently cursed himself for not noticing sooner. It couldn't be, could it? They were only in the stories his GrandPap told him and his siblings as small children by their family burro's hearth at night before bedtime, weren't they? He watched in sheer horror as the entire sky lit up bright, crimson red in the distance followed by a far less severe shaking underneath their paws that moved more side to side than up and down like the last shockwave--

"The threat is not MaRuu!" he called out to his mates with aplomb. "It was a bloody Sun Shock! Guard the perimeter! Raise the Red! Raise the Red!"

"Aye!" Chukk replied. "Wait...why?! What is a Sun Shock?! Where are you going?!"

"To find Ichabod!" Zed replied, pausing briefly, "if he's still alive, that is! Hope, my love! Hope!"

Dee dropped his shield and sheathed his blade in one fluid motion as he spun on his hind paws, spinning around with the grace of a dancer. He leapt at a full throttle back towards the remaining part of the HomeSpace gate that could be passed through safely and took off at a full clip, but nowhere near a match for Pi's graceful speed. If Pi and he were right, there would not be much time to evacuate HomeSpace. The sky was going to be falling to earth faster than any Quasi had ever seen.

The End was upon them, if his GrandPap's hushed, secret stories were to be believed, which meant that the Spirit and the Quasis were now at war... and the Spirit had just attacked them first and in devastating and blistering fashion-- and we don't stand a bloody chance, Dee thought to himself, weaving through the remnants of HomeSpace and refusing to let any tears fall in doing so. Not yet, he told himself. Save them for when you can afford them, mate. You have a mission and you have hope.

Right now, that was all Dee needed to know as he zigzagged towards the High Elder's Chamber in hopes that Ichabod would know what they did now, for HomeSpace would seemingly soon be lost to the ground in which it had been dug out over the millennia by his people after the Drying Draughts of generations long since passed. Since the Wailing Waters stopped running across the DryLands made sweetwater found only in cavernous streams beneath the surface. Since the Scorching Sun Days caused the vegetation to wither and grow frail, no longer producing luscious fruit or beautiful flowers for harvest back in a time Quasi were discovered to have been a farming people.

If they couldn't live beneath ground, Dee hoped against hope his GrandPap's stories happy ending was true: that the Called One would alone save the Quasi and restore the planet's relationship with the mighty Spirit to stop the Sun Shocks and save the HomeSpaces. Hopefully, whatever Quasi it was had already begun the trip to the Sun and all of this would be over soon. Their lives, all of them left anyways, depended on it. He prayed for Pi's aunt and others like her who he knew had lost their lives tragically and without warning or preparation in the first battle today, for they died warrior's deaths and would be remembered for such.

War, it turned out, was far crueler and more vicious than he, Chukk, or any of his other fellow Battler brothers would have ever imagined it could be. It should have been them, but it wasn't. Not one Battler fell today to the best of his knowledge thus far, as their barracks were right next to the HomeSpace entrance and all guards stationed at entrances were able to leap out of the way of the debris in time. But it was no miracle.

It was torturous to think that all of those who had pledged a blood oath to protect their fellow Quasi would have to live knowing they had all failed miserably. Instead, the Quasi had lost mothers, children, friends, and no one else who deserved to die. Dee cursed the Spirit under his breath, rounding the last turn before he would reach Ichabod's chamber. He cursed it to the core.

***

When Pi arrived at the remnants of the Elder Care and saw the look in Rhi's sad, soulful eyes when her friend's gaze met hers as Pi approached her, she knew Addy had been lost to the blast. New tears welled in Pi's eyes. Frick, frack, frick it all!

Rhi only said, "Gone, love. She's gone."

As Rhi flittered up to her, covered in quartz speckled dust, the two friends, who were never more like sisters, rubbed foreheads lovingly and ruefully. Pi found the tender embrace welcome. What Rhi must have seen was evident and nothing like what she had witnessed. Her friend had realized death, both bitter tasting and devastating to the soul. They stayed outside the Elder Care for a long while, helping to tend to the four souls who had survived the calamity. Thankfully, the remaining two Healers believed all could recover from their injuries. They were the lucky ones. Not like Addy and the six other residents who lost their lives in horrific fashion.

They whispered back and forth about what each had witnessed, and Pi had never been prouder of Scout and how he responded after the blast. Addy went to the Spirit knowing her meek and mild nephew was a true hero who saved the life of another without a moment's hesitation. Rhi even bragged that there would likely be no end to him bragging about the event when they all reconnected back at the burro, where Rex was waiting to tend to them with food and drink, she was certain.

The trip back to the burro was taken slowly, as Pi and Rhi took note of the extensive damage and stopped to assist any others path's they crossed who were in need of assistance. Neither wanted to be further than a paw's length from each other, clinging to each other's presence as if they might never see each other again if they did.

"She loved us, Pi," Rhi said simply after they left the latest cluster of hurt Quasi. "She wanted us to love life and love each other. They were last words."

Pi's shoulders went slack. "But, how can we? Look at this. We're ruined, Rhi."

There was a long silence as they neared the last turn of the spiral path before the burro.

"Not if we still have each other, Pi."

"There is that, I guess. The four squares, we are, aren't we?"

"Indeed. Now let's get in before there's no nectar left for me, er, us, I meant," Rhi said, sheepishly.

They entered the burro, pulling back the privacy skin door to find Rex, curled up on the floor in the far corner, crouched to the ground, his front paws wrapped around his two, long rear ones, muttering, "No, no, no…" over and over again.

Pi scanned the burro, looking for any sign of Scout. He was not in sight. She tore into the two sleeping hovels. Nothing. Pi felt something working into her chest that she couldn't explain. It was both a rising queasiness and a shaking tremor as she dashed back to the living area, where Rhi was now holding Rex's shaking front paw.

"Where, where is he? Why isn't he here? He was right behind me, Rex, I swear it..." Rhi shakenly asked Rex, her voice now weak and cracking.

There was no response.

Pi shook her head. This couldn't be. Her Scout was a hero! He saved Rhi from certain death!

"WHERE IS HE, REX?!" Pi screamed, breaking the noxious silence the three were sharing.

"They, they... told me, they told me, the artery tunnel and the Bugle Nests collapsed. They're, they're gone! The Bugles and Scout are gone! I am so very sorry! So sorry!!!" Rex blubbered, now reduced to sobbing made up of inaudible noises and cries.

"SCOUT!!! NO!!!" Pi screamed before collapsing to the burro floor, slamming her paws against the cold floor.

Rhi slipped down on the ground. Her people were gone? Scout gone? She went numb, unable to move.

Their world as they knew it ended in that moment. The Journey and everything associated with it had cursed them forever. They were alive but felt dead inside. It was the longest day of each of their lives, and it wasn't even over yet. And as of right now, being alive and having to bear witness to such tragic horror made them not to live at all. Nothing could be worse than this, or so they currently believed.

Pi suddenly felt an odd sensation, as her head and all the furs upon it began to softly tingle, as if coming alive.

Pi of the Quasi, you have it wrong. So, pay close heed where you truly belong. For your future will soon be close at paw but never forget what you just saw. Find the color and join the lyght and all will be made right.

"Stop," Pi muttered, banging her head. "Stop, stop, stop! Stop it now!"

Rhi and Rex both shot her concerned looks, being snapped out of their mournful dredges by Pi's outburst. "Pi?" they both asked, almost in unison.

"What is it, Pi?" Rex asked after another long, deafening silence filled the air when his sister offered no response.

Pi cried. "I keep hearing a voice inside my bloody head, it's telling me things I don't understand and don't want to hear! It started just before the blast. I just want to mourn my love, my Scout, in painful peace! Leave me bloody alone, whoever you are!!!"

Pi continued muttering things Rex could not understand. Rhi was no better, as she had paid no attention it seemed and returned to a curled-up ball on the floor. The two were in worse shock than Rex was, he was certain, having had more time to digest the news of Scout's and the Bugles' passing's.

"I should go there," Pi said, her voice cracking. "I can save Scout. I know I can." She began to rise.

Rex shakily rose to his paws, moving across the room and placing a comforting paw on her shoulder. "Don't move you two, okay, please? Unless it's a matter of life or--". Rex caught himself before finishing the sentence. Pi slunk back to the ground, defeated.

He needn't have asked. Neither Pi nor Rhi would be going anywhere for the foreseeable future. That was about the only thing he was sure of right now.

Ichabod better have survived, Rex grumbled, making his way into the kitchen to put on some tea for the wounded women he now found in his care. They needed him now more than ever.

The two women found their way into each other's arms a short time later, both feeling lost forever but needing each other more than they ever knew possible.

4

Ichabod was alone in his modest burro off to the side of the Elder
Chamber, a far more regal environment than his small dormitory
room. The massive enclosure's high walls, which earlier in the day had
pulsed with the soft yellow lyght vein energy which coursed through
them, had nearly imploded from the blast's fury. As with Ichabod's
smallish burro tucked to the side and kept separate by an ancient, thick
skin wall painted with the blue paint of the Ancients, the Elder
Chamber was previously filled from wall to wall with ancient Quasi art,
artifacts, and parchment shelves.

It was now a hot, cluttered mess. Parchments were sprawled
everywhere. Broken vases and pieces of art littered the quartz floor.
Debris and dirt covered most of the enclave.

"Too soon, too bloody soon," Ichabod muttered, the Arkelia and
the Journey Map nestled in his large pouch. "We were supposed to
have more time! Why her?! Why?'"

The old Quasi, wearing a dirt covered yellow cape and holding his
ornately carved birch staff in his front right paw, cursed under his
breath as he searched the remnants of his people's long history now
scattered haphazardly across the floor. Ichabod picked up and tossed
away the clutter in a sweeping circular motion. Whatever he was
searching for was proving incredibly hard to come by.

This was the scene Dee witnessed when he came crashing into the
burro, thanking the Spirit Ichabod was still among the living... and
being so in such a feisty fashion as to brush away any worries of serious
injury on Dee's part, eyeing the scene for any signs of impending

danger such as was the Battler's Way.

Ichabod was visibly pissed to all reckoning, but he was alive all the same. This vigor was what the Quasi needed right now, Dee thought to himself. They should be angry and ready to fight. Their lives would most likely depend on it. But how do you fight a sun?

"Dang the curses! Why her? Why now? I saw this differently! What's happening?!" Ichabod yelled, kicking a broken vase and sending it sailing across the burro, whizzing past Dee's head within a dib of his life. "Oh, spirits, Dee Battler, I didn't see you there. My regrets."

Dee shook it off. "We have more to worry about than errant, flying vases, don't we, Ichabod? That were Sun Shocks, weren't they? The stories of the End are true, aren't they?"

Ichabod puffed his chest, gripping his staff more tightly as if squeezing the life out of the inanimate wood. "Not as true as I thought they were it seems, lad. I officiated at yours and your partner Chukk's togetherness ceremony one planet turn before last, did I not? The day you take your lifemate is the best day of your life. You feel as if you can conquer the world together. Cherish that memory and hold onto it dearly, Dee. You'll need them in the days ahead. Here with a report for me, lad?"

Dee shook his head in the negative. "No, sir. Here to confirm that what happened are the first Sun Shocks of the End. They are, aren't they? Pi the Leaper said these were lyghtning blasts and the sky looks like the Tale of the Last War by GrandPap told me so many times I can't remember. It has to be, right? Not some MaRuu attack?"

Ichabod grabbed the parchment he was looking for, scooping it up into his pouch along with the Arkelian and the map Scout had been sent for. He rose to face the Battler, looking him straight in the eyes. "You know your parchments well, Dee," Ichabod said plainly. "Many thought them fantasies or lies."

"Guess many were wrong," Dee replied.

"Indeed. Many have been wrong about many things in our history, me included, it seems. But here we are. So, what now, lad? I've got things I need to attend to in a shorter amount of time than I had seen, er, thought. Speak or go."

Dee had always appreciated Ichabod's get right to it, matter of factness. Always being to the point meant you know where a Quasi stood on things, straight off. He admired that in a person. "Who is the

Called One? Would I know him and when do you expect his victory? I want to be the first to thank him for his service to the Quasi in our time of greatest need."

Ichabod eyed the Battler over. The idealism shone so brightly from Dee's stare, Ichabod thought he might need to shield his eyes. The lad's star shone bright. Maybe too bright but believing in something was better than no believing in anything at all. It was supposed to be him, he knew it. Ichabod sighed, clearing his throat.

"It's a her," Ichabod stated. "And she hasn't left yet."

Dee's jaw went slack and his face numb. "Excuse me, what? Who?"

"Your paths have already crossed. Pi the Leaper was chosen for the Journey. I told her not just yesterday."

Dee's brain was buzzing. "A leaper? A female? Why did you choose her of all Quasi?"

Ichabod frowned. "I didn't." He wasn't lying. The Spirit made him, not allowing any other way forward. No one else could understand how long they had been in this loop.

Dee was confused. "So, who did, Ichabod? And why?"

"The bloody Spirit did!" Ichabod barked. Why her, he had no idea either. He heard a voice tell him to choose her and until he did, his plan could not move forward. It must be her, the Spirit had said, and no other.

Dee's battler instincts were back in place. He was a soldier and soldiers don't ask questions when there is a task at hand. They don't think. They act. "Follow me and stay close. Watch your head for debris. I've got you."

Ichabod sighed. "To go where exactly?"

"To fetch Pi," Dee replied. "She has to get going if she's to save us, right?!"

Ichabod nodded. "Oh, of course. Yes, let's go. Good, lad." Under his breath, Ichabod swore to the Spirit. His ability to loop was gone. Otherwise, he would have avoided having this conversation in the first place. Now he was trapped into sending her on her way with both the map and the Arkelian. Why couldn't she have just turned him down like he had hoped? With his power having escaped him, Ichabod felt naked as the world continued to spin out of control without letting him steer it as he saw fit.

***

If there was anything to be thankful for, Rhi got word from one of the passersby checking in on their safety that many if not most of the Bugles were able to fly to safety before the lyght artery tunnel collapsed. Sadly, Scout was not so lucky. No one, Quasi or Bugle, saw him make his way out from either end before the tunnel collapsed on both sides.

It was beginning to be a little difficult in the growing confusion as the Quasi and Bugles began to emerge from the sustained wreckage to tell their tales of survival and of loss, as some were contradicting what others had said they saw. Pi, returning to the land of the living after being numb most of the night since returning to what was left of their lives, knew that people meant well. Talking about what happened was all any of them had at this point.

Pi had tried to go to where Scout was last seen but found herself restrained by Rex and Rhi on two different occasions now. There simply was no point, they told her. It was better to stay and be safe. She was frustrated, devastated, and angry--

But you are not scared...

Pi brushed the voice away, not bothering to mention it to the others again. They told her it was just her mind coping with such an insurmountable amount of loss, Rhi told her, now into her fourth mug of nectar, tea be danged. Pi just let it bubble beneath the surface as an annoyance.

He gave his life so that another could live. For that is the greatest gift one can ever give...

Pi found herself comforted by the words. A hero. Her Scout had died not a meek and mild worry wart but a true hero. He saved Rhi and sent her to save the rest of us without thinking about himself. Pi was proud of her partner through this unending sadness. He had joined the Spirit pure of heart. At least there was that. And if things kept going like this, she would hopefully be joining him in the Spirit soon enough.

If there is no Arkelia or Sun, then both die, both living and dead and the war will be done. All will lose, Pi, if you refuse to choose love.

Pi felt a depth of... something, brewing in her. The voice was most definitely not hers, and somehow, she knew although it spoke in rhyme, it was telling the truth. It felt as if it was becoming clearer, sharper somehow?

Dee appeared in the doorway with Ichabod and Chukk behind him.

Pi sprung to her feet while Rhi finished off her mug of nectar and Rex popped his head in from the kitchen.

"As today's events have demonstrated," Ichabod said sadly, "We have less time to save the planet than I thought. May we enter?"

"Oh, you can enter, all right," Pi quipped. "Scout and Addy are dead along with scores others! You have a lot of explaining to do! Addy told me the truth before she died!"

Ichabod nodded. "That it was all a hoax, right? A ruse to placate the people, right? A fallacy? A lie!"

Pi felt her head pound, confusion and rage smashing against each other. "Yes!"

Those around Ichabod didn't look that impressed with his explanation. "I didn't send you to summon the other HomeSpaces, Pi. I sent you to warn them that the lyght energies were starting to turn red. That danger was imminent. To be ready for the time of the Journey-"

"Oh Ichabod," Rhi said, "you knew?"

Ichabod shook his head. "Not the where nor the when, Rhi Bugle. We had little time to know and less to prepare and then... the notion that maybe one brave soul could save us was worth a fighting chance."

Rhi and Rex looked at each other, and then to Pi.

"The Spirit spoke to me, Ichabod. It told me to listen to you before I decide what to do," Pi said. "So, Rex, get Ichabod and the boys some tea, fetch me and Rhi some more nectar, and let's get this sorted. Ichabod, tell me everything you know. Now."

***

They were stories as old as when the Quasi started keeping track of things on parchment, millennia ago when the color of the planet's energy slowly started changing as the conditions of the planet itself did also. It was if the two things were intertwined and sadly, Ichabod told them, not realized in enough time by anyone, citizen or elder, to stop the tide of damage the inhabitants of the planet had caused Arkelia since time began and throughout the Ages.

So, as the planet inched closer to its unnatural end, the lyght energy turned more volatile, and the Quasi and Bugles were driven deeper and deeper beneath the planet's surface, the whispered fables of the Journey of Lyght bubbled back to the surface and became such a source of hope and inspiration. He never imagined that he would choose Pi, or anyone at all for that matter, especially at the request of the Spirit.

"You couldn't have known it would be me, Ichabod," Pi said, stopping the High Elder from chastising himself any further. "But I am telling you now that we need you more than ever before."

The rest of the assembled group backed up Pi's statements in the affirmative, especially Dee and Chukk, who still served Ichabod as Battlers. They all echoed the same sentiments: it wasn't his fault, none of this was. What Pi needed to know now was how this would now play out-

Rex, Dee, and Chukk looked around to Pi, while Ichabod and Rhi had never taken their eyes off Pi. Rhi took a swig of nectar, slamming her mug to the floor as Pi began to extend her paw towards Ichabod for the Arkelian.

"If she goes, I go!" Rhi said, swatting Pi's paw back down.

"Me too!" Rex said, with vigor, his paws clenched. "The three of us, go. None of the stories said we couldn't, and you aren't saying so now, are you, Spirit?! She goes, we go!"

Pi choked up. She was ready to give her life to save the lives of the other Quasi but mostly she would do it to save her family's lives above the rest. That Rhi and Rex would demand to go with her, knowing they would never return, made her prouder of them than ever before.

As a reward for their courage, there shall be added one more to bring the total for the journey to four and no more.

Pi looked at the eyes in the burro all looking at her. It was her choice, and even though she was the only one hearing it, she knew her family would support her. She sighed. "I accept." The others looked at her oddly, her she was talking to herself again. Pi the Crazy Chosen one...

Very well, Pi. Four and no more. It is best time you checked the artery tunnel floor once more. The journey begins tomorrow at first light. If you are not on the path north by a click to three, the next blast to hit will kill all who breathe.

"Rhi!!! Fly to the artery tunnel!!! Now, Rhi! Now!"

Pi, Rhi, and Rex all looked at each other confused before leaping to their feet.

"On it!"

POP!

Rhi was gone in a flash, through the door and into the dark

HomeSpace.

"What is it?" Chukk asked. "What did you hear?"

"Get food, water, and bandages! Now! To the artery tunnel! Let's move!" Pi yelped.

Rex tucked a sweetwater jug and a loaf of carrot bread wrapped in leaves into his pouch. Pi grabbed the Journey Map and the Arkelian from Ichabod, who seemed almost to grab after them when she relieved him of them.

They made their way to the door.

"You three start getting everyone out of HomeSpace and to somewhere safe on the surface, far from here," Pi said, motioning Ichabod, Dee, and Chukk towards the burro door.

"We're off," she continued, letting Rex leave first. "Ichabod, thank the Heavens, aye? You did what you were asked. The rest is on us. Go with the Spirit and hope it continues to guide both of us."

Letting them out before him, Ichabod took one last look around the small burro. These events were curious to him. He curled a devious grimace. "Let us hope so," the old Quasi said, departing. "I do not like this."

***

Rhi couldn't believe it. She absolutely couldn't believe it. The bugle rubbed her eyes and blinked twice before approaching any closer. It was him. Scout, covered in dirt and soot, laying on his back and breathing heavily in front of the collapsed tunnel. There was a burrowed hole that he must have crawled through to arrive at this location. Both his legs were intact. In fact, he didn't have a scrape on him from the looks of it. He just looked... tired?

"Scout?" Rhi asked, finally summoning up the courage. There was heavy breathing but no reply. "You, uh, okay there, mate?"

"Did you get to the others? They make out it okay?" Scout asked. "Better yet, Rhi, how in Arkelia am I okay? I fell asleep dying and here I am awake and praying never to fall asleep like that again. My rear paws were crushed and now... not?"

Scout wiggled his paws back and forth. "Why are you crying? Oh Spirit, please tell me Pi and Rex and Addy are okay?!"

"Addy didn't make it, Scout. But she died knowing you were a hero, she did. She said for you to love life and for us to love each other. She wasn't in pain, chum. Her vessel was just too damaged to keep afloat. Pi and Rex are fine, just... as you are..."

As soon as Scout rose from the ground, Pi nearly tackled him. "My love!!!"

Scout had never felt such a warm embrace. He wasn't entirely sure what was going on but being feted as a hero was something he was quickly warming up to. "I'm here, Pi, I'm here. Your Scout's here."

The couple kept the embrace well until after Rex arrived and handed Scout the sweetwater jug, which he drank all of, and the carrot bread, which he ate all of. He told them in between gulps and bites that he suddenly awoke, found a strength within him he never felt before, and pulled himself the ten dats or so until he was free of the wall collapse. He had thought his rear paws had been mangled but here they were, better than ever. It was a miracle through and through, as each of the four kept repeating to each other. Scout eyed the Arkelian Pi now wore on her chest.

"Surprise," Pi replied. "We've been tasked with saving the planet."

Scout shook his head. "We?" he repeated, smiling impishly.

"The four of us, together as one," Pi said, simply yet with incredible conviction.

And so, it has begun. Your gifts have been granted.

Rex sighed. "Welcome aboard the one-way, crazy ride of our lives, buddy. We win, we die but the planet lives. We lose, we die and everyone and everything else dies along with it."

Scout scanned the group. "Better than staying dead, I suppose. Grateful to think the Spirit thinks so highly of me, all to be had."

They nodded and began to make their way back to the burro to gather their items before embarking on the quest route the map laid out. Rhi wished to visit where the Bugles had re-nested and say her goodbyes before they left. Somehow, Scout *felt* Addy within him, telling him that *love would lyght the way.* Scout felt comforted. He believed her.

"I think we stand a fighting chance, family," Pi said, as if sensing both Addy and her interaction with Scout. Since she began wearing the Arkelian, Pi felt as if she could feel the energy of those around her somehow. She couldn't explain it. It was different.

"Was just thinking the same thing, my love," Scout replied, a wry smile formed on his lips. "Just because something's never been done doesn't mean it can't be, aye?"

Rhi chirped in agreement. "If whoever it is speaking to us can bring Scout back from the Spirit, I'd reckon anything is possible now. Has to be."

Rex remained silent. He had a striking suspicion Scout had been lying there outside the rubble all along but spoke nothing of it aloud. He was just happy his brother was alive, for now. Rex felt so conflicted. The world was crumbling around them, strange voices were filling Pi's head, and Rex started to wonder if they would all just be better off dead. There was a rhyme for them.

"We have one small issue to contend with," Scout said, looking at the Journey map and the Journey stories.

"What's that, Scout?" Pi asked, still trying to get the Arkelian to sit comfortably across her chest.

"Do any of you read ancient Origin?"

There was a long silence, only the sound of their movement through the caves registering in the air.

"That's what I thought," Scout went on. "None of us can read the texts on the bloody map."

There was a collective groan.

Pi kicked at the ground. "So, what now?"

Pi, and then the rest, stopped to look at each other. Their initial excitement over finding Scout alive had now dampened. This was proving to be as hard as a quest to save the planet should be. Each decision brought with it a new hurdle to overcome.

Possibilities are put in your place for obstacles to be faced. Your decisions will determine the route of the race. Some for the better and some for the worse, everything you do will alter the course. Fortune and fate, we do not understand, for not everything in life goes according to plan. From here on out, you are on your own, but you do not have to go it alone.

Pi spun around. She repeated what she just heard as best she could "They're riddles! Meant to confuse me! No, wait. They're rules, as if to a game! We're just players, not the judges making the rules!"

Rhi looked concerned. "Pi, sweets, whatever it is you're hearing, you sure you can, uh, you know, trust the information?"

"I say we need all the help we can get," Scout said. "It makes sense to put our best paws forward, don't it?"

Rex nodded. "It's like stacking your best deck of berry beads against an opponent before you start to maximize your chances of winning."

"Right," Scout agreed. "We need to stack our deck, best we can."

He paused. "So how do we best do that?"

Pi let out a grunt. "We're going to have to shuffle our berry beads first. We'll get to the burro. Rhi, find where Ichabod, Dee, and Chukk got to and have them meet us there. Quick!"

Rhi nodded. "Just quickly before I jet off, has anyone noticed how bloody fast I can fly now?"

Pi rolled her eyes. "Just go!"

"Right!" Rhi said.

POP!

The bugle left nothing but a vapor trail behind in her wake.

"She's not kidding," Rex said, letting out a low whistle. "That's one fast Bugle. She really shouldn't drink and fly. Rhi's bound to hurt someone eventually."

"Only four can go," Pi repeated. "Me and three others. Now we know one has to be able to read the map. That leaves two spots between the three of you. Spirits, this is excruciating."

Rex cleared his throat. "I've always been more the type to tend to others and have dinner ready for them when they get home, you know? You just got this big lug back, so he's definitely going. And with Rhi being able to get just about anywhere in the blink of an eye, she'll be useful. I'd just drag you down, being hilarious of course while I do it, but a burden all the same. You know I'm right, Pi."

Hers and Scout's silence confirmed this to be true. It was decided in silence that Rex would remain behind, giving his place up for one who could read ancient Origins text and be more useful for the upcoming endeavor. Rex felt almost relieved in a way. He would have willingly gone into the bowels of death for his family if it served a purpose but if staying behind gave the Quasi a better chance of surviving the Journey of Lyght, he was all for tending to the sick and needy left scattered through HomeSpace.

Rex felt an odd sense of relief wash over him in the time it took them to return to the burro. Pi and Scout felt the same feeling, knowing that Rex's unease above ground on the surface might have made for difficulty ahead. Pi felt no qualms in agreeing that it was for the best this way. The decision in her mind was final. Rex would stay in favor of a better suited choice. Pi said nothing but allow herself the hint of a small grin in the corner of her lip. The Spirit wasn't lying to her. Somehow, Pi just knew it.

***

Dee, with Chukk by his side and holding his paw, stood silently as Pi implored Ichabod to come with them on their journey to no avail. There was no way the High Elder would leave his wounded people to the elements alone and without the leader who inadvertently led them there in the first place. As determined as Pi was, she was no match for the old Quasi's mettle. Their talk quickly derailed into a shouting match. Dee caught glimpse of Chukk's eyes, locked directly onto him. He knew his partner well enough to know that look. Dee attempted to shrug him off, but Chukk, like Ichabod, wasn't having any of it--

"Stop," Dee interjected, cutting both Pi and Ichabod off in the middle of their latest heated exchange on the subject. "Ichabod need not go. My partner and lifelong love here, Chukk, would like me to let you know that I read ancient Origins and should nominate myself to join the others on this journey, or risk his eternal damnation."

Chukk smiled. "Took long enough. You're a warrior poet, Dee. Now put it to good use and don't even think about not making it back to me in one piece. I love you and I believe in you. All of you. Ichabod, Rex, and I can marshal the forces, tend to the sick, and hold down the HomeSpace until the four of you see this through, aye?"

Pi looked to Rhi and then to Scout. Scout looked to Pi and then to Rhi. Then they all looked to Dee. "May I join you on your quest, noble journeyers?"

"Rex and Chukk," Ichabod proclaimed, "under my direct command, you two will be. Rex, you will be in charge of the healers. Chukk, you will be in charge of the fortification efforts to ensure HomeSpace collapses no more before we can evacuate to a safer location. I'll keep these two hard at work in your absence, Journeyers. We will live on, thanks to you four. You do not go into the darkness. You bring us the lyght, even now." Whatever was to come, Ichabod was damned sure going to be at HomeSpace to do it. He even considered using the damage to HomeSpace to his advantage. If they were to evacuate, perhaps Ichabod could get his plans back on track.

Pi soaked in the events of the last day, her mind awash in an odd, numb, sensation, as if she was questioning whether or not all of this was really happening to her and those she loved. It was certainly no dream nor a nightmare. The Leaper knew what she was experiencing was real in so much that it was occurring, but she began to wonder if there was something else at play that she couldn't quite put her paws on. Why was it that a leaper, a battler, a scout, and a sentry all came to be together here, right now, getting ready to embark on a journey to save the very lyght of the planet, the Spirit of all that had come before them, pulsing through their minds and souls in a strange unison with them, to decide the fate of their world? Why, Spirit, why, Pi asked silently.

You ask me why? I ask you, my inquisitive Pi...
Why not?

Pi took the response both to head and to hearts. They were subjects to the rules and reign of the Spirit. They might be heroes or failures but there was one thing they definitely were: variables waiting to be tested out. This was no sick or twisted game, Pi decided. It was the culmination of a world defining test for the fate of them all.

***

Having now read through the Journeyer Map, it was evident that this might be a very short trip. The first stop was above the Northern Ridge, where there was to be a cave opening. According to Ichabod's ancient Origin histories, it is in this location that each of the last Journeyers had been killed, leaving only the map and the violet stoned Arkelian behind and leaving not a trace, not even a whisker, of their existence beyond that.

They packed lightly, bringing only a thick blanket and their silver blades, in addition to sweetwater jugs and carrot bread loaves. Scout carried Rhi's water and nectar jugs without a moment's hesitation, under the stipulation that he could mock her for bringing nectar with her on a quest to save the planet. She agreed without a moment's hesitation.

"If I'm to sacrifice my life for you lot," Rhi replied, "you better believe I'm going to be buzzed as I do it!"

Dee, who Pi had always admired for being as much a philosopher as a warrior and also for being such a doting life partner to Chukk when most battlers opted for a solitary existence, was a welcome addition to their small gang of misfits. He cleaned them up nicely, Pi thought. There was never anything wrong about doing the right thing first. She loved Scout and his squirrelly nature, even more so now that she had been granted a second chance to share her life with him and found it funny how she could find such polar opposites be such admirable qualities.

On one end, Dee's way was full of precision and regimen whereas Scout's was full of passion and verve. Pi considered herself lucky to have both of them by her side. Not to mention having Rhi flying circles around all three of them in constant patrol.

Their goodbyes had been bittersweet and poignant, with Rex, Ichabod, and Chukk refusing to believe that they would never see the foursome again. The mentality of false hope which Addy had explained to Pi went to the wayside. Hope was hope, in her opinion. Pi would take anything positive minded she could get her paws on now. Who was to say they would meet their ends? Maybe there would be another way, just as Scout had been returned to them.

All Pi knew at this point in time was that none of them really knew much of anything. What could and couldn't be seemed to be up for grabs at the present. Anything was possible, she told herself. Anything. Pi cursed herself silently for losing hope so easily after leaving Addy's earlier. From now on, Pi would decide things for herself just as she always had. Figuring things out was what she did best, after all.

The group reached the top of the Northern Ridge in good time, even as the weather turned far worse. Dee proved to be an adept climber and Scout amazed even himself with a newfound strength and perseverance. He seemed to be unstoppable in his zeal to navigate the jagged rocks and slippery slopes they faced. Rhi did her best to fly ahead and scout the past course to navigate but the thunder snow weighed heavily on her wings, causing her to spend a fair amount of the time nestled in Scout's large pouch instead, providing moral support in between nips of nectar.

"I've never seen anyone drink that much nectar and still be cognizant," Dee mentioned when they reached the mouth of the cave. "How do you do it, Rhi?"

Rhi chuckled. "How do you think? Practice! And lots of it."

Pi nuzzled Scout. "You were amazing in your climbing, love! I've never seen you move so strongly before!"

"That makes two of us, it does," Scout replied, returning the nuzzle. "Feel as though the Spirit is coursing through my very veins, I do. I feel as if I could put the whole mountain on my shoulders!"

Pi smiled broadly. "If we only have this time together, I thank the Spirit for it. I'm forever grateful to have you back, my love."

"And I, you," Scout replied. "You have always been my world, Pi. If we're to go, I'm glad it will be together."

Dee smiled, thinking of Chukk and how brave he was for telling Dee to spend their last days alive separated for the greater good of the planet and the Quasi people. He was Dee's hero the same as Scout and Pi were each other's. Rhi couldn't stifle a snort.

"Stop gushing and keep mushing, people!" the little Bugle barked playfully, flying towards them. "We got us a planet to save! The entrance is just ahead, see?!"

Rhi flew back down to the ground. No more than a click ahead, the Bugle could make out a massive cave entrance. It was a jagged slice out of the side of the steep, snow-covered North Mountains.

Dee double checked the written map and the crude diagrams. He nodded in affirmation. This was it. It had to be.

"She's right," Dee said, pointing to the map. "We made it to the first marker!"

"Of course, I'm right," Rhi said. "When you're Rhi, your right, as I like to say."

"Often," Scout mused, "and never have being asked first."

They shared a laugh before making their way towards what the Journeyers would soon learn was the end to any semblance of reality as they had ever understood it to be. Everything was about to change once more, in ways none of them could right now understand. Pi felt an odd twinge in her mind as a sense of awe struck her. She going to save the world and no one or heavenly Spirit could stop her. But first, she had questions she wanted answered.

"Break here," Pi called out. "I think we should rest before diving right into this thing, whatever it is."

"Shore up our strength, good thinking," Scout said, nodding in agreement. "These tired paws could use some elevated rest, if only for a short time."

Dee didn't voice any opposition, even though he wished to push on. He was nearly nervous with excitement. While he had read the directions to this place aloud, Dee kept his further reading mum, mostly because it didn't make any sense. It was just gibberish beyond the first set of instructions leading them this far. It made sense knowing none had ever made it any further. Why write more than you need to? The directions not making sense now made perfect sense from his new point of view.

Dee did not share this information for fear he would not be allowed to remain in the group. Although it meant his life, something within him told Dee he needed to be on this one-way mission with these three. It was his destiny, as Chukk had said back in the burro. He took this opportunity to sit on a nearby rock and take to writing in his journal while the others rested.

Pi crouched into a resting position and focused her thoughts on the Spirit she felt coursing through her veins, intertwined in her thoughts and soul. She called out to the Spirit.

You killed my parents. You killed Addy. Why?

You would not understand.

Try me.

If others had decided on different things in the past, they might still be alive so hold on fast. You might be the one dead. The Chosen One could be Rhi instead. I do not know the future nor control destiny or fate. I just arrange the board and set the players to the gate. It is your decisions that guide the path, not some type of spiritual wrath. The probabilities of possibilities are what define us all, Pi. Everything, both the big and small. The deep and the shallow, the wide and the narrow, so do not think me either cruel or callow. The tip of the blade does not feel the same as the hilt when it is thrust into thick flesh for the kill.

As if a lyght went off in Pi's mind, she suddenly pictured every decision she could think of ever making, all at the same time. It was like watching her whole life flash before her eyes in a flash. Every move of every muscle ever sent a shockwave through her brain, causing Pi to be feeling like she was carrying the whole world in her head. She nearly lost her breath before it stopped, leaving Pi panting.

Now you know I feel every moment of every day and every night. So, Pi of the Quasi, are you and your mates ready? The Journey of Lyght has begun and if you find your way to me your people and planet will live on. If you do not, all be undone, and we will all be no more.

There was a celestial silence. The voice of the Spirit was gone from her. Pi opened her eyes, seeing both her mates resting and also the mouth of the cave in the distance. She rose.

"Let's get this started, aye?" Rhi asked, leaving the comfort of Scout's pouch.

"Aye," Pi replied. "We're on our own from here on out, mates. The Spirit will leave us until the End."

"Is this some sort of game?" Scout asked. "Because if it is, it's a pretty sick and sordid one, if you ask me."

"And one with horrific historical odds," Dee added dryly.

"The Spirit said this is called the Journey of Lyght," Pi said. "So, let's shine bright, shall we?"

"Bloody lit, I am!" Rhi drunkenly called out. "To fight I go!"

Rhi flew towards the cave entrance, her fist in the air, triumphantly but somewhat wobbly.

"How she is able to fly in that condition amazes me," Dee said.

"She's been through a lot in her life," Scout said. "Besides Pi and me, nectar's about the only other constant in her life and it's gotten her this far."

Pi remained silent. She did not judge. Never had. Never would.

"Guess we don't have that much further to look forward to, I guess," Dee replied. "As long as she doesn't cause me harm, we'll be right as rain with each other."

Scout nodded but wasn't sure he believed it. Their new friend seemed to have a bone to pick with Rhi and her nectar drinking. He hoped Dee would just let it go. She was who she was, and they didn't to be having any rows with each other through all this. Sacrificing themselves for the planet was one thing but asking Rhi Bugle to do it without the aid of nectar would bring about an instant verbal annihilation not even the strongest of Battlers would be able to defend themselves against.

"Come on, let's get this started," Pi said, quickening her pace. "We have a planet to save. Enough small talk."

The three turned their attention to the leaping at hand, navigating up the rocky slope towards the growing mouth of the cave. Pi was both proud, and a bit surprised, to see Scout moving with such strength and vigor. It seemed the Spirit had returned him to them a bit stronger than he was before the blast. His leaps were forceful ones, still a little clumsy and flailing, but definitely more powerful than she had ever seen him maneuver in the past. Pi was, in a word, impressed.

Dee was not used to taking orders from others as Battler Commander but felt oddly at ease doing so for Pi, mostly knowing that she had been the one called for this. What a burden to have, he mused. He had known her since in passing but not well enough to call a friend. They travelled in different circles, his, the Battlers, and hers her small family unit. Dee knew now that they were both made up of people who would fight for each other to the death, so he found a kinship with them... even the little drunkard bugle.

Nectar was a fool's drink, in his opinion. One that dulls the senses and the mind from what needed to be done was nothing he found comfort in. Life was to be faced, not hidden from in his opinion. Regardless, if Rhi was able to stay on point, she would have no quarrel from him.

Scout was amazed at his leaping ability, feeling stronger than he ever had before. I should die more often, he joked to himself! Being able to keep up with Pi was a feat he never thought would be capable but here he was, staying on her rear right in flanking position right along with Dee the Battler, no less. If only Addy could see him now. And then, a strange sensation entered Scout's mind. She can see me now, he thought, as if feeling her presence somehow. It was a comforting feeling. He felt as if he was being guided and then it happened. In an instance, he felt himself falling--

They were nearly to the top, leaping over a series of flat rocks balanced over a steep, jagged precipice when the one Scout had chosen to mount a leap from broke free, and flipped over, sending him plunging into the cavernous jagged rock below. He let out a sharp yell as he began to crash down with it. Dee watched what was happening to his right and immediately dove into action, spinning and springing down and to his right in one swooping motion. He was barely able to catch Scout's left hind paw before grabbing hold of the rock above with his own hind paws.

Pi spun into action by sliding to the edge and holding Dee's paws in place.

"We've got you!" she yelled, as the three of them swung dangerously close to the steep cavernous edge.

"There!" Rhi yelled, flying next to them and pointing down to Dee. "Fling yourselves there!"

Using Pi's weight and his own momentum to guide him, Dee used his strength to swing the two of them to the safety of a small ledge not far below their position out of harm's way. He never would have seen the move had it not been for Rhi's viewpoint. The two Quasi lay on their backs, breathing deeply while Rhi helped Pi to her paws up above.

"Thanks mates!" Scout called out. "True life savers, you are! All of you!"

"Stop dying, Scout!" Rhi exclaimed. "We can't take much bloody more of this!"

"Seriously!" Pi added, chuckling. "I don't reckon the Spirit is going to give you a second, second chance, Scout! Watch yourself! You hear me!"

"I'm not trying to be died," Scout replied. "Just seems I've gotten pretty good at it."

"Well then, get worse at it, Scout," Dee said, panting. "Because there isn't any way I could manage to pull that off twice. Watch your back, your front, and your sides at all times, okay?"

"Yes sir," Scout said. "I owe you one."

"Better make that two," Dee said. "You're pretty heavy, Scout."

Once the two battered Quasi climbed back up to the rock's edge, the rest of the journey to the mouth of the cave went without incident. Rhi would fly ahead and return back telling the three Quasi the best route for them to take. She took extra care to make sure Scout had the easiest route possible up the jagged rock in hopes there wouldn't be a repeat performance of his near fatal plunge down the mountain's side earlier. He was proving to be a walking disaster, that one, Rhi cursed under breath.

***

Rex was beginning to regret his decision to stay behind. It wasn't that he minded helping the blast survivors but the ones he really wanted to be helping was Pi and the rest of the journeyers, as Ichabod now called his other family members. He missed them terribly. He felt like such a coward, even though Rex knew it was the wise choice to make. Having just finished organizing the caregivers and providing them all with schedules to tend to their duties, Rex found himself wanting to see how Ichabod was doing.

He took his slow time going to the Elder Chamber, thinking back to nights around the hearth when he, Pi, Scout, and Rhi would tell each other scary stories to see who could frighten the others the best. Pi always won. Her stories were the most creative and freaky, always giving Rex the shivers before she was through. He missed his sister and couldn't fathom losing her. Rex pictured her smiling and nuzzling into Scout, happy in love.

If wasn't for her, he never would have gotten over the death of their parents all those planet turns ago. And now, Pi, Scout, and Rhi were giving their lives to the Spirit to save all of them. What good was being saved if Rex couldn't share it with those he loved the most?

Rex reached the Chamber, entered, and walked through the darkness towards Ichabod's chamber. As he approached, Rex heard Ichabod talking to someone. His curiosity got the best of him and Rex found himself slowing to a near slink so he could hear the conversation.

"--yes, I sent her," Ichabod was saying, "and when she and the others fail, we blame them and claim we had no choice in sending them because she swore the Spirit spoke to her, so the rest won't turn on us. We'll maintain control and keep the Quasi together through this for as many future generations as we can."

Rex's heart leapt in his chest. Wait? What?!

"Ichabod," the Bugle elder named Bha replied, "that's genius. And you are certain that if we move our people to the Southlands, we will be able to survive these severe storm blasts and the MaRuu? And what of the lad, Scout? They claimed him dead."

"We both know the dead don't rise, Bha," Ichabod replied. "He was pinned down and then managed to escape before losing consciousness. A simple problem with a simple explanation. He's no ghost, that one, believe you me. The Southlands will serve us well, thanks to you. They are far enough from the Lyghtning Fields so any storm blasts like this one will not affect us and our fellow Quasi in the existing Southern HomeSpace will no doubt help us. It was foolhardy for my predecessor to dig our HomeSpace here. And now, with Pi, we'll have the emotional capital to get the Diggers from the other satellite HomeSpaces to carry the heavy burden for us. Political maneuverings are far easier to accomplish when you get the people to believe in mystical forces behind them rather than old, jaded Elders."

Bha chuckled. "This is good to hear, Ichabod. Sending fools in search of fool's gold, aye?"

"Indeed," Ichabod replied.

"And the Leaper, hearing the voice of the Spirit?"

Ichabod sighed. "That was beyond me. Her being guided by voices is fine in that they guided her in the direction I wanted her to take!" But he knew she had, as he had, and the Spirit was doing everything it could to stop the inevitable. Bha was so easy to lie to, Ichabod rationalized, spoon feeding the grizzled Bugle what he wanted to hear instead of the more complicated truth.

The two laughed heartily, meanness dripping from the voices.

Rex could take no more. He slowly backed away from Ichabod's chamber, biting his lower lip. If he knew the first thing about fighting, Rex would beat the both of them to a pulp. But his mind was now clouded with despair, in addition to a new hateful disdain for Ichabod.

Pi had heard the voice of the Spirit! She was spoken to in rhymes, for goodness sake! Scout had died, his rear paws mangled! And then resurrected! Right? Rex asked himself. Only Pi had heard the voice, sure, and Scout had said he dug himself out of the ceiling collapse but, they had no reason to lie. Did they?

Rex was feeling his grip on reality start to cave in not unlike HomeSpace had the day before. What to do? Who to tell? Rex thought of Chukk, who seemed trustworthy since their lives intertwined, and decided that he deserved to know the truth about Ichabod's intentions seeing as his life partner was giving his life right along with his family members. Slipping out of the Elder Chamber, Rex went off to find Chukk to see what he thought they should do about this serious turn of events. But suddenly, something stopped him.

Rex could take no more. Rage filled his hearts.

He ripped open the skin blind, staring down the two shocked politicians. "You bastards!"

Bha looked on fearfully. Ichabod stayed perfectly still. Rex, breathing heavily, took two steps towards them.

"How could you? We trusted you!" Rex snarled, his snouts flaring.

As Rex inched closer, Bha began to back away and to the side of the smallish burro. Noticing this, Rex leapt into the air for Ichabod.

"Rex, no! You don't--"

He tackled the old Quasi and began fighting with him as Ichabod swatted at Rex's face, landing a blow right across Rex's snout and sending him flopping onto the floor. Stunned, Rex began to get up when Bha grabbed hold of Ichabod's birch staff and hit Rex with it in the head full on--

Rex blinked. He was back outside Ichabod's burro? He heard the two elders talking on the other side... the exact same words he heard before? Rex felt odd and dizzy. What was happening here? What was happening to him? Rex backed away slowly, as he did before, only this time, he did not turn back. The frightened Quasi turned on the balls of his paws and crept away from words he had already heard said.

Find Chukk, Rex told himself. And find him quick. He didn't know what was going on, but whatever it was, they had to get to the others. Damn what the voice Pi heard had told her. They were risking their lives to save the reputation of the elders and nothing more. The Journey of Lyght was not just a myth, it was a death sentence.

After leaving the Elder Chamber, Rex ventured to the Barracks where Chukk was directing the mobilization efforts. Surrounded by his fellow Battlers, Rex noticed that Chukk was as confident a Battler as he had ever seen. Directing his troops on how to best help others seemed to come naturally to him. Rex could see why Dee and Chukk were both so happy together and now knew they deserved to be together once again in this life. Dee had been at the wrong place at the wrong time and now would die a martyr because of it. None of this was fair at all, Rex grumbled to himself. What happened back in the Elder Chamber with Ichabod and Bha was confusing to say the least, but maybe it happened for a reason.

After asking for privacy with Chukk, Rex told the Battler everything. When he was done, Rex noticed that Chukk was holding his silver blade hilt so tightly he thought it would shatter the shiny metal into shards. Chukk's eyes met his in an icy stare. Rex swallowed hard.

"So, what do we do?" Rex asked when he finished. He could see the gears moving in Chukk's mind.

"First time I saw Dee, I knew I loved him," Chukk said. "They say it doesn't happen like that but for me, I knew right off he was the one for me. Since that first day in mid-tier schooling, we were inseparable from each other. Pups were picking on me because of my size, I was a runt of a thing, but in swooped Dee to save the day and every other day thereafter. He's kept me safe damn near my whole life. Made me love myself and be the best me I can be. There's not a damn chance some politician is going to rip him from me to save their own skin. I don't care how you heard what you heard as long as you're sure you heard it. It's not that I don't trust you. I do. But how can I trust that's truly the case, Rex? How do I know you're not just trying to keep your family from harm for your own sake and safety? You barely know me and Dee, for Spirit's sake."

Rex grimaced. "I know you well enough to know you don't want to lose Dee just as much as I don't want to lose Pi, Scout, or Rhi, if there's no need to. They're marching to their deaths for certain, Chukk. We have to stop them. How can I prove this to you?" Suddenly, Scout remembered something. "You and Dee both read Ancient Origins, right?"

Chukk nodded. "Aye."

"Like I told you, Ichabod has a replica of the map in his burro, but with directions written on it for us to follow in Quasi standard because none of us understand Origin. You're the Battalion Commander. You can go in there without anyone thinking twice. If it's there, I'm no liar."

"Fine," Chukk replied. "Then what?"

Rex thought hard. "Then you tell me what comes next. This as far as I've gotten, and I'm thought drunk already."

Chukk shook his head. "You are one odd Quasi, Rex. I'll hop into your burro tonight after the sun falls. Stay sharp. And... thanks for caring so much about my partner and I. Odd, yes. Caring, even more so. Now go, before someone notices you."

Rex nodded, backing away. "Chukk?"

"Yes?"

"Thank you for believing me, if only that you believe that I believe it."

Chukk nodded, waving him away as a group of Battlers appeared coming his way, probably to report in after patrol.

Rex turned, leaving the barracks behind but not his growing sense of concern and worry. That stayed with him all the way back to the burro.

***

It took Chukk a few dits to see Ichabod away from the Chamber in a position that would allow him to break away and investigate the younger Quasi's claims of deceit against their High Elder. The opportunity arose when Ichabod went to the Farmer's Den to consult with the root growers about storage containers for the evacuation. As soon as Ichabod was out of sight, Chukk took his chance.

It was remarkable how simple it was to prove Rex correct. The first place Chukk checked was the small refuse sack next to Ichabod's workstation area. Among the other garbage was a balled-up replica of the Journeyer's Map with Quasi standard writing in Ichabod's hand. He couldn't believe it. The map's route was identical to the one he had seen earlier when Dee took possession of it, only the directions had been rewritten just as Rex foresaw.

Chukk returned everything to as it was, save for taking ownership of the replica map, and left as quickly as he had arrived. Shoving the map into his pouch, Chukk began to grind his teeth in tension as he thought through what to do next. The oaf returned from the dead, the girl was being guided by voices, the bug was faster than light itself, and now the imp could see into the future? Chukk's head hurt. What lay in store next, he wondered ruefully? Dee growing a second head that could breathe fire? Oh Dee, Chukk thought, what in Spirit's name have you gotten us into?! He sighed heavily, deciding to pace for a bit through the caves before reporting back to Rex. And then, Chukk reiterated to himself his previous thought process and nearly kicked himself for his moment of hesitation. He prayed to his mother to forgive his transgression as he changed course to head to Rex's burro.

Chukk was met, as he suspected, with a very cagey and nervous Rex pacing the living area like a feral beast. "You need to calm down, Rex."

Rex shot Chukk a look of pure disdain. "You don't say. Really, calm down with all of this going on?"

Chukk sighed. "Let's sit down okay?"

After a moment's hesitation, Rex joined Chukk by sitting on the nearby pillows. "Well?"

"You say you saw something happen before it did, right?" Chukk asked.

"Aye, I did, I swear," Rex replied.

"Your sister told us she's hearing the voice of the Spirit in her head, right?" Chukk asked. "And Scout came back from the dead?"

"Yes," Rex replied inquisitively, "and yes."

"The bugle, all of a sudden is flying faster than her wings can take her. That I saw for myself and heard her mention it when we all met," Chukk added, his tone still even and measured. "Seems to me there's a good chance Ichabod and your Aunt were downright wrong about the Journey being a farce, Rex. Don't you think that's a possibility, with everything you've seen and heard?"

Rex was about to bark an answer when he stopped himself to ponder Chukk's words. "Go on then."

Chukk leaned closer. "If they're wrong about the Journey of Lyght, then how do we bloody well know they're right about anything having to do with it either? I'm thinking that we shouldn't be so quick to assume that my Dee and your family aren't doing exactly as the ancients foretold. I'm thinking that we've all been so worn down by our skepticism and selfishness that we forgot how to believe in anything greater than what we can touch with our paws, see with our eyes, smell with our snouts, and ear with our ears. What about faith? Hope? Love? What about what we believe in our souls and the Spirit again, Rex?"

Rex soaked this in. Chukk said nothing more, remaining quiet. Rex hadn't thought about it like that. His first reaction to everything was always to picture the worst possible outcome and then be mildly relieved when things didn't end up going as bad as he thought they might. Ever since the death of his parents when he was young, Rex had lived a jaded, fractured existence. The scenario of dying with the planet, and without his loved ones there to be with him at the end, was the worst of all possible outcomes, which is why he felt so numb to any chance of anything else. Rex forced himself to admit that what he learned about Ichabod's intentions just let feel justified in his decision to abdicate his place on the journey without a fight. The coward in him was not letting Rex let that go. He was, for the umpteenth time in his life, ashamed of himself and afraid to admit it.

"You think they can come back alive, either way?" Rex asked skeptically.

Chukk nodded. "I do, and it seems to me the Spirit might very well be looking out for them, and you too, to boot."

Rex nodded, feeling a rush of energy begin to flow through him. "If they do it, save us, that would be spectacular, wouldn't it?"

"When," Chukk corrected him, "when they save us, they will return home to us, Rex." He winked at the younger Quasi. "There's magic in the air. My mum always said so. Sometimes you just have to look for it longer and harder than other times, but all this? This is destiny, mate, and we should be thrilled to be a part of it until we know for certain otherwise. Seems to me, anyways. You're your own person. You do you."

They were silent for a bit. Rex swallowed hard. "What are we going to do about Ichabod and HomeSpace?"

"His motives might be dark, but his intentions are hopefully pure, Rex. They say not to trust the elders and that's because at the planet's turn, they're all just in it for themselves and their cherished power over us. Moving the burros will go against popular opinion, so this gave him a way of making it go down nice and easy for folks. He wins either way, just the way leaders like it. Now that being said, I saw the tail end of that Sun Shock and there's no way we'd survive a second one. No, we leave him be and get our people to safety in the South. There is one thing, though, Little One, I'm having you trained for battle and coming to Battalion Command."

Rex nearly fell out of his cushions. "Say what now?"

Chukk laughed. "As a Strategist, Rex. If you can foretell the future, very well likely you can save some lives and do a world of good. Even if you, what shall we call it, ping, on something only once, it will be well worth it. We're putting you to good use doing good for the many instead of just yourself. The world's at stake and we need our best players playing and not sitting on the fringes twiddling their paws. You start tomorrow."

Rex shook his head. "Chukk, new friend, I am *not* the Battler type. I'm all bluster and no fight. I cook and clean. Sure, I can dress a wound with a firm bandage and apply pressure but I'm not the Quasi you want next to you in battle, mate."

Chukk rose from his cushions. "You will be. Be at the Barracks at sunrise and bring your best." Chukk pulled the crumpled map from his pouch. "And if Ichabod gives me, you, or anyone else trying to do the right thing by the Quasi any trouble or starts behaving badly, the map will give us leverage. Good night, Rex."

Chukk disappeared into the night, leaving Rex in awe of his new protector and boss.

***

The trek up the North Ridge left the Journeyers winded and tired, save Pi. As a Leaper, she was used to navigating rough, vertical terrain and making good speed doing it. Scout, though showing signs of great strength Pi found remarkable to say the least, hadn't learned how to harness it very well and was left in near tatters after his day of digging himself out of the ceiling collapse and then proceeding to venture up the cliffs with the group. Dee's frame was built for power and resistance, which served him well, but having to rescue Scout late in the climb had caused his paws to weaken to the point that a night's rest was much needed. Rhi had fallen asleep nestled in Scout's pouch as soon as the group had broken camp for the night.

They found a cluster of lyght veins near the mouth of the cave, which the map and guide listed as the beginning of the first stop on their one way ticket to the Sun, and made camp there to take advantage of the heat the pulsing lyght veins provided while the wind wickedly whipped around them, interspersed with large, fluffy indigo snowflakes that blew around in the yellow swirls of lyght left by the vein arteries surrounding them.

Pi couldn't sleep as the others were so easily able to. Her mind was too busy spinning with the past day's events. As she sat pondering things both trivial, such as if they had packed enough carrot bread or not, and grave, such as if any of the rest of them would be afforded a second chance at life if they faltered or met a bad end as Scout had, she found herself wishing upon wishes that her father and mother were still alive to nurture and champion her and Rex. Losing them had nearly been the death of Pi and Rex both and even now, all these planet turns later, she still had no real grasp on what had exactly happened to them or any of the others who had gone on the expedition.

Neither Pi nor anyone else even knew where it was they had travelled to; Ichabod, Addy, and the other Elders saying that the information was still a matter of HomeSpace security and unable to be divulged for fear others would meet the same fate. She never understood how Scout's parents or any of the other survivors could keep such information secret either. Them especially, for as much nectar as they drank to drown their sorrows, in addition to treating Scout as poorly as they did.

Pi heard a noise behind her. Wasting no time, she whipped around, grabbing her silver blade and quilling up in one, fluid, deadly movement to find she had nearly beheaded Dee, who froze in an instant.

"You should have been a Battler with moves like that, Leaper," he said drolly, pushing the blade away from his head slowly.

"Leapers have to think fast and move faster when we're alone out here. My apologies," Pi said. "I thought you were all asleep."

"Don't apologize," Dee replied. "We need to have instincts like that if we stand half a chance to reach the Spirit Chamber before getting killed by the MaRuu or Spirit knows what else that might come in our way. I had my eyes closed but sleep is escaping me at the moment. Those two, I don't know how they are managing it. Quite the pair they are."

Pi let herself smile for the first time since seeing Scout alive back at HomeSpace. "That they are. You have to love them. I do anyways."

"For that I'm certain," Dee said, sharing the smile.

"Spirit Chamber, you said?" Pi asked.

"Aye. It's our final destination. The map says it's the planetary residence of the Quasi Spirit here on Arkelia. Hopefully. I finished making out the map before we went to bunk."

"So, what do we have in store for us, Dee?"

"To be honest, Pi, I'm not entirely sure. It doesn't read the way our Quasi texts do now. It speaks in prose, sort of. It's hard to explain. What I can tell you is that the map isn't geospatial. Rather, it's allegorical. I know for certain it starts in those caves but from there, your guess is as good as mine until I start to see how things play out and hopefully make more sense out of it as we go along."

"Dee," Pi replied, "nothing about any of this makes one lick of sense."

They two Journeyers shared the first muffled laugh of their burgeoning kinship. Both would have admitted that it was good to laugh. It warmed their hearts and souls, even in this cold, dark place as they faced the weight of the world and the end of their existence together.

"Can I ask you something?" Pi went on after the laughing had concluded.

"You just did," Dee replied, smiling. "But go ahead. Ask again."

"Do you believe me that I've heard the Spirit's voice in my head, that it's talking to me?" Pi asked, trying to catch snowflakes on her silver blade.

There was a moment of silence as Dee watched the leaper play with her sword and the elements, not sure if she was feeling inquisitive or nervous.

"I wouldn't be here if I didn't," he replied, taking his own, longer bronze blade out and joining in trying to catch the snow. "The real question you should be asking is if you do."

Pi didn't respond. They sat in silence, playing with the snow.

"You have an advantage," she said finally.

"And what's that," Dee asked, unsure what she was getting at.

"Your blade is bigger than mine," Pi said plainly, pausing. "At catching the snow. Nothing to do with whether or not you've followed a crazy weirdo and her back from the dead partner into the Arkelian wilds with a buzzed Bugle in tow on a half-baked journey that's going to get us and everyone else living underneath the rocks killed."

"Chukk and I both believe in the power of the Spirit, Pi," Dee said. "And none of you would be here if you didn't too. Trust yourself or else you'll never be able to trust another... and we need to all trust each other now. Our lives depend on it. I'm going to lay back down and see if I can muster some sleep. I think you should try and do the same. Good night."

"Night," Pi replied. She stayed in her seat, letting him go back to the camp alone.

Afraid to sleep for fear she wouldn't wake up, Pi forced herself to take Dee's advice after a few dits time. Returning to the camp, she nestled herself in next to Scout, with Rhi's buzzing snores gently passing through his pouch, and nuzzled into his nook. This immediately tempered her excitement and allowed her to begin falling asleep. Her last thoughts were of Rex. She missed him already.

***

Ichabod was used to lying to get what he wanted accomplished. Having to shovel the Bugle elder Bha such drivel seemed beneath him though. Who among the elders would believe him if he told them he too had heard a voice in his mind other than his own that told him not to select any other than Pi for the Journey, not any of the Battlers they were to choose from? Being High Elder meant doing what was best for all the Quasi at all times and moving HomeSpace was paramount after the Sun Shock blast. Ichabod knew better than to question the future, for he saw how to protect them all.

Pi was technically, the seventh of the seventh called, with forty-eight past Journeyers disappearing into the ether. But they were all ferocious male Battlers, warriors through and through, who had all gone were all chosen on by their reigning High Elders. The Quasis needed to think he was still in complete control, for if Ichabod could not move his people quickly, they would surely perish if another Sun Shock hit the lyghtning fields. That it helped him move one step closer to facing the MaRuu need not be known by anyone else. Ichabod sighed. His head was dizzy from all this. He feared another sleepless night was in his future.

5

Pi awoke, covered in sweat. She was shaking. Her head felt odd and tingly. What was that, Pi thought to herself. It was as if the Spirit were having a battle royal in her mind. She remembered her dream vividly but could not picture what she saw in her mind, only the feeling of agitation and fear echoing now through her body.

Scout was awake now. He yawned. "You all right, love? Bad dream?"

Pi nodded. "I sure hope so."

Scout looked at her inquisitively. "What's that mean?"

She looked around, as if to make sure she really was lying here in Scout's embrace, with Rhi snoring away in Scout's pouch, and Dee off to the side, lying underneath their blankets and tucked under the warmth of the lyght vein artery at the top of the Northern Ridge. "It wasn't all a dream, was it?"

Scout shook his head. "No, love. We're off to save the planet. The Sun will start rising soon. Our quest begins in a bit."

Pi sighed, rubbing the sleep from her eyes. "If that's so, then I'd say we've already started it with what we've been put through so far, aye?"

Scout chuckled. "Fair enough. I have to admit that I feel oddly optimistic, Pi. Like we have a chance to go back home again. Foolhardy, I guess."

Pi nodded as, strangely; she thought the same. Pi thought back to her talk with Addy. Hope, she thought. It was if it was an indestructible feeling. Fully knowing there was no return from this, still she thought there might be some way to defy the fates and somehow return to

HomeSpace alive. She didn't mind it.

"I feel the same way, Scout," Pi replied. "Who knows, maybe this time will be different."

"What do you mean this time?" Scout asked.

"I don't know why I just said that," Pi replied. "It just sort of came out. Spirit, Scout, I've lost my mind, haven't I?"

"Only as much as I've lost my life," Scout replied. "Come on, lets wake this buzzer in my pouch and get Dee up. We're going to have to get going pretty soon."

"I'm already up," Dee replied, opening his eyes. "Been up for a few dits now. Listen, we're all crazy for doing this, Pi. In a way, I think we have to be."

Scout softly shook his pouch. "Wake up, Rhi."

The buzzed snoring stopped. Rhi climbed out of the pouch, stretching her small arms skyward and letting out a little yawn. "Did I miss anything?"

"If you mean breakfast," Scout replied. "The answer is no."

As the journeyers tucked their blankets back into their pouches and shared sweetwater and carrot bread, there was an odd silence between them as the inevitability of what lay ahead creeped closer and closer. The only sounds were the whipping around of the wind and Rhi's wings fluttering ferociously to fight them. It was both eerie and calming for them at the same time, not being sure what to say to each other before entering into the cave and whatever lie ahead. They could be facing a quick death, as each secretly expected, or worse - the unknown. Not being able to conjure up in their minds what they were facing was nearly excruciating.

Pi, though, found herself oddly excited by not knowing what was to come. Something inside her always pushed her to want to know it all, for only with all of the information available to her did she feel comfort. That mindset had both helped and hurt her throughout life, hurt mostly with what had happened to her parents, and helped with everything else. Pi knew she was incredibly smart and that gnawing need within her to learn everything she didn't know was why.

She just hoped it would help them on their journey. Knowing that none of the chosen had made it further than here gave her a feeling of fear but Pi brushed it away with the hope that she and the others would be the first to prove the legends wrong and that this trip into the unknown wouldn't end in sacrifice. How she longed to see Rex again.

"All right," Dee said once they were all packed up and ready to go, "Here we go." He read from the map. "If you enter here, you have faced fear. Prepare to face it once more. Find your courage to persevere."

There was a long pause between them.

"Wait, that's it?" Rhi asked. "That was no bloody help at all!"

"I think that's the point, Rhi" Pi replied. "We have to find the answers within ourselves. That being said, before we go any further, I want to give each of you the chance to turn back now. There won't be any hard feelings on my part. If you want out, now is the time to say so."

There was another silence. Scout broke it by chuckling. Loudly. "What kind of family would we be if we left you to this all alone, love?" Scout asked Pi. "And besides, we need Dee to read the bloody map."

They all laughed, Pi the loudest.

"We're in this together," Rhi said. "No way around it, Pi. We're on this journey with you. Let's see it through."

"I know I don't know you all very well but from what I've seen in the course of one day lets me know you all share a love for our peoples and for each other," Dee said. "I am honored to stand beside each of you and read the bloody map."

There was more laughter.

"Right then," Pi said. "Let's go meet destiny at its door, shall we?" She took hold of Scout's front paw. They walked towards the cave entrance together, with Rhi flying next to them and Dee bringing up the rear. Pi held out her other front paw. "Dee, take my paw. Rhi, take Scout's. We enter together as one."

The four journeyers hopped forward methodically, entering the dark cave. As they crossed the threshold, they saw only darkness. Firmly inside the bowels of the cave, the ground beneath them seemed to start pulsing with yellow lyght as energy raced beneath their feet. It grew with each step they took forward. Looking behind them, it appeared pitch black. They followed the lyght and felt themselves moving lower and lower in altitude, entering the heart of the mountain.

After a long hop, continuing deeper and deeper inside the cave, they four journeyers froze in their tracks.

"Unreal," Rhi whispered. It was an understatement.

"Blimey," Scout said shortly thereafter. "It's--"

"Beautiful," Dee finished, his eyes wide.

Pi remained silent, studying everything the light was refracting through her sparkling eyes. They had been walking through walls of pure quartz crystal from the floor to the cave's ceiling. And now, yellow lyght from countless vein arteries filled the enormous cavern they found themselves in. The lyght bounced from crystal to crystal, causing rainbow lyght prisms, full of red, orange, yellow, blue, indigo, and violet, to bounce from wall to wall. Only the gravel and dirt floor under them was spared from sharing the beauty in front of them.

Pi turned around. And behind them. She looked left. And to their left. She looked right. And to their right. They were surrounded by these crystal walls somehow? How had they let that happen? She looked up, seeing that the crystal walls ran right up to the ceiling.

Rhi was looking around as well, feeling as if the walls were closing in. "I'm going up and above!"

"I don't think that's going to work," Pi said, but it was too late.

POP!

Off Rhi went.

BANG!

And then, down she came.

Rhi fell back to the ground after slamming into the cavern's crystal ceiling with great velocity. "Ow!"

"You okay, Rhi?" Scout asked, leaning over to check on her. "Quite a bang that was!"

Rhi shook her head clear. "Bloody trapped, we are! Walls go all the way up!"

Pi remained quiet while the others began asking each other how they had allowed themselves to get trapped like this, how they must have followed in the paw prints of all the journeyers before them, and what to do next. Perhaps they could retrace their steps and get out that way.

But wouldn't that bring them back to where they started? Was that the point? Wouldn't the others have done the same thing? Each question that had no answer was making them more and more flustered.

"Dee, read the map again," Pi instructed. This whole time, Dee had been studying it as Scout and Rhi threw unanswerable questions back and forth to each other.

"Okay, it says 'If you enter here, you have faced fear. Prepare to face it once more. Find your courage to persevere'," Dee read. "Wait,

I swear this wasn't here before. There's a new line of text that says, 'Finding courage means you will find the way.' I swear on my life that wasn't there before!"

Rhi scratched her head. "But what does it mean?"

"I don't know but I think I've got this place figured out," Pi said. "It's a maze. There must only be another way out and it's up to us to find it."

"But... If it turns out there's only one way out," Scout replied, "that means there was only one-way in. Meaning that it's a bloody dead end. We retrace our steps back and we'll end up back outside the cave. Makes no sense."

"I agree," Dee said, studying the map. "There's a progression to all of it. It doesn't say anything about going back. There must be two entrances, the entrance which we already came through and another that allows us to move on."

"All right then," Pi said. "Seems we explore. I vote we stay together. If we get separated, we might never find each other again. Agreed?"

"Agreed," the others replied.

"And away we go," Pi mused, slowly advancing ahead.

The others followed suit as the maze twirled and twisted around them. As the lyght bounced from one wall to the next, they grew more and more disoriented. Never had such beauty seemed so deadly to any of them.

Time seemed to have no meaning after a while as the journeyers fell further and further into the maze. Each new pathway found led to another new glimpse of hope only to be vanquished when a dead end would be found. Rhi's frustration at not being able to fly above the walls became well established quickly.

After an extended period of twists and turns that led to yet dead end, Scout stopped them before they began again. "Wait a moment. I have a thought."

"What is it, love?" Pi asked, taking a drink of sweetwater. "See something we don't?"

"Aye," Scout replied, pointing down. "Tracks. Our tracks. We've been here, looks like, a few times before doesn't it?"

Dee let out a groan. "Circles. We've been going in bloody circles!"

"If we could just get to the other side here," Pi said, pointing at the far most wall, "we could get out. I can make out the other entrance through this wall!"

Suddenly, the lyght began shifting around them and the maze was filled with grinding sounds. As the four journeyers stood paralyzed in fear, the maze seemingly closed in around them. They found themselves trapped where they were.

Rhi grimaced. "There's no way out now if we can't even find our way back to where we came in! We're trapped, we are!"

They all banged on the four crystal walls surrounding them. For what seemed an eternity, they yelled and screamed for help to no avail.

Scout's punches seemed to shake the cave in its entirety, but nothing came as a result. After Pi, Dee, and Rhi had finally succumbed to fatigue and took a seat to rest, Scout continued pounding away. Without saying anything to embarrass him, Pi knew her partner was scared straight through. Rhi kept looking to Pi, as if she would somehow magically save them.

"What is it, Rhi?" Pi finally asked, mostly just to break the monotony of listening to Scout's wall punches thunder through their ears.

"Now would be a good time for that voice in your head to something, wouldn't it?" Rhi asked. "Is it saying anything now?"

Pi shook her head. "No. Not a peep."

"Some help the Spirit turned out to be!" Rhi spat. "Tricked us into coming in here just like the others. Just to leave us here to dig our own graves, it bloody did."

Pi looked to Scout and Dee, to the ground, and then back to them once more. Then she smiled. And then she laughed.

"We're through," Dee said. "There's no other way to go and Pi's gone wonky. I'm afraid the bugle's right. We're going to die here."

"I'm not sure we should be laughing, love," Scout said, putting a paw on Pi's shoulder.

"I figured it out. Rhi, you're a genius! Courage means you dig your paws in when the going gets tough, right?" Pi asked. No one answered.

"Afraid you three are, aren't you?" Pi asked again.

"And you're not?" Rhi replied. "Might I ask why?"

Pi looked down, scratching her taloned rear paws into the dirt and gravel below. "Our people are diggers. So, I say, when there's nowhere else to go above, the Quasi way is to go... below." She pointed down at the ground in front of the end of the wall.

"We'll dig our way to the other side of the wall!" Scout exclaimed. "Bloody brilliant, you are!"

"The map doesn't say how we move on," Dee said. "It just says we persevere. I like it!"

Rhi looked on in astonishment. "I'm in agreement except for one thing, bugles are no diggers."

"Oh, come on, Rhi," Pi ribbed. "Every little bit helps. Let's go!"

The three Quasi used their massive hind paws to begin digging through the maze floor where the crystal wall came to a dead end. As the dirt and gravel gave way, Scout reached down and felt inside the hole they had dug thus far. He raised his head, a smile on his face.

"The crystal only goes as low as the maze floor," Scout said, still smiling.

"Which means we can dig beneath it!" Dee said. "Pi, you're a genius! And courageous unlike any I've ever seen!"

As they dug deeper and deeper, it seemed the lyght in the maze began to shine brighter and brighter. In the time it took to dig a proper tunnel underneath the crystal, prism filled wall, the four journeyers began to have trouble hiding their excitement. It only helped them dig faster and more furious.

When the tunnel to the other side was complete, they embraced and thanked Pi repeatedly for thinking of such an audacious solution to their problem. They amazed that a tunnel big enough for all them to pass through was even possible and how remarkable it was that the crystal was not attached to the floor but the ceiling above it.

"Does the map say what happens next? After we make it through?" Pi asked Dee, who just finished taking a long drink of sweetwater and dusting himself off from all the digging.

Dee looked at the map. "A different place from what you know, to the land of purple snow you will now go…"

"Ugh," Rhi exclaimed. "Snow? I hate everything about it save for letting it melt so we can drink it as sweetwater."

"Means we can refill our jugs when we're there," Scout replied. "No need to keep rationing!" He reached into his pouch for his sweetwater jug, only for Pi to swat at him to put it back.

"We wait until we're sure, Scout," Pi scolded him. "Let's go see what this is about, shall we? Dare say I'm a little excited!"

"All for it," Dee said. "Let's go!"

As the four journeyers slip through their makeshift tunnel and onto the other side of the crystal cave maze, they became the first ever journeyers to pass the first marker. After they passed through, there was a loud rumbling in the cave. Suddenly, the large crystal they had just passed under crashed downwards, plunging deeply into the ground. Shards of crystal began falling around them.

"I see lyght ahead!" Pi called out, pointing to her left. "Go to the lyght! Do not stop and do not look back! Go! Go!"

POP!

Rhi was gone in an instant.

Pi and Dee followed, with Scout bringing up the rear as the cave collapsed behind them in spectacular fashion. Reaching the mouth of the cave, they dove out into the hazy, indigo mist as the cave fell in on itself for good, sending out glittering dust of pulverized crystal and quartz.

As the three Quasi lay on the snowy ground, Rhi swooped down from her position above them. "Guess we're not going home that way. If we go home at all, that is."

They turned to see the mouth of the cave filled with debris, dusty ash still shooting out of it in thick plumes. They looked up, and up again, at a mountain face that seemed to extend to the heavens and then some. Truly massive, it was unlike anything any of them had ever seen. From this perspective there seemed no way to climb it and it appeared to stretch on forever in each direction. Wherever they now were, the journeyers were trapped here.

***

Rex had never been so tired in his life and was thrilled to find out he had graduated from what he guessed was a very paired down version of Battler's training. For the past twelve days, he spent his mornings training with Chukk and his regiment and his afternoons helping them prepare the HomeSpace for the upcoming Caravan to the Southland. And now, here they were, moving out as a herd for the first time in a millennia to seek out a new home.

It was all so surreal, nothing more so than his newfound ability to take a peek into what his future held. It was after the second occurrence, when Rex was able to predict a massive lyghtning blast hitting the outpost wall where he was stationed, that Chukk decided that it was something Rex could learn to control and use as a predictive tool to keep them safe at all times.

With Chukk's help, Rex was able to determine that he could indeed spring himself back, but only able to seemingly do so for a few dits at a time thus far and usually when his actions caused him peril or harm. They proved this when Chukk threw his bronze blade into Rex's rear paw as a test. Even now, having not endured it again, Rex could still feel the sharp, blinding pain like it just happened.

Giving Rex a silver blade of his own, Chukk said, "You get into a spot that proves treacherous to either you, us, or anyone else, you stab yourself in the hind paw and snap yourself back to warn us. Got that?"

Thankfully, that had not been the case as everything was going as smoothly as moving a herd could be. Ichabod and the other elders remained at the very rear, claiming to be too old to travel at the front with the Battler battalions. Chukk said it was more likely the leaders wanted to stay clear of any trouble they might run into at the front. The herd was flanked by the Leapers on the left and the Scouts on the right. The young and able bodied were in the front behind the soldiers with the older Quasi, the Healers, and then Ichabod bringing up the rear with the other Battler Battalion protecting them from a flank attack.

Five days in, and Rex was amazed at just how little life was left on the surface. Indigo, red, and orange storm skies were constant, as was the swirling, hazy mist of Indigo vapor that clung in the air like soup. Lyghtning rippled constantly above the sky. The ground was always either jagged rock or thick sand and there was hardly any vegetation anywhere to be found except for thorny, bramble bushes and thick milkweeds, which constantly blew in the heavy winds.

Besides the normal cloth sash that each Quasi typically wore around their lower body to cover their extremities, most of the herd was also wearing full robes to protect themselves against the elements. Even with this extra layer of warmth and his natural protective coat, Rex could still feel the sting of cold against his skin.

Chukk spent his time travelling the length of the herd, checking in on the various sentries he had established for status updates and feeding this information to Ichabod in the rear for guidance. As he approached from the rear, Rex slowed his gallop to catch up with his new friend. He was still wondering when or if Chukk would talk to Ichabod about the circumstances of selecting Pi as the Called Journeyer. Now seemed as good as time as any to ask about it.

"How'd it go with Ichabod?" Rex asked, drawing next to Chukk.

Chukk shot him an inquisitive look. "What are you getting on about? What about him?"

Rex returned the look. "What am I getting on about? What are you getting on about? You were back checking in with him just now, weren't you?"

Chukk shook his head. "You are an odd one, Rex. I'll give you that. I was checking in with Bha."

"Bha?" Rex asked, startled. "Why him?"

Chukk looked truly puzzled at this point. He put his paw on Rex's shoulder, slowing both of them to a stop to let the herd pass them by. He studied the younger Quasi's face, as if waiting for him to snap out of a trance. "Ichabod's dead, Rex. You know that. He died in the Sun Shock blast with the others."

Rex shook his head, a sharp pain now pulsing in his skull. "No, no, no. He tricked Pi and the rest into going. You know that. You have the map he forged! Remember?" Rex pointed at Chukk's pouch. "Let's see it! Stop this madness! It's not funny!"

Chukk ruefully withdrew the map from his pouch. It looked to Rex like the same parchment, but only now the writing was oddly different. It was just poorly drawn scratching looked to have been done in haste. There were blood stains speckled across it. "In his last breaths to you and my Dee, he drew us this map to the Westland Caves and made sure we undertake this caravan to the Southlands. You know this, Rex. Come on now, snap out of it!"

Rex looked around. He went to grab the silver blade from his pouch only to find it missing. All that he found were food rations, a sweetwater jug, and his medicinal herbs sack he had given away to one of the Healers at the start of the journey. "No, this isn't right," he muttered. "This is wrong, all wrong. He's alive. Please believe me."

Chukk lightly rubbed Rex's shoulder. "Mate, you and Dee were the ones to find him. You were there when he drew him the map before his vessel gave out. What's gotten into you? And why aren't you with the Healers in the rear? What brought you up here with the Battlers, anyways?"

Rex felt everything beginning to spin. "I've lost my mind; I think I've lost my bloody mind."

"Ichabod asked Dee to take care of you three, so I'm here for you, mate," Chukk said calmly. "Take in the air and get yourself straight. Have some sweetwater."

Rex did as he was told. He did his best to slow his breathing for fear of losing consciousness. And somehow, he began to remember the events Chukk had just described. It was an odd sensation as his memory now held two timelines of events, both leading him here to this time and place. He began to weep thick tears.

"It's all right, Rex, it's all right," Chukk consoled him. "What's going on? You can tell me."

"Something's happening," Rex said. "I think things are changing and I'm the only one who knows it."

Chukk eyed Rex up. "Changing how? What in bloody damnation are you going on about?"

"I don't know, Chukk," Rex said, "but things are either getting better or worse. Oh, I just don't know anymore. We're all going to die, aren't we?"

"None of that now!" Chukk replied. "Not today we're not. We've been on caravan now for nearly a week and we're well on our way to the Southlands. We'll have our brethren there to help us start to re-dig a new HomeSpace and that's not even mentioning the journeyers' mission. Think positively!"

"Do you really think they stand a chance?" Rex asked, the dizziness fading.

"Of course, I do," Chukk said. "My Dee doesn't know the meaning of failure. I reckon your sister is the same way along with Scout and the little one. Give them a chance. For all we know, they're already on their way to saving us."

Rex swallowed hard. "Can I tell you something? It might take a dit or two."

"Aye," Chukk said, truly wanting to help Rex regain his composure. "Go on then."

When Rex was done telling Chukk all that he had just encountered with time now seemingly changing around him, he stared up the Battler with scared eyes. "What do you think it means?" he asked Chukk, meekly.

Chukk did not do what Rex expected. He smiled. "If you're telling the truth then it seems time might be starting to straighten itself out, Rex. Ichabod died a hero's death instead of living a coward's lie. That's proper, young one. You notice anything else, you tell me, okay?"

Rex nodded. He hadn't thought about why things might have happened, just that they had. "What do you think it could mean, Chukk?"

Chukk smiled even broader. "I think it means my partner and your family are making good progress, Rex." He reached in his pouch, withdrawing his secondary weapon, a silver blade, and handed it to Rex. "I guess I'm giving this back to you in an odd way," he joked. "Don't go cutting your paw unless you need to. We don't even know if you can still pull that trick off and I think I like things just the way they are right now, don't you?"

"Why's that?" Rex asked.

"Hope, Rex," Chukk replied. "We have hope."

Chukk leapt off with a magnificent long leap towards the Battlers in the front, leaving Rex to choose where to go - to the rear with the Healers or to the front with the Battlers. Rex thought about it for a moment and finally decided to join the Healers in the rear. He fancied himself more of a helper than a soldier.

***

The two MaRuu watched the large herd of Quasi invaders at a safe distance so they would not be detected. Perched on a nearby hilltop covered in thick bristle bushes, the creatures used their jet-black scales and horn spikes to their best advantage to blend in with their surroundings. The wind did not bother them in the least. The cold was to their liking as that was what their home always was like - frigid cold. The Bugle had been right. The Quasi meant to move into the Southlands, their lands. Unspeakable!

The scene was disturbing to say the least. It appeared the foreign conquerors were once again making moves to spread across what was left of their homelands. This could not be. They will need to be stopped, for certain, the MaRuu said to each other telepathically, as was the way they communicated with each other. Retreating as quietly as possible down the far side of the hills, the MaRuu agreed to return to their base and begin to send out the call for as many Spikers as they could muster. The Quasi of the East were on a southern trajectory and this could not be.

Death would come to them all, the MaRuu said, both in agreement. The battle lines had been drawn. War was coming for the Quasi invaders once more and this time, none would survive to tell the tale.

***

The Journeyers had spent the better part of a day hiking away from where the cave entrance had collapsed through thick wilted brush and more thorny brambles than any of them had ever seen. None were too pleased with Scout very much, most of all Scout himself. As they had started off on the day's journey, he quickly fell behind the rest. Pi and Dee were eager to reach the next challenge and did not enjoy his seemingly lackadaisical approach to what they were going through as it appeared, he was, as Scout tended to do, daydreaming and not paying attention to the terrain in front of them.

Pi watched as Dee chopped his way through the thicket with his bronze blade, not missing a step, and wondered why her Scout seemed to leave the hard work for others to do for him so often. Rhi would routinely buzz back to check on him, but also chiding him for keep falling in the bramble brushes. He didn't find it at all funny, as each stumble brought with it a new, painful scratch to his bottom.

Scout could hear his father teasing him, mocking him for never being good enough while he was drunk on nectar. He could hear his mother chiding him to be extra careful because he wouldn't be able to tend to her needs if he was incapacitated or hurt somehow, as she had made Scout never be too far from her beckoning call. Their constant criticism had left an indelible mark on his psyche, bringing painful memories bubbling to the surface frequently. His childhood fears had stayed with him long after his parents who had cultivated them had passed on.

Scout never felt confident on his own. He relied on Pi's strength to carry him through life. Scout knew he should trust himself more but when you were told your life that you were a failure, it had a long-lasting effect on someone. He had accepted he was not very good at things and fearful of making any decisions that might tilt the fragile balance he kept with himself and others, mostly Pi. Scout could tell she wasn't presently pleased with him. He reached back into his pouch and took hold of his half empty sweetwater jug, taking another pull of liquid to quench his growing thirst.

"Take it easy on the sweetwater, Scout," Rhi said, buzzing towards him. "We don't know when we'll get more!"

Pi spun around. "Scout! For the love of all things, put your sweetwater away! You've been slurping it down all day, for Spirit's sake! Make it last! This is the last time I tell you!"

Scout hated when Pi got angry at him. Why was he so incapable of being better than he was? She had already chastised him for getting into his carrot bread rations and now here he was getting scolded for not minding his sweetwater supply better. Dang it, Scout, he scolded himself, be better and don't make Pi mad!

"Sorry, love!" Scout called out. "So sorry! Terribly sorry!"

"Stop apologizing, Scout," Rhi said softly, feeling bad for getting him in more trouble with Pi. "Just take better care of your rations and try to stay on the trail Dee is cutting out. Your rear end can't take much more abuse there, mate."

Scout nodded, thankful for Rhi's sense of humor. How he wished he could be more like them, confident and courageous, decisive and determined. Here he was, covered in scratches, through half his rations, and battling the ghosts of his dead parents in his head just trying to figure out why of all Quasi, he was the one who deserved a second chance at life? Was his act of selflessness worthy of such a prize? Oh, how he questioned himself even now! What a mess of a Quasi he was. Why did they even want him with them on this important mission. He questioned losing his life again so soon after being granted a spiritual reprieve.

Scout didn't remember any of what happened before he woke up and started digging himself out but Rhi said he saved her and sent her to save the others. He hardly believed he was capable of such behavior. She must have imagined it. Scout was starting to think he was never pinned down at all. In fact, he felt sure of it somehow.

The giant rock that fell landed above him, wedged between the bench and the ground, providing him cover. He remembered it now. It was odd because in the back of his mind, he vaguely remembered being pinned down also. What was happening to him?

Scout got scared, wandering off in his mind once more and losing track of where he was on the jagged trail. His left hind paw was caught up in a tangle of vines, causing him to stumble. His sweetwater jug went flying, landing on the ground in between Pi and Dee, its contents dribbling out onto the hard rock beneath their paws.

"Scout?! Really?!" Pi chastised him. "Are you all right?"

Scout picked himself up, dusting himself off. He earned himself a scrape on his right hind paw in the fall. "Aye. Guess I won't be tempted to drink anymore of my sweetwater, will I?"

"Seriously, Scout," Pi said, picking up the jug and bringing to him.

"You need to mind yourself better. We can't do it for you all the time."

"Can I talk to you for a moment?" Scout asked quietly. "Alone?"

"Fine," Pi said, "if it helps you get your bearings straight."

"Excuse us, you two," Scout said to Dee and Rhi.

Once they were a little ways back, Scout said, "In the cave collapse, I remember the rock missing me now. Never being pinned. Never-"

"Dying," Pi finished. "Oh, this is bloody weird. I remember them saying you died but now I can also remember you saying the rock missed you. Is that why you fell just then?"

"Aye," Scout replied. "I got stuck in my head for a moment. Pi, I don't know that I belong here with you. I'm no good to any of you. I just get in the way. I'm a liability. I don't know what's happening but I'm bloody scared, I am."

Pi rubbed his front paw. "It's going to be okay, Scout. You hear me? Whatever this all is and whatever we're doing, everything is changing somehow. But we're still here and we're still together. You hear me?"

Scout nodded.

"Good," Pi replied. "I know you worry and doubt, well, everything, but I know you don't doubt me, do you?"

"I trust you with my life, or lives, er, but yes, I trust you," Scout said. "What am I to do?"

Pi sighed. "Figure out how to answer that question yourself, love."

She turned and heading back towards the others, leaving Scout to wonder if Pi meant that lovingly or in haste. Stupid, Scout, he chided himself. You even worry about good advice you've been given. He sighed a heavy breath and returned his attention to keeping up with the rest of the journeyers, who had returned to the trail in front of them.

***

"So, what now?" Rhi asked. "Which way does the map say?"

Dee studied the map and then read, "Which way to go is up to you. Choose your path and see it through. The end result will be one of two."

Rhi was visibly flustered, looking in one direction and then back in the other. "That doesn't help! There's only two bloody paths to choose from!"

Above them, the sky sent yellow lyghtning streaking out in all directions. Loud booms of thunder echoed out constantly. Yet there was no rain, which was oddly scary. Pi kept waiting for the sweetwater to fall, hoping it would break the increasing storm clouds, to no avail. There was also none of the promised indigo snow, so Scout's wasting of sweetwater now gave the others something to grumble at him about.

Their solidarity was fraying and now this, they had reached an impasse where there were only two paths they could take to go on, one downhill to the left and another uphill to the right. Pi and the others had been debating which trail to take for nearly as long as it took them to get here. It was growing more and more frustrating as the debate lingered onwards.

Scout had taken to sitting on a nearby rock, never one to want to argue over much of everything. He had been mostly quiet as Dee, Rhi, and Pi debated if they were missing something, each anxious to reach the next challenge and take one step closer to saving everyone. He scratched his chin and cleared his throat. "Pi, what are you thinking, love?"

Pi faced him. "Oh, I don't know what to think at this point, honestly. I just want to figure this out and get back on the journey. We've wasted too much time as it is." She paused. "I'm also thinking you shouldn't have lost your sweetwater. Now I'm not just worried about which way to go but also if we're all going to run out of rations!"

"Aye, it was stupid of me," Scout said. "As I tend to do. What about you two? What do you think?"

Rhi and Dee stopped their near combative quarrel, turning to face Scout.

"I think you're trying to change the subject," Rhi replied.

"About the route," Scout said. "What are your thoughts on which way to go?

"I honestly have no clue, Scout!" Rhi spat.

"Dee, mate?" Scout asked.

Dee looked to the map, then back to both paths. "You've got me, Scout. No idea where to go from here."

Pi looked at Scout inquisitively. "What are you getting at? You have that look you get when you're turning something over. Spill it."

"I couldn't decide upon anything except for how much I love you my whole life," Scout said. "It's brought me a lot of sleepless nights, I tell you. Could I do this? Should I have done that? Just pure indecision at every turn. I'd either decide on something and beat myself up for what I'd done or not do something and then worry that I'd made the wrong choice, full of regret and doubt about it for planet turns. Indecision would lead me to fear myself and my actions. It robbed me of trusting myself, it did."

Rhi flew to him, resting on his shoulder. "We love you just the way you are, Scout. You know that, you big fur ball."

Scout cleared his throat. "But I didn't, Rhi. And if I've been given a second chance at life, I want to go out knowing I can trust myself and the decisions I make. And that's how I figured out this right here, us standing here not knowing what to do, is our second challenge."

Pi, Rhi, and Dee looked at each other in shocked silence before returning their attention to a Scout none of them, not even Pi, had ever seen: a confident one. The map now made sense. This was a test, one none of them had realized. Pi felt like crying tears of joy at seeing Scout not just discover this about himself, but of recognizing the challenge in front of them before she did. She had never been prouder.

"Okay then," Dee said, breaking the silence. "So, what do we do about it, Scout? We still have to choose a path, don't we?"

Scout nodded. "Aye. There is that. I have my thoughts on it. In life, things can be hard. Other times, easier. I can't speak for you but for me, climbing up a hill is harder than going down the other side. I saw we take the uphill path. Such as in life, this is not an easy task we're faced with so neither should the route we take."

There was another silence. In this one, Scout knew it was one focused on how simple the rationale he had reached was if they came to think about it themselves. "Just my thoughts, though."

Pi was the first to move, bounding up to Scout and wrapping her paws around him, sending Rhi off kilter and back into the air nearby. She nuzzled her head to his. "You followed me and now, I say we follow you."

Rhi collected herself, balancing herself in the air. "Way to go there, Scout! Good thinking, that is! Let's go!"

Dee tucked the map into his pouch. "So up, up, and away we go. Well done, Scout. I'm in for a climb. After you, mate."

Scout rose from the rock, feeling stronger than he ever had both in mind and body as he led the others on their chosen path and further into the unknown. Pi was by his side and for the first time, he felt closer to her equal than in the past. Her love had kept him going for longer than he could remember, the constant nagging of his father's harsh criticisms and his mother's unhealthy dependence on him finally free from shackling his thoughts and soul. Scout felt a new sensation coursing through him- confidence. It felt... good!

As the group climbed the uphill path, Pi was pleased to note that the terrain beneath their feet was growing less jagged and softer to the paw, slowly turning from rock to earth beneath them. As a leaper, she spent much of her time traversing the geography between the four HomeSpaces and was used to rocky terrain. This new ground they were encountering felt nearly spongy beneath her paws and was foreign to her, not that she was complaining. Nearing what appeared to be peak on the large hill they were on, Pi caught sight of it before the others, as she was trained to scan her surroundings both near and far.

"Scout, you were right!" Pi said, grabbing his arm.

"How do you know?" he asked, surprised by her exclamation.

Pi didn't answer. Instead, she pointed a paw above them and to the right. The rest of the group's eyes followed her paw point. There it was. Covering a rock formation in front of them was the unmistakable site of indigo snow.

Scout collapsed on the ground, banging his paws both left and right. "I was right?!" he asked no one in particular, staring up at Pi.

Pi nodded, smiling. "You were right, love!"

"I'm never right!" he replied, laughing merrily.

"Guess you can't say that anymore, eh?" Rhi said, chuckling.

"Well done, mate! You got us to the next marker!" Dee exclaimed.

The yellow energy wave rippled across the land without any warning, washing over everything in a bright rippling flash. As it passed through them, each of the Journeyers felt all of their fears disappear in an instant. It was like a bath of positive energy cleansing each of their souls. In place of their fear, they now felt only courage.

"Anyone know what that bloody was?" Rhi asked. "Map say anything about it?"

Dee pulled the map out and after studying it, replied, "Nothing that I can make out except the caves were marked yellow."

The second energy wave, this time indigo, washed over them. Their indecision was taken away, replaced with steely reserve and acceptance. The energy ribbon disappeared as quickly as the first yellow one did.

Dee returned his attention back to the map. "The second marker was indigo," he said. "I think it means we've made this much progress."

"Sounds right to me," Scout said, picking himself up off the ground. "I want to thank all of you for not ripping my head off back in the brambles and giving me the chance to redeem myself. I owe you all thanks."

"Mate," Rhi replied, "you owe us nothing. We all fall every so often. And you know what?"

"What?" Scout asked.

"We tend to pick ourselves back up too," Rhi replied, smiling. "Now hand me my nectar. Time for a celebratory nip!"

Scout dug the small jug out of his pouch, tossing it to her. "Have one for me, will you?"

"Certainly!" Rhi replied, taking a swig.

Dee did his best not to frown. "I say we break here for the night. Thoughts?"

Pi nodded. "Agreed. It's been a long day, especially for my sweetwater slugging, clumsy as an oaf partner over there," she said in jest.

"Still proud of me, love?" Scout asked her.

"Of course," Pi replied. "Now get over here so I can tend to those bramble scratches on your bottom unless of course, someone else wants to?"

"All you, Pi," Rhi said.

"Go right ahead," Dee laughed. "His ass is definitely all yours to deal with!"

Scout laughed. "I can tend to myself, thank you very much."

There was a pause, in addition to a look of skepticism from Pi as he tried to reach his rear end to pluck the brambles free with no success. "A little help might be nice, I reckon."

The Journeyers laughed heartily as Pi bent Scout over and began tending to him. His bottom was quite scratched with scrapes and cuts. There were a good lot of thorny brambles stuck in his undercoat, which Pi dug out one by one. She couldn't see the wide grin on Scout's face during the whole ordeal as he relished these newfound feelings of courage that had washed over him.

I was right, Scout told himself proudly. I was right.

***

All at once, Rex felt his thoughts changing. In the rear of the herd caravan with the other Healers, Rex suddenly felt... different. It was the oddest feeling he ever felt. He couldn't explain it, really. Rex just felt... better. For the first time in days, he let himself smile thinking of his sister, Scout, and Rhi. He didn't know what they had done but Rex somehow knew they had done... something, and it was a good thing not just for them, but for the planet as well.

"Woo hoo!" Rex called out, startling the others surrounding him.

The curious stares of the other healers didn't bother Rex one bit. He did something he hadn't done in a long while - he laughed out loud.

"Er, are you alright there, Rex?" one of the healers asked him cautiously.

"Yes! And no! Oh, I don't know," Rex replied. "They did something!"

"Who did what?" another of the healers asked.

"My family is saving us, and I don't know how but I know they just did something for us!" Rex exclaimed. "I can't explain it, but they did!"

"Well tell them to hurry the heavens up," another Healer said. "Our paws are killing us."

Rex grew quiet. "I wish I could. I truly wish I could."

The moment passed and Rex found himself returning his attention to the terrain beneath his paws and in front of him. He prayed for their safe return. He missed them terribly.

***

Pi was, yet again, awoken from sleep covered in sweat and shaken. The voices at odds with each other from her dream still fresh in her mind. It was definitely more irritating than anything else because, yet again, nothing she could remember save for the feeling that the Spirit was as uncertain as she was to what the future held for them all whether it be life, death, or something in between. Pi slipped out from under Scout's paw, took her sweetwater jug, and quietly made her way to the top of the crest where they had bunked for the night.

Feeling the snow underneath her paws and hearing the sound of it crunching from her weight, Pi gazed out into the dark night. The sky still rumbled with thunder and lit up infrequently with streams of orange lyghtning, giving Pi glimpses of what lay in front of them tomorrow. It appeared to be snow plains leading to another set of mountains that reached far into the sky. She noticed that the lyghtning had seeming changed color, from yellow to orange and wondered what it meant. Pi also wondered where they were in relation to the HomeSpace, because it wasn't anywhere she had been before.

Pi often wondered about most things. She couldn't help it. Every angle needed to be explored in every way possible. It wasn't enough to just think about life absent-mindedly. Rather, Pi did her best to think of each nugget of information her mind stumbled across purposefully. She believed if she thought on something long enough, the solution would manifest itself from her own mind's eye. Pi had grown accustomed to working over multiple rationales throughout the course of her life.

She felt as if she was the center of a universe of her own making and it was up to her and her alone to find victory in it. And here she was, at the precipice of the end of the world and no other than her own Scout had proven that this was a shared journey to take, not a singular one as Pi had first imagined. Addy would have been proud of Scout today, for his inner, spiritual growth. Pi knew that for certain.

She thought of what they knew of the map and its vague instructions thus far and how the first two challenges seemed to test Scout and his failings like they were designed for him. Pi knew this couldn't be the case but was happy at how the day's events had turned out all the same. To see her Scout find his courage and decisiveness was awe inspiring. It seemed to her that his second chance at life was proving to be something he would not take for granted and for that Pi was grateful.

Still, she thought that challenges would be for her alone. She was the chosen one, wasn't she? Shouldn't she have been the one to figure out the right path to take earlier? Should she be even thinking this way? Pi brushed the thoughts aside as she watched Rhi fly up to join her.

"Morning, Rhi," Pi said simply. "Not like you to get up before sunrise."

"Bad dreams," Rhi replied. "Pictured Scout as my partner and it scared me to death!"

They shared a chuckle.

"Never thought he had it in him," Rhi said proudly. "He's come far in a short amount of time."

"Maybe dying does that to you," Pi replied. "He became whole yesterday. To see him take charge like that, out of bloody nowhere-"

"Oh, it wasn't out of nowhere," Rhi said, cutting in. "He was like that with me in the blast. I think Scout has just learned he can do it on the regular now."

"And for that I am grateful," Pi replied. "Are the others up yet?"

"Aye," Rhi said. "I got sent for you. Time for another vague message from the map of agitation. That's what I'm calling it anyways."

"See the lyghtning?" Pi asked, pointing to the sky above them. "It was yellow yesterday."

"Seems orange now," Rhi commented. "Wonder why?"

"I was thinking about that," Pi said. "I'm starting to wonder if the lyght energy is tied somehow to the map and our journey. Dee said the map calls it the 'journey of lyght'. The yellow and indigo lyght flashes we saw came after the first two challenges too. What if it's all connected to us and what we're doing? Or not doing?"

"You know what I think?" Rhi asked. "I think you think too bloody much. Now come on!"

Pi followed Rhi back to where they had camped the night before, finding Scout filling the sweetwater jugs with snow and Dee studying the map. Pi saw that her blanket had been neatly folded, and a portion of carrot bread sat on top of it, waiting for her. She felt a pang of guilt for not doing anything to help prepare for the upcoming day's journey before brushing it away to engage with the others.

"Where are we at, Dee?" Pi asked, scooping up the carrot bread and taking a hearty bite.

Dee showed them the map, pointing to an image of a horizontal indigo line pointing towards three vertical blue, wavy ones. "Straight ahead the line you go, through the fields of snow. Where it will take you to the edge that turns to blue. All you must do then is find the way through."

"Like I said," Rhi quipped, "The Map of Agitation speaks again."

"At least there's only one way through," Dee said. "Seems we follow the trail due south across the fields on the other side of the crest and keep our eyes open for something blue. Fairly straight forward."

Pi leaned forward, extending her paw to Dee. "Can I see the map, please?"

Dee handed Pi the map. "You see something I don't?"

Pi studied the diagram. She had seen those three wavy blue lines before. Then it hit her. Could it be?

"What is it, love?" Scout asked her.

Pi pointed to the wavy blue lines. "The Southern HomeSpace has an ancient stone carving in their Elder Chamber that describes our early times. This symbol, the lines, is part of it. It's impossible, though. There's no way."

"Oh, my goodness," Dee said, taking the map back. "I should have remembered this. She's right. This means rushwaters."

"What are rushwaters?" Rhi asked. "Tell us already!"

"In ancient times, it is written that rushwaters were moving bodies of water that ran from massive pools stored on Arkelia's surface," Pi replied. "They were deep and fast. Carrying our people across the various lands in vessels made of thickwood."

"Thickwood is a myth," Scout said. "Nothing that big could grow on the surface. I doubt these rushwaters ever existed either. We would know it. Wouldn't we?"

Dee looked to Scout, and then to Pi and Rhi. "I do not think we are presently anywhere that has ever been mapped, Scout. When we went through that cave at the beginning, we came out on the other side of the Northern Slope. No Quasi has ever been where we are now, mainly because none could get over the top of the mountains-"

"Because we went bloody under it," Rhi said. "Unreal."

"I was thinking we were off the chartered maps," Pi said. "That being said, who knows what we'll see."

Dee pointed to the map again. "Best I can make out, we'll know where we're going when we get there. I wish I had a better answer for all of you."

"Well," Rhi said. "One thing is for certain. We're further along today than we were yesterday and no reason not to think we're one step closer to tomorrow, aye?"

"Let's get on then," Pi said. "We have a planet to save."

Scout surprised them all by doing something which Pi felt was simple but extraordinary. He started moving first, taking the lead. "Come on now, you heard her," Scout said, puffing his chest. "On to the next challenge that awaits us!"

Pi followed first, followed by Dee and Rhi. All had smiles on their faces. Each in their own way felt stronger than they did before, a feeling of kinetic energy coursing through them. For only right now, they felt victorious.

***

Never before had Chukk seen such a sight. Having ventured ahead of the herd to gauge the terrain awaiting them, he found himself staring in awed disbelief at what appeared to be a massive lyghtning field, rippling with the planet's energy, sending plumes of lyght energy into the sky and then plunging back beneath the depths of the planet's crust. Sure, he had seen a lyghtning field before, but never one like this - the energy was not the yellow color he was used to but also, red, orange, indigo, and blue, and constantly changing. The beams of lyght were swirling and twirling in the air, almost as if they were dancing with each other. It was, in a word, beautiful.

It also wasn't on the crude drawing Ichabod had given them, which would cause an issue as they would be forced to divert around it. It was a smaller field than others Chukk had seen in his travels but would still take them the better part of a day to navigate around. He wondered how long the field had been here, and also what the different colored energy streams meant, if anything.

Ichabod had said he thought the trip would take them seven days and they were already into their sixth day now. How much longer the herd could take, Chukk didn't know. He wondered if Dee and the others had made more progress in reaching the Spirit and that was why the planet's energy was changing. Or was the planet dying faster than Ichabod had estimated? Was the whole trip with the herd caravan a waste of time? So many questions and no answers to be had, he thought ruefully.

No, they would continue to move ahead in hopes of reaching the Southern HomeSpace as quickly as possible. There was no other option. It was then that Chukk saw the massive blue colored lyghtning beam rocket skywards. He knew what would come next without a doubt in his mind. Chukk watched partly in awe but mostly in horror as the beam came crashing down in the distance. The force of the second Sun Shock sent out a tremendous blast of energy in all directions, sending him flying through the air and back to the ground with so much force, he nearly lost consciousness. Lying on the ground as the huge dust wave blew over and past him, Chukk let out a long painful groan.

His Battler mind did not let him rest, though. Instantaneously, he climbed back to his hind paws and surveyed the scene. Being out in the open had saved their lives for certain. He wondered if the three other HomeSpaces had suffered as they had in the East and if the lyghtning fields in their regions were behaving them same way in sending these Sun Shocks hurtling through the ground. They hadn't stayed behind long enough for any leapers to either arrive from the other HomeSpaces and the three Bugle sentries Bha had sent to warn the other regions hadn't caught back up to the herd caravan yet and might not in the remaining time it would take to reach the Southlands. What a horrific mess, Chukk thought to himself.

He began as fast of a gallop as he could muster to return to check on the herd. Dee, Chukk thought, wherever you are and whatever you're doing, for the love of the Spirit, please don't waste any bloody time doing it. There won't be much of an Arkelia left if you do. If you can hear me, love, carry on and battle strong. We need you now more than ever. Chukk made a point to tell himself to find Rex when he got back, remembering the odd little Quasi saying he could manipulate time. If there had been any casualties in the blast, Chukk thought, that might be useful.

***

The fifty MaRuu watched the Quasi invaders closely. How foolish they were. The Quasi had violated not only the trust of the MaRuus but of the Mother Planet herself, and now they were all suffering for it. The planet was angry with the Quasi, the MaRuu were certain of it. Only they could restore the balance by eliminating the vermin threat themselves, having sent their contingent to the Great Well armed with the Red Rock that held the collective spirit of the MaRuu to be offered in sacrifice to the Mother planet herself. This turn of events with the Quasi yet again invading their lands seemed to be destiny calling - save the planet and also get the chance to exact revenge and decimate a quarter of the Quasi concurrently? Fortune must be smiling on the MaRuu!

Since taking notice of the Quasis' exodus from their eastern living abode, the MaRuu now had their herd migration in their sights. Being careful to keep their numbers small, the MaRuu kept themselves away from detection by remaining in the foothills that flanked the Quasi position. They only moved in the shadows and by nightfall, sending only one at a time back to their nearest outpost. This way, they always had sense of what the Quasi scum were up to. Not that there was much to report as of yet. The Quasi were moving in a pattern due South, most likely to the housing abode their kind kept there. The Quasi left their home in disarray, and it seemed a good portion of it had collapsed in the first large scream from the Mother planet. It was a shame it had not killed them all, as the MaRuu were certain the Mother planet had surely intended.

The MaRuu counted the Quasi number to be in the many hundreds, with their useless soldiers at the front and again in the rear, leaving the long stream of weaker Quasi in the middle of the pack helpless. This was where they would strike, most likely, unless a better plan of attack made itself known to them.

A new energy pore had opened after the first blast just in front of the Quasi position and the MaRuu were certain the Quasi did not know this based on their current trajectory. Depending on how the invaders decided to navigate themselves around it would determine when and how the MaRuu would send their first wave of attack.

The Quasi deserved to be annihilated as far as the MaRuu were concerned. They had arrived as pilgrims, fleeing their lands on the other side of the Shining Sea after drying their homeland of all its natural resources. The first set of Quasi came in peace. But sadly, that peace wilted away with each new arrival of their kind, all seeking game to eat, flower to grow and harvest, and sweetwater to drink. Lest they forget the main reason the Quasi began eradicating the MaRuu from their own homes: lyght energy. Once the Quasi realized the lyght energy could extend their lives fivefold, the Lyght War began as both sides fought to take possession of the areas surrounding the four lyghtning fields in the north and south and to the east and west.

The MaRuu, who never had violence in their way of life before the Quasi arrived, were not fighters of any kind and were not prepared for what would happen when one MaRuu life was taken - every single one of them shared the pain and experience. The Quasi used this to their advantage and won very quickly. But never again would the MaRuu suffer such a defeat. In the three millennia that had passed since, the MaRuu had evolved their minds and bodies to become perfect weapons, able to block each other out when need be and to kill their prey in a quick barrage of brute physical force and blinding speed.

Banished to the Snowlands, the MaRuu took this newfound feeling of rage that rippled through their collective minds and put it to good use. They trained themselves to survive in the elements, their thick frames evolving from raw skin to a thick plated hide which kept their bodies warm in the cold conditions, their teeth becoming elongated in sharp tusks to pierce the thick layer of indigo ice covering most of the land so they could draw sweetwater from beneath the surface, and each of their four long limbs growing long, curved talons perfect for cutting ice sheets or, slicing through an opponent in a heartbeat.

Yet, they were not ones to go back to war, for the MaRuu, having experienced collectively what dying a vicious death truly feels like en masse, decided to leave the invaders be. They had been defeated and it was not the MaRuu way to question the Mother planet's decisions, nor oppose her intentions. If the Quasi stayed in their conquered realms, the MaRuu would let them be but, if any Quasi came looking for them, they would not like what they found.

Over the millennia, the MaRuu and their evolving physiques had become quite adept at killing Quasi invaders to the point the vermin knew now, thanks in part to the last batch of them to unwisely wander into the Snowlands, that the MaRuu were not to be interacted with.

But this, a mass exodus across the Plainlands in direct violation of the truce? It might prove to be the MaRuus last chance to punish the Quasi for bleeding Arkelia of all of its natural resources, essentially killing Mother planet. They killed the Eastlands and now would attack what was left of the West if the MaRuu did not intervene to put a stop to it. Thanks to the Quasi's greedy, gluttonous ways, Arkelia had no remaining flower, hardly any vegetation, and scarce amounts of fresh water. They disrespected life by squandering the balance which would supply future generations, both MaRuu and Quasi, ample to live from. The Quasi were a cancer upon Arkelia, plain and true.

This shared sentiment among the MaRuu made biding their time somewhat nerve racking. The full swarm would arrive in no more than two days' time and by then, the Quasi would surely be aware of their presence. It did not matter. The MaRuu knew that the Quasi fighters could never stop them. It would be a glorious sacrifice for the Mother planet indeed. For now, they made themselves content watching the Quasi slowly near their coming end and started giving thought to if now was the time to conquer their remaining enclaves. The MaRuu felt the anticipation of revenge surging through their shared consciousness. It thrilled them to no end. If Mother planet willed it, the MaRuu would not stop until every last Quasi pup and elder alike, fell to the ground, dead. Then the second energy blast went screaming out in their own blue color energy, sending them reeling. It was if Mother Planet spoke to them directly saying, 'Attack'!

6

The Journeyers were tired, but none more so than Dee, although he didn't let this on to the others. To them, he was the Battler, the warrior who carried on until the mission had been accomplished and all of the obstacles in his way had either been eliminated and enemies vanquished. The Quasi with the mighty blade who saved the day, every day. But this was not how he felt on the inside. Inside, he had a growing feeling of sadness and remorse for leaving Chukk behind at HomeSpace to deal with the aftermath of the Sun Shock. What had he been thinking, he chastised himself ruefully?

At this point, the indigo snow was getting thicker underneath their paws, the winds were whipping fiercely, and the air grew colder and colder with each passing moment it seemed. Rhi was now unable to fly, her crystalline wings freezing together, sending her to the confines of Scout's large pouch to stay warm. She was the lucky one and Dee resented her for it, as his teeth chattered, and his eyes stung wildly.

Neither Pi nor Scout had complained yet and Dee did not want to be the first to do so. It went against everything Dee had been trained to do since pupdom and he was growing more and more sullen thinking that all they needed him was read the stupid, nonsensical map. Dee cursed himself for not just offering to transcribe to bloody thing for them in the first place. If Ichabod hadn't asked, he and Chukk to protect Pi, her brother, her partner, and her friend, Dee doubted he would be here right now... in this role, his mind whispered to him.

Wait, Dee asked himself, did Ichabod ask him that? He felt like he had two sets of memories in his mind, somehow knowing that both had been true. It was an odd sensation. His mind brought him back to the present, reminding him that he wanted to be the one tasked with saving the planet. If it had been him, Dee never would have let others risk themselves by tagging along. The prophecies were very specific, and Dee would have followed the rules set out by the ancients in precise, Battler fashion. What they were doing now seemed wrong somehow.

Dee liked the others, it wasn't anything they had done, and they had progressed further then he had expected them to but being a Battler didn't mean he didn't have doubt and reservations. He was the odd one out here. There had been no mortal danger for him to save them from yet, meaning they had not encountered any MaRuu, which he secretly admitted was one of the things he was looking forward to on the trip.

He lived for danger and all things considered, Dee's growing sense of frustration stemmed from boredom. They were essentially hiking to Spirit knows where, to do what he did not yet know besides sacrificing their lives in the process. Finally, Dee let himself think about what was swirling around his mind since this all started: he was not ready to die, for these three or for the good of the planet. He felt ashamed and guilty for doing so.

Add to that his growing sense of loneliness, and now arctic, unyielding weather to was making Dee quickly miserable. He missed Chukk's tender embrace when they cuddled together when they were lucky enough to be off patrols on the same nights. He missed home. And here he was playing sitter to a ragtag lot with no self-discipline. But they have each other, Dee thought. I'm alone here with them and the farther we go, the less Dee wanted to be there.

The bugle bothered him the most. If Rhi wasn't yapping, she was drinking. It was incredibly bothersome to watch and witness, especially as neither of the other two seemed to give the little one's behavior a second thought. It was Dee's opinion that Pi and Scout were enabling Rhi to be as self-destructive as she could turn out to be. To think that Dee's life, hanging in the balance the same as theirs, might be felled because a drunken flying nuisance had a misstep or error in judgement irritated Dee to no end. And then what he thought was going to eventually happen did. The Bugle crossed the thin line Dee had drawn in his mind as how far he would tolerate her.

The Journeyers found the path had grown rockier and was leading them down through the crevices of the steep hilly plateaus as they left the mountain path behind to flatter ground. They were winding around a bend and out of the sunlight, as odd hissing and bubbling noises began to fill their ears. Dee sniffed the growingly acidic quality to the air.

"Sulfur," he said to the others. "I've smelt it before. We should pause before we go any further. No knowing what's ahead but there could be burnt or scorched ground. Perhaps we should find a way around."

"I'm sure whatever it is isn't as bad as that smell," Pi said. "It's almost as bad as smelling Scout's hind paws when he gets back to the burro at night."

Scout and Rhi snickered at Pi's joke while Dee furrowed his brow. "Not likely. My Battler ways are telling me we're walking into something nasty." Dee unsheathed his blade from its hilt.

"Oh, calm down, Battler," Rhi said, taking yet another swig of her nectar jug. "It'll be fine, it will. Probably just, er, well I don't know what sulfur is but whatever it is can't be that bad. We've seen nothing but this path since we left the cave, we have. Relax!"

"For the love of the Spirit," Dee pleaded to Rhi, "will you shut up and show some caution for once, Rhi? This could be serious trouble we're to be facing! Stop drinking your damn nectar long enough to see that!"

"Uh oh," Scout whispered to Pi, who had covered her face with one paw as if to say the same.

Rhi took another swig from her jug. "No. My thing is to do my thing and my thing is to do what I bloody want. No one tells me what, when, or how to do anything, they don't. Why? Because that's how I bloody like it. Understood?"

Dee looked to Pi and then to Scout. "You two coddle her and let her behave this way. Why?"

"Don't you talk to them about me," Rhi spat. "You talk to me about me, you do. Got that do you?"

"Fine," Dee huffed. "I don't even know why I'm here besides to read you what nonsense is in the map. Follow the pictures to stay on the right path. I'm out of here." Dee threw the map on the ground in front of Rhi, spun on his paws, and began walking back the way they came.

"Where do you think you're going?" Pi asked.

"Home," Dee called over his shoulder. "Let the drunk decide your fate. None of you mean anything to me anyways. If we're to die, I'd rather do it in the company of my partner. At least he listens to me!"

Pi went to follow him, but Scout put his paw gently on her shoulder. "This isn't for you to make right, love."

"He's right, Pi," Rhi said. "Agree with Scout on this, I do!"

"It's for you to fix, Rhi," Scout replied. "You went too far too fast and you know it, little one. The only thing bigger than your ego is your mouth sometimes, I swear it."

"But-" Rhi started.

"He's right, Rhi," Pi said. "Scout and I are going to check around the corner and see what's around the bend. Why don't you go apologize, eh? You know better than to assume people can take the way you are right away. He's our friend, not a foe. Go make nice."

Rhi crossed her arms. "Fine."

She flew slowly to catch up to him.

"Dee!" Pi yelled suddenly. "Come back! We need you, okay?! We need you!"

Up ahead, Dee and Rhi saw Scout and Pi reappear from up around the bend ahead. As he approached them, Dee tried to look ahead to see what had caught their eyes. He soon saw what they did, and he couldn't believe his eyes. It couldn't be... could it?

"How is this possible?" Pi asked as Dee and Rhi neared her and Scout. "Why would anyone in the right minds plunk themselves down at the edge of sulfur pits?"

"Don't bloody ask me," Scout replied. "Dee, thoughts, mate?"

Up ahead past the last of the sulfur pits, Dee could clearly see a figure sitting alone, wrapped in a burlap blanket of sorts. From their current position it was difficult for Dee to make out much more. Dee felt his insides tingle with excitement. Finally, he thought, something to do!

"What do we do?" Rhi asked from the confines of Scout's pouch. "What's the map say about where we are, Dee? See, I need you. Also, I'm sorry for telling you how it is with me. I'll play nice from here on out, I will."

Dee frowned, pulling the map out and scanning it. "To yourself be true. Only then will you find true blue?"

"What's true blue?" Rhi asked.

Dee placed the map back into his pouch and removed his bronze blade from its hilt wrapped around his waist. "I don't know but I'm sure as Spirit going to find out. You three stay here. I'll be back. Especially the drunk here. And if I don't like what I see, I might still go. Consider me undecided presently."

Dee didn't wait for any conjecture from the others, bounding down the hill towards the mysterious figure coming into view ever faster still. His excitement at some adventure in check, Dee felt his grasp on his blade tighten with each hop he advanced with. He was ready for anything.

Seeing the distinct shape of a Quasi's large hind paws, Dee grew more and more curious as he neared the figure. Whoever it was, they were of the same kind. This was a Quasi.

"You can put your blade down, son," the figure said as Dee approached, now moving slowly and taking measured moves forward. "I mean no one but myself harm."

He sounds ancient, Dee thought, sizing up the threat level he faced. Threat level? Zero, Dee bemoaned, sheathing his blade. "Who are you and what are you doing here?" Dee asked, puffing his chest and doing his best to project a steely disposition to the stranger. "What's your name?"

"So many questions and only one of them important," the old stranger, his fur gone nearly white and eyes sunken so far into his skull Dee was surprised he could see anything through them, replied. "Sit next to me? It's been a very long time since I've seen anyone, let alone a Battler such as yourself. Call for the others, please."

Dee sighed. Some Battler. "I think I'll stand if it's all the same to you."

He turned back, seeing the others had heeded his instructions and were waiting at the top of the hill awaiting his command. Dee saw no reason why the others shouldn't share in such a thrilling development such as this. He waved them down, yelling out for them to come down.

"You look tired," the old Quasi said. "You should sit and rest your paws from your journey."

"Who are you?" Dee asked again, more forcibly.

"No one important," the ancient Quasi said.

"You said I asked one important question," Dee said, getting frustrated. "Which one was it?"

"Now that's a better question. You asked me what I was doing here. I'll tell you if you'll take a seat next to me."

"Fine, old one," Dee grumbled, sitting across from the old Quasi.

"Much better," the old one said. "I've been here for longer than I ever thought one could live. Unable to move forward. Unable to return from whence I came. Trapped here, knowing only that I failed my mission to restore the balance between the Sun and the great Quasi Spirit, having to relive my grief every day as if it had just happened yesterday. Cursed to die with the very soul of our planet for not mending the error of my ways."

Dee's eyes grew wide. "You were chosen for the Journey of Lyght? You didn't die?!"

"Son, I die every day," the ancient Chosen one said. "And wake up sitting here, forced to relive the torture of my broken soul every day. Except for today, because now you, Dee of the Quasi, are here. I have been waiting for you."

"Me?" Dee asked incredulously, excited once more. "I knew it, they were going to choose me for the Journey, weren't they?"

"No way to know because they never did, did they?" the old one replied. "I've been waiting to tell you what happened to me for over a millennia. That's all. And all you have to do is listen. So, will you listen to my tale or would you prefer to just forge on ahead just as you are? The choice is yours; it matters not to me. All I must do is ask you and now I have. You have until your fellow journeyers arrive to decide. Shouldn't be too long now. They approach quickly."

An eerie silence grew between the two Quasi as Pi and Scout drew closer. Dee, although he had just met him, felt oddly in the presence of the stranger. He wanted to say something, anything, to this old Quasi but no words came. And then-

"Tell me," Dee blurted out. "Before they get here, tell me your tale."

The ancient one chuckled, clapping his front paws together loudly. "Very well."

Dee was shocked to see the falling snow frozen in time all around them. But it wasn't just the snow. The wind had also stopped blowing. It appeared the old one had frozen time itself. "What are you?"

"A friend," the old one replied. "Now hear me, Dee of the Quasi, for my tale will end with one of two doors for you to choose. One goes forward and the other, back. You can ask me one question before making your choice. May I proceed?"

Dee said nothing, opting rather just to nod that he was in agreement.

"Good. I'll begin. I was a Battler, just like you. The time of the Journey came upon us, the Spirit in turmoil, and I was picked... along with others. The elder said the Spirit willed it. I was honored at first but then, I grew remorseful once we set out. I wanted to do it on my own. I didn't want anyone else to slow me down. I slowly grew more and more resentful. At the same time, I cursed myself that it didn't go the way I had originally wanted it to. I grew restless."

Dee knew the feeling. This adventure wasn't exactly what he thought he was signing up for. Weird, yes, but exciting, not so much.

"My resentment gave way to sadness and bitterness," the ancient one continued. "It got to the point that all I wanted to do was go home. If havoc was going to rain down on our people, I thought I would be better suited to defend the ones I had left behind. I told the group I wanted to go home. They told me they needed me, but I was having none of it. They said they needed my support and that they valued me and what I could offer them, but I brushed them off. I was selfish, Dee of the Quasi, and I was belligerent. I envied how the others all seemed to get on with each other and unwisely made the biggest mistake of my worthless life."

"So, what did you do?" Dee asked, questioning everything that had begun running through his head since he and the others had left and completely forgetting that he had just asked his only question to the old Quasi.

"That will be your one question then," the ancient one replied. "When given the chance, I left."

Dee swallowed hard, feeling like kicking himself for being so rash in asking what the old Quasi had done. "Guess that means I have a decision to make. You said I had two choices to make."

"I did," the old one said. "You have two choices. You can either leave the others behind and return to where you came from just as I did or you can give me your bronze blade, your sweetwater jug, and your rations, to continue on ahead with your mates."

"They're not my mates," Dee said defensively.

"Then leaving them be and returning home might make more sense."

Dee's brain was spinning. Home! The journey! Chukk! Arkelia! Oh, he felt torn. He so desperately wanted to ask the old Quasi more questions! This felt like torture. After what seemed like an eternity, Dee thought about what he thought Pi might do. She made her choices based on a clear-headed rationale. Dee found that Pi made her decisions first with her head and then with her heart. What would Pi do? He wanted to ask her for help, heck, even Scout or Rhi might have an idea of how he could decide, but that would mean telling them everything that was running through his mind, both good and bad. Then it hit Dee-

"Unfreeze time, old one," Dee ordered. "I want to ask my mates for help. I have no more questions for you, but they might."

The ancient one chuckled before clapping his paws once more. The snow resumed falling, the wind began blowing again, and the other Journeyers grew near. "As you wish. It seems you might need them more then you realized, doesn't it?"

Dee couldn't help but smile a bit. He threw his blade down, followed by his sweetwater jug, and his carrot bread rations. Oddly, the map had disappeared. Perhaps he had dropped it on the trip down here? "Take them. I've made my choice. Now I need them just as much as they need me."

It was the ancient one's turn to smile. He pulled out a withered piece of parchment. Dee recognized it immediately. It was the Journey Map, his map. He held it out to Dee, who took it with his eyes wide and his jaw slack. "You're... me?" he stammered.

"No, Dee," the ancient Dee said. "I was."

He disappeared, leaving Dee's items behind.

Pi, Scout, and Rhi sped up after the figure vanished into thin air. "What happened?" Pi asked, watching Dee gather his items back up. "Who was that and what did they want?!"

"A kindred spirit," Dee said, still smiling. "He truly meant none of us harm."

"Where did he go?!" Rhi exclaimed. "He just up and disappeared, Dee! What magic was that?"

"And what did he want, mate?" Scout added.

"To show me the way," Dee replied. "I'd like to thank each of you for letting me be a part of this and let you know I appreciate you."

Pi and Scout exchanged an inquisitive glance. Rhi was more forward. She climbed out of Scout's pouch and flew up to meet Dee at his eye level.

"Spill it, Battler!" Rhi spat. "Who was that and what did he bloody want? Where did he bloody go?!"

Dee did something none of them expected. He laughed merrily.

Dee laughed so hard his sides hurt. "Last week, I would have told you I just lost my mind. But now? Now I know I'm right where I need to be. Sit down and rest. I'll tell you everything."

As Dee told his fellow Journeyers of the dark, cloudy thoughts he was having and offering apologies for doubting both himself, his motives, as well as his actions and negative thoughts, Pi, Scout, and especially Rhi surprised him by saying they had each had similar moments of frustration and sadness. Dee was not alone. As he went on to detail his interaction with who he would eventually become if he didn't learn to trust others, Dee saw that they were fully engaged in what he was saying. They believe me, he thought to himself. They trust I speak truth. I owe these three the same. He told them that the old Quasi would be him if he let his doubt and lack of trust take him over.

Rhi was the first to respond. "You chose us over home?" she asked, choking up. "Oh Dee, your truly one of us now. You're family."

"Aye, mate," Scout said. "Proud to have you here and not just because you saved me from falling down that gorge."

"Thanks, you two," Dee replied, smiling. "I'm sorry I doubted any of this. I can't explain how I feel right now."

Pi had been silent, almost as if she was letting the scene play out before engaging. She cleared her throat. "You said he, you, said you had to give up your blade, sweetwater, and rations to continue with us. What did that mean to you?"

Dee looked Pi looked her in the eyes. Heck, she was smart. "It meant I would have to rely on the three of yours compassion for the rest of the trip."

Pi nodded. "What else does it mean? You're missing something."

Dee raised an eyebrow. Oh, he thought to himself. He smiled once more. "That I would have to trust you to protect me just as you have trusted me to protect you. It needs to be mutual. We need to trust each other. I need to know that you do need me, but I need you three also."

A bright indigo energy wave flashed in all directions, clearing out the indigo snow clouds and leaving only a clear blue sky and bright red Sun in its wake. Down and to their left, the Journeyers saw a blue stone trail emerge from beneath the ice beneath them. It rose above the ice cover and appeared to stretch towards a blue stone formation in the distance that none of them had noticed before.

"Good work," Pi said. "You just helped us pass the third marker, Dee. This journey is as much yours as ours. Now don't forget it."

"Forget what?" Dee asked, still slack jawed.

"You're one of us now," Pi replied. "Our friends are the family we choose, and we've chosen each other now. Never forget it."

Rhi flew up to him and hugged his front paw. It took him a moment, but Dee found himself softly patting her little arm, returning the gesture. Pi said no more. She began to hop down the new trail. As Dee watched her leave, he was almost bowled over by Scout's hug. Dee laughed merrily, feeling better already.

***

Rex was having issues. He slowly turned around again, looking at the group of elders behind him. He was still there, as impossible as it seemed. Ichabod was hopping alongside Bha, who was in flight, and the others. Rex thought his head was going to explode. Then he heard his name being called out by none other than Ichabod. Rex slowed his gallop, making his way through the group of Healers he was traveling with to hop next to the High Elder.

"Have you felt any more time shifts?" Ichabod asked a very confused looking Rex.

Rex shook his head, still unable to speak. He cleared his throat. "Big one, very big one…" Rex said, his voice trembling.

"Well," Ichabod replied, "Don't keep us waiting, Rex. What is it?"

"More like who is it," Rex replied. "You. You were alive. But then you were dead. And now you're alive. You didn't betray us now, so there's that going for you. You did right by Pi."

"Of course, I did!" Ichabod replied. "Are you saying I didn't?!"

"No, yes, oh, I don't know, Ichabod!" Rex stammered. "My head is getting mighty confused with all this! I'm remembering all these different events, and everything is getting garbled! You may not remember but you tried to bloody kill me a few days ago!"

Ichabod stopped, taking Rex by the shoulders. "The Spirit gave you a great gift, Rex. I know it's difficult for you, but your memories of the other timelines are the only way for us to know that the Journeyers are still making progress. We need you now more than ever, Rex. Believe that, son." The bastard has the power of the eternal star, Ichabod fumed silently, my power.

Rex felt like the focal point of a swarming sea of chaos. Here he was, a week from home, travelling through the plains towards an uncertain future in the Southlands, lyghtning fields pummeling the planet with Sun Shocks, tired, restless, and afraid for Pi, Scout, Rhi, and the Battler, Dee. And that wasn't even including the shifting timelines swirling around in his head that was giving Rex a headache unlike any he had ever had. If only Pi were still here.

"Do you remember how many lives you saved in the moments before the Sun Shock, Rex?" Ichabod asked. "Do you?"

Rex thought back to that fateful day. He now remembered that he had experienced the blast and was able to loop back just far enough to hop through the burros, yelling and screaming for all he came in contact with to take cover in doorways, under tables, anything the Quasi could find to deflect the blast and the debris it rained down, even making it to the Elder Care and saving-

"Addy!" Rex exclaimed. "I saved Addy! Oh, my goodness, I saved Addy!"

"You did indeed," Ichabod replied, giving Rex the time to catch up on his new memories. He and Rex had been through this many times at this point. It was frustrating how slowly Rex was getting acclimated to the power of the star he now yielded. "It was her sending from the Spirit that told her to instruct Pi to take the others with her. Do you remember that now?" When I wanted Dee to remain behind with me to lead the charge against the MaRuu.

Rex did, and he also remembered her dying in his arms the morning after the Journeyers had departed. His hearts sank once more. This was just too much for him to handle. It was if he was feeling every emotion there was all at the same time.

"Thanks to you, she lived long enough to be able to say goodbye," Ichabod said. "Pi and Scout were-"

"Grateful," Rex said in a near whisper.

"You're here and you're safe, Rex," Ichabod said, trying to comfort him. I must keep the welp close by and in my good company, Ichabod reasoned. It would be the only way to try to steer towards the future needed for the Quasi to survive this.

Then Rex remembered the second Sun Shock. "There's another Sun Shock coming, Ichabod!"

Ichabod grabbed his horn. Finally! He blew the alarm call, bringing the herd caravan to a stop that moved from the back to the front. "How much time do we have, Rex?"

Rex spun on his paws, looking around. In the distance, he saw a flicker of lyght. "There, that's a new lyghtning field up ahead. Chukk went to investigate because it's not on the map you gave him and-"

Ichabod withdrew the map to the Southlands from his pouch. "You mean this one?"

Rex nodded. "Besides you being here now, that's what else changed. I think? I think there was something else, but I can't remember. But I know it wasn't good. Chukk never came back after the second Sun Shock and then, something bad happened, oh curses why can't I remember it!"

"So, let's remedy that," Ichabod said. "Go fetch Chukk and bring him back here so we can help you remember. Spread the word forward for everyone to get on the ground and prepare for a blast. Go!"

"Aye!" Rex said, taking off for the front of the herd caravan where Chukk and his battalion of Battlers were leading the way.

Ichabod turned to Bha, who he knew had keenly watched the exchange with Rex. "That boy has the weight of the world on his shoulders, doesn't he, Bha?"

"I don't know how he's doing it," Bha replied. "But if it wasn't for him, I think we'd all be dead by now. Who would have thought meek and mild Rex was up for all of this?"

Ichabod frowned. "The Spirit surely did catch me by surprise."

Bha chuckled. "It did indeed. Keep Bor's role mum, I have. He won't know that part, will he?"

"As long as the Journey of Lyght moves ahead, we all take a step closer to the balance being restored," Ichabod said. Or at least until I can use Rex to guide us back to where we belong.

***

Chukk watched Rex begin to approach him from within a cluster of Quasi moving directly behind his Battlers. "This can't be good," Chukk said as soon as Rex was in earshot. "We heard the Warning Horn blow. What are we facing now?"

"Sun shock," Rex said, panting. "There's a new lyghtning field ahead. You went to investigate it, but it must have been unstable and there was another Sun Shock, and then you didn't come back before..."

Rex trailed off, struggling with something. Chukk eyed him for a moment, wondering how Rex was still sane with all of this madness bubbling away inside his brain. He put his paw on Rex's shoulder.

"Before what, Rex?"

"Dang it, I can't remember, Chukk," Rex replied, noticeably frazzled. He rubbed his head with his paw. "But the Sun Shock is coming, I know that to be true."

"I take it that's why Ichabod blew the horn?" Chukk asked.

Rex nodded.

"So how much time do you reckon we have? How far ahead is the field?"

Rex pointed to the small glimmer off in the distance. "That's it there, mate. I think I looped back to when you told me you were going to investigate it so the Sun Shock will be coming soon and then... dang it, I can't remember!"

"In the Sun Shock were there any fatalities besides me?" Chukk asked.

Rex scanned his memory of the event. People were thrown to the ground and banged up a bit, but he didn't remember anyone receiving any serious injuries. Cuts and bruises for certain, but no fatalities until-

"There are MaRuu! Oh my, that's it! There are MaRuu out there," Rex said. "There are bloody MaRuu!"

Chukk spun around. "Battlers, brave! Fetch your blades!"

The Battlers' bronze blades were immediately drawn. They took their battle poses, facing Chukk. Rex saw a steely reserve in Chukk's eyes unlike one he had ever seen that dripped with pure, unadulterated determination.

"Rex," Chukk said. "How many?"

Rex scanned his memories again. "At least a hundred, probably more. And they're coming. There coming for us now."

"Where?" Chukk asked. "From which direction?"

Then Rex remembered the rest. "All I saw was the bodies they left behind before..."

Rex trailed off again.

"Before what, Rex?" Chukk asked, growing impatient.

Rex swallowed hard. "Before they killed me. I died. I think we all probably did. We're walking into a bloody massacre, Chukk."

"Only this time, we know they're coming, mate," Chukk said. "They don't know we have you." Chukk spun to the Battlers. "Battlers! Spread through the ranks! Keep your eyes open in all directions-"

The second Sun Shock blasted in the distance, sending plumes of blue energy racing out in all directions and shaking the ground beneath them with magnificent force, knocking them all to the ground. Chukk regained his composure quickly, lifting Rex back to his hind paws. The other Battlers were also quickly back upright.

"Battlers, brave!" Chukk called out. "Two by two formations, get the herd gathered behind you in a circle grouping! Now! Now! Now! Runner, get those instructions to the back! We are under attack! Go!"

Rex marveled at the flurry of activity taking place before his eyes. He knew he hadn't seen this before. This time would be different! It had to be, or he wouldn't still be here!

"Rex?!" Chukk asked. "I asked you where you were the first time they came?!"

Rex snapped out of his daze. "I was in the front waiting for you to come back from the expedition!"

"Then their attack didn't come from the front," Chukk surmised. "Battlers, brave! Regroup back, four by two! Push the herd up and away! Now! Now! Now!"

"What should I do?!" Rex asked as the kinetic energy of watching all of this commotion energized and frightened him.

"You and I are going back to protect Ichabod so we can figure out how to move further forward," Chukk replied. "Let's go! Now!"

The two Quasi took off in a fast gallop towards the rear of the herd caravan, dodging their random, flustered Quasi brethren as they went. Huffing and panting behind the much faster Chukk, Rex felt in his pouch and took hold of the silver blade he found there. Withdrawing it, Rex told himself that this time would be different. The monsters would be stopped by Chukk and the mighty Battlers and they would not be killed by the terrifying creatures filling his memories now.

As they made their way through the flattened herd, who were still struggling to lift themselves after this new energy blast, Rex kept scanning the horizon in all directions. Towards the rear of the herd, Rex saw Ichabod and Bha helping an older Quasi back to their feet.

"We need you right now, Ichabod!" Chukk called out, clearing a path through the maze of Quasi for himself and Rex. "Rex, start talking!" Chukk, with his bronze blade at the ready, pushed Rex in front of him.

"The MaRuu are coming!" Rex said loudly. "They're going to attack!"

As soon as the words were out of his mouth, Rex regretted that he had yelled it so loudly. All of the nearby Quasi starting shrieking wildly, running off in all directions, screaming his words for all to hear. The herd, which had been in a straight-line formation, was now scattering wildly. Quasi who had been injured in the blast were being stampeded over. Ichabod and Bha stared at him with consternation on their eyes. Chukk put his head in his paws.

"Not how I would have told him," Chukk said to Rex. "That was foolish, Rex. Truly foolish."

"Where are they, Rex?" Ichabod asked, scanning the horizon. "Where?!"

Rex spun around and around, seeing nothing. "I, I don't know. Or I don't remember! Or, oh, I don't know but they are coming, I swear it!"

Ichabod watched the herd disperse in all directions and also, the Battlers unsure whether to try to stop them or defend their current position. He saw the look of confusion of Rex's face, as well as the looks of frustration on Chukk and Bha's faces. Yet, he did his best to stay calm. He took a deep breath, attempting to look like he was weighing his options.

"It's better to not scatter," Ichabod said. "Separated we're disjointed and aimless, and easy to attack. Chukk, have your Battlers gather the herd into small groups, two Battlers to each group, and send them here." Ichabod withdrew his map and pointed to a location due South, "There is our spot, the abandoned Quartz Quarries. We can regroup there." That was where the battle would be won.

Chukk studied the map. "Are you sure? We'll be boxed in. There's only one way in or out, isn't there?"

"Better to prepare for an attack from one point of entry rather than one from all sides, don't you think?" Ichabod replied. Just as it would be at HomeSpace. The MaRuu's ability to hear each other's thoughts became too much to handle for them when they would swarm together, as if making each other's minds fill with chatter and noise. They became easy to kill when grouped together in a large swarm. It worked this way in the first millennia, and it would work again now.

"How do we know we'll even make it there?" Chukk questioned. "Thanks to Rex and his inability to show reserve, the herd is bloody scattering all over the plain. And the quarries are at least three dits away at a steady clip, Ichabod."

"Chukk," Ichabod replied, "Rex is doing the best he can. You know this so degrade him you will not. That stops here and now. You forget that we have something the MaRuu do not."

Rex smiled. "Bha's Bugles."

"That's right, Rex. Bha, get the Bugles in the air immediately. Have them find the MaRuu location and report back to us as soon as possible."

"We know they were not coming at us from the front," Chukk said. "Rex knew that much."

"Very well," Ichabod said. "Bha, instruct the Bugle sentries to scan our west, east, and south points of entry. I also want one per group with each of us. You'll be ours. Chukk and Rex will be with us also. Rex?"

"Yes?" Rex replied.

"If this goes sour," Ichabod said plainly, "you know what we have to do, don't you, son?"

Chukk patted Rex on the back. "I'll slice you so fast you won't even feel it, mate. That's a promise."

Rex sighed. "It's okay. Once you've been ripped through by a MaRuu, anything less can't compare." He paused, remembering something. "They came at night and not all at once put in small packs one after the other. It was after the moon fell beneath massive cloud cover. I remember now. We have time. We have time!"

"Good, good," Ichabod said. "Bha, go send your people out. Go now."

Bha nodded, flying away.

"Chukk," Ichabod went on, "you get the groups formed and meet up with Rex and I as soon as possible. Take the map for now to make sure your Battlers know where they're going, blades at the ready. Go."

Chukk nodded, spinning on his paws and leaving them.

Rex and Ichabod, facing each other, stood silently for a moment in the swirling chaos going on around them. Rex didn't know what to say, so just stood there eying Ichabod. Ichabod did something unexpected. He smiled.

"Rex," Ichabod said, "your sister would be very proud of you."

"Really?" Rex asked. "Why do you think that?"

"Because I am," Ichabod replied. "That's why. Why wouldn't I be when we have the Eternal Star?"

"Huh?" Rex asked.

"On every map, there is a compass showing how to make out the directions. You are the point right in the middle of where the directions cross, which is also the point between the Spirit and all of Arkelia. I only told your sister and the rest what they needed to know as I knew it to be then. You're our star, Rex, shining bright against the dark of night. We are all grateful for you. You are as important to us as the other Journeyers are, son. You are on the Journey of Lyght, too." This would help him to keep Rex nearby.

Rex smiled. "I never thought about it that way."

Ichabod returned the smile. "Well, now you can. Stay strong, Rex, stay strong. You're right where you belong. Come on, let's see if we can help gather our brethren up after the scare you gave them."

Putting his paw on Rex's shoulder, Ichabod led the younger Quasi towards the nearest Quasi to them. "I'm glad to have you like this, Ichabod," Rex said, "you and Bha were kind of jerky creeps when this all started. Nothing personal."

Ichabod laughed and Rex couldn't help but join in. Rex thought of Pi and hoped she and the others were doing as good or better than they were. If the MaRuu found the herd, that meant they could find Pi and the others too. This gave Rex a pang of fear, but he made himself brush it away, replacing it with hope that they were all okay and making their way towards saving them all-

The MaRuu attacked from in front of them, ripping through the Quasi as if they were wispy sheets of parchment. The air was filled with screams. The attackers moved faster than anything Ichabod had ever seen, the exception being Rhi's newfound flying abilities. The MaRuu moved in a near graceful swirl of destruction and chaos that left nothing in their trail except for the bodies of his fallen people. Looking in all directions, Ichabod saw nothing but despair. There was nowhere to go out here on the plain. The caves to the north were too far. He looked to Rex.

Rex met Ichabod's gaze, already knowing what the look meant. He saw the hopelessness in the old Quasi's eyes. He could tell Ichabod was seeing the eradication of his people take place right before their eyes. Rex reached into his pouch, withdrawing the silver blade. He handed it to Ichabod. "Do it."

Ichabod took hold of the blade. "When you come back, find me and tell me to alert the herd immediately, one Bugle and two Battlers to every ten Quasi in tight formation to the Quartz Quarry. You and Chukk with me and Bha. Tell me I said, fortune is no folly. Got that?"

Rex nodded. He closed his eyes and elongated his neck. Ichabod drew back with the blade and-

"There!" Bha yelled, pointing at Rex to a group of the MaRuu. "That's the one you want!

One of the MaRuu sent an icy blast from their mouth, blasting Ichabod and Rex with it and causing Ichabod to drop the blade. The two Quasi were knocked down by three more of the blasts sent by three more MaRuu. The rest came in a swarm, surrounding the two Quasi in what seemed like seconds, with Bha and a few other Bugles flying behind them.

"Bha," Ichabod asked, knowing that if he had the power of the star, he would have foreseen whatever it was that was happening. "What is this madness?"

"The younger one is your target," Bha said, disregarding Ichabod.

Rex was still stunned from his fall and was in shock watching Bha turn on them. "What are you doing helping them?!"

One of the MaRuu came forward. "Because," it hissed, "the natural order has been corrupted. You are not alone in attempting to stop our planet mother from dying. The MaRuu have undertaken the Path of Color and we will not be stopped by or usurped by Quasi scum. Bind them!"

The other MaRuu swarmed Ichabod and Rex, sending out thick icy clouds which turned to thick ice on their front and rear paws. The two bound Quasis watched helplessly as a sleigh bed dragged by four other MaRuu arrived. They were then unceremoniously lifted and thrown onto the vehicle before being frozen further to the sleigh bed. They were now fully incapacitated prisoners of a war neither knew was going on.

"Bha," Ichabod said. "You are a traitor to our people."

Bha shook his head, flying close to Ichabod. "No, old one, I'm a traitor to your people. To my people, I am their patriot. The Bugles will now fly free. No Quasi will ever control us again!"

"Good Spirits, Bha," Ichabod said. "When did you first betray us?" This would be useful information to have.

"Your little friend," the lead MaRuu hissed, "made the agreement when we saved him from death on your last expedition into our lands. He waited until the Sun Shock to alert us that we should make our move to end what had already begun. Go, little one," the MaRuu said, "Spread the word to your kind, you are now in truce with the MaRuu.

Fly away and leave us be. You are free."

"Let's see the Spirit save you now, Ichabod," Bha said, turning to a petrified looking Rex. "Can't turn the clock back again, Rex, can you? They're going to keep you stuck here like a knotted root."

Rex turned his head enough to catch Ichabod's stare. The old Quasi gave him a look of determination.

Ichabod whispered, "Not yet." Rex then looked back to the MaRuu and Bha-

Chukk grabbed Bha first, throwing him soundly to the ground before whipping around to face the MaRuu. His blade sliced and diced through them just enough faster than their attacks against him to land their targets. Sparks flew from their quilled fur armor as Chukk and then two of his fellow Battlers sent their blades spinning in deft, swift blows to the MaRuu.

Taken off guard by the rear assault, the MaRuu attempted to regroup in a small circle around the sleigh carrying Rex and Ichabod. Seeing this, Chukk leapt into the air, aiming his rear paw talons and bloody bronze blade right for the middle of the pack, with his fellow Battlers, now numbering four, following suit. The MaRuu were no match for them, in all of their furious rage. Rex watched all of this in both shock and awe. Never before had he seen any Quasi at war. They were in one word, vicious.

"Are you all right?!" Chukk called out, his breath heaving.

"We will be," Ichabod said. "Set us free and we stand a better chance!"

Chukk looked around. "Sorry, Ichabod, no time! Battlers, brave! Let's get them out of here now! Help me pull the sleigh to the rendezvous point! On your fours, go, go, go!"

The next few dits were a whirlwind. Rex and Ichabod found themselves being pulled by three Battlers, with Chukk steering and another apparently watching point as they thundered across the now dark plains. Every so often, they would find themselves being attacked by more MaRuu and each time, Chukk and his Battlers would repel them through sheer force. The MaRuu, smaller in stature than the Quasi, found their strength in sheer number, attacking in swarms. When it was only a few at a time, it seemed Chukk and the Battlers made quicker work of their opponents.

"Where are we going?" Rex finally asked, once the sleigh began again for parts to him still unknown.

"Somewhere safer than here!" Chukk answered from the front of the sleigh.

"Why didn't you just kill me? Or stab me or something?" Rex called back.

"Because we still need you here, Rex!" Chukk replied. "You have to know the plan I worked out first! Not enough time for a strategy session back there, was there?"

The Battler led sleigh was now seemingly clear of any visible MaRuu threat but Chukk and his Battlers drove it as if their attackers were right on their trail. Ichabod had been silent this whole time. In his head, he thought of Bha's and the other Bugles betrayal of the Quasi. The Bugles had been serving the Quasi as sentries and nectar providers since the third millennia in the Homelands, when the Quasi explorers had saved them from near extinction in their hives on the surface.

When the planet's weather kept declining, the Bugles surely would have died off if not for the Quasi offering them a home in exchange for their noble service. The Bugle Pact had been in effect for so long, Ichabod never realized that the Bugles saw it as an unbreakable contract instead of the measure of peaceful cooperation the way he and the other Quasi surely did. Bha's testimony otherwise seemed like treason to the highest degree.

As the sleigh began to slow, Ichabod wondered if all of the Bugles were working against the Quasi's interests out of a necessity to avoid the wrath of the MaRuu or their apparent deep seeded resentment of them and how the Quasi had treated them? Time would only tell, Ichabod surmised. And now, being pulled to Spirit knows where, he had the very survival of the herd to figure out. Ichabod wondered why Rex was still here in this place, lying next to him.

What more could they need to endure before Rex could loop back and stop this from happening? Then, Ichabod's hearts sank as he thought of the most likely possibility. He buried those thoughts away, interested to see what place Chukk and the Battlers could have found to keep them safe from harm. It truly seemed that for every step forward they made the Spirit drove them five backwards first. Ichabod was saddened to feel as if this was how his herd would die off, in a blood drenched massacre of his own making. He had been betrayed by who he thought up until now was his dearest friend, now his sworn enemy.

The lyght in front of them grew brighter as the sleigh came to a stop in front of a massive, glowing lyght vein cave sending the familiar glow of yellow energy off into the dark of the night. The Battlers and Chukk came to the back of the sleigh.

"Don't move, either of you," Chukk commanded, wielding his bronze blade. With four quick chops, he broke Rex and Ichabod free of their frost shackles sending the ice shards into pulverized wisps of ice dust. "Come on, we don't know how long it will be until they find us here. Battlers, take the sleigh back and fetch as many wounded as you can, three in the front and two in the back. Fetch one more from inside to go with you. Keep it going until your paws fall off and then swap out until you either get them all back safely or die trying. Go, go, go!"

The Battlers did just as they were told in a flurry of motion that amazed Rex to no end. No questions, no objections, no worry, just pure acceptance of their mission. He knew he could never be like that. Not for long anyways.

Following Chukk into the cave, Ichabod saw that the mouth was full of bruised Battlers, all with their blades at the ready. There had to be at the minimum thirty of them, all protecting those from the herd that had somehow also been rescued. There weren't many. Perhaps a hundred if Ichabod had to guess. He felt all of their eyes burn into him as he passed them by. They know this is my fault, Ichabod thought to himself.

"We think might be cave is fresh," Chukk said, taking a sweetwater jug from one of the wounded and taking a gulp before returning it.

"Fresh?" Rex asked.

"Fresh as in it most likely became accessible after the first Sun Shock," Chukk replied. "It's not on Ichabod's map, so it must be uncharted."

"Which also means the MaRuu don't know its whereabouts," Ichabod said. "Or even that it exists." Which meant Rex could end this timeline and start another...

"Right," Chukk said. "So, if Rex can loop back, we can redirect the herd here earlier on, shore up our defenses, and make our stand," Chukk replied. "That is, if you agree, Ichabod."

"What about Bha and the Bugles?" the elder Quasi asked. "He must have been sending the MaRuu our bearings all along the way somehow."

"It must only be Bha and one of his sentries," Chukk said. "As you can see, we have plenty of Bugles here who mean us no harm. I think he went rogue on you, Ichabod. All we need to do is to get to him before he gets to his sentry that alerted the MaRuu to begin their attack. We silence Bha and focus on getting our people here to this cave. Then we can properly defend ourselves while we send word ahead to the Western HomeSpace to send us enough reinforcements to defeat the MaRuu. What do you think?"

"When you say, 'silence him'," Rex asked. "What does that mean exactly?"

Chukk pulled out his bronze blade. "I'll kill him. Just make sure to tell me why."

"It will be the only way, Rex," Ichabod said. "He is a traitor and has caused mass casualties to our people. It must be done."

Rex sighed and then nodded. "Got it. All right, then."

He reached into his pouch, withdrew the gifted silver blade, and prepared to cut his front left paw. "Anything else before I go?" Rex asked, looking from Chukk to Ichabod.

"If we do not cross paths again know in your hearts we are proud of you, Rex," Ichabod said. "Destroy the MaRuu for us, all right?" Ichabod hoped this loop would not leave him deceased as the last one apparently had.

Chukk nodded, taking the blade to his paw. Then he stopped, frozen in thought. "I think I just thought of something. It's probably a stupid idea, though."

"What is it, Rex?" Ichabod asked.

"What if I tried bringing you back with me?" Rex asked. "Holding on to me when I go back might just bring you with me."

"Improbable, Rex," Ichabod said. "And if it did work, these Quasi and Bugles would be left here in this cave with no one to lead them or marshal defending them."

Chukk raised a paw. "No, you're thinking spatially, Ichabod. Think in a non-linear way. We would rewind with him, leaving all of this just as one future possibility but only one each of us is aware of. Darn, why didn't we think of this before? Rex, you're a genius. I'll do you one better. What if all of us here in the cave held paws and hands, Quasi and Bugle alike? We could all go back and while you and everyone else here are warning the rest of the herd to head straight for this lyght cave to fortify for attack and encampment, Ichabod and I can take on Bha straight on then regroup with you here, while the Battlers here and I can mobilize to the south where the attack came from and launch a preemptive attack on the MaRuu. Why send one back when we might be able to send a hundred to save a thousand?!"

"I don't know if it will work," Rex said. "But it's worth a try, isn't it, Ichabod?"

Ichabod shrugged. "I guess it is. But that means taking the time to tell all of these Quasi that there might be more hope than there actually is. If it doesn't work, there will be a lot of disappointment going around."

"Ichabod," Rex replied, "if I go back alone, they'll never know we even tried. I'll remember but they won't, and neither will you."

Ichabod let out a sigh. "All must be going to destruction if young Rex is making more sense than I am. All right, let's get them ready. Off you go."

Chukk headed for the Battlers while Ichabod and Rex began telling all the Quasi and Bugles off the plan to try to give them more of a head start to reach the cave. The instructions were simple: ask no questions and just hold another's hand or paw until we all connect, when you are back on the plains in the light of day tell all you see to head for this cave as fast as your paws or wings will take you.

Once they were all linked together, Rex extended his left paw towards Chukk, who had his blade at the ready. Rex nodded. Chukk swung his blade, going straight through Rex's forearm and lopping off his front left paw from the wrist up.

"Yeow!!!" Rex exclaimed, in blinding pain.

"Bet that hurt, didn't it?" Chukk asked, smiling.

"You cut off my bloody paw!" Rex yelled.

"Did I?" Chukk asked.

Rex looked down. His paw was not only intact but basked in sunshine. Looking around him, he could tell right away they were no longer on the Plains. Getting his bearings, Rex saw that they were back in front of HomeSpace?

"Not sure what you did, but it seems like we're right back to when we were before we got started? I don't know, I'm new to this," Chukk said. "We better find Ichabod and figure out what to do. People are going to be mighty confused in there, I reckon. Let's spread the word to just stay in place and hope Ichabod gets to Bha before any of the cave dwellers speak of what's going on. Let's go!"

Rex nodded, looking down once more to his fully functioning left paw in awe. He followed Chukk at a fast leap to keep up with him. Just when things seemed to be as weird as they could be, the Spirit threw everything off kilter anew. For what reason or purpose, Rex had no bloody clue.

As they made their way inside, Chukk and Rex both scanned their surroundings for commotion from the others who had traveled back with them. Oddly, everyone seemed to be going about their business preparing for the herd caravan to depart. No one seemed to be acting as if any of the events they just witnessed even took place. Nearing the Elder Chamber, Chukk slowed to a stop. Rex followed suit.

"I don't think any of them know what happened, mate," Chukk said, in a hushed tone.

"Me either," Rex said. "If Bha's in there with him, how will we know if Ichabod came back with us too?"

"Just stay mum and let me do the talking," Chukk said. "Come on."

As they passed through the Elder Chamber and towards Ichabod's burro, they heard strange noises being emitted. The sounds were muted by the entrance drape. Chukk put his hand on the drape, slowly pulling it back. Inside, Ichabod stood behind his desk while Bha lay tied up with sashes with his small mouth gagged with burlap.

"Guess you came back with us then?" Chukk asked.

"Aye," Ichabod said. "A bit further back than we expected it seems, too."

"And him?" Rex asked, pointing down at Bha.

"You were right, Chukk," Ichabod replied. "It was only him and one of his sentries."

"Which one?" Chukk asked.

"Bha has informed me that he won't tell us," Ichabod said. "I've been waiting for you to arrive to help jog his memory. Then we will be well on our way to righting this ship, won't we?"

"Aye," Chukk said. "Loosen the gag, Rex."

Rex neared Bha, reached down, and did as he was told.

"It doesn't matter," Bha said, spitting out blood. "I already sent him on his way. The MaRuu will know what you're up to. They'll know you lost HomeSpace. They'll still come... wherever you are. They find you and kill you all!"

"Gag him!" Chukk commanded, sending Rex to return the gag to a wriggling and writhing Bha's mouth.

"What now?" Rex asked, rising after fastening the gag around Bha's mouth. "If we stay here, we risk the place collapsing in on us and if we leave, the MaRuu are going to attack us halfway to the Western HomeSpace?

"The Spirit brought us back here for a reason," Ichabod said. "What is it in this time and place that affords us another option? We must think this through, lads."

"I have a thought," Chukk said. "I say we stay. We know when the second Sun Shock will crash down now. We get everyone out in time before it, see what more damage there is, and wait for the Battler Battalions from the South you're about to call for to arrive."

"And what of the MaRuu?" Rex asked. "What then?"

"Then we take the fight to them," Chukk said. "If they were willing to attack a multitude of unarmed Quasis, then they do not deserve to keep on living. Ichabod?"

Ichabod nodded. "I'll send for the Southern Battlers. By the calendar of days, we have eight days before the second Sun Shock blast. We have time to prepare. Not much, but enough I think."

Rex pointed at Bha. "What about him?"

Chukk withdrew his blade. "Rex, on your way. I'll meet you back up at the battalion dwelling. Ichabod, go call for a Leaper. Leave Bha to me."

As Rex and Ichabod left the burro, they heard the distinct sound of a muted scream, followed by an eerie silence that chilled both of them to the bone with each step they took further away from the burro. Once out in the main cavern, Rex suddenly stopped.

"Ichabod," Rex said. "Wait. Why didn't the Spirit send us back far enough to get out before Bha sent his sentry? Or better yet, why not send us back to before the first Sun Shock? That way we could evacuate everyone to safety."

Ichabod stopped, facing Rex. "I, I do not know, Rex. Those are good questions. But I already thought of that before you and Chukk arrived. I would wager that you are only to rewind time back so far as to when the Journey of Lyght began. You might have forgotten that this was the day the others left us behind to follow the Map of Lyght."

Rex sunk his shoulders low. "I miss them so much, Ichabod. Especially Pi."

"I'm sure she misses you too. So why don't the three of us go catch up to them and say goodbye one last time. They only left a few dits before you went off with Chukk if you remember. We just need to remember to come back here. If we go off with them, we'll sever the loop you've created off and never make it back here to prepare for the MaRuu invasion. Spirit only knows what would happen then." Perhaps if Ichabod could convince Pi to return the Arkelian to him, the power of the Eternal Star would be his once more.

"Nothing good," Chukk said from behind, catching up to them. "I thought about that very thing as we were making our way to you earlier. I say we leave them be. We can't risk it. Any of us says something strange or offsetting, this whole thing could come crashing down on us. Rex? You look uncertain there, mate."

Rex looked from Ichabod to Chukk. "You're right. We leave them alone to go on their journey. We can't risk it, even if we really, really, want to. We have to let things we want go sometimes. No, it would be greedy to need that, and I don't want to be like that anymore. Let them be."

A warm, orange energy wave rippled through HomeSpace and everything around them, causing their fur to stand up on its end.

"What was that?!" Chukk asked, drawing his bloodied blade from its sheath and spinning around to assay the threat.

Ichabod looked around, but slower. "Put your blade down, Chukk. I think it was a marker of the journey of lyght. Well done, Rex. You conquered your fears and just helped Pi and the others take one step closer to saving Arkelia." Or destroy it. It was difficult to tell, even for Ichabod, at this point what with all the timeline changes and course corrections taking place around them.

Rex looked confused. "Wait, what now?"

"You're on the Journey too, young one," Ichabod said. "And we're right here to help you through the rest of the tests we might face moving forward."

"Tests?" Chukk asked. "I thought all they had to do was follow the map wherever it took them so they could face the Spirit?"

"Oh, they are," Ichabod replied. "As are we now, apparently. The map is directions to a journey that is beyond our understanding, Chukk. It is a journey through the lyght energy that drives all life, both the positive and the negative. While orange symbolizes pride, it also symbolizes greed. Rex here just realized his pride by refusing to be greedy with his need for outside love. Apparently, the Spirit felt this was necessary for us to move closer to meeting what It wants." Or just pushed us further away.

"So, we're on the journey too?" Rex asked. "Even though we haven't gone anywhere?"

"I can't speak for Ichabod but seems to me we've gone just as far as they have," Chukk said. "Just in a different way."

Rex scratched his head. "All of this is making my head hurt. I think I'm going to go lie down for a bit. Is that okay?"

"Rest up, Rex," Chukk said. "Now, thanks to you, we have some time to think."

"Rex?" Ichabod said.

"Yeah, Ichabod?" Rex said, turning to leave.

"We're proud of you, lad," Ichabod said. "You saved many lives today."

"You're a hero in my book," Chukk said.

Rex smiled sheepishly. "Thanks. I'm going to go collapse now if it's alright with you two. Hopefully the fate of the planet can wait long enough for me to get some sleep?"

"You've earned that much and more," Ichabod replied, a smile on his face. "Go on then."

Rex turned, leaving in a near shuffle as his sore paws ached. Ichabod and Chukk watched him go, as slow as they had ever seen any Quasi hop. If not for the past day's events it would have been almost comical. Once he was out of ear shot, Ichabod took Chukk by the arm.

"I want you to start drawing up battle plans," Ichabod ordered. "This is the time for us to take the fight to the MaRuu once and for all know that we know what they're planning."

"We'll keep them far from HomeSpace, Ichabod," Chukk said. "I promise you that. We'll meet them in the middle distance between there and here. No more harm will come to our people."

"Good," Ichabod. "We've seen enough suffering for three lifetimes. Show no mercy, Battler." But the battle would be fought here. He had foreseen it.

"Aye," Chukk replied. "No mercy. They die. Every single bloody one of them."

***

Pi was tired. Her paws ached. Her head felt heavy. She was struggling and wished against wishes that none of the others noticed.

Pi had to be strong. She had to show them that she was worthy of being called to the journey taking place and that should the others falter or fall behind, she alone would be able to carry this heavy burden forward alone.

It had been two days since Dee had left them in his attempt to return home, only to meet with another figure who then disappeared from sight. Who he met, Dee refused to say, except that Dee had been wrong to leave them in the first place. Whatever he did, it had sent out another of the energy waves when Dee was through. He seemed reinvigorated and keenly more personable to all three of them, so there was that at least. There had been no more whispers about Rhi's drinking or Scout's clumsiness.

Dee seemed to be all right with Pi since they had set off, so his behavior now seemed more balanced in the group dynamic Pi knew they needed to have to survive all of this. But she was growing weary of how long this was all taking. Pi had expected to show up at the Sun Chamber by the end of the first night and here they were nearly seven days into the journey with nothing to show for it, save some flashing energy and improved behavior from a newly brave Scout and a freshly attentive Dee. Rhi was a feisty and funny as ever but Pi felt a sense of anxiousness that was slowly transforming into an air of exasperation. Can't we just get on with it already, she asked herself repeatedly.

Pi kept this to herself, not wanting the others to think any less of her or that she was ungrateful in any way for having the weight of the world placed squarely on her shoulders. That the others chose to come along was nice, it truly was, but Pi began to wonder if their involvement had caused her to miss something or slow down the trip. If she was going to give her life to save the planet, Pi wanted to hurry up and get it over with.

"You all right up there, love?" Rhi called out from behind Pi. "Been mighty quiet today!"

"Yes indeed!" Pi huffed. "I'm sure we'll be getting to where we're going soon!"

"Want me to fly ahead for another sweep?" Rhi asked as she flew up next to Pi. "Map is just a blue line pointing north towards those squiggly lines, but I could try to see where it's taking us. What do you think?"

Secretly, Pi wished Rhi would just leave her alone to stew in her thoughts until they reached the next destination. "Yeah, Rhi. Go on ahead."

"On it!" Rhi replied. She took a deep breath-

POP!

Pi was still amazed at just how fast Rhi seemed able to fly since the Sun Shock. It was incredible. That wasn't to mention Scout's jaw-dropping brute strength also. Why couldn't she have received some sort of superpower like that? She had heard the Spirit's voice twice and then, nothing. Had she done something wrong? Was the Spirit upset with how Pi had proceeded after the Sun Shock? What had she done?

The landscape around them was curious to Pi as well. While all of Arkelia was mostly barren of vegetation, covered in no more than moss and bramble bushes, the terrain she and the others were travelling through was thick with plants now, all having strange colored blossoms on them unlike any Pi had ever seen. Every color she had ever seen was on display on the different variety of plants they were know surrounded by.

Scout had been the first to notice that the plant stems and branches were made of a color unlike any they had ever seen before. It was impossible to describe, other than it seemed vibrant and fresh, lighter than blue but richer than yellow. It made the vegetation seem almost alien. Pi would not tell the others that this frightened her.

They would not know Pi was fallible like they were. She needed them to know that she was better, stronger, and more daring than they all were. Pi needed them to know she was worthy of this and whatever else lie ahead.

"Inbound!" Scout called out, bringing Pi back to her senses.

She turned to see Scout pointing to his right. Before she knew what was going on, Pi watched Rhi near them from the East, over a nearby ridge covered in the strange, yet beautiful, plant life. Rhi was flying towards them, waving her arms around like a mad person.

"Found it!" Rhi called out, her voice growing louder as she drew closer by the second. "I bloody found it; I did!"

"Found what, Rhi?" Dee asked as she slowed to a stop in front of them.

"The squiggles!" Rhi exclaimed. "Oh, just wait when you see them! They're epic, they are!"

Pi perked up at this. This meant they were getting back on track and closer to the end game if they had moved to the next of the map's markers. This meant they were drawing closer to the Sun Chamber and facing the Spirit. This meant she was one step closer to saving the Quasi, even if it also meant her impending death.

"How far, Rhi?" Pi asked.

Rhi landed in the middle of the group. "Not far. You can't see it from here, but the path is going to look like it ends up around the next bend." She paused. "But it doesn't! Lucky you have me along, you are! The colored plants cover up where it takes a sharp turn and down alongside where the Squiggles are! Not bad, eh?!"

Pi had to smile. Rhi's excitement was contagious and was about the only thing save for Scout's love that brightened her spirits these days. She thought of Rex and how they had cried after... saying goodbye to Addie? Wait, what?

"Scout! Rhi!" Pi chirped. "We got the chance to say goodbye to Addie?! Right? Or didn't we?"

Scout was the first to respond after each spent time contemplating the question. "It's happened again, love. I remember both. Her dying without us and then her being alive to see us go. Odd, this is."

"What's happening?" Rhi asked? "Wait, Scout didn't die? Or did he? And Addy, I, you, what is this?"

Pi took a moment to collect herself. "We're changing our history, the past and what happened since this all started. Somehow, things are getting... better? Or maybe different is a better word for it if that makes sense."

"It doesn't" Dee said. "But I met an old version of myself on the path back there and was told that if I didn't learn to trust you all, I would end up stranded out here for all of eternity, so at this point, I'm pretty sure we're not on Arkelia anymore. Or our understanding of it, anyways. We're someplace in between reality and-"

"The Spirit," Pi finished. "That cave wasn't just a cave, was it?"

"Now," Dee said, "seeing all of this? No, Pi, I don't think it was just a cave."

Scout scratched his chin. "Does it matter? Wherever we are, we are here now, aren't we?"

"He's right," Pi said with confidence in her voice. "We are here to complete a mission to meet the Spirit when it is ready to meet us. And if what we do somehow affect what we've already done, then we are only the better for it. We take each step forward not worrying about the step that preceded it. Agreed?"

They all nodded, silent.

"Good," Pi continued, "because all we have is each other now. Let's go see these squiggles Rhi has so excited discovered for us, shall we?"

"You're not going to believe it with your own eyes," Rhi teased. "I can surely tell you that, I can! Let's go!"

Moving forward, Pi brushed her negative thoughts away as they pushed on through the overgrown colored plants to continue on the blue earthed path beneath their paws. Those thoughts, still what she believed in her heart, made Pi feel almost guilty for how noble she knew she presented herself to the others in the group. Deep down, Pi knew she didn't deserve to be the leader of their group and probably not the Chosen one to face the Spirit.

Deep in her hearts, Pi knew she wasn't truly worthy. If Ichabod had chosen a Battler like Dee, maybe no one would have died in the first place.

"Do you see it?" Rhi exclaimed, buzzing next to Pi. "See it, Pi?"

Pi followed the direction Rhi was pointing in and froze in her tracks. "Impossible. It can't be."

"Improbable is more like it," Dee said. "Because... wow, there it is, isn't it?"

"My eyes have never seen such a beautiful thing," Scout said, his jaw slack. "The Spirit must exist to make such a place as this, doesn't it?"

"I... what, how?" Pi asked, staring down the hill towards such a cornucopia of brilliant light, color, and motion she thought she would cry right then and there. "Just look at it. It's-"

"Spectacular," Scout finished. "If Addy could see only see us now."

In front of the Journeyers, the blue path winded upwards, next to a mighty river of sweetwater, splashing over rock clusters sprawled out throughout the raging streams of water. Flashes of blue energy would leap out of the glowing, moving waters before diving back under the surface, sending pretty sparks out in a cascade of motion. But that alone was not the most impressive thing in the Journeyers line of sight.

High above in the distance, the water in front of them seemed to fall with the force of the very planet behind it over jagged rock formations protruding from the hillside ahead. Pi could think of no word but epic to describe the scene in front of her.

"Awesome," Scout whispered loud enough for the rest to hear. "What is it?"

Dee had the map out, smiling. He looked up from it. "The

Squiggles, apparently. This is our next marker."

"What does the map say, Dee?" Pi asked, she was excited now.

"Across this river one must go, the rest must go with the flow," Dee read. He looked up, a confused look on his face. "I don't get it."

"What's that mean?" Rhi asked. "Makes no sense whatsoever, does it?!"

"Are you reading it right there, mate?" Scout questioned. "Maybe you read your Ancient text wrong."

Dee looked back to the map. "No, that's definitely what it says." He read it aloud again.

"Does it say anything else?" Pi asked.

Dee shook his head. "After that, it just has a line drawn to the south pointing towards a bunch of red dashes and half circles. See?"

He showed them all the map. To Pi, the images ahead looked like red thunder snow falling over rolling hills. But that was not what they were facing in the here and now. She shrugged.

"We'll figure it out," Pi said. "Let's go."

Dee shot a quick look to Scout as if to say, really? Scout shrugged.

"You heard the lady," Scout replied. "On we go."

"Adventure!" Rhi nearly yelled. "Come on!"

They moved quickly along the lyghtning river's edge, following the blue path to its end, leading to a place where the rocks allowed for a jagged path across the river to the other side near the base of the cliff of falling water. Mist swirled around them, causing gentle sparks of energy to pop ever so often on the tips of their fur.

"This amount of sweetwater would keep the Quasi from having to collect rainfall canisters ever again," Dee said, his eyes wide. "I wonder where its coming from?"

"See, me," Rhi said, "I wonder where it's going. Guess we differ there, huh, mate?" She laughed heartily.

"I just wonder how, or who, we send to cross first," Pi said. "Because I think that's what the map is instructing us to do."

"It said only one could go before the rest," Dee replied. "So, who do we send?"

The Journeyers looked back and forth at each other.

"It should be me," Pi said, breaking the silence. "I'll go."

"Not so fast, love," Scout replied. "We need to make sure you get safely to the end. It could be a trap, because of course you'd say that. No, I'll go."

"Look, I know my place here now," Dee said. "I'm here because the three of you let me be. I bitched and moaned about taking care of you the whole way here, up until recently. No, I'm the Battler, remember? I'll go."

Rhi sighed. "You're all daft, you are! I can fly to other side in less than a dit! See?"

"No!" Pi exclaimed. "Ri, don't!!!"

It was too little, too late.

POP!

Rhi was gone from their sight... and yet, she did not show back up on the other side. Dits turned to dats. It was excruciating for Scout to watch Pi's face melt from one of confusion to sheer and utter disgust. The most excruciating part was wondering who would speak first.

"Stupid," Pi muttered. "Bloody stubborn and bloody stupid."

"She only ever listens to herself," Dee said. "I'm sorry but it's true. Most of the time, it's the nectar talking, not her. I'm sorry, you two. I truly am. But it's true. She's a stubborn lush."

"Oh Rhi," Scout said, chiming in. "Why'd you have to go and act all Rhi-ish on us? Foolish girl."

Pi felt like her brain was going to explode. Rhi didn't listen. She never listened. Pi was going to take the variables they had to work with, formulate a plan, and decide what they should do next. But now, everything had run amok. Rhi was gone, of her own free will, just because she thought she knew best. But it was Pi, who had spoken with the Spirit itself, had been the selected as the Chosen one, had been given the Arkelian she now wore over her chest, that should have decided.

Not Rhi, with no hesitation or regard for Pi. It was unfair and now, Rhi seemed to have paid the ultimate price. Pi couldn't help herself from cursing Rhi and her foolishness.

"It was supposed to be me!" Pi blurted out. "Why did she do that? I'm the one that was supposed to go! This is my journey, mine alone! No one else can do this!"

After another long silence, Scout spoke up. "Why don't you tell us what you really think, love?"

"Wow," Dee said. "Is that what you really think, Pi?"

Pi, both front paws clenched, looked to the ground. "I've been thinking it the past few days, yes. I wasn't going to say anything. But now, what does it matter? Thanks to Rhi, I've failed everyone, haven't

I?"

Scout hopped to her, putting his paw on her shoulder to offer some comfort. Pi brushed him away. "Not now, Scout. Leave me be. I need time to think about this."

Pi turned and hopped closer to the falling water where she found a cluster of rocks to sit on beside the rushing river of lyght water. She knew something like this was going to happen. All it took was one misstep and now, Rhi was gone and they had no way of knowing if the same would happen to them if they tried to follow her across. What a bloody mess her little Bugle friend had gotten them into.

Sure, Dee went to leave, but that turned out to be one of the journey markers, the test they seemed to be undertaking to move forward. Well, we're going sideward now, Pi groused. And as mad as she was at Rhi, Pi wanted her friend to be safe and sound and back with them.

Looking up and down the river, from the sparking, crackling waterfall to the raging rapids twisting into the distance, Pi saw only the one route they could take crossing on the protruding rocks in front of them. But then something caught her eye, hidden under mossy color plant cover off to the side of the nearest still pool, not far in front of where the waterfall was sending mist and sparks swirling out into the crisp, fresh air. Pi recognized the shape from her childhood picture books detailing the ancient times. She saw the hull of a boat.

"Boys!" Pi called out. "Come here!"

Scout and Dee hopped up as quick as their paws could take them.

"What is it, Pi?" Dee asked.

"You see Rhi?" Scout asked.

Pi shook her head. "No. I see something that would have let us all cross first, and together at that." She pointed to the boat.

"Is that a... boat?" Dee asked. "Like in the ancient times when there was still land water?"

"It sure looks like it," Scout said. "If only she-"

"Doesn't matter now," Pi said. "She did. She did exactly what she's done her whole life."

"What's that?" Dee asked.

"Whatever she wanted," Scout replied. "Only one way for Rhi... hers. Shame, it is."

"It was when we lost our parents in the expedition," Pi said. "Rex and I still had each other but Rhi lost everything. We were teens then. It's when she started drinking. That's why no one gave her any grief

133

since then."

Dee frowned. "Didn't do her much good in the end, did it? This journey opened my eyes a few days ago. Made me think outside of myself. I'm sorry she didn't get the same opportunity. It's sad."

"You know, mate," Scout said. "Same goes for me. This has changed me. I'm not afraid and worrying anymore. Found my confidence, I have. Thing was Rhi is she was in denial anything was wrong. Put out all jokes and giggles into the world, but on the inside? I reckon it was a much different story."

Pi swallowed hard at that, brushing away the similarities she was starting to draw between her and Rhi. They were not the same. Pi was smarter, better, and wiser than her friend. She knew how to keep things together, as long as Pi could control the variables and see all the angles. Like now, finding a boat to take them across the lyght river. If only Rhi had listened to her, she'd still be here!

"Let's get it uncovered and make sure it's sturdy enough for us," Pi said. "It's not dark yet but it's getting there."

Scout and Dee made quick work of cleaning the boat off of the overgrown color plants. The vessel looked to made of thick bramble wood and appeared to still be watertight once they placed it in the still pool off to the side of the waterfall. Pi appeared to be rustling around in the plant growth from where the boat had been, causing Scout and Dee to watch her with a mix of curiosity and apprehension as to where her mind was. Pi paid them no bother, finally finding what she was searching for. She smiled, proud of herself for her line of thinking.

"Looking for Rhi down there?" Scout asked.

"Nope!" Pi said, raising two long, thin at the top and larger at the bottom, pieces of bramble wood. "We're going to need these, lads!"

"What are they for?" Scout asked, befuddled.

Dee chuckled. "Steering this thing, Scout. Why didn't I think to notice that?"

Pi tossed one of the oars to Dee. "Because I did. That's why."

"So, let's get across so we can look for Rhi," Dee said. "She's got to be over there somewhere."

"We don't know that," Scout said. "She just up and vanished, mate."

"After everything we've been through and seen," Pi said, throwing the other oar to Scout, "we don't know anything, Scout."

"Well, whatever, love," Scout stammered. "But we still need to cross."

Pi had been thinking about that. "Do we?"

"Do we, what?" Dee asked. "Cross?"

"It said one would cross," Pi said. "But the rest-"

"Should go with the flow," Scout finished.

"What if that means not crossing the river at all?" Pi asked.

She picked up a small bunch of the small color plants and threw them down into the water. They moved downstream with the river's moving stream before being disintegrated by the lyghtning current running through the water. Dee and Scout looked from the plants to Pi.

"What if we take the boat and follow the flow of the lyght river?" Pi opined. "It makes more sense if you take the time to think about it, no?"

Dee and Scout looked at each other, and then back to Pi.

"Bloody brilliant, you are," Scout replied. "I never would have thought of that."

"Me either," Dee said. "Chosen One, indeed. I have a question for you two, though. This has all got me thinking on the journey itself."

"What about it?" Pi asked. Who was he to question the ancients?

"If there was only one Chosen one," Dee began, "then why do the map's riddles and tests mention others and their roles too?"

Pi and Scout fell silent. Neither had put any thought into that.

"I'll tell you, why," Dee said. "This map has different instructions and text than when I first read it. I noticed it when we arrived here but Rhi flying off didn't let me bring it up before now."

"What makes sense anymore is that nothing makes sense anymore," Pi said. "I just don't know if that's a good thing or a bad thing."

"Good thing," Scout said. "I hope, anyways."

Pi wondered why the Spirit graced her with its voice only to disappear into the ether once the journey began. Probably for that very reason, she thought to herself. It was up to her to see this through without any help from above. Pi, still believing that this journey was hers alone, hadn't thought that as variables changed so would the journey itself. That was stupid of her not to consider. So, if the journey was a shared one, what role did she play now? Den mother? Follower? Or was it something else? Problem solver, perhaps? Her mind was always whirring and spinning, thinking of probable outcomes and solutions to things. It was just how her mind worked.

"What if Rhi was supposed to be the one to cross?" Pi asked, drawing Scout and Dee's attention. "What if whoever crossed first was the right one to go and the rest were meant to go another way, going down the river. I'm thinking this might not affect us badly as I was thinking it would."

"Makes sense, if there's any to be had," Dee said. "That might just be Rhi's path to achieving another of the markers, or better yet, ours by trusting that we can soldier on without her."

"I reckon that speedy little Bugle will catch up with us as soon as she's able," Scout added.

"She may be stubborn," Pi said, "but along with it comes that raw determination and feisty persistence of hers. I saw we follow the river and see where it takes us. Lads?"

"Aye," Scout said. "Never been on a boat before. Heck, I've never seen moving water before either. As Rhi would say, 'Adventure ahead!'"

Pi and Dee laughed.

"I think you're right about the instructions, if you can call them that," Dee said. "I say we do it. She might just be better off for all we know."

"Or she could be gone," Pi replied. "But we move on just as she would have. So, what do you think? Is the boat watertight?"

Dee lightly jumped up and down in the boat, causing no ill effect. "Seems so. I am curious as to why I'm not getting zapped through with lyght energy, though."

"Now that I can't answer," Pi replied. "It must be made of energy resistant material. It's the only explanation I can think of."

"Or the Spirit protecting us until it eventually kills us," Scout surmised. "At this point, who bloody cares? Let's go."

With Dee on one oar, Scout on the other, and Pi in the front as point, they slowly maneuvered the boat out into the rushing water of the lyght river. As the current continued to quicken, pulling the boat quicker and quicker downstream, the three remaining Journeyers sadly left the last known location of their friend, Rhi. Each hoped they would see her again, but they knew nothing was for certain, now more than ever before. As a pastel colored sky called to the in the distance, Pi thought she caught a glimpse of something shiny moving on the other side of the far riverside and turned to see what it was.

"See something?" Scout asked. "Is it Rhi?"

Scout and Dee tried to dig their oars down to stop the boat, but the river current was too fast and the water too deep. They couldn't stop. Inexperienced boaters, the two Quasi struggled to redirect the boat towards the far shore. Pi scanned the location where she thought she saw movement, looking for any sign of Rhi-

POP!

Rhi appeared out of nowhere, flying straight towards them at breakneck speed. She crashed into the boat with a loud thud, her small body crackling with lyght energy.

"Rhi!!!" Pi cried out, reaching down to scoop her friend up in her paws to hug her lovingly. "We thought we lost you forever, you stupid, stubborn, beautiful little Bugle!"

Dee and Scout were both slack jawed. Scout spoke first.

"Rhi, you little bugger!" Scout exclaimed. "Beyond words you are! Don't be scaring us like that!"

"How long have I been gone?" Rhi asked, breathing hard. "How long?!"

Pi, Scout, and Dee looked at each other.

"Three dats, maybe four," Pi said, quizzically. "Why? Where have you been?"

"I, er, not important," Rhi said. "Listen, we have a problem. Well, they have a problem. But they said I can't tell you, so let's just move forward, aye?"

"What nonsense are you talking about, Rhi Bugle?" Dee asked, utterly confused. "Are you even more buzzed on nectar than usual?"

"Don't drink anymore, mate," Rhi replied.

"Anymore?" Pi asked. "Wait, how long do you think you were gone?"

"Long enough," Rhi replied. "Look, you lot, we have to be careful from here on out. We're not the only ones making passage for the Sun Chamber. The MaRuu are onto us. They're going for it too."

Scout dropped is oar, causing a loud clunk of a noise. "Sorry, wait, the MaRuu? What? Where?"

"That's just it, mate," Rhi said. "I don't know, except that some are ahead of us. That's all I can say. We need to move forward, but trust me you three, I will never, ever make a snap judgement without consulting you first ever again. That is a both an apology and a promise. There is no I in us, is there?"

"No," Pi said, "there's not. Apology accepted... sister."

"Good enough for me," Scout said.

"I want to know where you got your information from, little one," Dee said, rather sternly. "You can't just pop in and drop that on us without more information. Where were you?"

Rhi shook her head. "Better off this way, mate. I've trusted you. I'm asking you to trust me until I prove unworthy. All I'll say is that we need to do this. We cannot falter. We do this together as one or..." She trailed off, turning to face ahead.

"Or what, Rhi?" Pi asked.

Rhi sighed. "Or we'll fail. And everyone dies. And none of us wants that, do we? Now do you accept my apology, and will you trust me that I've learned my lesson and am here to help or is this going to be uncomfortable for the remainder of the trip?"

Dee studied her. "Fine, apology accepted but if this was just a rouse to get back in our good graces, you're going to regret it."

"I'll take that as a yes, Battler," Rhi said. "If memory serves me, we have some more weird shapes to decipher, right?"

The boat, with the four Journeyers abroad, moved down river at a good clip into the approaching sunset. Rhi, just happy to be back with her family, took little time before snuggling into the nook of Pi's front paw. Rhi had been told not to share any of the goings on back at HomeSpace with the Journeyers but to make them aware that there was a MaRuu threat looming, and that was all. Rex had been very specific on this point. Rhi hoped to never see such horror again in her life. It had been the longest month of her life and she would prefer not to repeat it.

Poor, poor Rex, Rhi thought, sadly.

***

"Rhi, don't!"

POP!

Rhi took one look at her surroundings before losing her coordination and crashing into the rocky dirt below. She looked around, puzzled to no end. "This... isn't possible?!"

Rhi was lying on the ground in HomeSpace, just shy of the tunnel that lead to Pi's burro. Some Quasi that passed her by, who were maneuvering around the fallen rubble left in the wake of the Sun Shock, gave Rhi quizzical looks as they hopped by. She banged her small hands against the ground in frustration. "No! No! No! What is this? Pi?! Scout?! Battler?! Where are you?!"

Rhi, panting, asked the air, "What is this? How is this possible? Rex, I have to find Rex."

She dusted herself off and flew the rest of the way to Pi and Rex's burro, hoping he would be there. Maybe Pi and Scout would be there too! Rhi could see the glow of a lyght lamp from the doorway. Well, someone was there! She flew inside.

Inside, Rhi saw Rex asleep on his sitting cushions in the corner of the living area. "Rex!"

Rex, startled, opened his eyes to find Rhi floating in the air above him? "Waaaaa!!!!"

"Ahhhhhh!!!" Rhi screamed, matching Rex's yell. "Stop! Rex, stop it!!! It's me, it's Rhi! I'm back!"

"Back from where?!" Rex asked, scared stiff.

"I'm back... from the future. I think I am, anyways," Rhi answered. "I don't know how but I am. I was flying across a giant stream of moving lyght water and now I'm here! Are the others here? Are Pi and Scout here?! The Battler bloke, Dee?!"

Rex shook his head. "No, this is impossible! You, you just left, uh, wait, this is so confusing at this point... um, yesterday?!"

"That means we'd already gone in the cave and gone to the Journey Place," Rhi said, turning to leave. "I have to leave! I have to get back to them!"

"No, stop!" Rex said, grabbing her by the arm and pulling Rhi down to the ground. "Cool off and wait a dit! Heck, you're a force of nature! Just relax. The them who just left here aren't the them you just got separated from, if that's makes any sense. If you go and interfere with the journey, you could cause it to never get started in the first place and who knows what would happen if you ran into yourself. So just stop. Can you do that?"

Rhi floated to the ground. "So, I am in the past. Bloody heavy, this is."

"Your past," Rex said. "Our present. Me, well, I'm kind of all over the place in this mess. Essentially, your present is now our present too, but it's also in your past."

Rhi looked at him quizzically. "What's that mean?"

"It means we need to figure out your place in this and what it means," Rex said. "You stay here. Try not to interact with anyone or anything until I get back with the others, okay? Just stay in here and calm yourself. You're safe, at least for the time being, I hope."

Rhi climbed up on the cushions. "I think my head's going to explode, I do. I need me some nectar to calm down. Fetch me some?"

"The nectar jugs are just how you left them, Rhi," Rex said. "Empty."

Rhi sank into the cushions. "I don't think this can get any worse."

"Welcome to the party," Rex said, turning to leave.

***

"And then, Pi wanted to cross the water first, but Dee and Scout thought they should go first to protect her," Rhi explained. "I knew I could fly over it faster than they could get across on the rocks, so I just, er, did. And the next thing I knew, here I am telling you three my tale. So, there it is." Rhi took a swig of her new, but now half empty, nectar jug.

Rex looked to Ichabod. Chukk was still out doing something with his Battalion and hadn't joined them yet. Ichabod had been silent since asking Rhi to recount everything that had happened to the Journeyers since their departure from HomeSpace. His let out a long breath through his nostrils, as if decompressing.

"I see only two possibilities here," Ichabod said, breaking the silence. "Either your part of the journey lead you back to this place and time for a reason or... it didn't, and you were sent back here to sit out the rest of the trip because your actions somehow failed the Spirit."

"Ouch," Rex said, causing Ichabod to slap him upside the head. "I was kidding!"

"She's been through a lot, Rex," Ichabod said. "As we all have. Be kind."

"Says the guy who went around trying to get everyone killed," Rex muttered. All of Ichabod's niceness was not what it seemed, Rex now realized somehow seeing through this charade of comradery.

"I still don't think that is accurate, Rex," Ichabod replied. "I never have anything but the best intentions for the Quasi in mind. I seriously doubt some of your earlier recollections of me."

"Look," Rex said. "I'm thrilled you're in our corner now, Ichabod, really, I am, and we need you to help us make sense out of all this, but I'm starting to see that people's natures aren't changing in the new

140

timelines. I've watched you try to get one step ahead of this in your own way since this all started and all it did was stop you from politicking behind closed doors and keep Chukk from lopping your head off for it. You just wait for me to tell you what's going to happen next and frankly, I'm starting to get sick of it. I want to trust you but part of me wonders if you're up to something I just haven't picked up on yet. Now, Rhi's here from the future, my sister and Scout are stuck out in the middle of Spirit knows where with a grumpy Battler, and the MaRuu are going to attack us, again, and where and when does it bloody end?! I need some air."

Rex leapt from his cushions and left the burro, leaving Ichabod and Rhi alone to face each other in awkward silence.

"He's off his rocker, that one," Rhi said. "Rex is bloody losing it. And I bet I'm next. What is he talking about?"

Ichabod sighed. "It's complicated, Rhi Bugle." It seemed Rex had caught on to his manipulations. Oh well. He would not be needed much longer.

"Try me, especially the part where you tell me when you tried to kill us. Now." Rhi folded her arms.

"Whatever has taken place since the Spirit called to me to select Pi to the Journey of Lyght and Addy to ask the three of you to join her, well, that's apparently not how it all really began. History is changing around us by the dit, and young Rex here is the only one not changing with it. He, like you, are from the original timeline. The world and everything that happened has been changing around him. It is a heavy burden to bear, but he plays an important part of the journey, Rhi. He's how we know what came before and what is coming next. Without him, we'd all be dead by now." Ichabod took a sip of sweetwater, eyeing Rhi's reaction to his explanation thus far.

"Let's get back to you killing us," Rhi said, stoic. "How about that? Go on then."

Ichabod chuckled. "Apparently, according to one of Rex's visions, an earlier version of me told your leader, Bha, that I was sending you four on a wild pup chase and intentionally into the hands of the MaRuu. Preposterous! And that's if Rex was even right and not confused as he tends to get. Rhi, it was just one possibility out of countless others and also the first time Rex remembers seeing the future, so it must be taken with a speck of dirt and a drop of water. It means nothing, really."

"Fine," Rhi said. "Speaking of Bha, I'd like to see him."

"Oh, Ichabod said, "I'm afraid that's not possible. He turned on us, Rhi. On all of us. He turned out to be the true traitor to our people. He's sent a Bugle sentry to alert the MaRuu to our misfortune. In one possible future, they will return and decimate our people in a massacre unlike any you have ever thought imaginable, both Quasi and Bugle peoples will be eradicated."

Rhi dropped her now empty nectar jug to the ground in shock. "When?"

"When?" Ichabod reiterated. "That is becoming a difficult question to answer these days."

"When did he send the sentry, Ichabod?" Rhi asked. "How long ago?"

Ichabod thought for a second, replaying the events in his mind. "He would have sent whoever it was yesterday, I suppose. Why?"

"Because he would have sent the only Bugle sentry that's been to the South where the MaRuu are. It must be old Bor, the chubby, salty bloke that came back with him from the expedition years ago! They were the only two who returned!"

Ichabod raised an eyebrow. "So, what, Rhi? What does it matter who Bha sent?" he asked. "He's already gone."

"But I can catch that slow, fat bastard!" Rhi exclaimed. "I'll stop him before he ever gets there, I will."

"He has a full day's start on you, little one," Ichabod said. "He's probably halfway there, already. Let it go. We have this under control."

"No," Rhi said, lifting herself in the air. "I can help. I bet that's why I'm here. To help you. Ichabod think about it! I flew through bloody time to get here!"

"And what will you do when you catch him?" Ichabod asked. "Are you prepared to kill another Bugle for the greater good? That's a heavy burden to bear."

Rhi paused, but then nodded. "Whatever it takes. I got sent back for a reason, Ichabod. Let me help. Please. I'm bloody begging you. This has to be why I'm here. Because I don't spend time thinking, I just do what needs to be done. Just like right now. Please!"

Ichabod was quiet for a moment. He played the scenarios out in his mind before speaking again. "How fast are you, Rhi?"

"Faster than light itself," she replied.

"Do you know how to wield a blade?"

"No," Rhi replied. "But I learn as fast as I can fly. Teach me."

"Follow me," Ichabod said, rising. "We need to meet up with Chukk the Battler as soon as his Battalion returns from some, er, maneuvers."

"What about Rex?" Rhi asked, following Ichabod out of the burro.

"Let's keep your mission a secret for now, Rhi," Ichabod said. "Rex has enough to worry about as it is. There will be plenty of time for us to bring him up to speed once you've returned and life can settle back down. He's had about as much as he can handle, I'm afraid."

"Fair enough, that is," Rhi said. "I thought he was about to strangle you back there for a moment, I did."

As they moved through HomeSpace, Ichabod thought of how much more time there would be to mount an offensive against the villainous MaRuu if they were able to attack with the element of surprise. If the bugle could catch and kill the sentry, that time loop would be forever closed and it would allow Chukk as much time as he needed to plan out a full-on offensive to wipe the MaRuu preemptively out so that images like he had seen on the Plainlands from the previous timeline would never, ever have the remotest possibility of coming true.

The MaRuu were heartless, soulless creatures who had taken advantage of the Quasis in a time of need and the traitor Bha had tried to add further insult to injury by inferring that the Quasi were somehow responsible in all this? Ridiculous! The Quasi won these lands fairly in the first millennia from the MaRuu and had shown the Bugles nothing but compassion since taking them in from their dying home islands on the journey over the Shining Sea.

The Quasi, Ichabod knew in his hearts, were the strongest race on Arkelia for a reason: The Spirit rewarded both cunning and compassion. That was why they were tasked with the Journey of Lyght to add a thousand more planet turns to Arkelia's future. And then they would go again. If there was one thing the Quasi never did, it was stop... for anything. It was as the ancients willed it to be, stop never, live forever. Even now that the End Beacon had made itself known.

For as long as the Quasi lived, breathed, and bred, the Spirit would continue on through them. If all the Quasi were to die, the Spirit would be no more and then, all of Arkelia with it. On that battlefield in the Plains, Ichabod felt as he was watching the finality of life itself take place. He shuddered. No, it would not be. Threats such as the MaRuu could be conquered with enough cunning and courage, just as they had defeated them when they were first attacked after colonizing the Last Continent.

If there was to be war, Ichabod thought, he wanted it to be on their terms and not on the MaRuus'. Their opponents had evolved into killing machines whose swarm like behavior must somehow be turned against them. How do you kill a killer, Ichabod thought as they neared the Battalion quarters? He could make Chukk out as they approached. Rhi, for the first time in her life, had been silent the whole time the two had spent walking. It didn't bother Ichabod.

"What's she doing here?!" Chukk asked, throwing his hands up.

"She's from the future, Chukk," Ichabod said, taking him aside and putting a paw on his shoulder. "Seems the Spirit has seen to it to give you more time to plan, er, our defenses. Your Dee is doing just fine and the Journey of Lyght continues on, but Rhi here and her lyghtning fast speed have come back in time to assist us with our little problem of the MaRuu being alerted to our misfortune. She thinks she can catch up to Bha's sentry before he reaches the MaRuu. She can close the loop so that the MaRuu have no idea HomeSpace has been struck and they'll return to simply resenting us from afar."

Chukk eyed Ichabod, realizing that the plan to strike the MaRuu preemptively was not common knowledge for the others yet.

"We'll avert a war, we will!" Rhi exclaimed. "I'll save the day, I will!"

Chukk looked back to Ichabod. "What do you want of me?"

"She needs a blade she can carry and a very brief, but detailed tutorial on how to use it," Ichabod said. "Think you can help us?"

Chukk chuckled. "This keeps getting weirder and weirder, mate. Aye, I can help her. But a blade her size? I'll have to have one made special. Might take until tomorrow. What if I teach her paw to paw combat instead? If you can kill with a blade, you should be able to snap a neck. That's the Battler way."

Rhi swallowed hard. "Er, of course. Yeah, I'll snap his neck, I will!"

"How is it you can fly so bloody fast now, bugle?" Chukk asked.

"Don't know," Rhi said. "It just started after the Sun Shock. Don't know how I traveled through time either, so who knows anything really? You know?"

Chukk laughed. "Fair enough. My Dee, how is, was, oh, just, is he all right?"

It was Rhi's turn to smile. "Grumpy and feisty, but he's had our backs when it's mattered the most. He almost left at one point because he uh, missed you so much, he did. But he came back stronger than ever, he did. Loves you lots, I reckon. Last time I saw him, he was safe, mate." No need to complicate anything regarding Dee, Rhi thought. It wasn't her fault Dee didn't like her personality.

Chukk nodded. "Good. Now come on, little one. Let's teach you how to grapple. This other bugle won't know what hit them."

Ichabod watched as Rhi followed Chukk away towards the training range. He turned and made his way into the HomeSpace, not stopping until he was back in the confines of his small burro. He sat on the edge of his bedding cushions and dug into the corner, retrieving a small woven thistle root box, with the Quasi insignia on it.

Opening the box, Ichabod retrieved an old, torn, and tattered parchment written in the ancient text. In his paws, he was holding last known relic from the first age, from the first Quasi High Elder to arrive on the Last Continent, and the first to send a Chosen one for the Journey of Lyght. He turned to last written scratching and read aloud:

"He was told the Great Spirit was the beginning and the end, nothing and everything, and all else in between. None would ever know its pain, being alone yet making up all life, those feelings together at the same time. It was too heavy a burden to bear. So, the Spirit split in two and set fire to the air without a care. If the misery is to continue, take the journey if you dare. The final sign of the upcoming end will be known when all time will begin to bend. The future and past will end, at last."

Ichabod sighed, rubbing his old, tired eyes. He carefully put the parchment back into the box. "If we're doomed to go, Spirit, we're taking the MaRuu with us. And that is a promise."

Ichabod got up, moving to his desk. He began drawing up communiques to the three other HomeSpaces. He hoped Rhi was able to complete her mission because either way, they were going to war. And in war, the element of surprise tended to favor the victors. There was no question in his mind now that the Spirit was on their side.

He gave a moment to pause to the MaRuu speaking of a path of color and their own attempt to stop the Ending. Most likely foolish nonsense meant to scare him into assisting them, but if not, something that could be troublesome. If the MaRuu were also aware the planet itself was slowing in its orbit around the Sun, and by some miracle beat the Quasi in finding a way to reverse it, then the Quasi would certainly face extinction at their hands. No, it had to be the other way around, for this Ichabod was now more certain than ever having seen what he had seen.

The MaRuu had to die. All of them.

**

"And that, little one," Chukk said, "is how you snap a neck. Force and motion. Can you remember that?"

"Force and motion," Rhi repeated. "Got it, I do. He won't know what hit him."

"Oh, he will," Chukk replied. "But if you do it right, he won't be able to stop you before the deed is done. Are you sure you're up for this?"

Rhi, as was her way, didn't spend time wallowing in thinking things through. If her gut told her to do it, she did it, and didn't spend any time worrying about it after the fact. The type of thinking had gotten her into a good deal of trouble throughout the planet turns, but it also let her know that she, Rhi Bugle, decided her fate and no one else. This was no different. There was something that needed doing and Rhi knew she was the only one who could do it.

"I know this is why I'm here and not there," Rhi said. "It must be my test."

"Test?" Chukk asked.

"Your life partner and Pi think the journey of lyght is more about winning tests of mettle that it is covering distance," Rhi said. "I didn't really believe them until now. I'm meant to stop the war, I am."

Chukk just nodded in agreement, knowing this would not be the case. "Get there and get back. Report in as soon as your able. I can't send anyone to come looking for you so if it this goes sideways on you, Rhi, you're on your own. Understood?"

"Aye," Rhi replied. "I'm not one for goodbyes, so-"

POP!

She was gone in a blur of motion, leaving nothing but a swirling vapor cloud in her wake.

"That's going to come in handy," Chukk said, marveling at the bugle's speed. "That is, if she makes it back here in one piece."

Chukk turned to return to his barracks, where his battle plan parchments were waiting for him. He wondered how Dee was doing and prayed that the Spirit would somehow see to it that they might be reunited in the future. If the world couldn't be saved, Chukk would want no one else but Dee standing next to him on the field of battle squaring off against the MaRuu. Cunning and swift the MaRuu might be, but Chukk now had the advantage.

He had seen how they fought, coming in swarms of ten to twenty at a time and trying to encircle their prey, pushing them into one central location. But one on one, the Quasi, their raw strength, and their thick quilled armor, gave them the advantage. The battle would be strength versus speed, and now thanks to the return of Rhi, the Quasi would now have a way to communicate with each other faster than the MaRuu could attack.

Chukk allowed himself a small smile. Things were starting to look up.

***

Rex had been sitting on the edge of the Wisher's Well, the sweetwater reserve that provided HomeSpace with their drinking water, for what must be at least three dats by now. Watching the lyght veins underneath the surface of the water sparkle brought him great peace. It gave him time to quiet his mind and think back to how this had all started, for Rex had lost track of the beginning of the journey in all of this time travelling madness. His headache finally retreated, a newly resolute Rex was about ready to leave when he felt a paw on his shoulder, causing him to leap up, started. It was Ichabod.

"Don't worry, Rex," Ichabod said. "I'm not here to kill you, I promise."

"To be fair," Rex replied, "I rewound time before you could strike the blow, so there is that. I was on my way to find you regardless. Speak, Ichabod."

"You've been through so much in such a short amount of time," Ichabod replied. "I think your thoughts might be betraying you, Rex. I want to put this for rest once and for all. If I used to be the type of Quasi who was capable of such a terrible thing, I am not that Quasi now. I need you to believe that I only have the best of intentions in wanting to save our peoples, both Quasi and Bugle. How can we get past this?"

Rex rose from the rock ledge he had been sitting on. "I want you to pledge on the life of the Fallen, that you mean no one no harm. I also want to stay with you, share your burro, go where you go, and see and do what you do until this is all sorted, one way or the other. Agree to that, and we can move forward. Those are my terms."

"Can't you trust me, Rex?" Ichabod asked, pleadingly.

"No," Rex replied. "I don't think I can. And if you have nothing to hide, then my terms shouldn't be a problem, should they? So, are they, Ichabod?"

"I don't need to prove anything to you," Ichabod said. "This is foolhardy of you, Rex."

"Maybe, Ichabod," Rex said. "But I'm remembering I shouldn't be surprised. Count me out of your invasion."

"Er, excuse me?" Ichabod replied, caught off guard.

"You made my friend a murderer and then an instrument of war," Rex said. "You killed innocent people."

"What are you talking about?" Ichabod asked. "I have done no such thing!"

"But you will," Rex said. He tapped his forehead. "Remember me?"

"Wait, you-"

"Leapt ahead and back again," Rex said. "Three times now and nothing changes anymore. It all goes to pot. Whatever I say to convince you not to attack the MaRuu and not to use Rhi as your tool to do it, fails. And then I'm right back here, making a wish at the Wisher's Well. Only it never comes true. What a simple twist of fate, eh?"

"Rex, I-"

"Shut up," Rex interjected. "I've heard enough. You should leave them be, Ichabod. They only attacked us because we invaded their space. Space you knew to be theirs! But now, an all-out war?! And if you don't think you could kill me, I have news for you. You'll try again. But I'll save you the burden. I'm out. Done. I want no part of any of this. Leave me be and I'll gladly return the favor. And if you don't, we'll just be right back here again, only I'll be the only one to remember it. This was no gift from the Spirit I received. It's a bloody curse."

"But your sister-"

"Will die," Rex finished. "We all will. Thanks to you. So, I chose to spend my final days alone with my thoughts. Good night."

Rex pushed past Ichabod and into the darkness, leaving Ichabod, his jaw slack, to think on what he just heard. They had come too far!

No, this couldn't be. Give the lad time to rest and then bring his new friend, Chukk, with him to persuade Rex otherwise.

They truly needed him now more than ever. How else could they insure to win the upcoming offensive than to foresee every enemy parry? No, Rex would come to his senses. And Rhi? A weapon of war? What nonsense was Rex talking about?

Ichabod decided to give Chukk the Battler a visit. He would need to know what was said. Together, they could help Rex regain his mental balance and help him to see that this time, apparently, it would be different. If they could convince him to share what led to their failures and shortcomings in the other future timelines Rex had lived through, they could devise the perfect plan of attack now. But if he didn't? Well, Ichabod reasoned, they'd kill him to start the loop anew.

Only this time, Ichabod decided, Rex would not go back alone.

***

Rhi, to her thinking, was moving faster than life itself was happening. She tore through the Southlands at a clip that was so fast, she almost misrecognized where she was geographically. At this rate, Rhi knew she'd be catching up to Bor sooner rather than later. She was not incorrect in this assessment. She knew she'd been traveling for less than a dat, for that she was certain.

At this rate, Rhi could take care of Bor and be back to HomeSpace in time for a late slurp of her sweet, sweet Nectar. They would sit around the lyght fan in Pi's burro and be regaled with Rhi's tale of victory and honor, they would!

Tearing through the Winter Mountain Flats, Rhi saw the heavyweight Bor ahead of her and to the left. How such a slovenly, obese bugle could still keep himself in the air under all that weight was a mystery to Rhi. She was surprised Bor's wings hadn't snapped clean off yet.

Chukk instructed her to attack from the rear, wrap her strong arm around Bor's neck, and twist around and up. Easy peasy. Dead he'd be at the hands of Rhi, she thought. She slowed her herself to make sure her trajectory wouldn't bring her to a stop in front of Bor, ensuring that she would stop right behind him, make her move, and be done with it.

POP!

Bor turned just in time to see Rhi attack him, screaming. Throwing his hands up in self-defense, Bor found himself being grappled with incredible force. He was able to push Rhi off, sending her to the purple snow below. She landed with a thud, sending a puff of snow into the air where she landed. Bor changed direction, heading for a nearby cluster of bramble thicket where he could decide what to do next in response to her attack.

Rhi sprung back into the air. "Argh!"

She saw him heading for the bramble and knew this would provide Bor with a strong defensive position. Rhi had to reach him first!

POP!

Rhi flew as fast as she could to catch up to Bor, without realizing her velocity was faster than she thought it was...

SPLAT!

What happened, Rhi asked herself, feeling all of a sudden wet from head to toe. Coming to a stop, Rhi looked all around for Bor, who was nowhere to be found. She looked herself over. Rhi was covered in pink, bloody mucus. It's him, she realized. I flew right through Bor, killing him. And I didn't even feel it.

Rhi floated to the snow ground below, rubbing the purple snow over her arms, legs, and torso. I bloody exploded him, I did, she thought to herself. Unbelievable, but remarkable, as it was, Rhi felt dirty... and somehow, evil. She took a life while in flight, preparing to... take a life? She sighed heavily. "What am I? What have I become?" she asked aloud.

She waited for any answer, hoping the Spirit would speak to her as it had Pi. No response came. After Rhi had spent a long while wondering what to make of her situation, she decided it was best to return to HomeSpace. She rose into the air.

POP!

And Rhi was gone, leaving only the pulpy remnants of her enemy drizzled over the purple snow behind her. Flying as fast as her four crystal wings would take her, Rhi felt Bor's goopy remains hardening around her like a thick shell. It sickened her to no end. How was she supposed to revel in her first victory in battle with the innards of her prey covered all over her?

Oh, whatever, she had done it! Rhi averted a war and now knew she had it in her to take the life of any who might cross her simply by flying straight through them! She was a proper killer, she was!

"Wait a dit, I'm a killer," Rhi said. "I'm a killer?" What have I done?!

***

Rex stood, leaning against the main wall protecting the front HomeSpace gate. He watched and listened to the growing rumbles emanating from the lyghtning fields to the east. The thick cloud cover rumbled in time with bright yellow and orange lyghtning strikes in the distance. A soft but steady rain fell, drizzling his fur with moisture when the wind would whip up. He continued waiting for-

POP!

Rhi slowed to a stop, lowering herself to the wet ground in front of Rex. "Don't look at me, Rex. I'm a monster, I am."

Rex did not look away, but rather, locked eyes with Rhi. "I've seen it before and I'll probably see it again, Rhi. You'll get past this. You had no idea what it would feel like to take someone's life, especially by accidentally flying right through them, did you?"

"How, how do you know that?!" Rhi asked.

"Because you've told me before," Rex replied. "And if I don't get it right this time, you'll end up telling me again."

"I don't understand," Rhi replied. "Wait, you traveled into the future again, didn't you?"

"Aye," Rex said. "Problem is, I seem to be stuck in a loop. This is now my fourth time seeing you come back covered in the entrails of another Bugle. First three times, you sought me out looking for condolement after reporting into Ichabod and Chukk first. Thought I'd save you trying to find me this time and also try to find a way to delay the inevitable just long enough for Pi to complete the journey of light."

"What are you talking about, Rex?" Rhi asked. "You're freaking me out, you are."

"When they find out you can kill as fast as you can fly, they are going to convince you to be a weapon, Rhi. You'll tell me not a chance right now but let them ply you with enough nectar in the days ahead while you bask in your new role. Pretty soon, the idea of being a war hero will start sounding pretty good." Rex kicked a pebble with his rear paw.

Rhi stood there silently. "New role? You're crazy, Rex, you are. I wouldn't do that, and I won't kill anyone ever again."

"When the Quasi are pinned down behind enemy lines and their only hope is a little Bugle who can take out twenty MaRuu faster than her heart beats and who also blames them for the death of her parents," Rex replied, "you might surprise yourself. Trust me, Rhi, you want no part of this."

"Swear on Pi this is true," Rhi said.

"On Pi," Rex said. "It's all true. Which is why I'm begging you now to listen to me. We have to send you back where you came from. You don't belong here. You belong on the journey with Pi."

Rhi flew up and sat on the wall next to Rex. "Do I though? I mean, I didn't listen to her at the river and it got me booted back here. I offered to kill Bor without a moment's hesitation and now look at me. Maybe I am what you tell me I am, a heartless killer. Maybe that's all I was ever meant to be. I belong here with you, I do."

Rex sighed heavily. "Why am I even bothering at this point?"

"Don't say that!" Rhi replied. "Ichabod says your super important, he does!"

"Yeah," Rex replied, "to him and his maneuvering. Now that you've stopped the sentry and Bha's dead, that loop is closed. They... won't... come. But now Ichabod and Chukk, having seen what the MaRuu are capable of are going to take the fight to them to disastrous results."

"Is it a slaughter?" Rhi asked.

"You could say that," Rex replied.

"Do, do they defeat us?" Rhi asked.

"I don't know, Rhi," Rex said. "I don't make it to the end. But I've seen both sides have the advantage and the outcome is still the bloody, and I mean bloody, same."

There was silence. Rhi fidgeted with her little legs for a bit, know more uncomfortable than ever. Rex rose to leave.

"Listen," Rex said. "I think I know how we can send you back. It's not going anywhere. Go check in with Ichabod after you've cleaned yourself up and hear him out. After you've done that, for the first time in your life, stay sober and think about your options. Decide what you want to do and then find me. And if you decide to stay, don't say I didn't warn you."

"Why no nectar?" Rhi asked, puzzled.

"It clouds your judgement and it's a crutch you no longer need," Rex said. "I think anyone willing to do what you did tonight for the good of the whole HomeSpace doesn't need any liquid courage. You have the real thing. Good night, Rhi."

Rhi nodded. "Night, Rex. And... thanks, mate. Hey wait. Bha's dead?"

"Yeah," Rex said, walking away. "Ichabod had Chukk kill him. You all have blood on your paws. I'm just trying to stop there from being anymore."

Rex hopped away, leaving Rhi alone on the wall. No nectar? He must be crazy. But to call her courageous? Doubly so. But Rhi knew Rex well enough to know that whatever it was he said he saw, he did.

She wanted to believe him, but at the same time, she also felt the need to see what Ichabod had to say also. Rhi's first inclination was to grab a few drinks after she washed Bor's remnants off her, but Rex had a point about staying levelheaded. One night off nectar wouldn't hurt.

***

"That's... remarkable, Rhi," Ichabod said. "You say you killed him just by flying at your full velocity, er, through him?"

Rhi nodded. "Killed him, I did. Straight through. The MaRuu threat is done with. Finished. We can turn to other problems now."

Ichabod sized the bugle up. She seemed almost dazed, as cautious with her word choices. He sensed there was more Rhi wasn't telling him.

"You seem to be taking this all rather well, Rhi," Ichabod said. "Are you sure you're alright?"

Rhi wanted to trust the Quasi leader, truly she did. He seemed heartfelt and concerned but there was... something else behind his words of compassion. Her talk with Rex had made Rhi think in advance to question everything Ichabod might throw at her. Was she imagining this? Did she imagine her talk with Rex? Was she dead and was all of this a dream?

"Bit of a headache," Rhi replied. "And a twinge of a stomach ache but all in all, fit as a bugle. As you do, as they say."

"Good, good," Ichabod replied. "Chukk the Battler will be proud of his student. For that I am certain. How you, er, seen Rex at all?" In his mind, he was envisioning the next evolution of Quasi battle, led by a flying arrow spear.

"No," Rhi lied. "I'd like to though. He's family. I could use a fuzzy shoulder to cry on after all this."

153

Ichabod straightened. "Oh, Rhi Bugle, I think that might be unwise. You heard how he was before you left. Well, I'm afraid Rex's madness has only gotten worse. I fear for your safety, little one."

The short, bristly white hairs on Rhi's skin shot straight up. "What do you mean?"

"He's taken a turn for the worse," Ichabod replied. "Talking of things yet to come that never could be. He accused me of terrible things."

"Me too," Rhi blurted out without thinking. Damn, her mouth!

"Oh, please tell me," Ichabod replied. "That way we can help him, together."

Rhi did her best to think quickly. "He said you're going to get a lot of us killed fighting the MaRuu and that I would be... your weapon?" You just said exactly what he told you, Rhi, she cursed herself. Why did she drink all that nectar before coming in here?! She couldn't keep her thoughts straight. Rhi was blazingly drunk and tended not to be able to lie very well when that took place.

"I see," Ichabod replied. "Well, now. That is essentially what he told me. You don't believe it. Do you?"

"Not really," Rhi said, truth speaking. "Seems to me there's no room for doom and gloom, personally. We stopped the MaRuu. All's said and done now. We don't attack them, and they won't attack us. Seems pretty straightforward if you ask me."

"It is indeed," Ichabod replied. "The Quasi would only ever attack an enemy if they struck first. It is our way. And our Bugle friends would agree with that sentiment as well. You know Rhi, with Bha banished as a traitor, your people need a new leader. I think it should be you."

Rhi's eyes went wide. "Wait, what?"

"You're the first Bugle warrior ever and more notably, you've faced the Spirit of the Journey of Lyght," Ichabod said. "I can't think of a better candidate. Will you work with me, and Chukk also, to protect and serve the HomeSpace? Please don't hesitate in your reply!"

Rhi leapt up, flying to Ichabod with her hand out. She shook paw to hand. "I'm in!"

Ichabod smiled. "And I, as well as the Bugles, will be grateful for your service to our people. Welcome to leadership, Rhi, leader of the Eastern HomeSpace Bugles!"

"I just wish my mum and pa were here to see this," Rhi gushed. "They'd be so-"

"Proud," Ichabod said. "It is such a shame those MaRuu bastards chopped them down, the peaceful explorers looking to find us more lyght veins they were. Such a tragic loss, indeed."

Rhi's head was spinning. Rex was wrong, she decided. It was Ichabod and Chukk that would help her find her way again. She made her mind up. Rex was dead to her and that was that. Or at least until she sobered up. But for right now, Rhi felt the bliss of being ignorant towards him and his ramblings. She knew who she was and what she could or would do.

Ichabod raised the nectar jug in the air. "A celebratory drink, Rhi?"

Rhi smiled. She was home. And now, she was in charge. She would let no harm come to HomeSpace. She would protect them all. "Cheers!"

***

Rex sat alone. It wouldn't be long now. He sighed.

"By now, she must have caved... again." He buried his head in his paws and wept. "Right on schedule."

Leaning back on his cushions, Rex felt the timeline shift take place in his mind. He could now tell the differences immediately, no longer feeling any sense of disorientation or bewilderment. He was mentally sharp now, his abilities strengthening just as everything around seemed to be falling apart.

Rex's plan was in full effect now. He hoped the three prior loops had given him enough information to plot his course more wisely this time. He wanted them on their toes and to want him nearby. That way, he would know how Ichabod, Chukk, and Rhi were up to at all times. He just hoped he hadn't overplayed his anger.

Ichabod was the trickiest to read, as his character seemed to shift with each new timeline and at this point had become quite muddled to Rex. Ichabod's intentions seemed to shift with the tides. Was he an ally or a foe? Rex truly had no idea. But his desire to protect the Quasi by attacking the MaRuu was going to be disastrous, to the MaRuu. And that would bring about the end. The planet would rip apart at the seams around them, taking no mercy on anyone.

The first time around, Rex believed in Ichabod and Chukk but wound up seeing that they would all die. The second go round saw Rex having reservations and trying to see what they did wrong that upset the Spirit. They all died again. By the third time, Rex began to wonder if the attack was a good idea and found himself being blown up and the planet right along with him.

Rex's best guess right now was to put a stop to the attack before it ever took place, but it was still only a guess. For as flimsy as his intentions had been, Ichabod seemed dead set on the attack. It was if remembering what could have been was the same thing as what will be, and Rex had come to understand that just wasn't the case. Things were changing faster than he could remember them. Every indication was that Rex had been granted this ability to avert calamity, so why was he now so bad at it?

Rhi, Chukk had come to see, believed she was sent back for the wrong reason. She wasn't sent to kill anyone, Rex surmised. She was sent to save herself. Only as stubborn and drunk as she tended to be, Rhi just couldn't see it. Rex decided this before he was sent back the third time. It had to be her.

It was only after Rhi gave the rest of the Bugles her gift of speed and ordered them into the attack that the end drew near. If he could somehow convince her not to join the fight at all and return to her own timeline with the warning about the MaRuu ahead and behind them, hopefully it would be enough to correct their course.

Rex really thought he had said enough to change her mind. He began to cry. Why him? Why not someone like Ichabod? A leader? An elder? Anyone else for that matter?

Suddenly, a small shadow cast across him. Rex looked up to see Rhi hovering, wobbly in the burro entranceway. She appeared to be drunk. He sighed. Now she's going to tell me I'm dead to her... again.

"A Bugle never turns down nectar, Rex," Rhi said, burping. "But they also trust their friends."

This caught Rex off guard. He wasn't expecting that! Something changed! "What, really?!"

"Hear me out," Rhi said. "I went back and turned down Ichabod's offer to lead the Bugles. I left to go sleep this off and I thought about everything you said. Ichabod too. You both make good arguments, you do and at one point, I didn't think I ever wanted to see or hear from you again. But I don't trust him and for as much as we've squabbled through the planet turns, I love you, I do. I thought about it and I believe you Rex. I know you wouldn't steer me wrong. I'm sorry I doubted you... brother. I'm done doing things just because I want to."

Rex smiled. "You have no idea how glad I am to hear you say that, Rhi!" He cried tears of joy. "We have to find some way to get you back to where you came from, Rhi."

"You said you thought of a way?" Rhi asked.

"I lied," Rex replied. "Had to play my best berry bead game against you, Rhi. Hope you don't mind. I've been fighting a losing war over here."

Rhi sighed. "It's all right, Rex. Let me sleep this off here and we can attack this conundrum in the morning, we will."

"Sounds great, Rhi," Rex replied. "And thanks."

"For what?" Rhi asked.

"Listening to me," Rex said.

An indigo energy wave filled the space of the burro, washing over all of HomeSpace.

"You get those here too?" Rhi asked.

Rex smiled. "We do now. I'm proud of you. Now flop down over here and let's get some rest. We're both going to need it."

Rhi flew up, weaving from the nectar, and cuddled up next to Rex.

"Rhi?" Rex said.

"Yeah, Rex," she replied.

"Sleep well," Rex said, weary, "I'm very, very proud of you, Rhi."

Rhi didn't reply. She just smiled from antenna to antenna. She was proud of herself too. It was a nice feeling. And tomorrow, she told herself, no more nectar. It had caused her too many problems and on top of that, with all that was afoot, Rhi knew she had to be sharp and keep her wits about her.

Her drinking days were now behind her. She had mourned her parents for long enough. It was time to start living in the present and stop dwelling on the past.

Rhi knew, deep down, it was the only way she and the others would live to see a future.

***

"I don't like this," Chukk said. "He hasn't been wrong yet. Why doubt him now?" Something's wrong, he thought but didn't say.

Ichabod shrugged. "The Spirit only knows. How he could doubt me and all we have been through together; I just don't know. He's like another person. Mean spirited. Vengeful."

"This is Rex we're talking about, right?" Chukk asked. "Listen, if he says your plan fails, that means it failed and will fail again. It was foolhardy to think we should mount any type of attack. You saw how they fought. They were ruthless and ten times our speed and kill efficiency. We were lucky to escape that slaughter with our lives."

"But," Ichabod said. "Consider for a moment what has taken place today. Rhi Bugle returning from the Journey of Lyght to help us has given me an idea. A few ideas actually. With her speed, we could be in constant communication with each other, giving advice, sharing strategies, and avoiding danger. And if need be, she could rip through a MaRuu's heart in the blink of an eye. She will prove useful to us, I promise you that, Chukk. It must be why she is here; I'd bet my life on it."

"From the sounds of it," Chukk replied, "you did just that and we lose... three times in a row! How can you even be considering this at this point?"

"I expected more cunning and courage from you, Battler," Ichabod mused.

"Oh, I'm fine as I am," Chukk said. "You've been different ever since the battle. You sound as Rex described you when this all first began."

"I am my own Quasi," Ichabod replied. "As the Spirit wills it."

"Wills what, exactly?" Chukk replied, his anger growing with his leader. "What does that even mean?"

"That pup does not define who I am, who I was, or who I will be," Ichabod hissed. "I do. And I intend to everything in my power to keep our people safe from harm-"

"By leading them into a battle that does not need to be fought, got it," Chukk finished for him.

"How do we know they will not attack?" Ichabod asked. "How can we be certain that only one sentry was sent? We can't, can we now?"

"No, we can't," Chukk replied. "So, until we know for certain the MaRuu mean us harm, the Battlers will remain on the ready. We'll extend our patrols out to the southern border and out as far as Rock's Crest. HomeSpace seems sturdy now but if there was to be another Sun Shock in those lyghtning fields up there, we'd have to evacuate all over again. And that apparently, leads us right into MaRuu territory."

"It's not their territory!" Ichabod exclaimed. "They stole it from us! We should have been safe on that caravan! They had no reason to attack us!"

"But they haven't," Chukk reminded Ichabod. "And without that sentry letting them know about it, we probably could have passed through it undetected on our way to the other HomeSpace. I still think that's our best bet. But I'm no gambler."

"If Pi and the others are successful," Ichabod said, "we will be on Arkelia for another thousand planet turns with the MaRuu ready to slice us down and exterminate us. Now that I have seen first-hand what they plan on doing, expanding their dominion and eradicating those who cross them, I have decided that it is in the Quasis' best interest to eliminate the threat before the threat eliminates us."

"Not with the Battlers you won't," Chukk replied. "I may report to you, but they report to me. We will not attack first. Is that clear?"

There was a short, awkward silence between them. Suddenly, Ichabod reached his paw out for a shake.

"You offer a fair deal, Battler," Ichabod answered. "Agreed. We will only mount attack if the MaRuu attack us first."

"Good," Chukk said, shaking Ichabod's paw. "I'm glad we're in agreement. Now let me find Rex and calm him down. His nerves must be in tatters right about now."

Chukk left Ichabod alone in his chambers. The elder scratched his head and hopped back and forth, almost frantically. He seemed at odds with himself.

"I'm right on this," Ichabod whispered. "I know I am. I just need a plan and then they'll understand. They need me to lead them, not him."

He wondered what they would think of him if they knew he, like Rex, was also from the original timeline of events and remembered everything from when this all first started. His game with Pi and Rex was closing in on him and it would take all his mettle to help them see that his way was the true way to a better existence.

He felt no remorse for deceiving them. With Rex apparently sharing the same gift from the Spirit, Ichabod could better gauge his own actions. Little did they know how many times it had taken him to get them this far. He was getting closer to stopping Rex and his attempts to stop the upcoming battle. Rex was incorrect in thinking the Quasi would lose at the hands of the MaRuu. Rather, the Quasi would be victorious over them.

He had seen how this all would end and the only place that would remain livable on the planet after the Journey of Lyght would be the

SouthLands where the MaRuu were now. One of the three last species left on Arkelia would have to go and that would be the MaRuu. Although he hadn't been able to leap ahead or behind in time since giving the Arkelian to Pi, Ichabod reasoned that the future he had foreseen was inevitable as he alone was the High Elder and Keeper of Secrets. There was no way he could be wrong. He was unquestionable.

He would let Rex and the others dither about trying to avert the conflict, but Ichabod had already planned on how to stop them. When he was ready to initiate that course of action, the Quasi people would once again rally behind him with unadulterated support for a military campaign. Ichabod smiled. He couldn't lose!

7

"We want you to take the leadership role, Rhi," Rex said.

Rhi, huddled under Pi's woven blankets, continued to shiver uncontrollably. "I can't bloody take much more of this, Rex. I feel like I'm dying, I am. Why are you talking about this now?"

Rex brought her a fresh mug of root tea, holding it to Rhi's small, quivering lips, as she took a long sip. "You're in withdrawal from nectar. You'll feel better soon. I promise. You just need to keep taking in tea to help cleanse your system. You need to be clear headed and strong to stand beside Ichabod as the leader of the Bugles, so I'll know what he's up to. Here, have some more."

Rhi took another big gulp of the warm tea. It reminded her of better days spent with Pi at Addy's bedside, chattering on about the boys and other trivial things. How she missed those days... and Pi. Her teeth were chattering less now but she still felt so weak and shaky. It was if every drop of nectar she had ever drank was now coming back to haunt her. Rhi was miserable.

"So, you want me to take the job, do you?" Rhi asked, after Rex helped her finish off the mug of warm liquid. "Why the change?"

"It was Chukk's idea," Rex answered. "Whatever you did by standing up to Ichabod had a positive effect on the timeline, Rhi. It brought Chukk back into the lyght and I already told you it helped me see there might be ways through this for us. All hope wasn't lost, after all. Thanks to you."

Rex placed the mug down on the ground next to her, lifting himself from the cushions to fetch a fresh pot of root tea for her. "What I can't figure out is Ichabod. He seems to blow with the wind as far as all this is concerned. It's almost like he's somehow sailing through the timelines like... oh, I don't know. But he's dead set on us going to war with the MaRuu. I wish I had been seeing the timelines this clearly since the beginning. It would have made all of this so much easier."

"Don't be hard on yourself, Rex," Rhi said. "But if you two think I should do it, then I'll do it. I'll lead my people... hopefully to safety, that is. How's that tea looking? I feel like I could drink the entire Shining Sea, I do."

"Coming right up," Rex said, returning with the kettle. As he filled up her mug, Rex looked her in the eyes. "I'm really proud of you for kicking your nectar habit, Rhi. You're one strong Bugle."

"All it ever did was dull my senses and get me into easily avoidable trouble," Rhi replied. "Let me try on my own, eh?"

Rex gently extended the mug to Rhi's shaking little hands. She took hold of the mug. When Rex knew she had it completely in her grasp, he let go of it. He was pleased to see that Rhi was able to hold onto it on her own. She was getting stronger, for certain. Rex was glad to see it.

Rhi had been under his care for three days now and from when she had begun the process of denectarication to know, she had been through terrible bouts of both physical and mental illness while the nectar worked its way out of her system. The root tea acted as a calming remedy that lessened the effects of withdrawal, but Rhi had shown just how tough she truly was through this arduous process by not complaining about her ordeal even once. She seemed to accept that her near constant nectar drinking had made her body functions almost need it to exist, and for that reason, ceasing its intake would take a heavy toll on her.

"You know," Rhi said, after draining this newest cup of tea, "I was starting to think the nectar was what gave me my newfound gift of speed, I did. Silly, aye?"

Rex smiled. "Not at all. But I highly doubt it. For all we know, giving up nectar might even make you fly faster."

"I don't see how that would be possible," Rhi huffed. "I bloody flew right through someone without even feeling it, I did. Any faster and I think I might be the one to pop."

Rex chuckled. "Well, at least you haven't lost your sense of humor without the nectar coursing through you."

"Hope that's a good thing, I do," Rhi said. She allowed herself a smile. "How long until these jitters run their course?"

"Not much longer now, I reckon," Rex said. "With root tea and rest, you should be back buzzing around by tomorrow morning."

"I'm worried about Pi," Rhi said. "She was getting upset before I left. Oh, I should have listened to her more."

"Upset?" Rex said. "What did she say that makes you think that?"

"Nothing," Rhi replied. "She got all quiet on us. You've seen her get like that when she feels like she's lost control of a situation. You know how she gets."

"Frustrated and angry," Rex replied. "Not a good way to be on a journey of lyght, is it?"

"It's strange, it is, Rex," Rhi said. "We were feeling like the journey hadn't even really started yet, but the last time Dee showed us the map, we we're nearly to the end of it. None of it was making much sense, I tell you. It was trying all of us. But Scout and Dee both had these choices they made that made them feel better, so there is that."

"What choices, Rhi?" Rex asked, now very curious.

After asking for a minute to relieve herself and also for more tea when she returned, Rhi walked Rex through all they had encountered on the journey thus far and how the events had seemed to improve the characters of both Scout and then Dee.

"It explains the timeline shifts better," Rex said. "Whatever the four of you were doing, it was changing things both before, here in the present, and hopefully, the future to come. It means you were succeeding. It must explain the energy waves too. Heck, even you deciding to think before you act and coming back here to me had an effect. Crazy. We're changing the fabric of who we are and what we're capable of, Rhi. You being here must be a part of the journey, your part counts just as much as the rest. You must see that now."

"When did you get all, and nothing personal intended, wise and smart, Rex?" Rhi asked.

Rex smiled sheepishly. "I've grown up a lot in a short period of time, not that time seems to matter much anymore. Everything it seems, is relative."

"You know, Ichabod sure knew a lot about what you've been going through, hasn't he? Why do you think that is?"

"Now that's a good question, Rhi," Rex said. "Beyond reading ancient texts, something is telling me Ichabod knows a lot more about what's happening than he's letting on. He's been too wishy washy. And you're right, he does seem to know a lot about being the star. Makes me wonder how it was he came to pick Pi and set you all off in such a hurry. Do you have the memory of him opposing Addy's sending that you three should go with her? Because now I do."

"I didn't pay much attention back then, Rex," Rhi admitted. "I've been more drunk than sober in my life up to now, but I believe you if you say that's how he was. Somehow, I just know you're telling me your truth. I can almost just feel it. Who would have thought Rex the Jokester would become Rex the Wise, eh?"

"From the sounds of it, stranger things have happened," Rex replied. "Which leads me to how you got here. You say you were flying across a river of lyght energy fueled water?"

Rhi nodded. "I could feel the ambient energy coursing through me, I did. Why?"

"Because when the time comes," Rex said. "I think I just figured out how to send you back and I don't think you're going to like it very much."

"Tell me!" Rhi barked. "I need to get back to the journey, Rex!"

Rex sighed. "You sure you want to hear this? It's just an idea."

"Yes!" Rhi replied.

"I think if you fly into the lyghtning fields at full speed," Rex said. "We can send you back to the future."

Rhi couldn't help but laugh. "Rex the Jokester, you are! Too funny, mate, too funny! I'd be fried to a bloody crisp!"

Rex shrugged. "It has to be tied to the lyght energy, Rhi. Think about it. Without the lyght energy, the planet and all of us on it would die. It binds us all together. And it's been changing. We only ever saw yellow energy but now it flickers orange and red. You saw that indigo energy wave. I think the lyght energy itself is what's guiding your journey, not a Quasi Spirit of the Dead. Look, it's just a theory at this point, okay?"

Rhi could tell she had bristled Rex's fur with her laughing. "Rex, I didn't mean to laugh, mate. And we have time to think about it and figure it out. Wait a dit…"

Rex noticed the puzzled look on her face. "Rhi, what is it?"

Rhi cleared her throat. "I was about to say that I can't be here when I get back or there'd be twice as much of me to handle but then I remembered I'm not coming back. Am I?"

"Hey, look at me," Rex said. "I have news for you. Ichabod has not been trustworthy as far as I can tell. For all we know, he said that to scare you four. How would he know? No one ever passed the first marker, remember? You're beating the odds every dit of every day they remain out there fighting the good fight. Who knows, maybe there's a chance that there's a happy ending in this for all of us."

Rhi nodded. "I sure hope so, I do. Now if you'll excuse me, I have to tinkle again." She flew towards the refuse room.

Rex laughed. "At least some things never change."

***

Some things never changed, Ichabod thought as he watched Rhi take a long pull from her nectar jug. "How's the nectar these days?"

Rhi wiped her lips. "Good as always, it is. So, you'll let me lead the Bugles as long as I let you know what Rex and Chukk are up to?"

"Aye," Ichabod said. "Those two have lost their mettle, Rhi Bugle. To keep us all safe, I need to know if they mean the Quasi and Bugles harm. Their confusion as of late confounds me."

"Well," Rhi said, "I've got mettle to spare, I do. And that's fine by me. Look at what following Pi got me, sent back here the worse for wear, it did."

"I was honest when I told you I thought you four you would not return," Ichabod replied. "But look, here you are, Rhi. Just in time to help me reign in the herd and protect us from harm. The Spirit must have seen your true potential."

"Thank you, I do," Rhi replied. "So, what do you want me to do first?"

"I want you to allow me to help your people become more than what they are, Rhi Bugle," Ichabod said calmly. "I want to make them able to defend themselves as well as you."

Rhi took a swig from her nectar jug. "And how will are you going to do that?"

Ichabod smiled. "We're going to share your Spirit gift of speed with the rest of the Bugles."

Rhi almost dropped her jug before composing herself. "What now?"

"We will harness the yellow lyght energy and bind you all together with it," Ichabod said. "When the same energy course through all your bodies, so will your gift of speed. The Bugles will be our greatest defense against a MaRuu attack, Rhi. I've been waiting for this day for a long time."

"What does that mean?" she asked, nonchalantly taking another pull from her nectar jug.

"It means we must prepare for the MaRuu," Ichabod said. "Are you doubting me?"

"Oh no, not at all," Rhi said. "I'm just a curious Bugle. You should know that. We're all itchy and scratchy for the truths behind the truth."

"A truer sentiment was never said," Ichabod replied. "I am sorry I doubted your conviction, little one. We must act quickly. The MaRuu are in front of Pi and the rest on the journey to the Spirit and if the MaRuu arrive to the Spirit first, all will be lost. Once all the Bugle can fly as fast as you, we'll send you back through the cave and on your way to saving them while the rest of the Bugle can help us lead the impending MaRuu attack."

"Er, what now?" Rhi asked, utterly confused at this point. "What attack?"

"I received word from the scouts that they were attacked by the MaRuu in the Southlands just a short time ago," Ichabod said. "That is an act of war against us."

"Wait," Rhi said. "Who? Which ones?" How many?"

"Those are not questions for you to ask, Rhi," Ichabod replied. "My intelligence is sound. All Quasi Battlers cannot help but heed the call. I am on my way there after we're done here. So, are we done here?"

"I didn't write anything down," Rhi replied, "so just to make sure I'm clear, we're electrifying all the Bugles with my speed and then taking off to attack the MaRuu?"

"Because they attacked us first," Ichabod added. "Yes, that is correct. I will have the materials I need to give the Bugles your power by the moon rise tonight. Tell them to join you in my outer chamber then. And Rhi, please know you made the right choice. You've saved both the Quasi and MaRuu from utter destruction in trusting me. Thank you, little one."

Rhi nodded. "You know me. Drink first, think never. I trust you, Ichabod, I do."

***

"I don't trust him!" Rhi barked. "Not in the least!"

Chukk looked to Rex and then back to Rhi. "He bought that you were still drinking nectar?"

Rhi nodded. "Aye. I drank enough tea in front of him to make me piss for a week, I did."

"How does he know there are MaRuu in front of Pi and the others?" Chukk asked.

"Because he's lived through it," Rex said.

"Wait, what now?" Rhi asked.

"That makes two of us," Chukk said. "What?"

"I think Ichabod has what I have," Rex replied. "I think he's got the gift of the star, or at least, used to. I think he's seen the future too, only we're steering away from it and he doesn't like it very much."

"You know," Chukk said. "That would make sense, wouldn't it?"

"But not this impending future," Rex finished. "He's basing his decisions off old information and it's going to get a lot of folks killed."

"I don't follow?" Chukk asked.

"I think Ichabod used to be the eternal star," Rex said. "I'd reckon each High Elder has been. But somehow, his power got transferred to me. I get the feeling that he's probably also from the original timeline from when this all started but I don't think he can loop back anymore. That's why he's been so dependent on me. You see, before Rhi found her mettle, this all ended differently. I wasn't privy to what he was planning. Rhi and you weren't on my side. He kept killing me to restart the loop when the end came. He saw he had failed and couldn't accept it. But now, now I think we stand a good chance at getting past this."

"The end?" Rhi asked.

Rex sighed. "I said that didn't I?"

"Yeah you did," Chukk replied. "Spill it. What happens?"

"We invade," Rex said. "They repel us. The Bugles get sent in. The Quasi are victorious-"

"So, we win?" Chukk blurted out.

"Not so fast," Rex replied. "It won't matter. I've seen it both ways. They win. We lose. We win. We lose. Either way, the end comes for all of us."

"I'm sorry, Rex," Rhi said. "But I don't understand?"

"Somehow, someway," Rex said. "It has to do with Pi. She needs to not join the fight. I've seen her fight and win, and I've seen her fight and lose. Which means, to me anyways, that she needs to not fight at all, Rhi. And that's your mission. We're going to send you back to the future with a simple message: the enemy is behind you and in front of you but somehow find a way not to fight them."

Rhi shook her head. "Not possible. You know your sister better than me. She's a feisty one, she is."

"I have to agree with the bugle," Chukk said. "You're surrounded by MaRuu? You fight, no question."

"Look," Rex said. "I don't know how much longer I'm going to be able to loop back! For all I know, this could be it. I treat every time like it could be last. Otherwise, I think I would have given up by now. My sister, a bundle full of pain and logic, is the one chance we have to save this planet from collapsing in on itself! She needs to find a way. She needs to find peace for herself and for the planet. Pi has never gotten over the death of our parents on that stupid expedition, just like you with yours. But now look at you Rhi! You're clear headed and thinking things through! Anything is possible!"

"What are you saying, Rex?" Chukk asked.

"I'm saying that Pi holds the key to all this," Rex replied. "She just doesn't yet. That's where you come in, Rhi."

"How?" Rhi asked.

"She has to figure it out on her own," Rex said.

"Figure what out?" Rhi asked. "You're not making any sense, Rex!"

Rex leapt up. "I don't know! Because I haven't seen it! We all die, Rhi! We all die! All of us, Quasi, Bugle, and MaRuu!"

Chukk put his paw on Rex's shoulder. "Calm down, Rex. We're still here."

"Yeah," Rex said. "Now. But we'll end up just like I saw before, dead but you'll be gone, and I'll be right back here trying to find another way around it. Do you think I'm enjoying this? Do you think I like being caught in a loop that watches me die seeing all of you in mortal pain and there's nothing I can do about it?"

"But you said this time was different," Rhi said, in a near whisper. "You said we could find a way."

Rex collected himself, realizing he had gone too far. "I'm, I'm sorry. Neither of you deserve that. It's just, it's hard, you know?"

Chukk took hold of Rex, embracing him. "I can't even imagine, mate. But you're here now and we're with you. We can bring this to a close, together."

Rhi flew up, joining in the embrace. "It's okay, Rex. This times different. Now you have us and we're not going anywhere."

Rex gently broke free of their grasp. "But that's just it, Rhi. That's what's going to be different. You're going back to the future."

"Why is that different?" Rhi asked.

"Because we've never tried it before, Rhi," Rex replied. "It could kill you."

"Or it could make us all stronger," Rhi replied. "I'm game, Rex. I am. Through the lyghtning fields, you say?"

Rex nodded.

"Let's go then," Rhi replied. "I'm not one to wait on eternity. It waits on me."

Chukk nodded. "Now that's the Battler way. I'm with you, little one."

Rex wiped a few tears that had formed from his eyes. "I love you two, I truly do. Don't change again, okay? I love you two just as you are, right now."

The three embraced once more.

***

They stood underneath a rainy, thunderous sky, as orange and red lyght flickered across their faces with each new lyghtning burst that rose from the planet's core and subsequently slammed back underneath the surface. This was the closest any of them had ever stood to the lyghtning fields, and the moment was not lost on any of them. Rhi looked first to Chukk and then to Rex. They both looked as solemn as she felt.

"This doesn't work," Rhi said, "and I'm counting on you two to find a way to make this work without me."

"This works," Rex said, "and I won't know what comes next. It has to, Rhi, it has to."

"Either way," Chukk said, "Don't worry about us here. My Battlers won't go into anything without my okay. And I'm in no way okay with Ichabod or his plans. We stand a chance, Rhi Bugle."

Rex looked sadly to Chukk. "He's going to kill us both, Chukk. You know that."

"He can try," Chukk said. "Have hope, Rex. Good will prevail."

"But how?" Rhi asked.

Rex smiled. "Guess you'll have to tell us after the fact. Go on, Rhi.

Remember, the MaRuu are ahead and behind. She has to find a way not to fight them. Fly as fast as you can right over the lyghtning. Don't stop for anything. Go!"

Rhi wanted to say more but knew there was nothing left to say. Instead, she nodded. And then-

POP!

Rhi appeared out of nowhere, flying straight towards Pi and the others, who appeared to be... on a boat? When and where the bloody hell was she? She came crashing down right beside Pi in the vessel.

"Rhi!!!" Pi cried out, reaching down to scoop her friend up in her paws to hug her lovingly. "We thought we lost you forever, you stupid, stubborn, beautiful little Bugle!"

***

"What am I supposed to do with that?" Pi asked. "It's not much to go on, Rhi."

"All I've said is all I can say, Pi," Rhi answered. "The MaRuu are in front of us. You have to find a way not to fight them. Rex was very clear on this."

"The fact that Rex was clear on anything is itself something to be questioned," Pi replied. "Come on, there must be more. Tell us. Tell me."

Rhi knew she was beginning to waiver. They had been on the river for over a day now, with no signs of anything except more and more of the vibrant color plants cascading on both sides of the river of lyght's shores. Pi was growing antsy, she could tell.

"Look," Rhi said," all I know is what I saw and what I've told you. It will be enough, I'm sure. Rex is on his game, he is."

This talk of Rex holding supernatural powers over time gave Pi reason to doubt that Rhi hadn't lost her mind when whatever happened to her happened. None of it was adding up to make much sense, if you asked her. Pi thrived on making sense of things and none of this was computing in any way. They had been on a near loop discussing Rhi's message from the past, but Pi had to admit that Rhi was stone cold sober, and that was enough to give pause and listen.

"So, you were in the past, things happened, and Rex sent you back here to help me figure out how to *not* fight the MaRuu that are closing in on us," Pi said.

"Exactly," Rhi replied. "Now you're making sense of it, you are!"

"I don't think you're getting anywhere," Dee said.

Pi covered her head in her paws. "Rhi, you're not doing us any favors."

"I am, I am!" Rhi replied. "If you knew what I saw with Ichabod, you wouldn't be doubting me like this, you wouldn't!"

Pi's ears pricked up. "What about Ichabod?"

"Oh dang," Rhi replied. "I shouldn't have said that, I shouldn't."

"Sounds to me as if we're only getting a part of the story," Scout said. "Come on Rhi, you might as well tell us because, according to you, it already happened in the past, now didn't it?"

Rhi hadn't thought about it like that. There didn't seem to be any way around this, either. Maybe telling them would help?

She spent the next few dits telling her fellow journeyers of everything that happened and all she came to know from Rex, Chukk, and Ichabod since Rhi left them. By the time she was done, the other three Journeyers seemed nothing less than numb at all Rhi had said. Maybe she should have held some back?

"They can't put this kind of pressure on me," Pi whispered loud enough for the rest to hear her. "I can't be the only thing standing in between here and the end. Can I?"

"And what about me?" Dee said. "He didn't mention anything about me playing any part in this. I don't believe it."

"Seems we've played our part, mate," Scout said. "Who says we haven't done our part already? Right, Rhi?"

Rhi was flustered to no end. What had Rex been thinking? Of course, she had to tell them. "You all realize that everything I said happened in the past, right? We hadn't fought anyone yet. I didn't weaponize the other Bugles either."

"So?" Pi asked.

"That means we're still in it, Pi," Rhi said. "Whatever happened, well, happened and we're still here floating down this river, aren't we? What I'm saying is that whatever happened back then didn't happen to us now, did it?"

There was a long silence.

"She's right," Pi said, finally. "Our fate isn't theirs, whenever or whatever that may be. We stay true and we stay strong. We go on."

"Like we have a choice?" Dee asked, pointing to the river beneath them. "Seems we're going wherever this goes, doesn't it? We're sure can't steer with the current as strong as it is."

"Maybe we're not supposed to steer," Pi said. "As if we've been in any control since this all began. Maybe it's a test or maybe it's just a metaphor for how helpless I, er, we all are in this."

Rhi looked up at Pi. "Come on now, Pi. You don't mean that."

"Oh, I don't know anymore, Rhi," Pi replied. "I want to say we can guide our fate but the further we go and the more I see and hear, the more I think this is just our destiny, our fate. For all we know, we'll never face the Spirit and just be on this quest for the rest of our lives. Ever think of that? What if this is all there is and while were stuck in here running to and fro chasing wavy lines on some ancient map, those promised thousand planet turns are taking place out there at the same time?"

"Wow, that was deep," Scout said. "I only caught half of it, love, but I think you're thinking too much about it. Sometimes you just have to do like the map says and go with flow. Have some faith."

"In what, exactly," Pi asked. "I feel like we've been fooled, Scout. That this is just some trick somehow. I don't trust what I don't know and none of this is making any bloody sense anymore."

"What did you expect?" Dee asked. "Because, personally, I had no idea what we we're getting into when we went into that cave. But I knew I believed that you believed you were the one to save us. I still believe that, Pi. The real question is, do you?"

Pi did not respond. She sat down in the front of the boat, turning her back to the others. She was angry, but not with them. She was mad at the Spirit, and now, Ichabod, and anyone or anything else that meant her or her people harm. Pi wished she could just wield her blade and slice all the evil from the world in one foul swoop, vanquishing them all. Gah! She was so angry with the world!

Pi scratched at the Arkelian draped over her chest. It was if she could feel the energy contained within it coursing through her now, fueling her desire to see this come to an end. Pi just wanted to find the Spirit and be done with it at this point. Suddenly, bright red energy shot out of the Arkelian, it's formerly violet stone coloring now a bright red, throwing Pi to the back of the boat as the energy shot up in the air in all directions.

"What did you do?!" Rhi called out, shielding her eyes. "The MaRuu! They're going to see that, Pi!"

Pi couldn't make it stop, as she and the others tried covering the powerful beam of red energy emanating from the decorative chest piece. And then, as soon as it started, the energy ceased to exist any longer, leaving all in the boat stunned into a shocked silence. Pi took the Arkelian off, wrapping it in the small blanket she kept tucked in her pouch.

"I don't know what that was, I swear!" she said.

"I think I do," Dee said. "It was a homing signal. That just lit up the sky, Pi. If there any MaRuu out there, they're sure to know we're coming now. I think we just lost the element of surprise."

"I think it means that wherever we're going," Scout said, "we're almost there."

"What makes you say that?" Rhi asked.

"Because we've stopped moving," Pi replied.

Dee pointed to the horizon in from of them. "Look at those mountains! I swear they weren't there a dit ago!"

"And look to the far shore," Pi said, motioning with her front paw. "I don't remember there being snow cover a dit ago either."

The landscape had seemingly morphed around them while the Journeyers weren't looking. All around them now were purple, snow covered, tree lined hilly forest thickets heading towards the rocky mountains now visible in the distance. Blankets upon blankets of snow, no less. They each marveled at the scene while getting their bearings by spinning around to look in all directions.

"Well," Rhi said. "I guess there's your answer, Pi. Maybe the Spirit was listening."

"But is that a good thing or a bad thing?" Scout asked.

"Only one way to find out," Pi replied. "Dee, those mountains sure look to me like the next drawings on the map. I'm thinking the energy blast from the Arkelian was the red line going towards them. Can you two steer us towards the side towards the mountains?"

Dee and Scout lifted their oars and maneuvered the boat to the shore. Pi spent little time hopping out onto the snowy ground and trudging off in direction of the mountains, as Rhi buzzed right behind her. While Pi was anxious to see what they would encounter next, Rhi wanted to get off the boat as quickly as possible for fear she might be sent back in time again. Also, Rhi was growing concerned that Pi was acting a bit too eager to move ahead before weighing their options. Rhi's newfound sense of caution was in full effect.

"Careful, Pi," Rhi cautioned. "Let's make sure the lads get off the boat safely before we go stomping off through the snow, aye?

Pi came to a stop. "Rhi, did I just hear you advise caution? You really have come back to us different, haven't you?"

Rhi smiled. "Not different, better. I can think clearly now, you see."

"And I'm not?" Pi asked.

Scout and Dee hopped out and pulled the boat out of the lyght river.

"We might still be needing the boat," Scout said, throwing his oar down on the snowy ground.

Dee looked around. "I think we should send it down the river. According to Rhi, we're not the only ones out here. Remember?"

"That's a good point," Pi said. "But still we might need it also. I say we leave it here. Pull it up further and then let's get into the snow forest. Looks like we have quite the hike in front of us."

"It's your call," Scout said. "On it."

Scout took hold off the heavy boat with one paw and dragged it further up the shore and away from the water's edge. Dee pulled out the map and was studying it. Rhi flew over to a small rock and set herself down to sit.

"From here you go," Dee read, "through the forest of snow. Face your wrath when the winds do blow."

"The MaRuu," Pi said. "It must mean them."

"Well, hopefully we can avoid them," Scout said. "Do have any idea how many, Rhi? Did Rex say?"

Rhi shook her head. "Not that I can remember. Just that they were on the path ahead of us. Apparently, Rex heard it from the MaRuu during the attack on the herd that ended up not happening. If that makes any sense."

"I won't be running away from them," Dee said. "If they're looking for a fight, they'll get one. Battlers don't run away."

"Says the guy who wanted to bail on us," Pi said. "Let me guess, whatever happened when that orange energy shot out made you see the error of your ways?"

"Yeah, Pi," Dee said. "It did. I was wrong back there. I've already said I was sorry. Do I need to say it again?"

"Forget it," Pi huffed. "Let's just get going. I think I see our way." She pointed to the purple snow behind Dee where there was now a red stoned path leading into the thick forest woods.

"That wasn't there before," Rhi said. "Just like how the blue one showed up. It must be the way ahead."

"Only one way to find out," Pi said. "Let's go, shall we?"

Pi began heading for the path before anyone could answer. Dee and Scout exchanged looks of concern while Rhi flew to follow Pi. Although they didn't say it aloud, both could sense Pi's growing sense of frustration and anger. Scout had an idea.

"Hey Pi, love," Scout said, catching up to her. "The Arkelian stone was yellow when you first got it. Now it's turned red. What if it might be having some sort of effect on you?"

"What type of effect?" Pi asked hastily. "What are you trying to say, Scout?"

"Er, look," Scout replied, "maybe I could hold onto it for a little while. I think it might be getting you all sorts of jumpy. It's not like you to huff and puff like this."

Pi looked from Scout to the others. "Do you all think I'm behaving... poorly towards you?"

While Rhi shook her head no, Dee stepped towards Pi. "I think Scout might have a valid point. Let him tuck it in his pouch for a while. At worst, it will lighten your load for a spell. It couldn't hurt."

Pi knew she was feeling angry and bitter, but to realize that the others had noticed it too gave her pause. She reached into her pouch and removed the wrapped Arkelian. Pi held it out to Scout. He took the parcel and shoved it in his pouch, a sense of relief on his face.

"I think you might be right," Pi said. "I've been feeling low and resentful because it seems like everyone has played a part so far except for me. I'm supposed to be the Chosen one and it's like I'm just here existing. I don't mean to sound ungrateful for the help or selfish wanting all the glory for myself, but it's been getting harder and harder to think the world even needs me to save it anymore. I despair because deep down, I've been yearning to feel like I belong since Rex and I lost our parents to the expedition. I strive for perfection because I think it will make the bad thoughts go away but more just keep on coming. I don't really ever think I'm good enough for anything or anyone. It boggles my mind anyone could even love me."

Scout took Pi in his paws for a big hug. "I love you, Pi. Want to know how much?"

Pi was crying now. "How much?"

"More than you'll ever know," Scout replied, smiling. "More than life itself too. Want to know why?"

"Why?"

Scout looked Pi in the eyes, his big brown saucers fixed on her sparkling, wet-eyed topaz ones. "Because you never, ever give up. Not on anything. So, you better not start giving up now. I'm betting the Spirit saved the best for last. The rest of us would be quaking on our hind paws thinking the biggest obstacles would be saved for us alone, but you? You can't wait to conquer them and save us all. But to do that, Pi, you've got to save yourself first, love. Do this for you, not just for us. Start with your own heart and the rest of us will follow. But that doesn't have to mean you do it alone. That's why the three of us are here: to help you. Why? You have nothing left to prove to anyone, most importantly yourself because you're worthy of light and love. Because that's what you share with us every day. Don't let that go away. You are already everything you ever wanted to be and more. You, Pi, are enough, just as you are."

Pi's tears had dried up. She wiped their remnants away with her paw. She looked up into Scout's eyes and then looked to Rhi and Dee. "You really think so?"

"We know so," Rhi said. "But I think what Scout is saying is, do you?"

Pi smiled. "I do now. I'm grateful to each of you for everything you've done so far and I'm sorry for how I acted. I was being foolish."

"I think the Arkelian amplified your emotions somehow," Dee said. "When it sent out that beam of red lyght energy, were you thinking bad thoughts by any chance?"

Pi nodded sheepishly. She felt shameful that her bad behavior could cost them their lives. "If my anger in some way gets us all killed-"

"Nope," Scout said, cutting her. "You're not blaming yourself. It's not allowed. Just let it be, Pi."

"Now that we're all back on track," Dee said. "Let's hit the trail and find out what lies ahead, eh?"

"I like that idea," Pi said. "Let's go."

As they made way for the path and entered into the snowy forest, Pi tried to shake the feeling of anger from herself but found it difficult. She had been angry ever since finding out that her parents had been killed when she was a pup. After that day, nothing was every truly good ever again. And the thought of facing the MaRuu who were responsible gave Pi a growing sense of vengeance that could not be abated. All Pi had ever wanted in life was revenge for those responsible for destroying her family and now, it looked like she just might get it. Secretly, Pi was happy the beacon had gone out, not that she would share that with the others. She allowed herself a smile.

"Feeling better?" Rhi asked Pi.

"With every new hop we take," Pi replied.

***

News of the attack on the Ichabod's leapers spread quickly and Chukk found himself out of favor with the Battlers for his cautious sentiment. Looking down at the shackles around his paws, he silently cursed Ichabod for having him jailed for his defiance and for helping Rhi escape to parts unknown. He heard scuffling outside and guessed what was about to happen. When the stockade cell's heavy door creaked open, Chukk saw that he was spot on with his guess.

"Hey there, Rex," Chukk said as his partner in alleged crime was brought in by the two patrol guards.

"Hello, Chukk," Rex said as they sat him down on the ground next to the Battler. "Told you it wouldn't take long."

Chukk leaned back against the wall, waiting for the guards to leave, closing the heavy door behind them. The two Quasi now sat in near complete darkness. Rex let out a low sigh.

"How are we looking?" Chukk asked.

"I told you," Rex said, "I was just guessing Ichabod would have you and I thrown in here for calling the leaper attack into question. I haven't foreseen anything since Rhi found her mettle. This is an utterly new timeline now."

"Think it's for the better or worse?" Chukk asked.

"Well," Rex replied, "it's going to be tough to tell from in here. I take it your troops decided against believing you?"

"Aye," Chukk said. "I should have guessed as much. You were right. They'll follow the leader and do as they're told. They weren't trained to think for themselves. Quite the opposite actually and Dee and I were the ones to do it sadly. You think the Bugle made it?"

"No way to know except that she never came back," Rex said. "I give it even odds if you're wagering."

"I get that you knew there were MaRuu in front of them from what you heard," Chukk said. "But what was that talk of MaRuu behind them. You never mentioned that."

"You're right, I didn't," Rex replied. "I wanted them to hurry up and be done with it."

Chukk laughed. "A little added incentive, eh? Ichabod best be careful. Seems we have another leader in our midst."

"Only I'm trying to save everybody while he's trying to wipe us all out," Rex replied. "That and through all this, I still had to give Pi and Scout a hard time. It's kind of my thing."

"So back to us being locked up in here," Chukk said. "Think we'll just kick it all locked up?"

"We have the upper paw, actually," Rex said.

"Oh really, mighty Rex," Chukk replied. "Do tell, mate."

Rex smiled. "I think I have Ichabod figured out. He needs me."

"He does?" Chukk replied. "How so?"

"Because we're going to tell him I foresaw all of this and we'll help him win his precious battle with my time looping and your military prowess."

"And why would we do that? So, I can get free to kill him?" Chukk asked.

"I'm fairly certain the Spirit doesn't want anyone killing anyone," Rex said. "But that doesn't mean you can't kill him if he turns out as nefarious as I think he might be. Or kill me. Or both if you have to."

Chukk whistled. "That's ghastly, Rex. Why on Arkelia would you do that to yourself?"

"Because Rhi said how long they had been gone and I did the math," Rex replied. "What I'm doing out here isn't affecting them wherever it is they are. They're in a different reality than ours now. We can keep looping here until they complete their journey there."

Chukk thought on this for a moment. "How are you keeping this all straight? Just hearing you talk makes my head go numb, Rex."

"It's gotten easier as I've gone along," Rex said. "But I still can't control where I stop when I loop. It's like that's up to the Spirit or something."

"What's the furthest back you've gone?" Chukk asked.

"With you and Ichabod to right after Pi and the others left," Rex replied. "The last four times I've landed right back at the Wisher's Well from last night right after Rhi returned."

"But you've gotten her back to her future and there was that energy wave," Chukk said. "Seems like your starting off point might depend on the timeline outcomes, no?"

"I never thought about that," Rex replied. "Which means it could change now that Rhi's gone. So, if we can manage to get out of here-"

"We can try to loop back and get ourselves out of this cell before we've ever put in it," Chukk finished. "Worth a shot. That is, if we're ever let out of here."

"Oh, he'll send for us," Rex said. "He might be a great politician but he's no military leader. He's going to try to get us back on board this sinking ship. The trick is, we're going to let him. Let's save the looping for when we're really going to need it. Agreed?"

"Rex, the mighty strategist," Chukk mused. "I never thought I'd see the day."

"That makes two of us," Rex said.

***

A week later, Rex and Chukk were in Ichabod's burro looking over the battle plans to attack the MaRuu. With the arrival of the Battlers from the other HomeSpaces except for the ones from the South, the size of the Quasi Army was quite a formidable one. The time for war was upon nearly upon them and there would soon be no time to turn back. Rex and Chukk kept waiting for Pi, Dee, Scout, and Rhi to arrive at any dit, but all was for naught. Either the journeyers were still on their quest or had been lost. There was no way of knowing, so with the charade they prepared for one last chance to reason with Ichabod.

Rex looked at Ichabod. "You were the eternal star before me, weren't you?"

Ichabod smiled. "I see I've been found out. With the power of the star in time comes clarity, doesn't it, Rex?"

"You were right, Rex," Chukk said. "He's been playing you and I this whole time."

"Oh, not at all," Ichabod said. "I truly just want to help the Quasi survive the next thousand planet turns, Chukk. Everything I've done was done for the good of all."

"Except the MaRuu," Rex said. "Them you're okay with annihilating. Thing is, Ichabod, whatever future you saw didn't bring us here. Pi and the other journeyers have changed the timeline so much by now, you have no idea what will happen. The future you saw was one based on fear rather than hope. Admit it, that's why you've been so chummy with me. You wanted to be able to have a way to loop back in case things didn't go the way you wanted. So, you allied yourself to me, didn't you? And you just can't think that there might be a way to keep us alive without killing the MaRuu, can you?"

"You're going to kill me, aren't you?" Ichabod said. "What are you waiting for?"

"If you answer one question for us," Rex said. "We'll spare your life. Why Pi?"

Ichabod smiled. "Oh, that's an easy one. The Spirit wouldn't let me pick anyone else. Believe me, I tried. The Spirit willed it. Anyone else I tried to give it to brought me right back to when the Spirit told me to pick her to begin time anew. And as soon as I did, I lost the gift of the eternal star. I guess it was the part I was meant to play. I've spent every moment since trying to get us back on course to attack the MaRuu and now, here I am, finally successful in the endeavor."

"Successful?" Chukk said. "There's still time for us to stop this. Just because troops are assembled doesn't mean they have to march on a warpath."

"I ordered the Battlers from the South to attack straight from their HomeSpace," Ichabod said. "The war has already begun. And if you were to loop back, I would know what you were up to and be ready for you. I've been with you since the very beginning, Rex. And now, whatever bleeding-heart mission you two think you're on has come to an end. You have lost. Deal with it. Guards!"

As Rex and Chukk hopped to leave, five guards rushed into the main chamber. Chukk put up a valiant effort fighting two of them in paw-to-paw combat but soon found himself, and Rex, detained and in shackles. Ichabod sauntered from his burro into the chamber and was surprised to see Rex look almost calm. Chukk writhed against his restraints but remained quiet.

"Take them to the stockade," Ichabod ordered. "And keep the shackles on. Don't worry, Rex. It's just for the night. Tomorrow, the two of us will be making our way for the front with our own Battlers."

"The front?" Rex asked. "Why?"

"Why do you think?" Ichabod replied. "If the situation demands it, you and I will loop back to plan better for the next go round. I knew you two would turn on me again. Such a feeble attempt to deceive someone such as myself would take far more cunning."

"We know. Could you ever loop back without hurting yourself?" Rex asked.

"In time, but I still couldn't control where I returned to," Ichabod said. "Wait, why?"

Rex closed his eyes... and then reopened them.

"Oh, not at all," Ichabod said. "I truly just want to help the Quasi survive the next thousand planet turns, Chukk. Everything I've done was done for the good of all."

"Kill him," Rex said. "Now!"

Chukk threw the dagger he had been hiding in his left paw straight through Ichabod's chest. The elder slumped to the ground, dead.

"Your plan worked, Chukk," Rex said. "I got what we needed. He's was one bad, bad Quasi."

"You came back right to this point?" Chukk asked. "How far ahead were you?"

"Just a dit or two," Rex replied. "I suppose that means this as far back as I can go now?"

"We must be in sync somehow with the progress the others are making," Chukk mused. "Seems we're nearing the end, doesn't it? Think we still have time to stop this before it starts?"

"The war already started, Chukk," Rex said. "He didn't send for the Southern Battlers. He ordered them right into an attack against the MaRuu. Whatever future he lived in must have been the one that brought about the end only he never got that far before losing the power of the star. The ones I've seen all ended, er, badly."

"How badly?" Chukk asked. "I still don't see why fighting our mortal enemies is such a bad thing."

"Because the MaRuu aren't our enemies, Chukk," Rex said solemnly. "We're theirs. According to the MaRuu, Ichabod and I came across in a previous timeline, this all started with the Quasi invading their land during the first millennia."

"I know my history," Chukk said. "We came here peaceably across the Shining Sea because this is the last continent. There was no way around the First War."

"They were here first," Rex said. "We could have tried asking for a place to stay as opposed to stealing theirs from them. Just a thought."

"Well, Chukk replied, "it's not like we can change the past. We did it. It's done. No way of going back now."

"If any of this has taught me anything, Chukk," Rex replied, "it's that being bad in the past doesn't mean you can't do good in the present. It makes for a better future, believe me."

Chukk sighed. "So, what do we do now?"

"Apologize," Rex replied, "and hope it's not too little too late."

"And how do you do you reckon we do that?" Chukk asked.

Rex shrugged. "I haven't got that far yet. For the time being, we need to get the people here behind us. Are you certain the Battlers will back us?"

"I told you, mate," Chukk said. "The Battlers aren't the HomeSpace guards. They answer to me. But there is a leadership vacuum now we've rid ourselves of Ichabod, isn't there?"

"You're right," Rex agreed. "How should we get to lead the Quasi?"

Chukk smiled. "I'm looking right at him."

"You're kidding, right?" Rex asked. "Me?"

"You are our eternal star now, Rex," Chukk answered. "Aren't you? I think the Spirit knew what it was doing when it gave you your gift... by taking it away from one who would inflict harm and granting it to one who would risk everything to save all we hold near and dear. It's your power to yield to protect your people, Rex. You just didn't realize it until right now."

"And how do you know that?" Rex asked.

"Because I'm the one who gave it to you," Chukk replied.

"Wait," Rex replied. "Say what now?"

"I serve you, Elder Rex," Chukk replied. "And if I serve you then the Battlers do as well. And if the Battlers follow you, all of the Quasi will follow you too."

"We never discussed this, Chukk," Rex objected. "I'm no leader."

"Ichabod is dead," Chukk replied. "And we're still here. Must mean the Spirit wills it. Don't worry about the Council, either. Just disband it so a fresh one can be called without Ichabod's minions."

"Whoever said anything about a rebellion?" Rex asked.

"You did," Chukk replied. "As soon as you said to kill our leader."

"Oh, right," Rex said. "I kind of thought you would be the one taking charge, honestly. Me? Not so much."

"If you were to lead," Chukk said. "How do you think you might go about it?"

I think we should do it together. A Healer and a Battler have very different ways of approaching things, neither of them bad. And if Rhi makes it home, I say we include her, so the Bugles have an equal say. And someday, maybe even a MaRuu too. Majority vote will rule the day. What do you say?"

Chukk smiled. "I think, Rex, you just devised a system of governance. Until a Bugle, whomever it is, is chosen, I grant you their vote, two to my one. The idea of the MaRuu joining with us is pretty wishful thinking! I don't think it's going to happen in our lifetime."

"I think they might hold the key," Rex replied.

"Key to what?" Chukk asked.

"Saving the planet," Rex replied. "Something's been telling me Ichabod and the elders before him had it backwards. We attacked them and drove them from their lands. They retaliated by wiping out our expedition and anyone who crossed into what lands they have left. We attack them for an assault they are never actually going to initiate. They retaliate against our offensive. They are a reactionary effect to the causes of our aggression and always have been."

"I never really thought about it like that," Chukk said. "So, throughout our shared history, the Quasi picked the fight and the MaRuu simply retaliated. Sad, really, isn't it?"

Rex nodded. "The more I think about it, I think we should try to loop back further. Maybe I can get to Ichabod before he sent the battle orders to the southern HomeSpace."

"Go on, then," Chukk said. "I'll see you when I see you."

Rex closed his eyes. He reopened them.

"I'm still here, aren't I?" Rex asked.

Chukk nodded. "Maybe we need to do it like before." He unsheathed his bronze blade.

Rex extended his left paw. "Just cut my forepaw. No lopping off extremities."

Chukk gave Rex a stab in the forepaw as requested. "Yeow!"

Rex grabbed the wound. "Uh oh, we have a problem."

Chukk went in his pouch and removed swathing, tying the gauzy garment around Rex's forepaw. "Guess we've reached the end of any time jumping shenanigans. You had a good run, Rex. You helped us out a lot."

Rex winced, holding his paw. "I hope it was enough. I wonder though, do you think the gift of being the star went to anyone else?"

Chukk shrugged. "Only way we'll find out is if you notice a shift in the timeline moving forward. That is, if you kept that part of your gift."

"So, what do we do in the meantime?" Rex asked.

"First," Chukk said, "we get control of HomeSpace locked down with us in charge."

There was screaming out in the outer burro. Chukk and Rex hopped as quickly as they could and came face to face with a pair of bloodied Battlers wearing the Southern HomeSpace markings. They looked dehydrated and weary.

"What is it?" Chukk asked.

"The MaRuu were fiercer than we thought," the one closer to Rex said. "They wiped us out. Ichabod's message said the MaRuu wouldn't be able to fight if we surrounded them. He was wrong."

"We got away by hiding," the other one said. "We found a route out in the darkness."

"Where are the others?" Rex asked.

"Gone," the first said, panting. "And that's not the worst of it."

"It gets worse?" Rex asked.

"They took the southern HomeSpace by force," the other replied. "So, we just kept hopping as fast as we could hoping we'd find you all like this."

"And how's that?" Chukk asked.

"Alive," the first weary Battle said. "We feared you all dead. We must have beat them here."

"Here?" Rex asked.

"Rex," Chukk said. "This is it. It's time."

"Time for what?" Rex said, flustered.

"To prepare for the end," Chukk replied. "We're going to have to fight the MaRuu. There's no way around it now. I control the Army. You control the rest. As we agreed, aye?"

There were whispers from the other Quasi gathered that Rex and Chukk had taken control from Ichabod. Rex was not used to hearing a crowd send his name about through hushed murmurs. It was difficult to focus. But suddenly, Rex felt his fear dissipate into the ether as if the Spirit itself was guiding him.

"Ichabod led us into this and has been accounted for!" Rex called out, louder than he thought his voice could ever be. "Chukk and I stand here together, Battler and Healer, ready to help and stand at the ready for whatever might come! Heed our calls to action and tell the rest that we are here to help and not hurt you! We will defend our home to the last breath! All guards and Battlers are to report into Chukk and his battalion immediately! Begin fortifying our defenses! Healers, prepare triage stations both near the entrance and in the Elder's Chamber! The rest of you store as many carrots and sweetwater jugs as you can fit in your burros and stay there! Go!"

There was a flurry of activity as the crowd dispersed into a hundreds of moving figures. Chukk watched the scene with a sense of pride. He patted Rex on the shoulder.

"You sure sounded like a leader to me," Chukk said. "They don't need a committee right now, Rex. They need you."

"Yeah, well," Rex said. "I might have the shortest reign in Quasi history. And they don't need me, Chukk. They need us."

"I appreciate that, Rex," Chukk replied. "If by the grace of the Spirit we come through this alive, I'll gladly defer to your best judgement in all things political."

"If we somehow get through this mess," Rex said, "I'm giving the power to all Quasi to decide our future. Having only one person in charge is what started all this trouble to begin with. Now go, you've got an invasion to squash!"

Chukk gave a salute and turned on his paws to leave. He stopped. "Rex?"

"Yeah, Chukk?" Rex replied.

"I think the Spirit did right by picking you and your sister and your friends for the Journey," Chukk said. "I'm proud to call you my friend. I'm sure Dee thinks the same of the them, too. We're lucky to have gotten to know you."

Rex smiled, waving him off. "Get out of here, Battler. You have a battle to win, now don't you?"

"For our sakes," Chukk replied. "I sure hope so."

"Can you have Ichabod's body taken care of?" Rex asked.

"Oh right," Chukk said. "I'll have him out of there within the dat. To the lyghtning fields he goes."

"Good," Rex said. "And Chukk?"

"Yeah, Rex?"

"Thanks," Rex said. "For everything."

Chukk began to hop away. As Rex began reliving the three futures he had lived through, the new leader replayed all the death that followed in the attacks on the MaRuu he had witnessed. Even though the Quasi had proved victorious in all three scenarios, the end still came for them all. Think, Rex told himself. What could we do differently? Then it hit him like a lyghtning bolt.

"Chukk! Wait!" Rex called out, hopping to catch up to Chukk.

"What?" Chukk asked. "What is it? See something?"

"I'm, er, back," Rex lied. "Back from the future. I know this will go against everything you believe but I know what we need to do."

"You looped again? I thought you couldn't. Your arm, even."

Rex nodded. "It just, happened. There's no way for us to win this and stop the end from coming the way we're going. We have to try something else entirely."

"And what would that be?" Chukk asked.

"Surrender," Rex replied, calmly. "We need to surrender to the MaRuu."

"That's not the Battler way, Rex," Chukk said. "We fight until we die."

"But that's just it, Chukk," Rex replied. "We're in the wrong. Ichabod ordered an attack in a time of peace between us. Like you and I were talking about, don't you see? We have to end the cycle. We need to let the MaRuu win."

Rex saw from the look on Chukk's face that this was not going to be an easy sell.

"Look," Rex said. "I'm your leader. You gave me your vote, remember?"

"And I'm beginning to regret it," Chukk replied. "Why do I feel like you're just trying to buy time somehow."

Rex smiled. "Exactly. For all of us, Quasi, Bugle, and MaRuu alike. The longer we all live, the longer until the end comes."

"And you've seen that defending ourselves gets us nowhere?" Chukk asked.

"I've seen us win three times," Rex replied. "Every time, the end still comes for us all. I've seen us lose, uh, twice now. And the end still comes for us all."

"So what can we do different?" Chukk asked. "I'm confused. Again."

"Not fight at all," Rex replied. "I, as the Elder, will offer myself in surrender and request a meet up with their elders to determine how to end their engagement with us peacefully. I'll offer terms to avoid more warfare."

"And just how do you intend to keep yourself alive with them long enough to get to their nest beyond the Southlands?" Chukk asked.

"Good point," Rex said. "I might stand a chance if I've got you and your Battalion by my side. What do you say?"

Chukk huffed under his breath. "This is not our way, Rex."

"I know, Chukk," Rex replied. "That's why it's going to work. It has to."

Chukk was silent for a moment. "But if they attack us, we can attack back, right?"

Rex nodded. "If those are your terms, then yes."

Chukk was silent again. He spit in his paw and extended his paw to Rex. "I'm in. Shake on it."

Rex smiled, spitting in his paw and accepting the embrace. He did his best to grasp Chukk's paw as firmly as he was grasping Rex's.

An energy wave rippled around them, filling HomeSpace with bright light for a moment before dissipating. The color was unlike anything any of them had seen before. It was both vibrant and beautiful.

"I hope we just made the right decision," Rex said, looking around.

"I just hope the MaRuu will recognize our blades lying on the ground in front of us as a gesture of surrender and not just an easy kill," Chukk replied. "This could be a bloody quick defeat. Emphasis on the bloody."

***

Pi felt different somehow but couldn't put her paw pad on it. Ever since they had seen that odd colored flash go off, she had been doing nothing but thinking. Pi's mind was whirring with images of what had come before, what had changed around them, and oddly, of events she must only be daydreaming about for she would have no way of knowing. She felt like her brain was filling up with memories that were not hers but another's, namely Rex's, and then in an instant Pi felt a sense of strange awareness with it all as if the information she was receiving was complete. She stumbled on the red path and collapsed.

"Pi!" Scout called out from behind her. He hopped up to her, sliding to the ground next to her and cradling her head in his paws.

"What happened?" Rhi asked, flying to the pair and landing on the other side of Pi.

"She just slumped over," Dee said, standing above them. "Is she still breathing, Scout?"

"Aye," Scout replied. "We all seen she's been off her game the closer we get to wherever it is were going. Maybe she just got so knackered she collapsed under the weight of it."

Scout reached in his pouch with his free paw, putting the wrapped up Arkelian down on the path and then bringing his sweetwater jug out. He splashed a small amount of the sweetwater on her face. Her eyes blinked.

"Oh no, oh no, oh no," Pi whispered.

"Oh no, what?" Rhi asked, flying down and taking Pi's paw. "What is it, Pi?"

"I, saw home," Pi replied, quietly. "Rhi, I saw you. And Chukk. Oh, Ichabod, how could you? Rhi's told you the truth, Dee. About everything."

"And just how do you know that?" Dee asked.

"Because I was there," Pi answered. "I saw everything Rex saw; he's been through it all."

"Is anyone else confused right now?" Dee asked.

On the path next to them, wrapped in the small blanket, the Arkelian began to glow red once more, sending red lyght out through the cover of the blanket.

"In my head," Pi said. "In my memories. I can see it all. The MaRuu are coming for HomeSpace and Rex is going to just give it to them?! What is he thinking?!"

"What do you mean, just give it to them?" Scout asked. "Rhi, you said, you averted the war by killing Bha's sentry."

"Ichabod sent the Southern Battlers into the MaRuus territory to attack," Pi said.

"Oh no," Rhi replied. "We thought he would only attack if he managed to give my gift of speed to the other Bugles."

"Sounds like Ichabod made sure to make war inevitable," Dee said. "If that's what happened. I'm having trouble buying this, Pi."

"Look at that!" Rhi said, pointing to the glowing Arkelian. "It's doing the glowy, shiny thing again, it is!"

"Give it to me," Pi said. "I'm pretty sure I should put it back on."

"Yesterday we decided it was making you miserable, love," Scout said. "Do you really think it wise?"

"Whatever just happened," Pi replied, "was the Spirit wanting me to know everything Rex and Chukk have been going through back at HomeSpace to buy time for us to see this thing through. So much so that they are about to go out and surrender themselves and all the rest to the MaRuu! All so I can have more time to save them! So yes, I want it! I want all the power I can get!"

SWOOP!

Pi grabbed the Arkelian from the ground and put it back on so quickly her paws were a blur.

"Er?" Rhi said. "How'd you do that! You were as fast as... me?"

SWOOSH!

Pi leapt to her hind paws in a flash. "Speed! I'm fast now too, Rhi! Just like you!"

Scout somehow felt weaker all of a sudden. "Are you strong too? Strong like me?"

SWOOSH!

BANG!

Pi darted to a nearby tree and hit it as hard as she could. The tree splintered in two as if it were a twig, sending splinters in all directions as it fell to the snowy ground with a loud thud. Pi faced the others, a wide grin on her face.

"She is the One," Dee said. He lowered himself to a kneeling position.

Scout saw this and followed suit, kneeling in front of his life partner.

"I'm not kneeling," Rhi said. "Sorry, but I'm not. She didn't bloody kneel to us when we had those powers, now did she?"

"Rhi's right," Pi said. "Get up already."

Rhi looked into the distance. "Be right back."

She started flying into the distance, buzzing her wings as fast as she could. "Damn it. Gone, it is! The speed's all but left me now, it has!" Rhi turned around, rejoining the group. "What about you, Scout? Still have any of that super strength left?"

Scout shook his head. "Naw," he replied. "I felt it leave me. No use in hurting myself to prove it. Guess we were just placeholders, Rhi. They were Pi's gifts to have along."

"I'm sure you had them for a reason," Pi said. "But it makes more sense that I would be the one to have them. I'm not trying to rub it in, but I was the Chosen one. Um, where'd Dee go?"

Scout, Rhi, and Pi looked all around them. Dee was gone.

"That's bloody impossible," Scout said.

"He's just vanished into thin air, he has," Rhi remarked.

No, he didn't.

Pi whipped around in a flurry. "Show yourself!"

I'm in everything you see and do. And now the end nears just for you.

Pi spun back around. It couldn't be? Could it?

189

Rhi and Scout were gone, just like Dee. She was here on the red path, nearing the mighty mountains, all alone. She called out their names repeatedly to no avail. Her fellow journeyers had disappeared.

"Bring them back!" Pi yelled out loud. "They did nothing wrong!"

Red wrath is your way to find the path. Your actions will decide right from wrong and in the Sun Chamber who truly belongs.

"You come back to me now?!" Pi called out. "Like this?! Some Spirit you are! Let me see you so I can knock your teeth out!"

A response did not come. Pi spent a long while listening to nothing but the chill wind that was whipping the snow around her. She seethed in anger. Of all they've encountered and done and now this? She spat on the ground. But-

"Wait," Pi said. "I'm the Chosen one. This was never their journey. It was always meant to be mine alone. That must be it! This is the way it should be! I'm meant to save everyone alone! You can't fool me, Spirit! I see through your games!"

In a way, Pi almost felt relieved. Everything from here on out would be the way she wanted it done and in her own way. With all they had encountered, Pi felt certain the others had been sent back to HomeSpace as Rhi had previously. No harm could have come to them. This made Pi feel a sense of relief. Finally, she could see this through her way, alone to decide which course to take. Just then, Pi froze.

"Dee had the map," Pi said. "Damn it! Dee had the map!"

Pi kicked at the snowy ground beneath her hind paws. She forced herself to take a deep breath. Relax, Pi told her herself. I'll find the way. I always do and I always will. I don't need anyone. I never have.

All of a sudden, the dusky sky was lit up by a blue energy lyght beam in the distance. Much like the red beam the Arkelian had emitted before Pi acquired her new powers, the energy shot into the sky, shaking about in position. As quickly as it had lit up the darkening night, the lyght energy vanished.

"The MaRuu," Pi whispered. "It has to be."

She could see and hear Rex learning the MaRuu were on a 'path of color'. She saw them savagely attack her people on the plains. Pi remembered the two Southern Battlers arriving at HomeSpace saying the MaRuu had taken the South and were on their way east. She had to complete the journey and stop them somehow. "I bet they have a map, too, don't they, Spirit?"

Pi drew her face into a furrowed scowl. "It's time to end this, once

and for all, isn't it, Spirit? Isn't it?"

Do what you think is right. Stop the wrath to save the lyght or our time will soon be nigh.

"I knew it," Pi said, removing her silver blade from her pouch. "They will not defeat me!"

SWOOP!

Pi took off in a tear, leaving the red path and going towards the direction of the blue energy beam, weaving around various snow splattered trees as she went. Feeling as if she was cutting through the air was exhilarating to Pi to no end. Pi outstretched her front paws and stiffened her fur into quills as the scenery whirred past her. Holding her silver blade tightly, Pi whipped through the forest and kept her eyes open for another sign of the MaRuu-

Pi, stop and listen before you choose. Show courage or you will surely lose.

Pi came to an abrupt stop, sending a whirlwind of snow into the air all around her. There in front of her stood a solitary figure, their skin a reflective silver, wearing a breastplate identical to her own, only adorned with a blue gemstone instead of the red like on hers. The figure looked right at her, causing Pi to take a defensive stand. She gripped her blade and approached slowly. Everything in Pi told her that this was a MaRuu and she should kill it immediately. But something else was at play in her head. What if it's not alone out here? What if this is a trap? Pi was, as she tended to be, curious.

"You can lower your blade, Quasi," the figure said, in a voice that was both measured and hissing. "I will not kill you... yet."

"Is that so, MaRuu?" Pi replied. "Here to help me, are you?"

The MaRuu laughed. "Do you know how many times you have asked me that? Twice now."

Pi raised an eyebrow. "Stop talking nonsense. What are you doing here?"

"Same as you," The MaRuu said. "We were on the path of color to save the Mother Planet just as you were."

Pi drew closer, her blade at the ready. "We? Where are the rest?"

"It is just us two here now," the MaRuu replied. "I'm tired, Quasi. I have been here in this forest for longer than you. I've killed you and you've killed me. Neither outcome brings about any change. We both end up right here. Alone and bloodied. We have failed, Quasi. Our people outside this place are at war, did you know that?"

Pi was utterly confused as what to do. She cautiously looked around for sign of any others. It did appear she and the MaRuu were alone in this forest. She nodded. "We do now because you just told us so."

"What is your name?" Pi asked.

"We are MaRuu," the MaRuu replied. "Even though we cannot hear or reach our brethren now, we are always one. What are you called?"

Pi studied her opponent carefully, cautiously. "Pi."

"Pi," MaRuu said. "We have decided that we would like to get to know you better instead of killing you now."

"Well, MaRuu," Pi replied, "I am undecided. You say we've faced each other before but I have no such memory. I have never seen you before."

MaRuu tapped the blue chest plate. "This gives us powers beyond your reality. Yours does not?"

Pi looked down to the Arkelian. "I suppose it does, now."

"This talking is not what we expected," MaRuu said. "You did not speak when we met before. Your words were your blade strikes."
SWOOP!

Pi whipped around and behind MaRuu, bringing her blade to the creature's neck. "Where are they? The others?"

MaRuu threw its head back into Pi's, knocking her back. It flipped itself forward, spinning around on its heels to face a stunned Pi. They stood facing each other in defensive positions now.

"This will not end well, Pi," MaRuu said. "Mother Planet does not want this."

"You killed my parents! You destroyed my life!" Pi hissed.

"You invaded our homeland and nearly wiped us from existence," MaRuu said, calmly. "And yet still you kept coming. We have only killed those who entered the only territory we had left. We have only defended ourselves. You must know this to be true, Pi."

Pi's mind was filled with the same information from Rex's point of view. Argh! This was getting frustrating!

"My parents were missionaries," Pi said. "They were carrying the message of the Spirit to you!"

"One we did not ask for, Pi," MaRuu said. "Those Quasi zealots tried to invade our minds after they had already invaded our lands. We could not allow it. They should have left us be just as the first Quasi should have let us be."

Pi could take no more.

SWOOSH!

SNAP!

With one blindly fast move, Pi swept in and broke MaRuu's neck. She threw the body to the ground and screamed in rage. "It is done!"

A blue energy wave rippled through the snowy forest.

"As we said, Quasi," MaRuu said, right back standing in front of Pi. "We always end up here. Now you see, no?"

Pi let out a sigh. "You've got to be kidding me. Just great. What now?"

"We do not know," MaRuu said. "This is where the path of color led us."

"Do you have a map?" Pi asked.

MaRuu shook their head. "We followed the Path of Color to this place."

"Well," Pi replied. "To do what exactly?"

"To find a way to carry on," MaRuu said. "Together."

Pi snorted, the steam from her nostrils billowing in the cold air. "Not bloody likely, MaRuu. I'm not falling for that. My journey does not end with you. I have a planet to save.

SWOOSH!

Pi took off, crisscrossing across the forest as fast as she could go. She zigzagged for what felt like dats, covering every nook and cranny of the snowy landscape. It got her nowhere. Everything she would stop; Pi was right back in front of MaRuu.

"It is futile, Pi," MaRuu finally said. "I have done the same thing. We are destined to end up here, facing each other."

"To what end?" Pi asked.

"Have you heard the Mother Planet as we have?" MaRuu asked. "She speaks to us, telling us to find a better way. If you haven't, you should listen to it."

"Oh, I've heard a voice all right," Pi snorted. "And it told me to end your wrath to find the path. So there."

MaRuu cocked its head to one side. "How do you know she did not mean your own wrath? We have come to terms with wanting to kill you. Yet, we can see in your eyes you still mean us harm. We've told you it is pointless. Why not listen to us?"

"I don't really listen to anyone, truth be told," Pi said. "Save for myself."

"Why is that?" MaRuu asked. "We MaRuu share everything with

each other. Our thoughts, our ideas, our triumphs, and our sorrows are of one collective mind. We overcome obstacles together."

"Because I find strength in my individuality," Pi replied. "I am the only me. The world through my eyes is my own universe and mine alone."

"But to what benefit is it if you do not share what you think and feel with others?" MaRuu asked. "It sounds selfish of you."

"No, it's not like that," Pi began to fume. "We find strength in our differences because one person might see things differently from another perspective."

"But if you don't share that perspective with anyone," MaRuu asked, "how can another learn from it? You sound as if you do not trust others to tell you they might know more about things than you do."

Pi stopped to think about that. "I, I listen to others. I do. That's not what I was saying. I'm just saying that we are taught that we don't have to force ourselves to share everything with each other, er, that sounds selfish, doesn't it?"

"We found ourselves alone when we thought we were better than the others we were with on the path," MaRuu said. "It is not the MaRuu way. That is the Quasi way, is it not?"

Pi sighed. "Yeah, MaRuu, I guess it is."

"Is this what brought you to us? These thoughts?" MaRuu asked.

Pi wiped a tear from her eye. What had she been thinking? Why did she feel like she always had to go it alone? Look where it brought her. Alone with a MaRuu in a snowy forest somewhere between the Spirit and the planet with nothing but her anger and resentment with her. Pi swallowed hard.

"I, I think I was wrong," Pi replied. "And it cost me what I thought I held most dear, my family. What has become of us, MaRuu?"

"We wish we knew, Pi," MaRuu said. "We have one last question for you if you will answer it."

"Go ahead," Pi said. "Seems all we have is time now."

"Will you let us help you reach the Sun Chamber?" MaRuu asked. "Together? Perhaps we can help our peoples learn to speak more and fight less with each other, no?"

Pi took a deep breath. This whole time, this was what the journey had been about, wasn't it? And she had missed the point entirely. It wasn't about defeating or killing each other, rather, the Quasi and

MaRuu were meant to work together, weren't they? But with a certain caveat, Pi now knew. The Quasi had been the ones to upset the balance in the first place. And now the planet was dying as a result.

"I haven't been hearing the Spirit, have I?" Pi asked. "I've been hearing you."

MaRuu smiled. "So, you have heard her. We thought you might to get this far. We hear her too. You are different, Pi. You have the power to help us stop this before we reach the End."

"Wait," Pi said. "So, we're both being guided by the Quasi Spirit?"

"It is not the Quasi dead you hear, Pi," MaRuu said. "You hear Mother planet herself. She is all of us, living and dead, MaRuu, Quasi, Bugle, and all species now extinct. She wants us to save her and it can only be done together."

Pi's head was spinning. All of this could be a ruse. Or it could be the way to salvation. "So, what do you want from me, MaRuu?"

"You can start by believing us," MaRuu said, plainly. "It is only together we can stop our people's warring with each other."

"How do you know that?" Pi asked.

"We don't know it," MaRuu said. "We hope it. We are their only chance, Pi. Trust us now or all will perish in the End. We offer you salvation for all the Quasi's past indiscretions. We will start anew but it must start with you. Concede your fight and admit we need each other."

Pi's brain was humming. How could she trust a MaRuu?

"How can I trust you?" Pi asked. "You killed my parents."

"What would the Quasi have done if we had sent a party into your territory?" MaRuu asked. "Welcomed us warmly?"

Pi's shoulders slunk down. "We'd kill them," she said in a near whisper.

MaRuu removed a small stone tablet from under its foot. "There were no others. We undertook the path of color alone, only to meet the Quasi vessel of lyght and offer this map and our Red Stone Arkelian in a partnership in exchange for your apology and trust."

"This is all because of the Quasi," Pi said. "For that I, on behalf of my people, are sorry, MaRuu. I let my anger and lust to do this alone cloud my judgement and it cost me my family. So, here alone, with nowhere to go but with you, give you my trust."

Pi extended her clawed, front paw. MaRuu extended their clawed right hand. For the first time in over three millenias, the Quasi and

MaRuu found a shared peace in a simple embrace. Both smiled at each other.

Red energy rippled through the forest all around them.

"MaRuu!" Rhi yelled, startling Pi.

Dee whipped out his bronze blade. "What is this?!"

"Where are we?" Scout asked, looking around.

"Stop, Dee!" Pi yelled as the Battler began to approach them. "This is not our enemy!"

"It's a bloody MaRuu, it is!" Rhi called out. "What on Arkelia are you doing?"

"Making an alliance," Pi said. "We have a shared interest and a common goal. MaRuu here enlightened me that I've been going about this all wrong and I hope you'll all accept my deep regret at how I've acted."

"What do you mean, Pi?" Scout asked, watching Dee continue to hold his blade at the ready.

"I thought it was up to me, a Quasi, to save Arkelia alone," Pi said. "When we were the ones to muck it up in the first place. The MaRuu are not our enemy. We are theirs." Pi felt Rex's sense of clarity coursing through her as she spoke the same words he had said to Chukk back at HomeSpace.

"You're clearly under this MaRuu's control, Pi," Dee said. "Step away from it now."

"MaRuu isn't an it," Pi said. "They're a them. We've gone about this all wrong, Dee. And we need them as much as they need us. I see that now."

"And what could they possible need from us except for the Arkelian?" Dee asked.

"Some common understanding for one," Pi replied. "MaRuu here spoke and somehow, I feel my brother saying the same argument to your Chukk back home. It's all coming together because we are all going to come together to save the planet from herself."

"I am utterly confused right now," Scout said. "Who did what now?"

"We have seen you attack us and now we attack you," MaRuu said. "We now say the only way to win is to not fight at all. We think we can save the Mother planet this way."

"It, er, they sound just like what Rex was saying when I went back home," Rhi said. "That the only way to win was to never fight in the first place. That's why I took out Bha's sentry. No good it ended up doing."

"On the planet surface, we fight each other," MaRuu said. "But here in the core, we can come together to begin anew for the better of all."

"I don't like this," Dee said. "I don't trust them."

"And we do not trust you," MaRuu replied. "We trust her." MaRuu pointed at Pi. "She wears the Violet Stone and we the Red Gem. We can bring them together and bind them to each other."

"So, you need our Arkelian to save the planet for yourselves," Dee said. "So, if you just want it all said and done, why not just give us yours?"

"The Tablet of Color," MaRuu said, lifting their small stone tablet in the air, "is clear that we must go together into the Sun Chamber. We must combine our powers to set the balance. Of this we are certain."

"What does the map say, Dee?" Scout asked. "Anything about that?"

Dee removed the map from his pouch. He scanned it and them scanned it again. "Wait. This can't be."

"There is nothing else written, is there?" Pi asked. "We've reached the end of it, haven't we?"

Dee threw up his arms. "So, now we need this MaRuu to find the Sun Chamber. Just great."

Rhi flew up to MaRuu and Pi. "So, a hello is in order. I'm Rhi."

"We are MaRuu."

Scout neared, slowly hopping up to the newly emerging group. "I'm Scout, Pi's partner."

"We are MaRuu."

"I'll save you the trouble," Dee said. "You are MaRuu. I am Dee. And if I catch even the slightest hint that you're up to something, you can expect to find your blood splattered across my blade in an instant. Agreed?"

MaRuu smiled. "And we are the evil ones to you. We find that funny. Agreed, hostile one. Pi, it seems singularity and individuality in your kind breeds anger and mistrust."

"Yeah," Pi said. "I'm starting to notice that too. From here on out, we do this together and act as one. Is that understood, all of you? Me included."

Each said "Aye."

"Good," Pi said. "Whether we like it or not, we need MaRuu right now just as much as they need us. If that changes, we'll take it from there. So, MaRuu, what does your tablet say we do now that you've convinced us to join you?"

"Wait," MaRuu said.

"Wait?" Dee asked. "Where is the Sun Chamber?"

MaRuu looked around and smiled. "We are already in it. We have been since we left our homes to undertake the path. Our destination is at the place where the Mother planet can communicate with the Sun. The top of the mountains in front of us at the Widow's Peak is where we will offer ourselves in joined sacrifice to keep them in orbit of each other. We will wait for them there."

"Widow's Peak?" Rhi asked. "What does that mean?"

"That, Bugle," MaRuu replied, "is what we will find out when we get there."

Are you prepared to die to save the rest for that will be your final test?

Pi looked to MaRuu. "This is what the Spirit, or your Mother planet wills of us. To sacrifice our lives to save everyone else. Well, we're ready to die, MaRuu, just like you."

"That's why we're here, isn't it?" Scout said. "Some of us already have too if you remember."

Pi smiled. "In another life, love."

"Well I've lived more in the past stretch that I ever imagined, I have," Rhi said. "Forward, sideways, and back and it's all led to here, hasn't it?" I'm with you both."

"I've been trained to face death my whole life," Dee said. "And I'm ready now more than ever. Bring it on, I say. For our families and friends to live on, I say we finish this as we started it… together."

"That each of you is willing to make the ultimate sacrifice alongside me makes me want to cry," Pi said. "I love you all."

"We are surprised by this," MaRuu said, their interest piqued. "Pi was meant to be here as we are, but the rest of you came here knowing you would not return?" Your choice was to die by her side?"

"Being of your own free will still means you can act in favor of the greater good, MaRuu," Pi said. "In some cases, anyways. You have the tablet so lead the way. We have a mountain to climb and our destiny to meet."

8

"This is it," Chukk said. "Lay down your blades, all of you! Do not pick them back up unless I order you to! Stand fast!"

Rex watched Chukk and the rest of his Battlers lined up next to him lay their arms down on the ground in front of them, each taking one step back after doing so. Rex took out his silver blade and followed suit. The MaRuu swarm could be heard, but not yet seen, in the distance.

"Battlers," Chukk called out. "Kneel on your paws!"

Everyone kneeled, Rex included.

"Rex," Chukk whispered. "Stand up. That's how they should know you're our leader."

"Oh right, I forgot you said that," Rex said. "Sorry!" Rex stood back up, feeling his hind paws wobble in nervousness.

In what seemed like a dit but was probably closer to a dat, the MaRuu swarm appeared. Rex, Chukk, and the Battlers found themselves surrounded with the MaRuu closing in on them until they were so close, they could touch each other. Rex's stomach was in knots with anticipation at this point.

"This is it," Chukk whispered. "You can do this, Rex. I believe in you."

Rex nodded. "Thanks, Chukk. If this all goes sideways, thanks for being there most of the times. I forgive you for the few times you sided with Ichabod."

"Er, thanks?" Chukk replied.

One of the MaRuu came out of the swarm to face Rex, standing a paw's length from him.

"What is this?" the MaRuu asked.

Rex cleared his throat and looked the scary looking MaRuu right in the eyes. "I am the High Elder Rex of the Eastern HomeSpace and I propose a truce with the MaRuu. You were attacked under false pretense by those that did not know a ruse to conquer your people was underway. This traitor and his conspirators have been killed. We mean you no more harm and are sorry for the harm that has been already done. We ask you to leave this place and let any survivors from our southern HomeSpace travel here to safety. I offer you our southern lands in return. I know one MaRuu shares their experiences with all, so what say the MaRuu to these terms?"

Chukk stared up at Rex in disbelief. He didn't just think like a leader, he acted like one too. Chukk was amazed at how controlled and measured Rex was acting. He looked to the MaRuu, who seemed to be relaying the information telepathically and hadn't responded yet.

"The MaRuu were not expecting an offer of peace," the MaRuu said. "We do not trust the Quasi. Why should we accept these terms?

"Because, MaRuu," Chukk said. "While we drew your attention to us, the full Quasi Army of Battlers from all of our HomeSpaces has surrounded this position. If you do not accept the terms, we will go to war and the Quasi will win for I've foreseen it."

The MaRuu hissed before replying, "This makes no sense. You have entrapped us to... surrender?"

"I have seen our future, MaRuu," Rex said. "It ends badly for all of us if we make war instead of find peace. The planet will die and all of us right along with it. Believe this to be true."

Chukk didn't like the way this was going. The more Rex had to explain why the MaRuu should accept his terms, the less likely it became they would do so. Chukk eyed the bronze blade in front of him, but also the two daggers he had hidden in his pouch... just as he had ordered his Battlers to do. If there was to be a fight, they would be ready.

The MaRuu moved closer to Rex. "So, you wish not to fight us?"

Rex nodded. "That's the idea, MaRuu. We have also sent one forward on the journey of lyght, your path of color, to save the planet from destruction. Why don't we shelve all this until one or the other succeeds or fails? Then, if you still want war, you'll know just where to find us."

The MaRuu was silent again, their head twitching slightly. Rex assumed this was how they conveyed information with each other. He too remained silent. He saw Chukk beginning to fidget. Calm down, Chukk, Rex thought. This is going to-

"The MaRuu accept your terms under one condition," the MaRuu said. "You and this one here who protects you come back with us as an assurance of good faith and a deterrent to others who would seek to attack us. What is your decision?"

Rex looked down to Chukk, who nodded slightly. Rex looked back to the MaRuu, extending his paw. "Truce?"

The MaRuu extended its clawed hand, shaking Rex's paw. "Truce, Quasi. You are not like the other soldiers we have encountered."

"Really?" Rex asked, surprised. "How is that?"

"You think before you act," the MaRuu said. We find this refreshing. If you do not raise arms against us, we will not attack you. This is fair, no?"

Rex nodded. "Very fair. Battlers, throw out your daggers on the ground in front of your blades. Now."

Chukk was caught off guard. "But?"

"Have them do it now," Rex said. "We're surrendering to save the others. If they found them on you in a search this all would have been for not. Just do it. Now."

"Battlers," Chukk said. "Disarm!"

The Battlers all went in their pouches and threw down their daggers in front of their bronze blades. A few grumbled under their breath but still did as they were told. They were now defenseless.

"You will be put to work with the others," the MaRuu said. "No harm will come to you if you do as you are told. We promise you this. For now, you will be bound at the wrists and led by chain until we reach the Southern Enclave. May we proceed?"

Rex looked to Chukk once more. He gave a brief nod as if to say, I don't like this, but I'll go along with it. Rex nodded back before returning his attention to the MaRuu.

"We are ready, MaRuu," Rex said. "Let the rest go so that they know to retreat from the field and then we will go with you."

The MaRuu circle began to shift, leaving a passageway behind the Battlers.

"You are free to go, soldiers of Rex," the MaRuu hissed. "Your leader is smart and wise. Forget him not."

Rex and Chukk watched as the Battlers retreated from the middle of the MaRuu swarm.

Chukk turned his head. "Tell Peet of the Northern Battlers he is the new Southern Elder until we return!"

"Aye!" the Battlers called out.

"Return?" the MaRuu said. "That will not be possible. You will be our prisoners for the rest of your life. Those are the terms."

"You didn't say that before," Rex questioned. "But fine. We will not try to escape from you. We promise, don't we, Chukk?"

Chukk sighed. "Right, whatever. Let's just get on with this."

Rex lifted Chukk to his hind paws. He leaned into his ear. "Who do you think they meant by 'the others'"?

"Pretty sure we're going to find out soon enough, mate," Chukk replied, holding his front paws out to be chained while they chained Rex's front paws also. "I sure hope this was the right play."

"No more talking Quasis," the MaRuu said. "Only speak when we speak with you from now on. Let's go."

Rex and Chukk allowed themselves to be pulled into the MaRuu swarm as it retreated from HomeSpace. A violet energy wave washed all over them and their surroundings, startling the MaRuu. They stopped and kneeled on the ground, bowing their heads.

"The Path of Color is a righteous one," all the MaRuu said in unison. "We move even closer to the Mother planet."

Rex and Chukk looked at each other. Rex smiled a bit. "I think we did the right thing again."

"Here's hoping, Rex," Chukk whispered. "Otherwise, you just imprisoned us to our mortal enemies for the rest of our lives."

"Those lives would have been incredibly short lived," Rex replied, also whispering. "At least now, I'm pretty sure we stand a chance of making it out of all this alive."

"And why's that?" Chukk asked.

"Because we all died on that battlefield when the planet erupted the last three times, I lived through this," Rex whispered. "This is the farthest I've ever seen!"

"Wait a dit," Chukk hissed. "You said you went into the future again a while back and saw us do this?"

"I, er, lied," Rex replied. "I had to, and I won't do it again. I needed yours and the Battlers help to pull this off. Sorry but not sorry!"

"You're lucky I'm in chains right now, Rex," Chuck growled.

"Quasis! Shut up!" one of the MaRuu hissed. "We will skin you alive if either of you say another word!"

Rex caught Chukk's glaring stare and did his best to fake a smile. Chukk's expression did not lighten. At all.

***

The Journeyers were nearing a clearing in the forest brush when Pi spotted what they had been looking for. Ahead of them and to the right was the red path that had led them into the forest and subsequently, led Pi to find MaRuu. It was a welcome sight as they had spent the better part of the past two days looking for it.

"Eyes on the prize!" Pi called out, pointing to the path ahead. "MaRuu, I give you, the red trail on the Journey of Lyght."

"MaRuu sees Violet," they replied. "This is odd. Your map and our tablet correspond. We did not anticipate this."

"It's clearly red," Dee said.

"You must have different vision than we do that doesn't allow you to see it properly," Scout said.

"Perhaps it is the Quasi who see improperly," MaRuu replied. "It is no bother. It is the same path as on the Path of Color. Where your map ends is the mouth of the mountain range. Our tablet goes further, leading us to the Great Gateway. This is our final destination. We will go there, together."

"I still don't see why you want us to go with you," Dee said. "What do you need, both Arkelians or something?"

MaRuu nodded. "This is not untrue."

"So why not kill us for ours and go alone to ensure you win?" Dee said.

"It would not work," MaRuu replied. "We have already tried that many times."

"Wait, what now?" Scout asked. "That sounded quite ominous."

"MaRuu has been trapped here for a rather long time," Pi said. "They tried to save the planet on their own many times and there was no way out for either of us unless it was together. So here we are. I encountered it myself. Spirit only knows how long MaRuu was in there with us."

"We stopped counting," MaRuu said. "We have faced all of you many times before. We like you much more like this."

"Like what?" Rhi asked.

"Docile," MaRuu replied. "Your anger has departed. We like this as ours has also."

"Who are you to be preaching pacifism?" Dee asked. "You and your people have murdered any and all Quasis who dared to enter your lands since the first millennia. You're no Spirit Guide, MaRuu. You're a warrior like me, admit it."

"Dee," Pi said. "That's enough."

"MaRuu does not disagree with him," they replied. "We were different before embarking on the Path. It has changed us. We hope for the better. Has this not been the same for all of you? Has the Mother planet not helped you?"

"It has, MaRuu," Scout said. "It's shown us a great deal actually. Mostly about places where we would in the past falter. It helped me find courage if that's what you mean. Er, is that what you mean?"

"I think the only thing MaRuu here has learned is that their only way out of here is by our side and as soon as they don't need us anymore, they'll have at us," Dee said.

"Maybe," MaRuu hissed quietly. "We have not forgotten how to kill, warrior. We just choose not to, for the time being we share a common goal."

"Wait," Pi said. "What?"

"Both Arkelians are needed in the Great Gateway," MaRuu said. "We will end this together, whether we want to do it with you or not. We have seen we have no choice."

"I don't believe that," Dee said. "But I'd rather have my enemy in plain sight than hiding in the trees in stealth."

"Bloody Battler pride shining through, it is," Rhi said. "Pay him no mind, MaRuu."

"He is of little consequence to us," MaRuu said. "His fate is sealed."

"I decide my fate," Dee shot back. "Not you."

"Let's just end this then," MaRuu said. "Face us in combat and we will see who the weak one is."

"Enough!" Pi barked. "Dee, shut your trap or go home! MaRuu, don't bristle his fur! Just stop it, the both of you. We don't have time for petty squabbling."

"We have all the time in the world," MaRuu said. "We should know. We have been here for many planet turns by now. We have killed you all many times. Too many to count."

Pi sighed. "Well, whatever, but shut the sass down now, MaRuu. You are a guest on our journey and if you lost the rest of your party along the way, something tells me that we did a better job getting this far seeing as we're all still here, so pipe down."

"Or what?" MaRuu asked.

"Or you'll never leave this forest alive," Dee replied.

"Then neither will you," MaRuu hissed.

"Fine," Pi said. "Then leave us be. Go then."

MaRuu cocked their head. "You saw what happens when you kill us."

"Exactly," Pi said. "So, we need to make the best of this. We're stuck with each other. So, Dee here will stop accusing you and you'll stop threatening to kill everybody. Deal?"

MaRuu spat on the ground. "We will stay, but we could kill him. He is unnecessary to the Path. We only need you, Pi."

"Well," Pi said, "I need them so cork it with all the murder talk, okay? You lay one of those clawed fingers on any of us and we'll end up right back to where we started, wouldn't we?"

"This is true," MaRuu hissed.

"Right, so for the love of the Spirit just lay off each other," Pi said. "Agreed?"

Dee took his hand off his blade. "Fine. Agreed."

"Agreed," MaRuu hissed.

"New friends to be made, they are," Rhi chirped. "Me and Rex started out the same way, remember Pi?"

Pi allowed herself a smile. "I do. I never thought you two would get along. And from what you said about your time back at HomeSpace, it sounds like your truly brother and sister now. I'll be forever grateful he's doing what he's doing back there."

"Who is Rex?" MaRuu asked.

"My little brother," Pi replied. "Only he's not that little anymore from the sounds of it. He's doing everything in his power to stop them."

"Them?" MaRuu asked.

"You, MaRuu," Rhi said. "The MaRuu are going to attack us. Rex is going to find a way to stop it, he is."

"Why would the MaRuu attack the Quasi?" MaRuu asked. "What has happened? Tell us!"

Pi wished Rhi had kept her trap shut about that. "A bad Quasi made some of us attack you first, but my brother is going to put an end to it. We do not want war with you. It was an evil act."

"So, did he stop it?" MaRuu asked. "Tell us!"

"I only saw up to when I was granted his power," Pi said. "He was trying. I don't know if he was successful. But I believe in my hearts that he will. Dee's partner Chukk is helping him and they stand a good chance."

MaRuu snorted. "We miss being connected to the swarm so we would know these things. We have not heard the others on the outside since we entered the portal cave."

"I knew it!" Dee exclaimed. "The cave was a portal! We're someplace in between the planet and the Spirit, aren't we?"

"That is not untrue," MaRuu said. "Best we can determine, we are in the Space."

"What's that mean, the Space?" Scout asked.

"As the large one said," MaRuu replied. "In between the Mother planet and the Sun. That is why we must bring them together, as the Tablet demands of us."

"Bring together the planet and the sun?" Rhi asked. "How do we bloody do that?"

"We must bind them together to share their energy with one another," MaRuu said. "The Mother planet has been absorbing all of the Sun's energy. We need to help them harness the color streams and share them with each other in perfect balance so we can save them both."

"That sounds a bit tricky," Scout said. "How do we do that exactly?"

"MaRuu do not know. We take it Quasi do not either."

"Nope," Pi said. But you do know we're both to enter this Gateway thing with our Arkelians, right? We sacrifice ourselves and that does it, right?"

MaRuu nodded. "That we do know, yes."

"Are you scared to die?" Pi heard herself asking.

"We are ready to die to save the MaRuu," MaRuu replied.

"But that's not the same thing," Pi said. "I'm ready to die to save my people but I can't say I'm happy about it. I'm scared. There I said it. I'm bloody terrified to die and for the rest of you to die with me. I wish it didn't have to be like this. Wow, I've had that on the stew pot for some time now but just found the words now. Weird."

"We're all scared, love," Scout said. "But I'd rather die with you than know you died alone."

"Same here, Pi," Rhi said. "I love you; I do."

"Chukk and I knew what we were signing up for when I came with you for this, Pi," Dee said. "But I'd be lying if I didn't say that knowing we're nearing the end isn't scaring me. I think that's why I was pestering MaRuu. I'm here, though, and I'm not leaving you now. Like you said, we're in this together."

Pi swallowed the lump forming in her throat. "Rex and Chukk were going to face the entire MaRuu swarm for us. Rex, the Quasi who never wanted to leave his burro, and Chukk, who only knew me in passing were facing an army for us."

"How far we've come," Scout said. "I can't speak for the rest of you but at least I'll die knowing I was at my best. Just a pity we won't live long enough to enjoy it."

"Do you love anyone, MaRuu?" Pi asked. "Do you have a partner back home?"

"The MaRuu have many couplings," MaRuu said. "We share everything with each other save love. That is reserved for the others who draw you in with the joining scent. Those few are the ones who share their emotions with us alone."

"Where are they?" Rhi asked.

"They are in the Swarm still," MaRuu said. "We miss them."

"If you don't mind me asking, MaRuu," Pi said. "Are you male or female, here alone away from your swarm?"

"We are female," MaRuu replied. "All MaRuu who find another to share the scent can respawn if that was what you meant. But we have not spawned yet as we are still here."

"What does that mean?" Dee asked. "I don't follow."

Pi grimaced. "MaRuu die giving birth, don't they?"

MaRuu nodded. "To grant life, we must also take one to keep the balance."

"Whoa," Rhi said. "That's morbid."

"It is our way," MaRuu said. "What of you, bugle?"

"Oh, I can't have babies," Rhi said. "See, I came out a bit different. I'm neither boy nor girl, I'm not. I feel like a girl but tend to act like a boy. All in all, I'm just me!"

"And we love you for it, darling," Scout said. "Never been one like her and never will there be again. Rhi's one of kind, she is."

Pi smiled. "See this is nice, isn't it? Just talking. I feel like we were all so wrapped up with lyght beams and tests of meddle, we forgot to enjoy each other's company along the way."

"You're right," Dee said. "Hey, look, we made it. The forest is ending up ahead!"

In front of them, the red, or violet from MaRuu's perspective, path came to an end just as the snowy trees gave way to the steep mountain in front of them. Standing in the distance was a red stoned and violet jeweled adorned archway which led to a path that looked to wind up the side of the mountain with steps jaggedly carved into the mountainside. As soon as the Journeyers left the path, the sun appeared through the clouds and shone down on them. Above them, different colors of lyght energy rippled through the sky.

"We made it," Pi said. "I can't believe we made it."

"We're not there yet, love," Scout said, pointing up. "We still have a mountain to climb."

Rhi looked up. "I can't even see the top from here, I can't. It's so tall, like it's kissing the clouds, it is."

Pi turned to face the group. "MaRuu and I have to go up there, but you all don't have to. You've all played your parts well, but this is our sacrifice to make, not yours. You can turn back now. I don't want any of you to die for me."

"That's really not your decision to make, love," Scout said. "I'm going."

"The same goes for me," Dee said. "Battlers battle to the end."

"You couldn't shoo us away if you tried," Rhi said. "Besides, you might need us up there. You go, we all go, we do."

Pi smiled. "Do you all know how much I love you? More than life itself, that's how much."

"Addy'd be right proud of us, wouldn't she?" Scout asked.

"I know so," Pi replied. "Especially of you, my proud and brave Scout. She's smiling on us for sure. So, shall we go face destiny or what?"

"Together," Scout said. "Let's get ourselves fried, or whatever lies ahead."

MaRuu leaned from side to side, as if weighing their words with their body. "But you can all go now? Why do you not go? We do not understand this. We sent our others back when we entered the forest. Why do you stay when it is not your path? This makes no sense."

"It's their decision, MaRuu," Pi said. "They make up their own minds. We don't decide things the way the MaRuu do."

"But you said one Quasi sent an army to attack us without cause," MaRuu said. "If that was the case, then why did they fight us?"

"Because they were following orders," Dee said.

"But that makes no sense," MaRuu said. "Pi told you to leave but you do not. Does she not lead you?"

"She is leading us here," Dee said, "but she is not our leader. Our leader can send our forces into battle."

"One can decide the fate of the many then?" MaRuu asked.

"It's not a perfect system," Scout said, "as this cluster mess has proven."

"We gave our trust to one who did not deserve it," Pi said.

"But it is how we live, MaRuu," Dee said. "It's just the way it is, and it is what it is."

"That's not true, it's not," Rhi interjected. "Look at Rex and Chukk going to set things right! Now those are some true leaders, they are! Isn't that right, Pi?"

Pi was still having trouble believing the memories she experienced were those of her timid, younger brother but this journey had changed them all for the better and he was no different. "If you were to tell me Rex would lead a revolt against our Elder for the sake of the whole planet before this all started, I would have been the first to call you a liar. But now, with all we've done and seen? I think anything is possible. We've changed, MaRuu, just like you."

"And we can't read each other's minds the way you do, either," Scout said. "We have to do it the hard way by actually taking the time to speak with each other. It's harder than it might seem when you have to learn to trust others first."

"And earn their trust in turn," Dee said.

"We find this peculiar," MaRuu said. "But we did not think that you cannot hear each other without speaking first. We apologize."

"There's no need to apologize, MaRuu," Pi said. "We can't understand how you could live having to share a consciousness with all of your people at the same time, so I guess this is where we might be able to start learning from each other."

"We will take what we've learned with us to our deaths," MaRuu replied. "We hope your brother completes his task, both for the Quasi and for the MaRuu."

"We do too," Pi said. "So, what does your tablet say? Anything?"

MaRuu looked at the stone tablet. "We are to climb to the Widow's Peak and enter the Gateway. That is all that is written."

"But what do we do when we get there?" Pi asked. "Go inside this Chamber or Gateway and then what? I know I'm working on my curiosity and all, but I'd like to know a bit more about what awaits in case it's just another test."

"It says no more," MaRuu said. "We will just have to see."

Scout chuckled. "Pi doesn't do very well with waiting and seeing, MaRuu. She prefers knowing what lies ahead at all times. It's kind of her thing, you know?"

MaRuu cocked their head to one side.

Dee had the map back out. "Well, I'll be damned. There's a message under the final drawing now. Unreal. Listen: Bind the red and violet to find the balance of the green. The Spirits will help to save our Queen."

"Queen?" Pi asked. "What's a queen? And what's green? That literally makes no sense. Does it?"

"Well," Scout said, "we'll have plenty of time to think on it while we climb, won't we?"

"He's right, he is," Rhi said. "These things have a way of making more sense after we face them, they do."

"Too bad we won't be here to know," Pi said. "Let's go."

***

After what seemed like a full planet turn, Rex and Chukk found themselves in unfamiliar territory, the Southern Enclave, home to the MaRuu. The rocky terrain was splattered with purple snow which came up over their hind paws and left a crunching noise as they hopped through it on their way to only Spirit knows where. Rex found himself aching from head to paw from the mind numbingly long days they had spent getting this far.

Making the trip in silence only made it seem that much longer. One of the MaRuu that were holding their chains suddenly turned around and made their way back to Rex and Chukk, carrying two large water jugs and a sack of rootsnips, the vegetable they had been fed since going into captivity. The MaRuu placed the water jugs and sack down in between Rex and Chukk.

"Quasi have been good prisoners," the MaRuu said. "Hold out

paws."

Rex shot Chukk a look of confusion. Chukk just nodded, holding out his front paws. Rex, in turn, followed suit. The MaRuu unhooked the locking mechanism first on Chukk's chains and then Rex's.

"I don't understand?" Rex asked. "Not that I mind in the least but still, aren't you afraid we'll make a hop for it?"

"That is our wish," the MaRuu said. "We are now safe in the South. You may go home. You are not needed. Now Elder Rex knows the MaRuu show restraint as he does. Go now and do not return." The MaRuu turned and sped ahead to catch up with the swarm still moving further southward.

"I'll be damned," Chukk said, rubbing his wrists. "You were right, Rex. I can't bloody believe it."

"Others," Rex said. "They said there were others who were their prisoners. We can't leave them. It's not right."

"Rex," Chukk said. "Count your blessings, mate. Your gamble, however, incredibly unlikely, somehow worked. You just averted a war. Take that as a win and let's get out of here."

"But-"

"But nothing," Chukk said. "When we get through this, our people are going to need a leader and that Quasi is you. If you want, send a delegation or something to open talks with them. I'll lead it myself, albeit fully armed. But for now, let's go while the getting is good. Okay?"

Rex frowned. "No, I'm going to ask them to let us bring their prisoners back with us."

"In exchange for what, exactly?" Chukk asked. "You have nothing to offer them that you haven't already. Come on, leave it for now. Our people need us back at HomeSpace. We still have the planet dying and smashing all of us into smithereens to deal with, don't we?"

Rex's eyes lit up. "It didn't happen. It didn't happen! The end came when we were all on the battlefield on the third day. We've been gone five! I didn't even think about it! It didn't happen, Chukk! They did it!"

"If that's the case even better we get home as fast as possible," Chukk said. "Maybe we'll find them there waiting for us."

Rex smiled. "You still think there's a chance they'll make it home alive?"

"I think anything is possible," Chukk said. "And for all we know, the end is still coming. We might have just delayed it a bit longer."

"At least we played our part," Rex said. "The rest is up to them. All right, Chukk, let's go home."

"Now you're talking," Chukk said, scooping up two of the water jugs and placing them in his pouch. "Grab the rest and let's get out of here before they change their mind."

***

"Quasis climb well for not having hands," MaRuu said as they reached a narrow straight away on the mountain trail.

Pi laughed. "Our talons serve us well enough. We're built more for speed than climbing though, you're right."

"I miss my super strength," Scout wheezed, catching up to Pi and MaRuu on the trail. "I've got hardly enough stamina to breath up here, let alone climb these steep rock formations. Some trail."

"And I miss my buzzing speed," Rhi said, flying up behind them next to Dee. "Why'd you have to go and steal them from us, Pi?"

"It wasn't on purpose," Pi said. "It just happened when you…" She trailed off.

"Touched the Arkelian!" Scout nearly yelled, his voice bellowing. "I reckon we can have them back if we do it again!"

"Not a bad idea, that's not!" Rhi chimed in.

Pi bristled at this. "I think I was supposed to have those powers, you two. You know, Chosen one and all. I might need them moving ahead. You both had your time to have powers, now it's my turn."

"Well, I haven't had any powers at all the whole time," Dee said. "Maybe I could have a go. Think what a Battler with super strength and lyghtning speed could do, eh? Stop an evenly matched MaRuu with the same powers, that's for sure."

"Let's just drop it, okay?" Pi said. "We're nearly to the top."

"We have no powers," MaRuu said. "Our Arkelian acted only as a beacon of lyght for you to find us. We do not need powers to kill you, Dee. We only need our hands and a short amount of time."

Pi grimaced at this exchange. It had been going on like this for the entire hike up the mountain with Dee threatening MaRuu, who would counter threaten him, and so on. It was frustrating to Pi that Dee seemed not to give MaRuu half a chance and instead hated her not as an individual trying to save her people but a member of the MaRuu swarm he had spent his whole life training to seek out and destroy.

Their friction with each other had no place on this climb and led Pi to wonder if they were in the midst of yet another test of some kind.

"We are on a spiritual journey the lot of us," Pi said, turning to face them both. "We do not need any 'I can kill you and you can't kill me' rhetoric from either of you. Dee, leave her alone or take your Battler butt back down the mountain. MaRuu, stop letting him get to you. I know you don't have to like each other but I highly doubt the Spirit or sun, or whatever it is we're going to face wants to hear you two squabble over who can kill who the fastest. Got it?"

Dee kicked at the ground. "I'm, I'm sorry. It's just I spent my whole life being told that they were vermin who deserved nothing but death. This is all just sort of hard for me. But you're right and I'm sorry."

"Don't be sorry," Pi said. "Be better. Give her the chance she's been trying to give you. You know, I saw in Rex's memories something that he told your Chukk. Want to hear what it was?"

"What?" Dee said, quietly.

"That the MaRuu are not our enemy, Dee," Pi said. "We are theirs. Now chew on that for a dit." Pi spun back around and found a rock to sit on.

"But the expedition," Dee replied.

"If the MaRuu came traipsing into our land looking for a spot to build themselves a new settlement," Pi asked, "what would the elders have had the Battlers do to them? Well?"

"Kill them," Dee said in a near whisper.

"Spot on," Pi replied. "Rex finally saw the lyght and because the Spirit allowed me to see what he saw, now I see it too. My parents were foolhardy, Dee. They never should have left us to go in the first place. I now see their deaths are on their own paws and no one else's. I'm just saying that when you get to know people and how they think, sometimes you learn something about yourself in turn. Give her a chance, okay?"

MaRuu cocked her head to one side. "Were your parents with others, Pi? Many planet turns ago?"

"Yes, MaRuu," Pi replied. "They went on an expedition into the Southlands to look for a new place for us to settle. Your people killed them and others for it."

"Your parents are not dead then," MaRuu said. "They were imprisoned for trespassing."

Scout dropped his water jug.

213

"What?!" Rhi screamed. "Our parents, Pi! Oh my! Oh my!"

"Hold on a dit," Pi said, now shaking. "Are you saying the MaRuu didn't kill our people? Our parents are still alive?!"

MaRuu made a clicking noise. "If they are who we think they are, then yes, they are alive."

"But, how?" Scout asked. "My parents came back and told us everyone had been killed in a massacre. Why would they lie about something like that?"

Pi leaned back on the rock. "My guess would be Ichabod had his paws involved knowing what we now know about him. You know your parents weren't the best, Scout. Maybe Ichabod had them say those things to keep any of us from trying to make a peace with the MaRuu. He was bent on us going to war with them. We know that now."

"If your parents are still alive," Rhi said. "That means mine might still be alive too, it does! MaRuu, are you sure of this?"

MaRuu clicked again. "We share all knowledge. The Quasi and Bugle prisoners tend to our crops. They are treated well. We swear this. There are perhaps two handfuls of them we keep in the dry caves. They are chained but may roam throughout the caves with the slack they are given. They were told we would destroy you all if they tried to leave but this is just to keep them fearful. We would not actually do this."

"The Quasi tend to do what they're told, this is true," Pi said. "I can't bloody believe it. All this time, alive." Pi began crying.

Scout hopped to her and took Pi into his paws. "I'm so sorry, Pi. They never told me the truth. I'm so sorry."

Pi looked up, still crying. "It's not your bloody fault, Scout! Your parents were horrible! How could they? All this time?!"

"Unbelievable it is," Rhi said. "MaRuu, would they ever think of freeing them?"

"With what we know now from you, possibly," MaRuu replied. "We might be able to find terms. The Quasi would need to offer us something in return. That is how we operate. We trade with each other and we might be able to trade something with you. But for certain we do not know. It would be up to the swarm. We decide together."

"With us stuck here, there's no chance," Dee said. "They'll never know what MaRuu knows. We're about to die here, remember? The Arkelians? The Great Gateway of certain death? Sound a horn?"

"But we don't all have to go in the gateway," Scout said. "Just one of us with MaRuu and the Arkelians, right?"

There was an uncomfortable silence. Suddenly, Pi realized what Scout was getting at.

"No, Scout," Pi said. "I know you better than you know yourself and the answer is no. This is my burden to bear, not yours. You're not taking my place. Without MaRuu with us, it makes no difference. It won't work. You're not sacrificing yourself for me."

"It never said the two had to be MaRuu and Quasi, Pi," Dee said. "Scout could take yours and I could take the other one from MaRuu. You, her, and Rhi can go save your folks. We've got this covered, right, Scout?"

"Aye," Scout replied. "That we do. Pi, it's the only way. Sounds like my parents destroyed yours and Rhi's life in exchange for being excused from labor and plied with a lifetime of nectar. Let me make this right. I need to do this for you. I owe you that much. Heck, I owe you even more for you still loving me knowing it. I can't let this moment pass. It's just not your time to die. It's mine."

MaRuu looked back and forth between the Journeyers, her head cocking left to right. "We are not leaving the Path. We have our mission and we have accepted this to be true. We will not leave to save your parents. We are sorry."

"And I'm not leaving either," Pi said. "I came on this journey to save our planet, not shirk away from it for the chance to reunite with lost loved ones, no matter how much I might like to. It's settled. MaRuu and I are seeing this through to the end."

"But Pi," Scout said. "It's my family's fault you lost yours."

"Scout," Pi said. "You and Rhi are my family. You are enough, just as you are. You're not them and it's not your fault. If anyone should leave, it should be you three. In fact, I'm asking you to. Go and see if you can save them for me. That's how you can help me the most. Live on, take Rhi, and find a way to save our parents. Dee, I'm begging you to go with them. Let MaRuu and I finish this alone, please. Your deaths will be worthless otherwise."

Rhi fidgeted. "You truly would prefer us to leave, Pi? That's really what you want? Because I want to save my parents if they're alive, I do. But I also want to be here for you, I do. I won't leave without either of you."

"Rhi, take Scout and go home," Pi said. "Take Rex and find our parents. It's better this way."

Scout shook his head. "No, I won't let you do this, Pi. Not like this.

It should be me. Give me the Arkelian. Please trust me, love. You have a family to save. That's how I can make this right. Please?"

"This is getting us nowhere, Scout!" Pi exclaimed. "I can't let you do this. It has to be me. I'm the Chosen one, remember?"

"But that's just it, love," Scout said. "You're doing this out of duty to who, Ichabod? I am choosing to do this out of love and respect for you. In that way, I'm choosing to be the one to sacrifice my life. I'm the choosing one. Give me the Arkelian. Now. No more arguments. No more lectures. Just do it already."

"Don't give it to him," Dee said.

"Finally, some reason!" Pi replied.

"Give it to me instead," Dee said. "Chukk and I said our goodbyes before I left. He knows I was leaving never to return. We live by the Battler code. We fight until we die, hopefully in glorious battle, and this fits the bill by a wide margin. This should be my burden to bear. You have a family out there, Pi. Give me the Arkelian and go find them."

"We are making no progress at all!" MaRuu hissed. "Who is joining me in the Gateway? You must decide this now. We do not care who comes with us as long as one does!"

"Seems we're all willing to die to save each other," Scout said. "So, I guess we finish this the way we started it?"

"Together," Pi said.

"We're all daft and stubborn, we are," Rhi said. "We'll make worthy sacrifices, we will."

Pi sighed. "I can't believe you two."

"Nor us you, love," Scout said.

"We think you are all odd," MaRuu said. "We wish we would have had more time to learn your confusing ways."

"Well, hopefully we'll have plenty of time in the Spirit to do just that," Dee said.

"If no one's leaving then let's just get the inevitable over with, shall we?" Pi asked. "It can't be much further ahead. We're nearly to the top now."

"Then we wish to go there now," MaRuu said. "Come."

The Journeyers and MaRuu returned their attention to the trail and in less than a dat found themselves standing at the Widow's Peak. They were facing a large stone enclave adorned with stones and jewels: red, orange, yellow, blue, indigo, and violet in color. There were six sides to the structure, each equally distant from each other.

"So, what now?" Pi asked. Both hers and MaRuu's Arkelians were pulsing with different colors now.

"We believe we go inside," MaRuu said. "It is time for us to face the end."

Pi looked to Scout and then to Rhi and Dee. "This is as far as you three go. Wait out here. That's not a request. That's just the way it is going to be."

"No," Scout said. "I go where you go. Forever."

"I go too, I do," Rhi said. "Love and hugs, Pi. We're in this together we are."

"I didn't come all this way just to turn around now," Dee said. "Sorry. You're stuck with us."

Pi wiped away a tear. "You're all idiots… but I love you. Mind if we hold paws and hands? We'll all walk in together. You too, MaRuu. Let's see what the end looks like."

They all took a paw or hand, with Pi holding Scout's and Rhi's.

"I love you," Pi said.

"I love you," Scout said.

"I love you, I do," Rhi said.

"I love you all," Dee said.

"We thank you for love," MaRuu said.

The Journeyers and MaRuu walked into the middle of the Great Gateway. The lyght energy from the two Arkelians began to shoot out all around them, bouncing and ricocheting off the six stone and jewel encrusted stone sculptures. The energy kept moving faster and faster. They felt themselves being lifted off the ground. Floating in the air, soon everything around them was filled with blinding lyght the same as they saw back at the lyght waterfall.

Green now binds the colors and the lyght. From this place it will shine bright.

"This color is green?" Pi called out. "What is it?"

It is the color of balance and of peace. It will allow us to harness the lyght of the sun with this moon and regulate the energy between the two. To all five of you, we say thank you. You played your parts well.

"Who or what are you?!" Pi called out.

I am you, Pi. And you, Scout, and Rhi. I am Dee and I am MaRuu. I am all of you. The moon you're now on and the sun in the sky. I am everything. I am the Queen of this Universe. My daughter, your planet, and you were learning a lesson. I am grateful. Thank you. She needed to learn to learn the truth about love, as did all of you. She learns by watching you. She now knows that somethings are worth dying for, but love can overcome death.

"This is it!" Scout called out. "We're all going to die now!"

Poor Scout, you have already sacrificed yourselves to me. Not one of you is the person who started the journey of lyght and the path of color. You've all become far greater beings now. Your old selves were the sacrifice. Not what you have now become.

"So, what of us now?" Pi asked. "And what of your daughter, our planet?"

Now that you have brought the two keys together my energy will now power this moon, which will then share the power back with me in infinite duality. Both my daughter and I are now safe, as are all your peoples.

"Queen, what does that mean for us?" MaRuu asked.

"Yeah, we're confused, we are!" Rhi chirped. "I am anyways!"

You have all proven to be powered by love. You will have each other for what lies ahead.

"What lies ahead?" Pi asked.

Your families will always be waiting for you as your world is now one without end. The green energy grants eternal life and you can always return to drink from it. You can see them now if you choose to. You may bring Rex and Chukk with you when you return to this place.

"How can we measure when we're to return if we're living in eternity now?" Pi asked.

When the Arkelians glow, you will be brought back here to me. For now, go home with love in your hearts and peace in your minds.

The Journeyers and MaRuu fell to the ground as green energy swirled all around them. Pi was the first to notice that Scout, Rhi, and Dee were all wearing Arkelians now too. Each of them, including Pi's and MaRuu's were now green gemmed. She leapt to her feet.

"We didn't die," Pi said. "We didn't die!" She grabbed and hugged Scout, kissing him repeatedly.

"We did it!" Scout yelled. "Woo hoo! We actually did it!"

Dee just shook his head. "I can't believe it. I just can't believe it."

"Heroes, we are!" Rhi chirped. "Heroes!"

MaRuu watched them celebrate, with her head cocked to one side. "We find this a bit anticlimactic. We were expecting more than this."

"So sorry you didn't burn in flames," Dee said. "Come on, MaRuu! We did it!"

Dee extended his paws to her. She realized he was opening himself up to an embrace of friendship. She accepted it and for the first time in a long time, smiled. "We are glad to have met you, Dee."

"We like you too," Dee replied.

"So how about we leave here how we came in, you lot," Pi said, holding out her paws.

They all held paws and hands, exiting the Gateway. "Together."

"So how do we get home exactly?" Scout asked. "Back the way we came?"

As they walked out of the Gateway, they found themselves no longer on the top of the mountain. The Journeyers and MaRuu were standing in front of the mouth of the cave they had entered to undertake the journey in the first place. Only instead of barren, rocky, snowy terrain, there was lush green color plants in bloom all around them. Off to the right side, a river of water ran down the hillside.

"Look at that!" Rhi said, pointing in the sky. "Look at the sun and the moon!"

Above them, the sun glowed a bright green, as did the moon on the other edge of the sky. A green line of energy raced between them. The sky picked up on this, a light green hue abounded.

"Look at the lyght veins!" Dee said, pointing to the ground. "They're green too!"

"Just... awesome," Pi said. "Come on, we're less than a day from home now!"

They took off down the hill, laughing the whole way.

***

Rex and Chukk had just returned to HomeSpace, their paws aching and raw, when the planet seemed to hum and vibrate in the new color again. They could feel energy ripple all around them. The lyght veins all throughout HomeSpace suddenly began coursing with this new color also. Around them, all the damage to HomeSpace reversed itself. Walls rebuilt themselves. Debris vanished. Ceilings refortified.

"Epic," Rex muttered.

"They really did it," Chukk said. "They must have! Look at this!"

Then, the reports started coming in from the Bugle sentries and Leapers that outside HomeSpace, the terrain was no longer jagged and rough. Plants and grasses of all shapes and sizes had taken over the landscape for as for as they could see. Flowers of all colors covered the ground. Root vegetables pulled from the ground regrew instantly. Fruit plucked from newly grown trees did the same. The fruit regrew instantly. Water ran in rivers across the land and none of it was electrified. They ran with sweetwater!

In the weeks that followed, only good news came in. The planet had been reborn. People were reporting ailments disappearing and feeling more energy than they had in planet turns. Nothing but joy and happiness ruled the day… save for two.

Rex and Chukk, sitting in the Elder's Chamber, drank nectar and wept tears of both joy and sadness. While they were witnessing the rebirth of their planet, both had lost family as a result and were not as prone to celebrate as the rest of the populous. Rex had sent Leapers to check in with the other HomeSpaces to see if they were experiencing the same results although he already knew they were. Pi and the others saved them all, trading their lives for the good of all. They would not be forgotten, ever.

"I think we should have a memorial service for them," Rex said.

"Wait, where did you get that?!" Chukk exclaimed.

"Get what?" Rex asked.

Chukk pointed to Rex's chest where the Arkelian breast plate now sat, it's green stone rippling with pulses of energy. "That!"

Rex looked at his chest and feeling the weight of the Arkelian against his body, began to shake. "This just appeared on me! I don't know! Ichabod gave it to Pi! How did this get on me?!"

"Did you time loop?!" Chukk asked.

Rex looked around. "I, I don't think so! Wait, you're wearing one too?!"

"What does this mean?!" Chukk asked. He too wriggled in the breast plate he was now wearing.

It means you two did what needed doing.

"Who said that?!" Rex asked.

"What is this?!" Chukk exclaimed.

You were on the journey the whole time. See you when I see you.

The Arkelians stopped glowing.

Rex sighed. "You heard that too, right?"

"Aye," Chukk said. "I heard it all right. It was the Spirit. It had to be."

"Actually, we think it was the sun," Dee said from the doorway. "She prefers to be called the Queen of our Universe though. Just remember that for when you meet her."

"Dee?!" Chukk yelled. "You're here! You're bloody here!"

Chukk and Dee hopped to each other and entered into a long, passionate kiss.

Rex kept his focus on the doorway. He felt a smile creep up on his face when Pi, Scout, and Rhi appeared before him. Rex thought he was going to pass out from joy.

"You're not dead!" Chukk exclaimed, hopping up to them. "Any of you! You did it! You bloody did it!"

"We missed you so much, Rex!" Pi said, hugging her brother as hard as she could. "You were so brave! I got to see your memories and you did me so proud!"

"Word out in the burro on the way in is that you and Chukk stopped a war with the MaRuu all by yourselves?" Scout asked. "Two Quasi against the whole MaRuu swarm and not a drop of blood was shed?"

"We got lucky," Rex said, smiling. "Just trying to help buy you two more time, you know how it is. I was able to loop in time for a bit, Pi! It was the weirdest, most surreal experience of my life, I tell you."

MaRuu stood in the doorway. Rex caught glimpse of her and let out a yelp. Chukk reached for his blade but found Dee taking his hand away from the blade's hilt.

"She's with us," Pi said. "Chukk, Rex, this is our new friend, MaRuu. She helped us complete the Journey of Lyght and we helped her complete her Path of Color. She's not here to hurt us."

"Oh really?" Rex asked. "What is she here to do then?"

"She's going to help us rescue our parents," Pi said. "Rhi's too. The other MaRuu are holding them as-"

"Prisoners?" Rex finished. "Our parents are among those they've taken prisoner?" They're alive? Mum and Pappy are alive, Pi?"

"As far as we know," MaRuu said. "We cannot promise but the prognosis is good. Now that the balance has been found and the planet springs eternal, there is no need for them to remain under our guard. Now that we are back home, we can speak for all MaRuu when we meet with your new leader."

Chukk chuckled. "You're looking at him, MaRuu. They voted Rex in as High Elder as soon as we got back from your territory. His actions saved thousands of lives and averted a war with your people that would have ended all of us. For his first act, Rex freed the Bugles from their service requirements too."

"Bloody good of you, Rex!" Rhi chimed in.

"Voted him in?" Pi asked. "What's that about?"

"I asked for a popular vote," Rex said. "Didn't seem right just to assume control. Look where that got Ichabod."

"We request peace with the Quasi," MaRuu said. "And we would like to stay here with our friends if you'll have us. We have never had friends like this before. In trade we will return your prisoners if we can stay here with the Journeyers."

"That sounds like a fair trade," Rex said. "I'm sure we'll have more to work out as we go so having you around will make sense. Peace then? Can we have our parents back?"

"Yes," MaRuu said. "They are being released as we speak. Rhi's also and the others. They will be treated well and brought here. We promise you this."

"Great!" Rex exclaimed. "I'm just glad this is all over!"

"Yeah," Pi said. "About that. The Queen has another request for us. Now that we saved her daughter, she's sending us to help others find their path."

"So, the sun, whatever a Queen is, is sending us to save... another planet? Us?" Rex asked.

"Yup," Scout said.

"Exciting, right?!" Pi asked, beaming.

"Er, okay, I guess?" Rex said. "Do I have choice in this?"

"Nope," Scout said. "When those things on our chests glow green, we're off once more."

"So, it took all this to find out it's not the end but just the beginning of a new adventure!" Pi exclaimed. "We have to help another race from killing their own planet!"

"This race, what are they?" Rex asked. "Quasi, Bugle, or MaRuu?"

"Something called human," Pi replied. "Don't worry, Rex. I bet this time it will be a breeze now that we've been through all this. This time both you and Chukk can come with us too!"

"Another planet? Me on another planet?" Rex asked. "Up until you coming in here, I thought we *were* the only planet. This is a heavy load, Pi."

"But it's one we can lift together," Pi said. "We saved this planet. We can do it again! Right everyone?"

Pi looked around to a roomful of tired faces. "But just not yet. I get it. We just got back. Our parents aren't here yet either. We get some down time."

"Let's just say this is to be continued, shall we?" Dee said.

"Hey," Scout said, raising his front paws to reveal long, leathery flaps of skin and fur stretching from his wrists to his pawpits, "anybody else have these now?"

Looking around, all the Quasi found they now had the same new appendages.

"We all have them," Chukk said, examining his own. "I wonder what they're for?"

"I have a pretty good idea," Pi replied. "I made a few wishes while we were in there with the Queen. She must have decided to make a few of them come true as a sort of reward for us."

"Wait a dit," Rex said. "Are these… wings?!"

"Guess we'll have to find out, won't we?" Pi said, a smile on her face and a glint in her eye.

And Then…

ABOUT THE AUTHOR

A.O. Zephryes can be found online at:

Facebook: AOZephryes

or

Twitter: @RainAngel77

Made in the USA
Middletown, DE
15 October 2023

40493819R00137